bests

"With suspenseful drama, fast-paced action and a sensual romance, Crouch's latest has all the necessary ingredients of a satisfying read. This series looks to have loads of promise."

—*RT Book Reviews* on *Countermeasures*

"Featuring a unique story line and passion that leaps right off the pages, the insanely intense *Infiltration* is a solid addition to the Intrigue line."

—*RT Book Reviews*

"Crouch doesn't disappoint with another spectacular Intrigue read filled with explosive action and well-developed characters and plot."

—*RT Book Reviews* on *Special Forces Savior*

"Smoking chemistry between the reunited leads and some harrowing action scenes. Bottom line: *Armored Attraction* is another standout in Crouch's series."

—*RT Book Reviews*

"Danger, double-cross, intrigue, and romantic push and pull...this one has it all."

—*Goodreads* on *Leverage*

Janie Crouch has loved to read romance her whole life. This *USA TODAY* bestselling author cut her teeth on Harlequin Romance novels as a preteen, then moved on to a passion for romantic suspense as an adult. Janie lives with her husband and four children overseas. She enjoys traveling, long-distance running, movie watching, knitting and adventure/obstacle racing. You can find out more about her at janiecrouch.com.

Books by Janie Crouch

Harlequin Intrigue

Omega Sector: Under Siege

Daddy Defender
Protector's Instinct
Cease Fire

Omega Sector: Critical Response

Special Forces Savior
Fully Committed
Armored Attraction
Man of Action
Overwhelming Force
Battle Tested

Omega Sector

Infiltration
Countermeasures
Untraceable
Leverage

Visit the Author Profile page at Harlequin.com for more titles.

USA TODAY BESTSELLING AUTHOR

JANIE CROUCH

Infiltration
&
Overwhelming Force

HARLEQUIN® INTRIGUE CLASSICS

ISBN-13: 978-0-373-20882-1

Infiltration & Overwhelming Force

This edition published by arrangement with Harlequin Books S.A.

For questions and comments about the quality of this book, please contact us at CustomerService@Harlequin.com.

HARLEQUIN®
www.Harlequin.com

Printed in U.S.A.

CONTENTS

INFILTRATION

To my sweet cuz, the real "Sophia."
Thanks for providing the strength, charm and beauty to model a character after (although the rest is sheer drama and not you, I promise).
I am thankful beyond measure to have you in my life—a cousin by birth, a sister in every other way. 143, FC1!

Chapter One

Cameron Branson had been telling the lies so long he was afraid they were becoming truth to him.

"Look, Tom, I don't have a lot of time," Cameron barked quietly into his cell phone as he sat on a bench and looked out at Washington, DC's Potomac River. Joggers ran by in front of him and a mother chased a squealing toddler, but Cameron paid them no mind.

He especially paid no attention to the man sitting on the other side of the bench next to him who was also on his cell phone while glancing at a newspaper.

Except neither man was actually talking on his cell phone. They were talking to each other.

"Protocol dictates that we meet twice a week unless circumstances prove it impossible," Cameron was reminded by "Tom."

"Yeah, well, I don't have a whole lot of concern about protocol right at this moment. What I care about is bringing down the SOB who killed Jason."

Tom sighed and turned the page on his newspaper, without ever looking at Cameron. "You've been under a long time, Cam. And you missed our last two scheduled meetings. I can only cover for you so much before higher-ups start noticing."

"Well, it's not always easy getting away from the bad guys so we can have our chats," Cameron all but sneered. He knew his anger at Tom was misplaced, but couldn't seem to keep his irritation under control. He just wanted to get back to work.

"Everybody knows your undercover work in DS-13 is critical for us and for you personally. But it's important for us to do things by the book."

Cameron sighed but didn't say what was on his mind: doing things by the book was probably what had gotten Cameron's previous partner killed.

"All right. I'm sorry. I'll try to do better." Cameron almost believed it as he said it.

"Is everything still on for tomorrow's buy?"

"Yeah. It should go without a hiccup. Just make sure the warehouse stays clear."

"Cameron, I needed to meet with you about something else." Tom closed his newspaper and then reopened it. He seemed to be hesitating. Cameron knew this was bad. He'd never known his handler to be at a loss for words. "The parameters of your mission have changed."

Damn. "How so?"

"Taking the members and leader of DS-13 into custody is no longer your primary objective. For neither their black market activities nor their presumed part in your partner's death."

"Dammit, Tom…"

"I know, Cameron. But recent intel notified us that

DS-13 has obtained new encoding-transmitting technologies that they'll be selling to terrorists."

Cameron sighed and waited for Tom to continue.

"It's called Ghost Shell. This technology is like nothing we've ever seen—it could cripple communication within government agencies. It would give multiple terrorist groups the edge they've been looking for, and open us up to attacks all over the country. It's critical that this technology doesn't make it to the black market."

"Why isn't the cyberterrorism unit on this?" Cameron murmured with a sigh.

"It's beyond cyberterrorism now. Straight into terrorism. Besides, it's already out in the open. And since you're already neck-deep in DS-13…"

Cameron just shook his head. He knew what Tom said was true. Technology like this in DS-13's hands—the group was solely focused on financial gain—was bad, but in the hands of terrorist groups who were intent on destruction and loss of life, it would mean disaster.

"Roger that, Tom. Change of primary objective confirmed. I'll be in touch when I know something." Cameron got up from the bench and walked away. Tom stayed, as Cameron knew he would, pretending to talk on his cell phone a while longer as he looked at the paper.

Yeah, Cameron's primary objective had changed. But he'd be damned if he'd let justice for his partner's memory suffer because of it.

THE NEXT DAY, sitting in the back of the extended SUV with windows tinted just a bit darker than what was probably legal, Cam Cameron, as he was known to DS-13, pretended to chuckle at a filthy joke told by one of the other riders. When a second rider chimed in with another joke—something about a blonde, a redhead and a brunette—Cameron just tuned them out. He stretched his long legs out in front of him. At least there was room to do that in this vehicle.

One thing he had to give DS-13: they may be an organized crime ring with ties to almost every criminal activity imaginable—weapons, drugs, human trafficking, to name a few—but they knew how to travel in style.

Cameron had been undercover with them for eight months. Eight months pretending to be a midlevel weapons dealer. Eight months of trying to move up in the ranks of DS-13, so he could meet the boss.

The man who had ordered the execution of Cameron's partner over a year ago.

Cameron had made very little progress in the meeting-the-boss area of his work. Instead he'd been stuck with lower-level minions, who evidently thought a punch line about high heels and a sugar daddy downright hilarious, given the guffawing coming from all corners of the vehicle. Cameron chuckled again, just so it wouldn't be obvious that he wasn't laughing.

Blending in was key. Cameron's looks—black hair just a little too long, dark brown eyes, a perpetual five o'clock shadow—made him particularly suited for blending in with bad guys. Cameron had specifically cultivated the dark and unapproachable look. His six-foot frame was muscular—made even more so over the past few months since a favorite activity of the DS-13 minions was lifting weights—and he was light on his feet.

All in all, Cameron knew he came across as someone not to be messed with. Someone who could take care of himself. Someone menacing. It had helped him in undercover work for years, this ability to blend in physically.

The problem was, he felt his soul starting to blend in, too.

"Cam, don't you know any good jokes, man?" the driver called back to Cameron.

The best joke I know will be on you guys when I arrest all you bastards.

"No, Fin. I don't know any jokes. I can't be this beautiful, able to outlift all you princesses *and* be able to tell jokes. Wouldn't be fair to the rest of the world." Cameron smirked.

This led to an immediate argument over which of the four people in the SUV could bench the most weight, as Cameron knew it would.

Cameron was tired. He was tired of the lies, tired of keeping one step ahead of everyone else, tired of spending every day with these morons. And yesterday's meeting with Tom had confirmed what Cameron had already known: he wasn't checking in with his handler at Omega Sector as often as he should.

But since Cameron worked for Omega—an elite interagency task force—there was a little more leeway about check-ins and staying undercover longer. Omega agents had more training, more experience and the distinct mental acuity needed for long-term undercover work, or they never were sent out in the first place.

They were the best of the best.

God, it sounded so *Top Gun*. And Cameron certainly didn't feel best of anything right now.

"Two-ninety clean and jerk, two-seventy bench," Cameron responded to one of the guys asking about his top weight-lifting ability.

A round of obscenities flew through the vehicle. Nobody believed him.

"I'll take any of you pansies on, at any time." Cameron looked down at his fingernails in boredom. "But you better call your mommies first."

Another round of obscenities about what they would do to his mother, then arguments resumed about lifting, leg weights this time. Cameron zoned out again.

Cameron had promised Tom he would check in with the handler more often. He wasn't particularly worried about what Tom or the agency would do if he didn't. But he was worried his brothers, one older, one younger, both with ties to Omega Sector, might decide to storm the castle if they thought Cameron was in trouble. Not to mention his sister.

He wasn't in trouble, at least not the type that required help from his siblings.

He knew he was starting to make some progress in the case; there were talks of taking Cameron to the DS-13 main base, wherever that was. That's what Cameron wanted. That's where he would meet the man who ordered his partner's death. And as soon as Cameron could link him with that or any other felony, that bastard was going down.

Oh, yeah, and Cameron would recover Ghost Shell, as ordered.

Cameron didn't take the orders about the technology

acquirement lightly. He would get it. But he would bring down the bad guys while he was at it.

And then Cameron could get out of undercover work for a while and try to find himself. Get away from lies and filth for an extended period. Try to remember why he started this job in the first place.

As the SUV pulled up to an abandoned warehouse in a suburb far outside of Washington, Cameron got his head back in the game. No point whining about how hard this job was; he'd known that for a while now. Five years to be exact. Cameron immediately pushed that thought out of his head. This wasn't the time or place to think about her. Or any of the disasters that had happened since.

Opening his car door, Cameron stepped out. "All right, ladies, everything should be in the back office, upstairs. Use the east entrance since it's least visible."

The driver, Fin, was the leader of the group. Cameron walked around the car to him. "How do you want to set up security, Fin?" Cameron knew it was important to make Fin feel as if he was in charge.

"Yeah, let's leave someone at the back door outside and someone walking around inside, just in case."

Cameron nodded. "Great." He knew there would be no raids by authorities or attacks by a rival organization—thanks to Omega Sector—but nobody else knew it. As a matter of fact, nobody but them should be around this area at all. "You're coming in with me, right? So we can get it all counted and tested?"

Cameron was the one who had set up this sale, in an attempt to prove his usefulness, again, to DS-13. The men inside the warehouse—bad guys in their own right—were business associates of Cameron's. They were going to buy the weapons, ones Cameron had gotten for DS-13 at a hugely reduced price, thanks to them actually coming from the Omega Sector armory. All in all, DS-13 would make a nice little profit for very little work. Cameron would come out looking like the golden boy and would hopefully be one step closer to meeting the man in charge.

Nobody in DS-13 would ever know that the scumbags buying the weapons would be picked up by local law enforcement a few miles down the road after leaving here. The weapons would go back into government lockdown.

Fin barked orders to the rest of the men then walked with Cameron up the outdoor stairs to the second floor of the building. Inside was an office that looked down on the expanse of the warehouse, except seeing through the windows was nearly impossible due to years of cleaning neglect.

Cameron introduced the buyers to Fin and then stepped aside to let Fin talk to them so the guy could feel as if he was in charge. Cameron walked over to stand by a window that looked out onto the road. He rubbed a tiny bit of the filthy pane with his finger so he could see out, all the while keeping his ear on the conversation between the buyers and Fin, making sure Fin didn't screw things up.

Looking out his tiny hole, Cameron noticed a car moving slowly from the warehouse next door toward them. He cursed silently. Nobody was supposed to be in this area at all except for them. Omega Sector should've seen to that.

When the car got out of his line of sight from that window, Cameron casually moved to another window. He leaned back against the wall for a few moments before turning nonchalantly to the window and once again creating a little peephole in the dirt. Cameron was careful not to make it look as if he was studying anything. The last thing he wanted to do was draw attention to that car.

Sure enough the vehicle stopped right in front of the warehouse. Cameron cursed under his breath again. He hoped Marco, the man Fin had left as guard, didn't see the car. Maybe he wouldn't. The minions tended to be a little slack when Fin wasn't watching. Marco may be out smoking by the SUV or something. Cameron desperately hoped so. The last thing he needed was some civilian caught up in this mess.

"Isn't that right, Cam?" Fin called out to Cameron.

Cameron racked his brain trying to figure out what they were talking about. He needed to be paying more attention to this sale. Cameron wasn't sure how to respond. He didn't want to let on that he hadn't been listening to the conversation when he was the one who had set the whole thing up in the first place. Cameron decided to take a chance.

"If you say it, then it must be true, Fin."

Both the buyers and Fin burst out laughing, so Cameron figured he had said the right thing. He watched as Fin began showing the weapons to the buyers.

When he turned to the window again, the driver had gotten out of the car. He couldn't see much, but it looked as if it was a lone woman.

Damn.

Cameron knew he had to get down there and try to divert disaster before it hit full force.

"Fin, I've got to take a leak. I'm sure there's a can downstairs somewhere. I'll be back in a sec."

Fin and the buyers barely looked up from their exchange. Fin shooed in Cameron's general direction with his hand. Normally this lack of regard would've irritated Cameron, but now he was thankful for it. He headed out the door leading into the main section of the warehouse.

He hoped whoever was in the car was just some poor idiot who had gotten lost and would soon be on her way.

SOPHIA REARDON WAS lost and felt like some poor idiot. She rolled her window down farther and took a few deep breaths of air, trying to refocus.

Was this warehouse really the place? All of them looked the same. If she could read her own handwriting that would help. Of course, if people would do their jobs correctly in the first place she wouldn't have to be here at the corner of Serial-Killers-R-Us Street and Shouldn't-Be-Here-Alone Avenue.

Sophia looked down at the napkin where she'd scribbled the address. Yeah, that was definitely an *8* not a *3*. Which meant it was *this* warehouse she was supposed to be at, not the just-as-scary first one she'd gone to.

All Sophia needed were a few pictures of the interior ceiling frame and doorway of the warehouse to help finish a computer rendering of the building. This warehouse was identical to one that had burned down in an arson case two weeks ago—the work of a serial arsonist who had hit buildings in four different states. The FBI had been called in to help local law enforcement.

Sophia muttered under her breath again as she grabbed her camera gear and purse. She put her FBI credentials in her pocket, in case some poor security guard needed to see them. She pushed open the door to the warehouse and walked in slowly, giving her eyes time to adjust. She cursed her office mate, Bruce, who had begged Sophia to take these pictures.

"'The new girl at the coffee shop said yes to lunch, Sophia,'" Sophia said in her best mimicry of Bruce's voice. "'But today's our only chance this week. Please, please, please go take pictures at the horror-film warehouse for me. I'm worth getting mutilated for.'"

Sophia sighed. Bruce owed her. Big-time. Sophia hated this cloak-and-dagger stuff.

Sure, she worked for the FBI, but would be the first to tell you she wasn't an agent. She didn't even do CSI stuff usually, although she was part of the forensic team. She was a graphic designer, for goodness' sake. She designed brochures and fliers and posters. Safe in the comfort of her office in DC, not in some warehouse in Scaryville.

As the door closed behind her, Sophia took a deep breath and reminded herself there was plenty of air in this building and nothing to be afraid of. She was not trapped back in that car like during the accident five years ago. Sophia went through a couple of the mental exercises Dr. Fretwell had taught her to get her brief moment of panic under control. Once it had passed she grabbed her camera and began getting the shots she needed.

The doorway posed no problems so she got those first. But the beams in the ceiling area were going to be more difficult to film. Looking around she realized the office in the back would give her much better access to the shots she needed of the ceiling framing.

Sophia cautiously made her way back to the steps leading up to the office. It didn't look as if there were any serial killers or cyborgs living here, but the place still gave her the creeps. Wooden crates and boxes were piled all along the stairs and landing, making getting up them precarious. Sophia kept a firm grip on the railing for as long as she could until she had to let go to step around a huge crate.

As she began climbing the second set of steps, Sophia caught something moving out of the corner of her eye. She turned to see what it was just as an arm reached out from behind her and covered her mouth, pulling her up against a hard chest and silencing her startled scream.

A deep voice breathed quietly in her ear, "What the hell are you doing here?"

to have to get herself out. Because screaming wasn't going to help.

"Are you okay?" the voice asked, the mystery man still standing directly behind her, hand still hovering near her mouth.

"Yes. Look, I was just here to take some pictures of the door and ceiling." She was breathing so hard she could barely get the words out, so Sophia lifted her camera to the side so he could see it. "Whatever you're doing here, I don't know anything about it and I don't care."

There was no response from the man behind her. Sophia didn't know if that was a good or bad thing.

"I haven't seen you. I have no idea what you look like. I'll just leave. There's no cell phone coverage out here, so it's not like I can call anyone or anything." Sophia didn't know if that was true or not. She had forgotten to charge her phone again last night, so it was sitting dead out in her car. But she wasn't about to tell him that.

She realized she was rambling, but the longer he was silent, the more she was afraid he was going to do something terrible to her, like kill her.

Or cover her mouth with his hand again.

"I'm just going to go, okay?" Sophia took a small step away from him. "I'm not going to look at you and I'm just going to go."

The arm in front of her dropped. When he didn't stop her, Sophia took another step. Then another.

"Just get in your car and leave immediately. Don't let anybody else see you or believe me, the trouble will be much worse."

Now that the voice wasn't whispering, it sounded

vaguely familiar. As Sophia took another step away she turned to look at the man behind her before she could stop herself.

But before she could get a good look at him she tripped over one of the boxes lining the stairs. She grasped for the railing but couldn't reach it.

Just as she began to plummet down the stairs an arm reached out and grabbed her around her hips, sweeping her easily off her feet and yanking her back against him.

"Are you trying to get us both killed?" the voice hissed.

Now there was no doubt in Sophia's mind that the voice was familiar. She shook loose from the arm that held her and turned to face the voice. When she saw him clearly she almost stumbled again.

Just as tall, dark and handsome as ever—a walking cliché. The man who had walked out of her life five years ago. Without one single word.

"Cameron?"

Sophia watched as shock stole over Cameron's face. He was obviously as surprised to see her as she was to see him.

"Sophia? What are you doing here?"

"I'm taking pictures for a friend, for an arson investigation."

"An arson investigation? Are you law enforcement?"

Sophia shook her head. "No. Not really. I mean kind of, but no."

Cameron stared back at her in confusion and Sophia realized she wasn't making any sense.

"I work for the FBI, but I'm not an agent. I'm a graphic artist."

"You work for the Bureau? You're here for them?"

Cameron seemed overly shocked at her mention of the FBI. Sophia shook her head again. "Well, yes and no. I wasn't supposed to be here at all, but I'm helping a friend out by getting some pictures he wasn't able to get."

"Is anybody else from the Bureau coming?"

Sophia didn't understand why Cameron was asking her this, but the only thing she could think of—the only thing that really made sense about any of his behavior here—was that he was some sort of criminal now and she had walked in on something illegal.

Sophia would never have thought Cameron Branson capable of a criminal lifestyle when she had known him before. He'd just gotten out of the military and had more of a love for his family than anyone she'd ever known. He definitely had not been any sort of delinquent then. Trying to figure out where he belonged, sure. But not a criminal.

But she guessed a lot of stuff could happen in five years that changed a person. Case in point, the man standing in front of her whom she both recognized and didn't recognize.

Sophia took a step back from him. His hand, which had still been at her waist, dropped to his side.

"No, I'm not officially here for the Bureau. Nobody else is coming," Sophia told him.

Cameron seemed to relax a little at that admission, which just confirmed Sophia's suspicion about his criminal activities. Who else relaxed at the thought of the FBI *not* coming?

Sophia looked more closely at Cameron. His hair was

much longer than the nearly crew-cut length he used to keep—it curled now at the top of his black T-shirt. His posture was less erect, more casual. His eyes…

Well, his eyes were still the most gorgeous shade of brown she had ever seen.

She'd nearly fallen in love with those eyes once, back when she was too young and stupid to know better. Back when she thought he was a stand-up guy who was interested in her and perhaps wanted a future together.

But she had grown up and left those dreams behind. He hadn't given her much choice, when he'd left without a goodbye and without a single word in the five years since.

So whoever this man standing in front of her was—despite his gorgeous eyes—she needed to get away from him.

For more reasons than one.

CAMERON FELT AS IF he was having an out-of-body experience as the tiny brunette who had been clawing at his face moments before transformed from a stranger into Sophia Reardon.

This was not possible.

Seriously? Of all the warehouses in all the world, she had to be in this one? And moreover, somebody from Omega should've had the roads leading down to this area blocked so nobody who wasn't supposed to be here—for example, a cute brunette with a camera—got through. Somebody was going to catch a load of trouble for this, Cameron would make sure.

But right now he had to get Sophia out of here before somebody from DS-13 saw her.

But man, she looked good. Cameron gave himself just a second to really look at her. He hadn't seen her in five years. She'd been twenty-two years old then, but she didn't seem to have changed much. Her straight brown hair was a little longer, now past her shoulders, but the natural blond highlights were still there. Through the dimness of the warehouse's lights he could barely make out the freckles that still scattered across her cheeks and nose. And her stunning green eyes.

Eyes that were glaring up at him right now. He took a step toward her but she backed up. "I'm not going to hurt you, Soph."

She stopped moving. "I know. I just… I'm pretty claustrophobic. I don't want you to cover my mouth again."

Cameron nodded. "Okay, no problem."

"Why are *you* here, Cameron?" she asked with a great deal of suspicion in her tone.

Cameron couldn't blame her for the unease, given the current situation. "It's a long story and I don't have time to explain."

She jerked away from him. "Yeah. Explanations aren't your strong suit. I remember."

Cameron winced. He reached for her again, but then let his hand fall to the side. Sophia had every right to be angry at him about how things had ended between them five years ago, even though he had never meant to hurt her. Cutting casual ties had just been part of the life he'd chosen when he took the job with Omega Sector.

Of course, the fact that he had thought about her every day since he'd walked away from her had proven to Cameron that Sophia had been more than a casual tie. Now, with quite a bit more perspective, he realized he should've given her more information and a proper goodbye.

Unfortunately, it looked as if he was about to make the same mistakes all over again: no information and no proper goodbye.

"I'm sorry, Sophia. But you have to leave. Quickly."

"And what? You'll explain later? We both know that's not true."

Cameron knew there was no real response he could give. They both did know it was true.

"Besides, I'm not sure I want to know," Sophia continued softly.

Cameron wished he could explain, at least about what was happening right now—about being undercover—but time was running out. He needed to get Sophia out of here immediately. Every moment she stayed there was more of a risk of her being seen by a member of DS-13.

"Sophia…"

She shook her head and continued before he could say anything further, reaching a hand out toward him. "Don't worry, I'm going. Whatever you're doing here, Cameron, I don't want to know. But you be careful." She drew her hand back to her side without actually touching him.

Cameron couldn't stand the look in her eyes. She thought he was a criminal. He wished he could explain. Before she could turn away, Cameron leaned down and put his forehead against hers. "I'm sorry, Soph. Again." Cameron stepped back from her. "Go as fast and as quietly as you can. Don't let anyone see you."

Cameron watched as Sophia turned and carefully manipulated her way down the stairs through all the boxes. He didn't stay to watch her go the rest of the way out. He turned and made his way back to the office.

"Get lost?" Fin snickered as Cameron walked back in.

Cam just snorted. Fin looked at him a little closer. "What happened to you? You look like you've been in a wrestling match."

Damn it. He had practically been in a wrestling match.

"Stupid boxes everywhere. It's like an obstacle course down there. I tripped." Cameron brushed his hair back into place.

That got a few chuckles. Nobody seemed suspicious, which was good. "How's it going here?" Cameron asked.

Fin was taking his time showing off to the buyers what he knew about the assault rifles being sold. Fin liked to show off whenever he knew anything about anything, and oftentimes even when he didn't, but Cameron just let him ramble on. If the buyers didn't know when and if Fin was full of crap then it was their own fault. They'd be sitting in a jail cell in a few hours anyway.

"Why don't you start counting the money, Cam?" Fin told him. Cameron barely bit back a groan of frustration. What he really wanted to do was get over to the window and make sure Sophia's car was gone. But the money was on the other side of the office.

"Sure." Cameron met one of the buyers over at the desk and pulled out a small cash-counting machine from the bag they'd brought. The machine would make things a lot faster, but not fast enough. He wanted to know—needed to know—that Sophia had made it safely out of the building. He fed the cash into the machine as quickly as he could without making it obvious that he was in a hurry. The second buyer watched him carefully the entire time.

After double-checking, because he knew Fin would ask, Cameron put the counter away.

"All here, Fin."

"Did you double-check?"

Cameron refrained from rolling his eyes. "Yes." He walked over and placed the bag of money on the table by Fin, then strolled as casually as possible over to the window.

No car. *Thank God.*

Cameron felt himself relax for the first time since he realized that the tiny brunette who had just been trying to fight her way out of his arms was Sophia. The thought of sweet Sophia being caught in the middle of this made Cameron a little sick to his stomach.

Maybe seeing her today was some sort of sign to him. Further proof he needed to finish up this case and take a break. Maybe he would call Sophia, try to repair the damage from five years ago. Explain to her his reasons for leaving.

And tell her that he had never stopped thinking about her.

But right now he had to concentrate on the case at hand. Fin was finally winding down his spiel about the assault rifles, quite a bit of it incorrect information, the buyers had the weapons they wanted and DS-13 had the cash.

Cameron could tell Fin was pleased. As the buyers left, he walked over to Cameron and slapped him on his back.

"Good job, man. Very smooth transaction."

"As always, Fin. That's what I do."

Cameron wanted to demand to meet Fin's boss, but knew that any request on his part to meet the man would push him that much further away from a meeting. He had been patient up until now. He could be patient awhile longer. Although with the Ghost Shell encoding technology becoming Cameron's prime mission objective, he couldn't be patient much longer.

Fin nodded. "It is what you do, Cam. And Mr. Smith, my…um…boss, has become well aware of that."

Cameron straightened, his interest piqued. He doubted Mr. Smith was the boss's real name, but this was the first time Fin had ever openly talked about him directly to Cameron. Finally, the slightest progress.

"Well, I'd like to meet Mr. Smith someday."

Fin slapped him on the back again. "And you will, buddy. Soon, in fact. Mr. Smith may need your help in setting up some meetings for some new stuff."

Cameron hoped that by *new stuff* Fin meant the Ghost Shell technology. Fin didn't have an expansive vocabulary, unless it came to dirty jokes.

"But now, let's get back to the house so we can see that weight lifting you were talking so much trash about on the way here."

Cameron followed Fin down the stairs. Two of the other three minions were already at the car. The third,

Marco—the one sent to patrol the inside of the warehouse—wasn't there.

Dread pooled in Cameron's stomach.

"Where the hell is Marco?" Fin demanded of the other two. Neither knew.

"He's probably in there smoking or on the can. I'll go find him," Cameron offered. He had a bad feeling.

"Fine." Fin shooed Cameron annoyingly with his hand again. But again Cameron didn't care. "Hurry up."

Cameron made it to the warehouse door, just as it opened. Through it came Marco, dragging a terrified Sophia behind him.

Chapter Three

Cameron knew he had to think fast. A single word from Sophia, any sort of gesture that she knew him, would mean both their lives. In a split second, Cameron made a decision.

But he knew it wasn't going to be pretty.

He stormed up to Marco and grabbed Sophia out of his grasp. "What the hell, Marco? Is this a cop?"

Cameron pushed Sophia, probably a little rougher than necessary, face-first up against the warehouse wall. He heard her indrawn breath, but steeled himself against any thought of her pain or fear.

It was going to get much worse.

Cameron kept his hand pressed against Sophia's back, keeping her forced against the wall. Behind him he heard Fin and the other guys draw their weapons.

He willed Sophia to keep quiet.

Marco, a little shocked by Cameron's aggressive behavior, stuttered, "I just found her inside. She said she was an artist and was taking pictures of the warehouse."

"Did you check to see if she was wearing a wire or anything?" Cameron demanded.

Marco looked sheepish and shook his head. Cameron made a big show of running his hands all over Sophia's body, as if looking for surveillance equipment. Behind him the guys made a couple of catcalls. Sophia shuddered.

When his body search led to her hands, he could feel Sophia press some sort of card into his palm—he wasn't sure what. He moved so he more clearly blocked her from Fin and the men's view, and palmed whatever she had given him without looking at it. As he turned, he slipped it into the pocket of his jeans.

"She's clean," Cameron said as he spun her around. Sophia attempted to straighten the clothes Cameron had lifted and moved during his search, her face burning.

"Listen…" Sophia began.

Cameron backhanded her.

Oh, God. He pulled the slap as much as he could without making it obvious, but he knew it still had to hurt. Her head flew to the side. He watched as a bit of blood began to ooze from a split in her lip. Cameron thought he might vomit.

But if she had said his name, they would both be dead, or at the very least his undercover work would be blown. He couldn't take the chance.

He stuck his finger in her face. "You shut the hell up unless I ask you a specific question, got it?"

Cameron prayed as he had never prayed before that Sophia would keep quiet. He felt a bit of relief when she nodded slowly, staring at the ground.

"Whoa, Cam. I didn't think you had that in you." Fin chuckled.

Cameron smiled a little bit and rolled his shoulders

as if he was getting rid of tension. "Yeah. Well, I hate cops. But it doesn't look like she is one."

Cameron took Sophia's digital camera and brought it over to Fin. Together they looked through the pictures. Cameron relaxed a little when they were all shots of the doorway of the warehouse.

"What are you, a photographer?" Cameron asked her. He hoped she wouldn't bring up the Bureau.

"Yeah. A graphic artist." The answer came out as little more than a whisper from Sophia. She was still looking at the ground.

"What were you doing here?" Fin asked.

"Taking pictures for a computer drawing I'm doing of old warehouses."

Cameron breathed another sigh of relief when she didn't mention law enforcement. Good girl; smart thinking.

Cameron walked back over to her. "Did you know we'd be here?"

Sophia shook her head, staring at the ground. Cameron grabbed her chin and forced her to look up at him—more theatrics for Fin and the guys' benefit, but Sophia was paying the price. "You had no idea we were here?"

"No," Sophia spat out. "I thought all these buildings were abandoned. I just needed some pictures." She was glaring at him, but Cameron could see the terror lurking just behind the anger.

"Yeah, I'm all for woman's lib, but I guess nobody would be stupid enough to send one tiny female with no backup or weapons to arrest all of us." Cameron leered at her. "No offense, sweetheart."

"Marco, did you find any ID on her?" Fin asked.

"Her purse was in her car, which was sitting out front. I moved the car inside the building just in case someone else drove by," Marco informed them.

Well, that answered the question about why Sophia's car hadn't been out front when Cameron had looked the second time.

Marco brought the purse to Fin. Fin glanced inside the bag, evidently finding nothing of interest, pulled out her wallet and let the purse fall to the ground. Fin took her driver's license out.

"Sophia Reardon. Twenty-seven years old. Alexandria address." Fin looked through the rest of her wallet. Cameron held his breath, knowing Sophia must have some sort of FBI identification, even if she wasn't an agent. But Fin didn't say anything, just dropped her wallet into the purse on the ground.

Cameron thought of the card Sophia had slipped to him when he was searching her. Feigning as if he was looking around, Cameron slipped the card out of his pocket and glanced at it. Sure enough, Sophia's FBI credentials.

A smart and gutsy move on her part—one that had just saved her life. If Fin had seen FBI anywhere on her or in her possessions, they wouldn't have cared if she was just a graphic artist and not an agent. As far as they were concerned, anybody employed by the Bureau was their enemy.

Cameron caught Sophia's eye. He patted his pocket and gave her a slight nod. He had no idea if she understood what he was communicating, but she had done a good job.

Cameron walked over to Fin and leaned back against the SUV, knowing he had to play it casual. "So what do we do with her?"

Fin didn't answer immediately. That wasn't encouraging.

The hardest part of undercover work—especially in a situation like this—was figuring out how far you could take your bluff. Pull out of the game too soon and lose eight months of undercover work with only a couple of low-level arrests. But play the game too long and take a chance of somebody calling your bluff…

Which in this case would end in Sophia's death before Cameron could stop it.

And this situation was all the more complicated due to this new damn Ghost Shell technology DS-13 had. If Cameron blew his cover now, Omega would be hard-pressed to acquire that technology before it went on the black market. That could result in the loss of thousands of lives.

But Cameron wasn't going to let Sophia die. Not here. Not today. He was leaning very casually against the SUV, but he had slipped the safety off on his weapon, although it remained concealed under his shirt.

But just like Cameron, everyone here had a weapon. If this came down to a firefight, the odds were definitely not in his favor.

"Let's just let her go, Fin," Marco said. "Smash the camera, break her phone, slash her tires so she can't get anywhere. By the time she walks to the nearest phone, we'll be long gone."

Cameron could've hugged the big lug. That was

exactly the suggestion he had wanted to make, but couldn't.

Fin looked over at Cameron, but Cameron just shrugged as if it didn't matter to him a bit what happened to Sophia.

"No," Fin finally said. "No loose ends. Kill her."

Cameron heard Sophia's indrawn breath and he looked over at her. Full-blown panic was visible in her eyes now. She looked as if she was about to make a run for it. Cameron hoped she wouldn't. He didn't think he could take out all four of the other men before someone got a shot off at her.

A quick plan came to Cameron. God, he hoped this would work. He pushed himself away from the car lazily. "Aw, come on, Fin, can't I at least have a little fun with her first? Take her back to the house so there's something for me to do instead of looking at your ugly mugs all the time?" Cameron used his most cajoling tone.

That got a couple chuckles from the men, but Fin wasn't convinced.

"I thought you didn't like her?"

Cameron smiled easily. "I don't like cops." Cameron walked over to Sophia and trailed a finger along her collarbone, just above her breasts. "But her, knowing she's not a cop? Hmm."

Cameron licked his lips and moved closer to Sophia. She shuddered and stepped as far away from him as she could. A tear fell from the corner of her eye.

The guys all laughed at her reaction to him. Cameron pushed her back against the warehouse wall angrily, as if she had embarrassed him. "Well, obviously

I'm going to have to teach her some manners. But I'm up to the task. Maybe I'll know some dirty jokes when I'm done." That got more laughs.

Fin shook his head. "She's too skinny for me. I prefer women with some meat on their bones."

Cameron grinned and reached out to stroke some of Sophia's hair. She wouldn't even look at him. "Plenty of meat for me."

The guys snickered. Fin looked down at his watch. "Whatever. Do what you want with her. I don't care," Fin told Cameron. "But she's your responsibility. And you have to get rid of her when you're done."

Cameron felt marginally better now that the immediate threat to Sophia's life seemed to have passed, and his undercover work was also relatively safe. But he was pretty sure the look in her eyes would haunt him the rest of his life.

One last finishing touch to the show. He grabbed Sophia by the nape of the neck and hauled her roughly against him. He brought his mouth down heavily on hers, and wrapped his other arm around her hips. For a moment Sophia did nothing, then without warning she exploded into furious action, pushing away from him and squirming in his grasp.

Cameron brought his lips up her jawline to her ear, holding her body firmly against his. Quietly, so no one could hear him but her, he whispered, "Whatever you do, don't let anyone know you know me."

Sophia was attempting so hard to get away from him, Cameron wasn't sure if she heard him. He hoped she did. He brought his lips back to hers. This time she bit his lip.

The men howled in laughter when Cameron jerked back from her.

"Ow, you little hellion. You're going to pay for that."

He grabbed her arm and dragged her to the car. Someone opened the door for them and Cameron all but threw her in, then climbed in after her. It broke his heart to see how Sophia scrambled as far away from him as she could get in the confines of the SUV.

He had saved their lives for now, but the danger was far from finished. And he hoped the trauma he'd dealt Sophia wasn't too much to repair.

SOPHIA WAS JUST trying to keep it together. She slid all the way over in the seat to try to get as far away from Cameron as possible. If she could've curled herself into a tiny ball, she would have.

Normally she didn't like being in the backseat of a vehicle, especially when there were no windows she could roll down. But right now her claustrophobia would just have to get in line behind all the other things her brain had to freak out about.

Like the fact that she had just been kidnapped by some gang that her ex-boyfriend seemed to be part of.

Except she didn't know if he was *really* part of it or not.

Undercover.

It would answer a lot of questions if Cameron was working undercover. Like why he had tried to get her out of the warehouse and hadn't said anything about her FBI credentials.

Of course, it could also be that he was now a member of this organized crime group, or whatever it was, and just didn't want his ex-girlfriend's brains to get splattered all over the pavement.

So back to square one.

Sophia peeked over at Cameron to find him watching her with a decidedly malevolent look in his eyes. Sophia shuddered. That leering look was not something she had ever thought she would see from Cameron. Maybe he really was a criminal now. Sophia tried not to panic. If that look from Cameron was real, she was in big trouble.

But then Sophia glanced up and saw the leader guy, Fin, watching her and Cameron in the rearview mirror. Maybe Cameron suspected that they were being watched and was playing a role.

Undercover.

Please, please, please let him be working undercover.

After Cameron had told her to go, she had done exactly what he had asked: gone straight to her car. But when she had gotten to the door, her car wasn't there. The big guy—Marco?—was driving it inside. Sophia cursed herself for leaving the keys in it, but she had thought there was no one around for miles.

Sophia had tried to sneak outside without Marco seeing her, but hadn't managed it. The next thing she knew he'd grabbed her and had dragged her out the back exit of the warehouse.

Where Cameron had proceeded to scream at, strike and humiliate her.

And maybe save her life.

Sophia touched her lip—it still hurt, both from the slap and his mouth-grinding kiss. She had no such misconception that she was really any safer now than she had been while at the warehouse. But at least nobody had a gun in their hands now.

As the men around her chatted and generally insulted each other, Sophia tried to watch out the window without looking as if she was watching out the window. She didn't want to give anyone—Cameron included—a reason to think she was a threat. But if she had a chance to get away, she planned to take it, and knowing where she was would help.

They were still pretty far outside of DC when they turned into a residential area. Definitely not high-end, the houses were old, but pretty large. They were far enough apart that neighbors wouldn't be forced to see what the other was doing unless they were deliberately trying to. All in all, probably a good location for people selling drugs or weapons or whatever else. Although it wasn't too promising, maybe Sophia would be able to call for help when they parked and got out of the car, and someone would notice.

Their SUV pulled up to the house on the corner. Although the house was probably built in the 1960s, someone had obviously refurbished the garage door with a contemporary opener. The SUV pulled straight into the garage and the door shut quickly behind them.

Sophia bit back a sigh. So much for calling out to the neighbors for help.

Cameron's scary, black look was back. And even though she hoped he might be a good guy, Sophia was frightened. Everyone got out of the car, but Sophia couldn't force herself to move. She shrank back into the seat when Cameron reached for her.

"Get out here right now," Cameron told her through gritted teeth.

She could hear the other men laughing in the doorway. Fin called out, "Regretting your decision already, Cam?"

"I'm not regretting anything, but someone else is about to."

One of the other men whose name she didn't know offered to come help Cam get her out of the vehicle, listing in very crude detail what he would do to her while he was assisting.

Cameron glared at Sophia through narrowed eyes for a moment before calling back over his shoulder, "Actually, that sounds like a pretty good idea, Rick. Why don't you come on in here?"

Sophia immediately scooted over to Cameron and out the car door. All the men doubled over in malicious laughter in the doorway. Cameron grabbed her arm and dragged her forcefully out of the garage past the men, and toward the back of the house into what obviously was his bedroom. Sophia could still hear the other gang members laughing.

Once inside, Cameron turned and locked the door. Then Sophia watched, standing in the middle of the room, as he went over and grabbed a wooden chair that was leaning against the far wall. He dragged the chair to the door and propped it under the doorknob—added defense against anyone entering.

Cameron turned from the door and walked slowly over to Sophia. He stopped only when he was just inches from her. He reached up and touched the split on her lip.

They both winced.

“I’m sorry for everything that happened today, and everything that’s going to happen tonight,” he told her softly. “But right now I’m going to need you to scream like you’re terrified out of your mind. Or else I’m going to have to force you to do it.”

Chapter Four

Cameron wasn't sure if this situation could get much worse, but the look Sophia gave him made him think it probably could.

"Wh-what?" she stammered, backing away from him.

"Scream."

"Why?"

Cameron took a step toward her, closing the space between them again. "Look, Sophia, I don't want to hurt you. I really don't," he whispered close to her ear. "But those creeps out there have to think that there is something pretty terrible going on in here."

Sophia looked around the room frantically, as if trying to find a way to escape. A tear seeped from the corner of her eye.

Cameron grimaced. Unfortunately, tears weren't going to cut it in this case. He had to prove to the men in the rest of the house that there was a reason he had brought Sophia here.

One she wouldn't like.

Ultimately, the worse it seemed in here for her, the safer she would be from the other men.

"You have to scream. Yell. Call me names. Do something."

But Sophia just shook her head, looking around the room, anywhere but at him. It was almost as if she was in shock. Which would be understandable.

"Need some help in there, Cam?" Somebody—it sounded like Rick—called out from the other side of the door.

Damn. "Everything's just fine," Cameron responded.

Cameron gripped Sophia's arms—hard—and shook her. "C'mon, Soph. Work with me. If they think you like it, they're going to want their chance."

She still just looked at him mutely. It honestly seemed beyond her ability to make any sort of sound whatsoever.

"Damn it, Soph." Cameron shook her again. "I need you to fight me like you did back at the warehouse. Before you knew it was me."

Then it occurred to Cameron what he needed to do. She had fought him like a wildcat in the warehouse. Not because she thought he was such a bad guy, but because she seemed so claustrophobic.

In his training and work for both the US Army Rangers and then Omega Sector, Cameron had been taught how to use perps' weaknesses against them. It was one of the reasons Cameron had excelled at undercover work—his ability to pinpoint fears of the enemy. And use those fears without mercy.

He never thought he'd be using that training and skill to manipulate the one woman he once thought he might spend the rest of his life with.

Cameron spun Sophia around and put his hand over

her mouth as he had at the warehouse. She immediately tensed up and started struggling. When he didn't release her after a few moments she began fighting in earnest.

Cameron, protecting his face as best he could from her clawing hands, dragged her over to where the lone dresser stood in the sparse room. She kicked at it, causing it to hit up against the wall.

He could hear laughter from the other rooms.

Cameron removed his hand from her mouth.

"Let me go!" Sophia yelled as soon as his hand was gone. Cameron released her for just a moment and she flung herself around to face him, breaths sawing in and out of her chest.

This wasn't going to work. They couldn't hear her if his hand was over her mouth, but she didn't scream if it wasn't. Cameron looked around. The room had a tiny walk-in closet. Maybe that would be small enough to terrify her.

Cameron steeled himself against the thought of Sophia's terror. He stepped toward her and this time she did scream as he reached for her.

"No!"

His hand covered her mouth again. He could hear whistles and catcalls from outside the door.

"Just a couple more minutes, baby. Hang in there," he whispered into Sophia's ear as he dragged her toward the closet.

When Sophia realized where they were headed, she fought him harder than before. Panic took over. She got a good punch to his cheek before he could catch her arm. That was going to leave a mark. But he didn't let it stop him.

He caught the door with his foot and pushed it open. The closet was practically empty, just a couple of his shirts hanging in it. It wasn't big by any means, with barely enough room for two people, but it wasn't tiny. Only someone who really struggled with tight spaces would have a problem being in it for a short amount of time.

Cameron dragged the struggling Sophia into the enclosed space, keeping her back to his chest. He pulled the door closed with one hand and released her mouth with his other.

Sophia screamed as if she was terrified out of her mind. Which she was.

Cameron had no idea what obnoxious comments or noises the members of DS-13 were making about this. He couldn't hear anything over Sophia's screams.

Sophia fought in a violent frenzy—kicking, clawing, throwing wild punches. Cameron just tried to keep her from hurting him or herself. He kept her as close as he could to his body. After what seemed like the longest period of time in the history of the world—and probably even longer to her—but was really only a few seconds, Cameron opened the door and let go of Sophia. She immediately pushed away from Cameron and all but dived out of the closet, landing heavily on the floor.

She pushed herself across the floor, as far away from him and the closet as she could get, sucking in deep gulps of air the entire time. When she reached the far corner of the room she dragged her knees up to her chest and rocked back and forth. Cameron stood just outside the closet, watching her, unsure what to do. He had no idea why she was so claustrophobic, but it was definitely not something she had any control over.

In that moment Cameron hated every single thing about his life in law enforcement. He was here to catch bad guys. But right now the good guys were the ones who were paying the price.

Cameron took a step toward Sophia and she cringed away from him, whimpering. "No, please…" She stretched out her arms as if to ward him off.

"No," Cameron whispered. "I won't do that again. Never again."

Sophia nodded her head, but still shied away from him. Cameron didn't want to move any closer to her. She'd been through enough. Down the hall, Cameron could hear the TV blaring. Evidently the guys thought the show in Cameron's room was over.

He hoped it had been worth it. Because looking at Sophia right now, Cameron didn't think there was any way it could possibly have been.

Cameron took a few steps toward her then sat down on the floor so he could be eye to eye with Sophia. Her breathing was still labored, and every last ounce of color was missing from her face.

"Sophia, I'm so sorry." Cameron spoke softly. He knew this room wasn't bugged, but couldn't take any chances on any member of DS-13 overhearing them.

Cameron moved a little closer to Sophia but she shied away again. Cameron rubbed the back of his neck, where permanent tension seemed to have lodged, at least since he had first seen Sophia again this afternoon.

He wanted to give Sophia the physical space she needed, but the things he needed to say couldn't be said from across the room. Moving slowly, he scooted over until he was next to her against the wall.

Sophia just huddled into her corner and didn't look at him. But at least her breathing was slowing down a bit, wasn't quite so labored.

"Sophia, I'm so sorry," he said again. As if saying it again would make everything okay. "I had to make them think that something bad was happening in here."

Sophia gave a quiet bark of acerbic laughter.

Cameron shook his head. "I mean, something *they* would think is bad. You know what they expected."

Sophia nodded her head slightly, but didn't say anything. They sat there in silence for long moments. Cameron tried to figure out what possible words could make this better.

"Things have changed since I saw you last, five years ago," Cameron said softly, close to her ear.

"I know," Sophia all but hissed, but just as softly. "The Cameron Branson I knew five years ago never would've done this." She gestured toward her face with her hand, then pointed toward the closet with a shaky arm.

"Sophia, I'm sorry I hit you earlier. I had to take action immediately. And the closet..." Cameron shrugged wearily. "It had to be done."

Sophia turned away from him again without saying anything.

"It's not like I planned any of this. Damn it, Soph, I'm just trying to keep you alive."

Sophia covered her face with her hands and began to cry. Looking over at the arm that was now exposed because her short-sleeved blue shirt was ripped at the shoulder, he could see some angry red marks on her arm. Those were from him, probably during the closet fiasco. They were definitely going to leave bruises on her pale skin, even though he had only been trying to help.

Although it pained him, Cameron hardened himself against the ache he felt at the thought of marring her beautiful skin. The bruises would help sell their story to DS-13.

"At least tell me you're here, you know…working," Sophia finally said to him.

Cameron appreciated that she left out the word *undercover.* That word could get them both killed quicker than almost anything else they could say. "Yeah. I'm with the agency."

Cameron knew he was being vague, but didn't think now was the time to go into Omega Sector and his life there. When they had known each other before, he had just been coming out of the Rangers. Sophia didn't know anything about Omega—even most people who worked in the FBI knew nothing about it.

Sophia let out a sigh and turned toward him slightly. "Well, that's a relief. I wasn't sure."

She wasn't sure? "Seriously? What did you think, I had left the Rangers and joined some sort of crime syndicate since we last spoke?"

"Stranger things have happened."

Cameron shook his head. "I guess." He must really have been undercover too long if an old friend couldn't tell if he was pretending or not. Maybe he had been in the darkness too long.

Cameron didn't have time for metaphors about darkness and light in his life. He had a job to do: justice for his partner's killer and retrieval of Ghost Shell. And now making sure Sophia got out of this alive and relatively unscathed.

He definitely did not have time to think about how beautiful she was, or how much she had meant to him five years ago, or how often he had thought about her since.

Keeping her alive. That was the most important thing.

WAS HE HONESTLY offended that she couldn't tell if he was really working undercover or not when she was sitting here with bruises and a racing heartbeat from what he had done to her?

Sophia looked at the closet again. From across the room, it looked so benign. Obviously there was plenty of air throughout both this room and the closet. She very clearly knew that now. But five minutes ago there had been no way to convince her mind of that.

She pulled her knees closer to her body. She believed Cameron when he said he was undercover. She even believed he was doing what he thought was best when he had hit her earlier, and everything that had happened since. But that didn't mean she wanted him to touch her again.

But part of her desperately wanted him to touch her again. She had wanted that for five years. But not here in this house with those filthy men in the next room.

Sophia glanced sideways at Cameron. He looked as exhausted as she felt. Sophia didn't know much about undercover work, but she was sure that her entrance into the picture had to have thrown a wrench into whatever mission he was on.

"Have I totally screwed things up for you? I tried to get out of the warehouse like you said, but that big guy was out there," Sophia offered softly.

Cameron looked surprised that she was talking to him at all. Now that she was calming down she was realizing that Cameron really had been working in her best interest.

But she still wanted out of here as soon as possible.

"Well, your presence was definitely unexpected. But so far it looks like there was no harm done to the case."

"Really?" Sophia couldn't believe that was true.

"Yeah, evidently how I've been treating you has been helping solidify my bad-guy reputation."

"How long have you been…working with them?" Sophia turned toward him slightly.

"This group is called DS-13. They're basically into everything—weapons, drugs, money laundering. And now it looks like they're expanding into full-on terrorism." Cameron gestured toward the rest of the house with his thumb. "I've been in this house for about three weeks, but first made contact eight months ago."

"What do you do? I mean, what do they think you do?"

"They think I'm a midlevel weapons dealer. What you walked in on today was a sale I had set up."

Sophia shook her head. Just sheer bad luck. If Bruce had gotten the pictures when he was supposed to have… "If they did a sale, can't you make arrests?"

Cameron shifted a little closer to her, but this time Sophia didn't feel the need to move away.

"I could've arrested everybody there, and would've tried if things had gotten much more out of hand."

"Tried?"

Cameron reached over and pulled up her ripped sleeve, as if he could reattach it to the rest of her shirt by sheer will. "There were four of them, all armed, against just you and me. And only I had a weapon."

"Not very good odds, I guess." Sophia shuddered thinking about it.

"No, I doubt if either of us would've made it out alive." Cameron shrugged and smiled crookedly at her. "But I would've tried."

"Don't you have a wire or something? Backup?"

"Sometimes. But not in deep cover like this. It's too complicated and dangerous to have surveillance all the time. DS-13 is smart—that's why they chose this house. Surveillance vehicles would be pretty easy to spot around here."

"But what if you need help?" Sophia couldn't believe they would just send Cameron in by himself.

He smiled at her again and she found herself shifting a little more toward him.

That cocky smile. Lord, how she'd missed it.

"Honey, I can take care of myself. But I do have ways to bring in backup, if I need it."

"Like today?"

"Believe it or not, today was mostly for show. The buyers were picked up not long after they left the warehouse. The whole thing was just supposed to show DS-13 how helpful and well-organized my buys could be for them."

Cameron stretched his long legs out in front of him.

"The agency was supposed to have blocked everything off so nobody would be around those warehouses."

Sophia rolled her eyes. "Yeah, well, I got way lost and ended up coming through some farmer's back field to get to the warehouses. If the FBI was watching the roads, that's why they didn't see me."

Cameron nodded as if she had just solved some puzzle for him. "I didn't want to make any arrests because these are just lower-level bad guys. I'm trying to get their boss."

Sophia watched, a little frightened, as Cameron's face and posture hardened right before her eyes. Whoever this "boss" was, Cameron wanted to take him down. Badly.

"No luck yet?"

"Haven't even met him. This sort of work is tricky—you can't push too hard or it backfires on you."

Sophia nodded. She couldn't imagine the sort of pressure being undercover would put on someone. Never knowing if you were making the right choices, or when you may be discovered.

It had definitely made Cameron Branson into a harder man than when she had known him five years ago. Then, he had still been strong—physically, mentally, in all possible ways. But now there was an edge to him that hadn't been there before. One that scared her a little.

One that had probably saved her life earlier.

Almost as if her body was moving of its own accord she turned toward him. He did look exhausted. His black hair, grown out from how short it used to be, was touching his collar. Before she could stop herself,

Sophia reached out and tucked a stray curl back from where it had fallen onto his forehead, nearly to his eyes.

For a moment they looked at each other. Sophia forgot where they were, the danger they were in, the fear she had felt. She only saw Cameron.

Something slid under the door before a fist beat loudly on it. Sophia jumped back at the sound, the moment—whatever it was—shattered.

"Cam, man, you alive in there? I need to talk to you."

Cameron stood up and walked over to pick up whatever had been slid under the door. "Yeah, Fin. I'll be right out."

Cameron walked back over to her, and reached his hand out to help her up. Sophia hesitated for just a moment before taking it. "What is it he put under the door?"

Cameron walked with her over to the edge of the bed then sat down with a sigh. He held up what was in his hands: plastic zip ties—used everywhere to secure and fasten all sorts of things.

Sophia shook her head, confused. What were the ties for? Whatever it was, Cameron wasn't too happy about it.

"Poor man's handcuffs," he finally said. "I guess Fin wants to make sure you don't try to escape or anything while he and I are talking."

Oh. "Okay, I guess." Sophia was determined to keep it together. Now that she knew Cameron was undercover, she needed to help him if she could. Not being hysterical was the most help she could offer right now.

"Just don't try to struggle against them. They'll cut into your wrists if you do."

Sophia swallowed hard and nodded.

"I'm going to run one set around your wrists and one around your ankles since there's nothing in this room to secure you to. It will look more authentic that way if someone checks."

Sophia's panicked glaze flew up to his. Someone checking?

A fist pounded on the door again. "Damn it, Cam. Hurry up. You can finish doing whatever you want to her after we talk."

Cameron spoke to her quickly as he pulled the plastic fasteners around her ankles. "I'll be as fast as I can, but sometimes Fin likes to hear himself talk."

Cameron tightened the ties so they were tight but not painful. "If anybody comes through that door that isn't me, start screaming your head off. Immediately. Don't wait to see what they want."

Sophia nodded. That wasn't a problem. She knew her screaming voice was definitely in working condition.

Cameron slipped the other ties around her wrists, and pulled them tight. He helped her so she was sitting up against the wall the bed leaned against.

Cameron leaned down and put his forehead against hers. "I'm going to get you out of this. I swear to God." He lowered his lips and kissed her gently, then turned and strode out of the room without another word.

Chapter Five

Obnoxious catcalls met Cameron as he walked down the hall and past the living room. He stopped and gave the guys a little smirk and bow—even though it made him sick to his stomach—before turning and heading into the kitchen to see Fin.

Fin sat at the table, nursing a beer. Cameron made his way to the fridge to get a beer of his own as Fin looked him up and down.

"Worth it?" the man asked.

Cameron gave his most sly smile. "Absolutely." He held his beer up in silent salute as he took the seat across from Fin.

Fin gestured toward Cameron's face. "Looks like she may have given you a bruise there on your cheek."

He thought of all the marks on Sophia's arms. "She'll have plenty of her own."

Fin cackled at that. "Well, I'm glad it was worth the trouble." Cameron settled back in his chair, somehow managing to keep the smile on his face.

"So, I spoke to Mr. Smith tonight, while you were having your…fun," Fin continued.

Cameron kept his best poker face and feigned disinterest as he took a sip from his bottle. "I didn't know Mr. Smith was interested in the details of that sort of fun."

"Mr. Smith is interested in anything and everything that has to do with DS-13. And he has taken an interest in you."

Bingo. Eight months undercover, and this was what he had been waiting for. "Oh, yeah? Why's that?"

"He was impressed—has always been impressed—with how the sales you arrange go down without a hitch."

Cameron nodded and took a sip of his beer. "That's what I do."

"Well, Mr. Smith would like for you to start arranging more meetings and perhaps find some other sorts of buyers for some items he's come into recently."

"What sort of items?" Encoding technology, perhaps?

"Mr. Smith wants to meet you and tell you about that himself."

Cameron could tell Fin was watching him closely to see how he would react. How he played this off would be key. Too much enthusiasm would most certainly be reported back to Mr. Smith, and perhaps cause the whole invitation to be pulled. Not enough enthusiasm would be reported back as an insult.

But insult was definitely better than suspicion, so Cameron took another long drag on his beer and remained sprawled in his chair.

"That's cool. Whatever. Just let me know when." Cameron yawned, then got up, as if the meeting with Fin was over. He could tell Fin wasn't expecting that.

"Whoa, hang on there a minute, Cam. I'm not done."

"Oh…sorry, man." Cameron sat back down as if he didn't really care much about what Fin was going to say next. Which couldn't be further from the truth.

"Mr. Smith wants to meet you *tomorrow*," Fin told him.

That was a little sooner than Cameron expected, but not too bad. If he could find a way to get Sophia to safety.

"Okay, that's fine. Is he coming here? Does he want me to set up something with a buyer for tomorrow? That's kind of hard when I don't know what he's selling."

Fin shook his head. "No, he only wants to meet you tomorrow. Let's just say that your actions with the pretty brunette have reassured him that you're not afraid of getting your hands a little dirty."

Cameron grinned despite his souring stomach. "Well, it wasn't my hands getting dirty, if you know what I mean."

Fin howled in laughter again before turning serious. "Mr. Smith needs you to begin setting up some meetings with people who may be interested in doing a little bit more damage than just with a few automatic weapons."

"You mean like missiles or something?"

"No, actually a specific computer program or virus or something that can do major damage to law enforcement. I don't really understand it. But Mr. Smith says it's going to bring in a lot of money."

Cameron nodded. "Okay, man, no problem. Tell Mr. Smith I can line that up for him."

"Actually, you can tell him yourself when you see

him tomorrow. He's having a bit of a get-together at his mountain home. Has some people he'd like you to meet."

Crap. "Mountain home? Where? And I don't think it's going to work real well to bring 'my companion' on a plane, you know?"

"Cam, DS-13's resources are much greater, and more organized, than you think. We'll be using a small jet, owned by one of DS-13's dummy corporations. And Mr. Smith's house is in the mountains of Virginia."

"Wow. I didn't know about all that." Actually, Cameron did know about all that, at least all of it except the mountain house. No wonder Smith was never spotted, since he had some sort of secluded retreat.

Damn it. All of this just got much harder for him and Omega Sector. He needed to contact them tonight and let them know about the location change.

But most important he needed to get Sophia out of here as soon as possible. There was no way he was going to let her be transported to some remote location where he had even less control over the situation.

"There's a lot you don't know about DS-13, Cam," Fin said, smiling knowingly, self-importance fairly radiating off him. "Just be ready to go in the morning. We'll have to figure out what to do with your little friend by then."

"Private jet. Cool." At least Cameron's cover persona would think so. Cameron himself didn't give a damn.

"You'll want to be at your best when you meet Mr. Smith," Fin told him with a grin. "So don't exhaust yourself with other things."

"Roger that." Cameron took the last sip of his beer

and stood up. “See you tomorrow.” As he walked out of the kitchen he grabbed a bag of chips and one of the post-workout protein shakes the guys had lying around. It wasn’t a great meal for Sophia, but at least it was something.

Cameron didn’t have much time. Morning would come fast. He had no doubt that when Fin said they’d “figure out what to do with” Sophia in the morning, he meant kill her. He had to think of a plan to get Sophia out of here. Quickly.

Cameron walked as casually as he could back to the room. As he opened the door, he saw Sophia, still tied as he had left her, about to start screaming.

“It’s just me.” He put down the food and walked quickly over to her. “Are you okay? Any problems?”

“No, I’m fine. Just ready to get untied.”

Cameron pulled out the knife he always kept in his pocket. He made quick work of the zip ties, first at her wrists then her ankles, allowing the plastic to drop to the floor.

Sophia rubbed her wrists to try to get some of the blood to flow back normally. Cameron reached down and gently rubbed her ankles.

“Better?” he asked softly.

Sophia nodded. “Yeah, thanks. Did everything go okay out there?”

Cameron reluctantly stopped rubbing her ankles, released her feet and went to put the chair back under the door handle. He handed her the food and she began to eat.

He turned to her. “Yes and no.”

Sophia drew her knees up to her chest and wrapped

her arms around them. "Yes and no? That doesn't sound too good."

Cameron came and sat back down on the edge of the bed. "Well, in a rather ironic turn of events, it seems that the horrible way I've treated you has made DS-13 trust me more."

"What?"

"Whatever doubts they had about me have evidently been eradicated since I have turned into a rapist slime-ball."

"But you didn't..."

"Yeah, but they don't know that. Evidently your screams were pretty convincing." Cameron rubbed an exhausted hand over his eyes. He didn't want to think about that again.

Sophia unwrapped her grip on her legs and crawled a little closer to him, reaching out and touching him on the arm. "Cam, you did what you had to do. I thought about it while you were gone. You saved both of our lives without a doubt."

"Sophia..."

She moved a little closer. "I'm sorry about all that stuff I said. I don't think badly of you. I can't stand you thinking badly of yourself."

Cameron turned so he was facing directly toward her. He took the hand that was touching his arm and held it in both of his. God, she was so sweet. He looked down at the hand in his—so tiny.

He couldn't stand the thought of her being in this room—around these people—a minute longer. And the thought of taking Sophia to that other house where Mr. Smith was? Totally unacceptable.

Cameron reached out and stroked her cheek. She was looking at him so intently, so concerned about his *feelings*. Cameron could barely remember the last time he'd had an authentic feeling. Until today.

"I'm fine, Soph. If anything, just glad that something good has come out of this situation."

She smiled shyly before easing away. "Me, too."

"It seems that the quite elusive leader of DS-13, a man named Mr. Smith, wants to meet me now because of how everything went down today."

"That's good, right?"

Cameron nodded and eased backward on the bed so he was sitting next to her. "Yeah. That's what I've been trying to do for eight months."

"So what's the bad?"

Cameron sighed. "He wants to meet me tomorrow."

Cameron watched as Sophia obviously tried to figure out what that meant for her. "Oh, okay," she finally responded.

"Even worse, he wants for me to go to his mountain house. That's not…optimal for the situation."

"Because of me?"

"Partially, but not totally. I wasn't aware of this other location until tonight. I don't know anything about it so it's hard to prepare for it."

Sophia nodded, worry plain in her eyes.

He didn't know if she was worried for herself or him. Probably both. "But you're not going, so you don't need to worry about anything."

"I'm not going?"

"We're going to get you out of here tonight."

Sophia sat up straighter, obviously ready for action. "We are? How?"

"Wait until late, when everyone is asleep, then I'm going to tell you how to sneak out."

"But won't that cause trouble for you? Won't your cover be blown?"

Cameron shook his head. "Not if we do it right. It's going to have to look like you knocked me unconscious. I'm going to need a pretty good goose egg on my head."

When Sophia just shook her head, Cameron continued, "If anything, it will help. They'll be in a panic that you'll call the cops and will want to get out of here even faster. Anything that throws them off their timetable can only help me."

"That's good, I guess." Sophia shook her head again. "But I don't want to hit you with anything."

Cameron reached up and softly touched her swollen and bruised lip. "C'mon sweetie, turnabout is fair play."

"Cameron." Sophia reached up and touched his hand. "You did this because you had to. I know that."

"And you'll do this because you have to. It's the only way, Sophia."

SOPHIA DIDN'T LIKE IT. She really had come to terms with what he had done while he was having his meeting with Fin. Everything that had happened from the moment she had seen Cameron in the warehouse today had been done to protect her.

She didn't want to hurt him. But it looked as if she was going to have to.

"There's no other way?" she asked.

"Not if we want to keep suspicions off me. I'll wake

up and notice you're gone. Then I'll tell everyone we should leave before you call the cops."

"They won't think you let me go?"

Cameron shook his head. "Absolutely not. Especially not after earlier. Although can you do something for me?"

"I can try."

Cameron leaned close and whispered in her ear, "Can you yell, 'Get off me, you bastard'? It's been a little too quiet in here."

Sophia shot off the bed. If she couldn't do it, would he drag her back into the closet? She looked over at it, then back at him.

Cameron wasn't making moves toward her—as a matter of fact, he was keeping himself very casual and relaxed on the bed—but Sophia still took a step back. Then she stopped.

Just yell. It's not hard. Just do it.

"Get off me, you bastard!" she yelled at the top of her voice.

Immediately she could hear guffaws of laughter from other places in the house. Perverts.

Cameron got off the bed and came to stand right next to her. "Thank you."

"Anything to stay out of the closet."

Cameron grinned. "Got it." He grabbed her hand and brought it up to his lips and kissed it softly.

They both seemed a little shocked by his impulsive gesture, but Sophia didn't pull her hand away and Cameron didn't let it go.

"I just want to get you out of here. That's the most important thing to me," Cameron whispered. He let go of her hand, wrapped his arms around her and drew her to his chest. Sophia snuggled in. After what she had been through today his arms felt like absolute heaven. This was what she remembered about them from five years ago: a closeness that matched the burning attraction between them.

She and Cameron had met at a diner that was just a couple of blocks from her tiny apartment in Washington, near Georgetown University, where she went to school. Hating her own cooking, Sophia had made a habit of going to the diner each morning and one particularly crowded day Cameron had asked to share her booth and they'd struck up a conversation. Then he had started showing up at the same time every morning, displaying a great deal of interest in her.

Emotionally, Sophia had fallen fast and she had fallen hard.

But physically, Sophia was shy and a little bit awkward, so she had taken things slowly with Cameron, thinking they would have all the time in the world. For three months, they went on dates, shared many passionate kisses, sometimes talked all night, just to end up back at the diner for breakfast the next morning.

Sophia had thought—had *known*—Cameron was the one for her. And his willingness to wait so patiently for her physically had made her love him even more.

And she thought he felt the same way. But then one morning he didn't show up. The thought still left her feeling a little sick to her stomach. Plus, he had waited until he knew she would be at the diner to call her home phone and leave a message. *Hi, Soph. Something's come up and I'm going to have to leave town permanently. I wish you all the best. Take care.*

She still knew the message by heart. At least now, five years later, she didn't cringe when she thought about it.

Sophia eased herself back from his arms. A nice hug in the middle of a traumatic event was one thing, allowing herself to dive into the past and drag out all the hurts was quite another.

Cameron didn't try to hold on to her when Sophia pulled back. And although she knew it was for the best, it still panged her just a little.

"Okay, so what's the plan?" Sophia asked as she moved away and sat back down on the bed, which was as sparse as everything else in this room. She looked around. Nothing was inviting or comforting in the least. And the little she'd seen of the rest of the house as he'd dragged her in here wasn't much better.

Plus it was pretty stuffy in here. There was only a tiny window, covered by cheap blinds that barely let in any light at all. The bedroom was attached to a bathroom, but that room wasn't much more appealing, even with its own window.

Cameron saw her looking around. "What?"

"Just…this room. This entire house. You've been here three weeks, you said? How can you stand it?"

Cameron shrugged. "It's just part of the job. DS-13 wanting me to stay here was actually a huge step in the right direction. It meant they were really starting to trust me. Took long enough."

"Eight months, right? Isn't that a long time for—"

she lowered her voice even further "—undercover work? Consistent work?"

"Yeah, it's starting to reach the outer limits. But I asked to stay on this case and keep this cover for so long."

"Why?"

Cameron came and sat next to Sophia on the bed. "Let's just say that I'm determined that Mr. Smith—leader of DS-13—is going down."

Fierce determination gleamed in Cameron's eyes, as well as frustration.

"Something in particular you want him for, or just because he's a really bad guy?" Sophia asked, wanting to understand.

"Him being a bad guy is enough, but yeah, for me it's personal. He killed my partner last year. Viciously."

Sophia had no idea what to say to that. She reached out and touched his arm. "I'm so sorry, Cam."

Cameron nodded. "Mr. Smith suspected Jason, my partner, was undercover. Then cut his throat when he found out it was true."

Sophia's expression shuttered and she rubbed Cam's arm. No wonder Cameron was so intent on arresting Mr. Smith. She didn't blame him.

Cameron stood, and Sophia's hand fell away. "I will get him, Soph. Don't doubt it."

"I don't." Sophia smiled at Cameron and stood up. "So how are we getting me out of your way so you can get your job finished? Because, honestly, I can't stand the thought of you living in this jackass-infested rat hole much longer." She gestured around the room with her hand.

Cameron chuckled softly. "Jackass-infested rat hole?"

Sophia raised one eyebrow. "Seems apt. Although perhaps my metaphor is a bit mixed. I just want to get out of here and let you get to the other evil lair."

Cameron chuckled again. "I'm pretty sure they don't call it an evil lair."

Sophia smiled. She had missed his laugh. "Well, they should. So what's the plan?"

They were both startled by a loud pounding on the door again. Whoever it was tested the doorknob to see if it was locked. Cameron hooked his arm around Sophia and pulled her behind him so he was between her and the door.

"I'm busy in here!" Cameron yelled out, making annoyance plain in his voice. "What the hell do you want?"

"Cam, Fin said to give you these." It was one of the men, but Sophia didn't know which one. More plastic ties slid under the door.

"Fine, Rick. But stay the hell out unless you're trying to see my naked ass, you pervert."

They heard Rick mutter something about wanting to see a naked ass, but not Cameron's. But at least he left them alone. If Rick decided to force his way through the door, that chair propped under the knob definitely wasn't going to stop him.

Cameron breathed a sigh of relief when he seemed sure Rick was gone. "We've definitely got to get you out of here."

A thought occurred to Sophia. "Why did you tell them your real name? Isn't that dangerous?"

"They only know my first name. I discovered a while ago that it was better to use my first name for covers. Less confusion, less possible mistakes."

Sophia wasn't sure she understood. "Mistakes?"

"Well, if bad guys think your name is Tom but some complete stranger happens to say the name Cameron and you react…"

"Game over."

Cameron nodded. "Game definitely over. It's easier to keep the lies as close to the truth as possible."

"But no Branson, right?"

"Nope. Cam Cameron, at your service."

Sophia rolled her eyes. "Cam Cameron?"

Cameron shrugged. "Hey, it works."

"All right, Cam Cameron, what do we do now?"

"Now we climb in bed and wait a few hours, so I can get you out of here as soon as everyone's asleep. You need to be long gone before tomorrow morning."

Chapter Six

Lying in bed with Cameron for the few hours before they were going to sneak her out, Sophia never would've thought she would sleep. But evidently her traumatized mind had other plans.

Cameron had lain down with her on the small bed and tucked her into his side.

"Try to rest, if you can," he had whispered.

The last thing Sophia remembered was snorting, "Yeah, right." The next thing she knew, Cameron was waking her up…

With a kiss.

It took her a moment to figure out what was happening. Even longer to remember where she was. But she shut that all out for a few moments and melted into Cameron.

Sophia twisted in the tiny bed so she could get closer to him. She wrapped her fingers in his hair and pulled him against her. Cameron's hand slid from her neck all the way down her back and splayed out over her hip. He pulled her closer and deepened the kiss.

Sophia could barely keep from moaning. She had

missed this passion between them that erupted without either of them being able to do anything about it.

Cameron's lips trailed from her mouth, over her jaw and down to her neck. Sophia shivered, her breath quickening. She gave herself over to the sensation.

But after a few moments Cameron pulled away.

"I'm sorry, Soph. I shouldn't have done that."

Suddenly, all the reasons why this wasn't a good idea came crashing back to her. Sophia jerked away from him.

"You're right. You shouldn't have done that."

Cameron sighed and got up from the bed.

"I think everyone is asleep. It's time for us to get you out of here."

Sophia decided to let go of her annoyance about the kiss. Kisses. Complete make-out session. Whatever. There were more important things to concentrate on here.

She got up from the bed. "What time is it?"

"About 4:00 a.m. It's late enough that nobody should be awake, but still dark enough for you not to be seen."

Sophia nodded. "Okay. What do I need to do?"

"I'm going to walk you out and show you where the side door is. We'll go ahead and unlock it."

Sounded easy enough. "Okay."

"Once you get out, I want you to run, as fast as you can. When you get to the main road, there's a gas station about half a mile down. Call the Bureau and have somebody pick you up."

"No 911?"

"No. That would wreak havoc on what I'm doing

here. I want them to think you've called 911, but I don't want to have to deal with any uniforms poking around."

Sophia nodded.

"After I show you the door," Cameron continued, "we have to come back in here. I can't hit myself hard enough for it to be realistic."

Sophia cringed. She didn't know if she'd be able to hit him hard enough, either.

Cameron opened the door and ushered Sophia out. Everything in the house was quiet. Cameron led her silently down the hall to the side door, past the garage. She watched as he unlocked the door, and cracked it just the slightest bit, so it wouldn't make any noise when she came out here in a few minutes.

Cameron turned and looked at Sophia. Sophia nodded. She knew what to do when she came back. They silently headed back toward Cameron's room. With every step, Sophia was terrified someone would wake up and catch them.

Would that mean death for both of them? Would Cameron be able to cover for them again? Sophia didn't know.

She was also concerned that he wouldn't be able to convince DS-13 that her escape was an accident. That he wouldn't be able to talk his way out of it and that all his time working undercover would go to waste.

Or worse.

Back in his room, Sophia turned to Cameron. "What if they don't believe I attacked you and got away? What if they think you let me go?"

Cameron put his hands on her forearms. "Soph, it's okay. I've been with them a long time. They'll believe me."

"But how will I know you're okay? How will I know something bad hasn't happened to you?"

Cameron's hands slid up from her arms, over her shoulders until they were framing her face. "I'm good at what I do. I'll make them believe me, don't worry."

Sophia nodded. Her hands were a little shaky as she asked, "Is this the part where I get to knock you unconscious?"

Cameron grimaced. "Yeah. You're going to need to use the butt of my SIG to hit me with. There's nothing else in here that will do."

Sophia didn't like the thought of hitting him, and liked the thought of using a gun even less. "I don't know if that's a good idea. I don't know anything about guns."

"Well, just don't point it at me and pull the trigger and we'll be fine." Cameron's smile didn't reassure Sophia much. "I'll make sure it's not loaded," he added at her worried look. "Once you've hit me, take the gun with you and go. You probably won't even knock me unconscious. All that matters is that it looks like you did. In about an hour, I'll stumble out and wake everybody up, pretending like you just got away a few minutes ago."

Sophia had to admit, it was a pretty well-thought-out plan. She prayed it would work. For both their sakes.

"Okay, where do I hit you?" she whispered.

"On the back of the head, toward the base of my skull. Contrary to what you might think, it's the sudden, jerking motion of the skull that causes blackouts from an injury like this. Not necessarily the actual force."

"You mean I could hit you as hard as I can and it wouldn't matter?"

Cameron quickly corrected her. “No, that would definitely cause brain damage or possibly death. You don’t want to rabbit-punch me.”

“Rabbit punch is bad?”

Cameron nodded. “Very. I just mean that you don’t necessarily need tremendous force to knock someone unconscious. It’s the motion that causes it.”

Sophia wasn’t sure if she could do it. Cameron could see her obvious hesitation. “Soph, I’ll be fine. But we’re out of time. I need you to do this and get going.”

Sophia nodded.

“I have a hard head, sweetheart. I’ve been swearing that was true every day for five years.”

Sophia couldn’t help but laugh softly. “You and me both.”

Cameron sat on the bed, facing away from her. Sophia ran her fingers through his thick black hair, then let it go. She raised her arm with the gun in her hand.

“Ready?” Cameron asked. “Remember, hit me hard. Having to do it twice would really hurt. And once you’ve hit me, go. Don’t wait around. I promise I will be fine. One, two, three.”

Sophia brought the gun’s handle down—hard—against the base of his skull. Cameron made a sickening groan and fell forward onto the bed. Sophia could see that he was still breathing. Blood was slowly seeping from a giant knot where she’d hit him. Tears slid down her cheeks as she glanced at Cameron once more before easing out the door of his room.

Sophia’s breath seemed unimaginably loud to her as she made her way down the hallway as Cameron had shown her. Every step was full of terror, as she was afraid someone might wake up and catch her. As she walked through the kitchen, her shoes sounded so loud she slipped them off and carried them. Finally she made it to the side door that led outside from the kitchen.

It was closed.

Sophia knew Cameron had left that door open. She spun around in a panic, expecting to see someone behind her. But no one was there.

Maybe it had closed on its own. Sophia tried the knob. It was still unlocked. It must have just caught some wind or something. Regardless, she couldn't let it stop her now.

Sophia eased the door open as quietly as she could, grimacing with every little sound the door made. When the door was open the barest amount for her to fit, she slipped through, and pulled it gently and slowly closed behind her.

Sophia breathed a silent sigh of relief. At least she was out of the house. She bent down to put her flats back on her feet and took a deep breath to get her bearings and get ready to run. That's when she smelled it: cigarette smoke.

From right around the corner of the house.

Sophia quickly moved behind a large trash can that sat against the house, in case whoever was there came around the corner. Now she wouldn't be able to run the way Cameron had directed without being seen. She'd have to go the opposite way and then double back to the gas station when she was farther away from the house.

"I don't understand why we have to stay up all night." It sounded like Rick, the mean one with cold eyes.

"Well, you know Fin's not going to stay up if we're going to see Mr. Smith tomorrow."

Sophia didn't really care about who had to stay up or why Fin needed his beauty rest to see Mr. Smith. She needed to get out of here, now.

"But I don't understand why Fin doesn't trust Cam. Cam's one of us." That sounded like the big guy, Marco.

Sophia was starting to ease her way around to the back of the house when she heard Marco's statement. Fin didn't trust Cameron? She stopped and eased her way back so she could hear the conversation better.

"Yeah, well, if the woman is still here in the morning, then we'll know Cam is on the up-and-up. But like Fin said, if Cam let the woman get away…" Rick's voice trailed off.

"That doesn't mean he's a cop."

"He's either a cop or someone who lets a hundred-pound woman get the jump on him. Either way, DS-13 doesn't want him. Fin will take care of that." Rick laughed and Marco joined in after a moment.

Damn it. Sophia realized she was, in essence, signing Cameron's death warrant if she left now. She couldn't do it. She would have to sneak back inside and they'd figure out something else. She needed to hurry back into Cameron's room before he came out and told everyone she was missing.

And got himself killed.

Sophia peeked around the side of the trash can and jerked herself back as the two men walked around the corner. She held her breath, praying they hadn't seen her.

Marco was talking about a football game coming on

that night as they walked in the kitchen door. Sophia felt her heart drop as she heard the click of the lock once they were inside.

She had to find a way back into the house. Sophia ran around to the back, having to make her way over a low wooden fence when she found the fence gate locked. From the back of the house in the dark, it was hard to tell which room was Cameron's.

Sophia knew she had to figure it out quickly. Cameron was running out of time and he had no idea about it.

Sophia definitely didn't want to climb into the wrong room. But one window was a little higher than the others, and smaller. That must be the bathroom, which would make Cameron's the window to the left.

Sophia ran to Cameron's window and began tapping on it. She had to get his attention before he went out and told them she was gone. She tapped as loud as she dared, not wanting to wake anyone else.

"Cameron?" Sophia cupped her hands to the window in an attempt to make the sound go through it, rather than out. "Cameron!"

Nothing. She rapped on the pane again but he didn't come to the window. Sophia tried to open the window but it was locked from the inside.

She had to get in the house. It might already be too late.

Sophia climbed up onto the air-conditioning unit so she could reach the small window of the bathroom. Someone had left it cracked, just a little bit, but it was enough.

Sophia got her hands under the frame and slid it up as

high as it would go, cringing as it made a loud creaking sound. She hefted her body up and into the tiny opening. All the buttons of her blouse ripped off as she scooted through, but Sophia didn't stop. When a nail caught her shoulder Sophia let out a cry, but still didn't stop.

She finally got herself through the opening and fell into the bathtub on the other side. She got up as quickly as she could, using a towel to wipe the blood from a pretty large gash on her shoulder. She rushed into Cameron's room.

But he wasn't there.

Chapter Seven

The crack Sophia gave him on the back of the head definitely wasn't too soft. Although Cameron didn't lose consciousness for more than a few seconds—at least he didn't think so—his head hurt like the devil. Lying on his bed doing nothing, giving Sophia time to get away before he "discovered" her gone, was no problem.

After a few minutes he decided to get out of the bed and make his way out into the main part of the house. Nobody should be awake yet, and being caught knocked senseless would look better out in the living room than lying in his bed.

The room spun dizzyingly as Cameron got up. He couldn't hold back a groan. He felt as if sirens were going off in his head, and on top of that he could swear he heard someone calling his name. Maybe Sophia hit him harder than he thought.

Cameron ignored the pain and started out his door. After a few steps at least the building stopped spinning. He stumbled—mostly not acting—out into the living room.

Where both Marco and Rick sat, wide-awake.

This was not good. Why were they awake and dressed? How had Sophia gotten by them?

Cameron tried to silently move back into his room, but Rick saw him.

"What's going on, Cameron?" Rick asked him.

Cameron had no idea how to play this off. Did they already have Sophia? "My head. That bitch hit me on the head."

Cameron watched as Marco and Rick looked at one another pointedly. Another not-good sign. Something was going on here that Cameron didn't know. He decided not to mention Sophia being gone yet. Give her as much time as possible.

"What are you guys doing up?" Cameron plopped down on the couch and gritted his teeth as the back of his head throbbed. Better play off the head injury until he knew what was going on.

"We're just up. Getting everything ready to go to the other house," Marco told him.

"At like—what time is it?—five o'clock in the morning?" Cameron saw Marco and Rick make that weird eye contact again. Something was definitely not right.

"Where is the woman?" The voice came from behind Cameron on the couch. Fin.

Cameron racked his brain for what to say now. To say she had just hit him and run obviously wasn't going to cut it. He had no idea how he was going to get out of this.

"In my room. She hit me on the head with a bottle and I clocked her. I used one of the plastic ties on her hands and threw her in the closet."

Cameron stood up and walked toward the kitchen.

Maybe they wouldn't look for her and wouldn't notice she was gone for a while. It would give him a chance to get out or at least get to one of the other weapons in his room.

"Marco, go get her," Fin told the bigger man.

Damn it. Cameron shrugged and kept walking toward the kitchen as casually as he could. He wondered if his partner, Jason, had faced some sort of situation like this. Feeling the walls closing in on you and knowing there was no way out.

Knowing unless there was some sort of miracle, you were going to die.

Marco came back into the kitchen. "She's not in the closet, boss."

Rick and Marco both pulled out their guns and pointed them directly at Cameron.

"Whoa, what the hell's going on here?" Feigned shock was Cameron's only option. "It's too early in the morning for this. What are you pointing them at me for?"

Fin pulled out a wicked-looking blade. Cameron knew how much pride the smaller man took in it. He suspected it was the same knife that had killed his partner.

"Where's the woman, Cam?" Fin asked, walking closer.

"I told you, I threw her in the closet."

Fin looked over at Marco, who shook his head. "She's not in the closet."

"Fine, she's not in the closet. Maybe she's under the bed or something. Everybody knows Marco can't find his keys half the time. No surprise he can't find a person, either."

Cameron got up and strolled purposely to his room, as if to prove Marco wrong about Sophia. He knew taking them by surprise in there would be his best option.

The best of really, really bad options. Two guns and a knife against his bare hands and the very slight element of surprise?

Cameron entered his room, thankful that at least Sophia had gotten away. He walked over to his closet and thrust open the door.

"See? Told you," Marco said.

"Screw you, Marco." Cameron still kept up the innocent act. "She's in here somewhere."

Cameron looked under his bed, hoping to find anything there that could be used as a weapon. Nothing.

He got back up. It looked as if the guys were relaxing just a little bit. Good.

Cameron walked toward the bathroom door. "You check in there, Marco?"

Marco looked sheepish. "No." The big man looked over at Fin.

"Check it out," Fin told him.

This would be Cameron's only chance. Marco's back would be to him. He'd have to take down Rick first, since he had the gun. And Fin's knife was nothing to scoff at.

Cameron took a deep breath and tried to center himself. He ignored any pain in his head and focused on making it through the next few seconds alive.

Marco opened the bathroom door. Cameron shifted his weight so he could pivot around.

"Don't you touch me, you bastard!" The yell came from inside the bathroom.

Sophia?

Cameron was already in the process of pivoting, so he kept going around to face the other men. But instead of striking them as he had planned, Cameron just glared at Fin.

Fin had his knife up and had obviously been ready for Cameron's attack. There was no way Cameron would've lived through it.

"Okay, maybe I put her in the bathroom, not the closet. So sue me." Cameron shrugged. "Now can we get some coffee?"

The other three men mumbled something to each other and turned to walk out of Cam's room. He heard Marco mutter, "See, I told you." But he didn't hear any response.

Cameron bent down next to Sophia.

"Are you okay? Why are you back? How did you even get in here?" Cameron shot off the questions, knowing he wasn't giving Sophia enough time to respond. There wasn't any time to give her.

Sophia pointed at the window above the bathtub. Cameron couldn't believe, even as slight as Sophia was, that she'd managed to make it through that tiny opening.

He reached down to help her up and heard Sophia's indrawn breath and immediately released her. He noticed the gash on her shoulder.

"What happened?"

"I cut it on my way in through the window. It's not too bad, I think."

"Stay in here. I've got to get to the kitchen and see

what's going on. I'll bring back something to wrap your arm with."

Cameron didn't mention that the danger to the operation, and especially Sophia, was more severe now than ever. Unless Cameron could find a way to talk Fin into taking Sophia with them to Mr. Smith's mountain house, things were still going to get ugly real quick. He grabbed his weapon on the way out of the room.

When Cameron arrived in the kitchen, Fin and the other men were sitting around the table. Marco and Rick ate some sort of sugary cereal. Fin was drinking coffee.

Cameron went over to the cabinet, grabbed a mug for coffee, then turned so he was facing the table with his back against the counter.

"So, what the hell, Fin? After all this time you think I'm some sort of cop?"

"Not me, Cam. Sorry, man. It's Smith. He didn't like the whole situation with the woman and told us to make sure everything was under control."

Cameron should've known Smith was the one closer to figuring things out. Fin and his goons weren't known for their mental prowess.

"We'll have to get rid of her," Fin told Cameron calmly, taking a sip of his coffee as if he wasn't talking about murdering an innocent woman. Next to Fin, Rick looked gleeful at the thought of violence.

A plan came to Cameron—it was a Hail Mary, but it was worth a shot. He didn't like the thought of dragging Sophia in deeper, but at least this would mean not having to end his undercover operation without ever meeting Smith. He was so close.

Cameron thought of his partner, Jason, who had been

killed by Smith's order. That made the decision for him. Cameron silently took a deep breath. He was placing all his chips on this one bet.

"Yeah, about getting rid of her." Cameron forced himself to remain casual against the cabinet. "I'm not sure that's the right thing to do."

Rick snickered, but Cameron ignored him. Rick was just upset at the thought of the loss of need for violence.

"Why's that?" Fin asked.

"Well, it ends up that she wasn't in that warehouse by accident yesterday." Now Cameron had everyone's attention. "It ends up that she was there to try to meet and talk to one of us—someone who could get her a meeting with Mr. Smith."

"That's not going to happen," Fin spluttered, obviously thrown. "Mr. Smith doesn't meet with people he doesn't know for no reason."

"Basically that's what I told her," Cameron continued. "I mean, hell, I've known you guys for a long time and I've still never met Mr. Smith."

Fin stood up. "Fine. Then it's settled. Plan still doesn't change."

"Yeah, no problem." Here it went, the Hail Mary. "Oh, yeah, she mentioned knowing something important about a Ghost Rock or something. I have no idea what that is."

Fin froze exactly where he stood, staring at Cameron. Finally he turned and pointed at Rick and Marco. "You two, out. Now." They left their cereal and headed out the door without a word. Fin turned back to Cameron.

"You mean Ghost Shell?" Fin asked slowly.

"Yeah, Ghost Shell. That's it. Not Ghost Rock."

"That woman in your room knows about Ghost Shell?"

"Yeah." Cameron shrugged and took a sip of his coffee, pretending not to notice how completely wound up Fin was. "She said she came to the warehouse so she could find someone who knew Smith and could get her a meeting with him. But then things got out of hand before she could make her play… Guess that's my bad."

Cameron could see the wheels turning in Fin's head, so he continued, "Evidently there's some problem with this Ghost Shell whatever and she knows about it and how to fix it. But she says she'll only talk directly to Smith."

"So make her tell us and we'll tell him."

Cameron shrugged. "She said it can only be shown with the Ghost Shell. Whatever that is. She said Mr. Smith would be very glad to have the information."

Fin began pacing back and forth. "Mr. Smith isn't available today. I can't get in touch with him at all."

Cameron breathed a sigh of relief. Dealing with just Fin was much easier than dealing with Mr. Smith, someone Cameron didn't know at all. "Well, it's totally up to you, Fin. You know best. But I say, what harm can there be in bringing her? We can get rid of her there just as easily as here, if Mr. Smith doesn't want her around."

Cameron could see Fin considering the idea. Obviously the man was not supposed to bring unvetted strangers to meet Smith. But if that stranger was useful… "You could save the day, Fin. Whatever Ghost Shell is, it's obviously important to Mr. Smith. If this woman knows something helpful, you could be a real hero."

The thought of being in Smith's good graces was obviously the little push Fin needed. "All right, fine, we'll take her with us to the mountain house. But she's your responsibility. And you're the one going down if she doesn't have the info she says she does."

"That's cool, man. I think she does, though. She seems really smart."

"Oh, yeah?" Finn scoffed. "When did you guys have a little heart-to-heart talk?"

"Whoa, nothing like that." Cameron laughed good-naturedly. "Just after we had our…fun, she brought it up."

"Yeah?" Suspicion came back into Fin's eyes. "Was that before or after she hit you in the head?"

Cameron thought fast. "What can I say? We both like it rough. She obviously can give as good as she gets. We're beginning to grow on each other."

Evidently that was enough to satisfy Fin. "Whatever. Just have her and yourself ready to go soon. We'll be leaving in a couple of hours." With that, Fin turned and headed out of the kitchen.

Cameron took a sip of his coffee, but found it had gone cold so he dumped it in the sink. His plan had worked. Sophia was safe. His undercover operation was still intact and he was going to meet Smith. Cameron was one step closer to bringing that bastard down, acquiring Ghost Shell and getting Sophia to safety in one piece.

But the dread pooling in his stomach told him the opposite was true.

Chapter Eight

A few hours later Cameron watched out the jet window over Sophia's shoulder as they came in for their landing in the Blue Ridge Mountains area of western Virginia. There was nothing around but trees for miles in any direction. The airstrip they landed at was tiny, similar to the small airport south of Washington, DC, they'd taken off from not too long before. Neither was being monitored by anyone who didn't work for DS-13, Cameron was sure.

Cameron looked over at Sophia, who stared blankly out the window. Dark circles of exhaustion, almost like bruises, ringed her eyes. She held his hand in a death grip.

After convincing Fin to take Sophia with them to meet Smith, Cameron had made his way back to his room. Sophia had still been sitting on the bathroom floor, almost in a daze, arm still bleeding. He'd cleaned the cut and wrapped it with gauze. It didn't look as if it needed stitches, but it still wasn't pretty.

He still didn't know exactly why she had done it, but her return had saved his life, without a doubt.

"Thank you," Cameron had whispered when he was

finished with her wound, putting his hands reverently on either side of her face and kissing her gently.

Sophia had just nodded.

Since coming back into DS-13's grasp, Sophia had hardly said one word to Cameron, although he had to admit, talking had been nearly impossible. By the time he had played out his wounded-because-you-don't-trust-me part for Fin and the gang, and gotten suitable apologies, it had almost been time to go.

Cameron found a shirt for Sophia to wear—hers had lost all the buttons, much to the delight of the DS-13 men. He had wanted to talk to Sophia about what had happened, but sending an encoded message to Omega Sector with his satellite phone had been more important. He had to let Omega Sector know they were moving—to an unknown location as of yet—and that there was now an innocent third party involved. Cameron would send more info when he had time and details.

As the plane came to a halt, everybody unbuckled their seat belts and stood. Except Sophia. She still stared vacantly out the window.

Fin opened the plane door and everyone began to file out. When Sophia still didn't move, Cameron squatted down in front of her. He took her hands, which lay limply in her lap, in his.

"Hey," he whispered. He watched as her eyes, shadowed with exhaustion, turned blankly toward him. "You doing okay?"

Sophia nodded slowly. "Where are we?"

"We're in the mountains. Going to the evil lair, remember?"

The ghost of a smile crossed her lips. "They don't call it an evil lair."

Cameron winked at her and rubbed the back of both of her hands with his thumbs. They were like ice. "That's right, sweetie. You going to be all right? I know this is really hard."

Sophia nodded again. "I just don't know what to do, Cam." She leaned in closer to him and whispered urgently, "I know I work for the Bureau, but I'm an artist! I don't have any training. I don't know anything about working…you know, in situations like this."

Cameron unbuckled her seat belt and helped Sophia stand. "Just stay as close to me as possible, and try to ignore everyone else. Can you do that?"

Sophia gave a short bark of near-hysterical laughter. "Uh, yeah. No problem wanting to stay away from them. Especially that Rick guy—he freaks me out."

Cameron knew Rick had a cruel, violent streak. He didn't blame Sophia for wanting to stay away. "All right, let's go." Cameron quickly sent out the coordinates of this landing strip in a message to Omega Sector—a risky move, but one he had to make. Then he led Sophia down the few short steps of the small plane and over to the SUV that was waiting just off the runway. He got in the backseat with Sophia, noticing how she avoided looking at anyone.

And how every man in the vehicle looked at her. Cameron would have to keep Sophia with him as much as possible. She was definitely not safe alone.

Cameron paid very close attention as they drove from the airstrip to the mountain house. If for some reason he was not able to get GPS coordinates to Omega Sector, he would have to rely on his own observation and memory to find the "evil lair" again. They were headed northwest on a pretty steady incline. Mr. Smith's hideout must be near the top of one of these mountains. The Blue Ridge Mountains of Virginia weren't tall and barren like the Rockies. There were little peaks of hills everywhere, where homes could be built and privacy abounded.

Many of these homes had one way in, and one way out. Which was obviously the case here, Cameron realized. There hadn't been a single turnoff or other car on the road since they'd left the airstrip. Smart move on Mr. Smith's part.

Cameron hated that Sophia was here, but was excited that he was finally making such strong headway in the case. Today, finally—*finally*—he was going to meet Mr. Smith. Cameron knew he couldn't arrest Smith right away, he'd definitely need Omega Sector backup first. Plus, acquiring Ghost Shell took precedence over any arrest, but he couldn't help but feel hopeful that he was going to be able to do both.

Cameron glanced over at Sophia, who was staring blankly out the window again. He just hoped she could keep it together. He reached over and took her hand, subtly, so nobody else in the car could see. She looked over at him.

She could obviously recognize his concern. She nodded slightly and gave an attempt at a smile. Cameron squeezed her hand, wishing he could do more.

After just a few more minutes the car started making an even steeper incline. It wasn't long before they were at the DS-13 mountain house, or evil lair, or whatever you wanted to call it.

It definitely was no jackass-infested rat hole. Well, maybe it was jackass-infested, but it certainly wasn't a rat hole. The house was gorgeous and huge—a surprisingly tasteful blend of wood and large stone. Giant windows made up huge sections of walls, providing unobstructed views of the spectacular hills of the Blue Ridge Mountains.

And unobstructed views of anyone who might be trying to get up to the house through those hills. Any sort of covert attack of any magnitude would be nearly impossible. Definitely something Cameron would have to communicate to Omega Sector, if they planned to take down Mr. Smith here.

The beauty of the building and the surroundings were breathtaking, but Cameron forced himself to stay focused solely on the job at hand. The SUV pulled into a four-car garage that attached to the house through a walkway.

They all got out of the vehicle, grabbed their bags and made their way inside. Sophia stayed almost glued to Cameron's side, clutching his arm. Rick was quick to comment on it.

"Seems like someone is a little friendlier this morning, Cam."

Cameron smirked at him. "Yeah, well, I guess I'm just that charming."

Rick smirked back. "Maybe you should give me a chance to be charming with her. I'm a pretty charming guy." Rick took a step toward Sophia. Cameron immediately felt Sophia's grip on his arm tighten.

"Not going to happen, Rick. So just run along." Cameron shooed him away. Anger flared in the other man's eyes, but he said nothing.

Cameron gave a short whistle as they walked into the house. It was even more impressive on the inside than it was on the outside. "Wow, this is quite a place," Cameron told Fin as he looked around.

Fin nodded, grinning. "Ten bedrooms. Eleven baths. Half a dozen offices and meeting rooms. A formal dining room and even a party area. Try not to get lost."

A man who was probably a member of DS-13, but looked like a butler, came through a doorway from the back and started walking toward them. Tension filled Fin and the other goons at the man's presence. As subtly as he could, Cameron put himself between Sophia and this unknown person.

There were too many damn unknowns in this situation.

The man obviously knew Fin, but spoke with a formal tone. "Mr. Fin, welcome. As you know, your uncle will be arriving later this evening, bringing some other guests for a weekend soiree."

Fin fidgeted. "Um, yeah, Thompson, thanks. My uncle told me about the party. This is Cam Cameron. Cam, this is Thompson."

Thompson nodded. "Yes, Mr. Smith mentioned his arrival. And Mr. Cameron's guest? She was not mentioned."

Fin looked uncomfortable. "Yeah. She's with Cam. Has some information for Mr. Smith that we think he'll be very happy to hear." Fin lifted his chin in an attempt to look confident.

"I will show you to your room, Mr. Cameron, and your guest, also." Thompson turned to Cameron. "Everyone else has been here before and is familiar with the house."

"Good, because I'm tired as hell since I had to spend most of the night convincing everyone I'm not a liar." Cameron gave a dramatic sigh. He picked up his duffel from where he had set it on the floor and began following Thompson, the butler guy.

"Uncle?" Cameron said with an eyebrow raised as he passed Fin. "Who's the lying SOB now?"

Fin just laughed and shrugged and headed off to another part of the house.

Thompson led Cameron down the hall with Sophia following close behind, still holding his hand. Every once in a while he could feel a shudder run through her. She was swaying on her feet and Cameron knew he needed to get her to the room soon. He breathed a sigh of relief when the older man opened a door for them.

Cameron ushered Sophia inside, then turned to their escort. "Thanks, man. We're just going to crash for a while," Cameron told him while shutting the door in his face.

Cameron locked the door and looked around the room. It was definitely much nicer than the DS-13 house in DC. A huge four-poster bed, made of the same wood as the rest of the house, dominated much of the room. There was a dresser against one wall and two sitting chairs over by the massive sliding glass doors that led out to a small deck.

There were two doors over on the far wall. Cameron walked over to them. One was a closet. He quickly closed the door, praying they wouldn't need to use it. The other door led to a bathroom. Cameron whistled as he took in the huge hot tub and separate shower. This whole place was gorgeous and tasteful.

Cameron walked back into the bedroom and saw that Sophia had wandered over to the windows and was staring out vacantly, just as she had on the plane. He wanted to talk to her, but first he needed to check that their room wasn't bugged.

Cameron took what would look like a smartphone to any casual observer and punched in a code. This turned on a scanner that allowed him to see if there were any electronic transmissions being sent from anywhere in the room. It wasn't a foolproof way of checking for surveillance, but it was pretty useful.

There were no transmissions being sent from anywhere in this room. Not surprising. Criminals rarely recorded what was going on in their own homes if they were smart. Too many ways for it to be used against them.

Cameron walked over to Sophia and put his hands on her shoulders, then looked out at the view with her.

"Beautiful, isn't it?" she asked softly.

"Breathtaking. I wish we were here under different circumstances." He pulled her back against his chest and was relieved when she didn't pull away.

Sophia nodded. "Me, too."

Cameron turned her around so he could see her face. "Soph, why did you come back? Don't get me wrong, I'm thankful that you did. But *why*?"

Sophia looked around the room. "Is it okay to talk here?"

"Yeah, I checked for bugs. The room's clean."

"I was on my way out and I heard Rick and that other guy talking. Fin still didn't trust you completely. I was the final test for you."

Cameron felt himself tense. He'd had no idea. Fin—on Mr. Smith's orders—had set him up, and Cameron had been oblivious.

"You saved my life," Cameron whispered.

Sophia just smiled and shrugged. "So I guess we're even."

Cameron saw Sophia wince at the shrug. "Is your shoulder okay?"

She nodded. "Yes, just stiff. How's your head?"

Cameron winced but grinned. "You've got a pretty mean swing there, Miss Reardon."

"I'm sorry I'm still here, Cam. I know I complicate everything."

Cameron trailed a finger down her cheek. "Well, if you weren't here, I'd probably be dead. So I'm pretty damn glad you're here."

Sophia swayed on her feet. Cameron caught her quickly before she fell and led her over to the bed.

"You need to sleep," he told her gently as he pulled the covers back on the giant bed and ushered her in.

Sophia didn't say anything, just slipped her shoes off and lay down, fully clothed. She was asleep before he could pull the covers over her.

Cameron slipped his own shoes off and walked around to the other side of the bed. He slipped under the covers next to Sophia.

She was right; her presence here did complicate everything. But hell, Sophia complicated his life just by breathing. He reached over and pulled her sleeping body into his arms.

Cameron didn't have a plan, and that made him nervous. If it was just his life on the line then he'd be willing to fly blind as long as possible if it meant his goal was accomplished.

He kissed the top of Sophia's head as she snuggled in closer to him. Not having a plan when it was Sophia in jeopardy was unacceptable to him. So he would need to come up with one. Fast.

WHEN SOPHIA OPENED her eyes again the sun was setting. She sat straight up as she tried to remember where she was and who she was with. And then it all came back to her.

She knew Cameron had slept with her in the bed. She remembered waking up in a panic and finding him right by her side, rubbing her back and easing her to lie back down on the bed.

She could tell he had been there next to her until recently. The pillow still held the indentation from his head. She didn't know if he had slept this whole time with her or not, but she was thankful he had been there, next to her. She touched the place where Cameron had lain.

Sophia laid back in the luxurious bed now and stretched. No matter what, this place was definitely nicer than the rat hole they'd been in yesterday. But somehow that didn't make Sophia feel much better.

She turned over to her side and saw Cameron staring out the window. He seemed deep in thought. He was wearing only his jeans and his arms were crossed over his naked chest. He was definitely more muscular than when Sophia had last seen him five years ago. He had been fit then, but now the muscles in his chest, back and arms were even more pronounced.

And that six-pack he had acquired was definitely mouthwatering. Sophia once again wished they were here under different circumstances. That there wasn't so much weight riding on his shoulders, even if they seemed broad enough to carry anything.

Sophia got out of the bed and wandered over to stand next to Cameron. "Hey," she whispered.

"Feeling better?" he asked.

"Yeah. It's amazing what a few hours of sleep can do."

"You definitely needed it. I don't know how you were holding it together." They stood in companionable silence for a few moments, looking out the window. Sophia wanted to wrap an arm around Cameron, but wasn't sure if it would be appropriate. Or welcome.

"So do we have a plan? What do I need to do?"

Cameron turned so they were looking face-to-face at each other. "I've been thinking a lot while you were asleep. I have a plan." He didn't look too thrilled with it, though.

"Hopefully a better one than me running down this mountain in the middle of the night by myself?" Sophia joked, but inside she was afraid that was what she was going to have to do.

"No, you won't have to run all the way down. I'll have an extraction team waiting."

Sophia shook her head. "Last time I *escaped*, it almost got you killed. What makes you think it's a good plan this time?"

"It won't be just you. We'll both be going."

"I don't understand. How will that work? What about this case?"

Cameron didn't answer.

Sophia wasn't sure she was understanding exactly what was going on here. "But what about all your work? The eight months with DS-13? The weeks in the jackass-infested rat hole?"

Cameron turned to the side and looked back out the window. He shrugged.

"You can't do this, Cameron. What about the justice for your partner?"

Sophia watched as Cameron took a deep breath and ran his hand through his thick, dark hair. "Soph, I watched you there while you were sleeping. You're covered in bruises. You have a huge, nasty cut on your shoulder."

"But—" Sophia tried to cut in but he wouldn't let her. He turned and held both of her arms in his hands, careful not to put any pressure on her wound.

"No, listen. You've been absolutely amazing. You've kept your head and you've kept it together, when you had every reason to fall apart." He brought her a little closer. "And then, when you had a chance to get away, you came back for me, Soph. You saved my life."

Sophia just shrugged. There hadn't been any option for her. She wasn't going to leave him there to die.

"I want justice so bad for my partner that I can taste it, Soph. And there's other stuff, too, that you don't even know about. But that will all have to be taken care of another way at another time. I'm not going to risk your life. I'm going to call in for help and we're getting out of here tonight."

A sudden vibration from a small cell-phone-looking thing on the nightstand by the bed caught both of their attentions. Cameron quickly walked over and grabbed it. Sophia watched as Cameron twisted the box inside out and began typing a series of symbols on it. Then he stopped and waited, saying nothing. A few moments later the inside-out box beeped.

This time Cameron brought it up to his ear and spoke into it. "Omega, go. Code 44802. Security confirmed."

Cameron listened for a few moments to whatever was being said on the other end.

"Coordinates are confirmed. Primary target has not arrived."

Whatever was being said to Cameron did not make him happy. "Roger that. Secondary target has not arrived, then. Primary target location has not been ascertained."

More talk from the other end.

"Request withdrawal assistance tonight."

Now whatever was being said was really making Cameron mad.

"Bystander in pocket, but too many unknowns. Immediate assistance requested."

Cameron turned and looked directly at Sophia while he listened. She could see his teeth grit and a vein flicker at his neck. "No, there is no immediate threat to bystander. But again I repeat—there are too many unknowns."

Sophia watched as Cameron's fist clenched at his side.

"Roger that. Primary objective understood."

Cameron poked a series of buttons angrily into the phone. He turned it inside out so it just looked like a regular phone again and placed it on the nightstand again.

Sophia wasn't completely sure what she had just heard, but it sounded as if they were completely on their own.

Chapter Nine

Cameron wanted to throw the satellite phone across the room, but knew it wouldn't do any good. He drew a breath and released it, trying to focus. Being angry at Omega Sector's unwillingness to send a rescue team in immediately was not going to help anything. He needed to work the problem.

And right now the problem was standing a few feet away from him, engulfed by his T-shirt, with tousled brown hair and gorgeous green eyes.

He couldn't get her out. Cameron had to face that. She was watching him with intent eyes, looking so tiny. But she was far from helpless. Sophia wasn't a trained agent—as she was so quick to point out—but she was smart, and quick-thinking.

Cameron wanted Sophia out of there. But according to Omega Sector that wasn't an option. So she was about to become his partner.

Cameron stretched his arm out to Sophia and she walked hesitantly to him, questions in her eyes.

"Moving to plan B?" she asked. "No backup from the Bureau?"

Cameron nodded. "Yeah." He hesitated. "Except I don't work for the Bureau."

Sophia took a step back. "You don't?" Cameron could see her trying to figure out who he was working undercover for if it wasn't the FBI. "Are you DEA? Some sort of local law enforcement?"

"No. I'm part of what's called Omega Sector. We're an interagency task force. All the advantages of having the resources of individual agencies—DEA, FBI, Marshals Service, ATF, hell, even INTERPOL sometimes. But much less red tape."

"So basically you're like your own Justice League."

Cameron smiled at the Saturday-morning cartoon reference. "Yeah, basically. But without superpowers."

"I've worked at the Bureau for four years now. I've never heard of Omega Sector."

"No, you wouldn't have. It's not something you can just apply for. You're recruited by Omega, or you don't get in at all. They're looking for specific skills, mindsets, abilities."

Sophia took another small step away from Cameron, frowning. "And you had all those things."

Cameron shrugged. "I guess so."

"How long has Omega Sector been around?"

"About ten years."

"And when did you begin working for them?"

Cameron grimaced. There was no way around this. "Five years ago."

Sophia's head snapped up and Cameron could see realization dawn in her eyes. Omega Sector was the reason he had never said goodbye to her.

Sophia turned and walked over to the window. Cameron stayed where he was over by the bed, giving her space.

"So they recruited you?"

"Yes."

Sophia continued to look out the window. "I'm not surprised. You're obviously good at this sort of thing."

"I wanted to make a difference in the world, Soph. Omega Sector was that chance."

Sophia nodded, still not looking at him. "And I suppose because it's all top secret and stuff, you couldn't tell anybody."

"Sophia..."

"You know what? I don't even want to talk about this right now. You wanted to make a difference. You joined your *Super Friends* group and have been doing that ever since. Congratulations."

Her back and shoulders were ramrod-straight as she stared out the window. What she didn't say stood like a giant between them.

You wanted to make a difference more than you wanted to be with me.

Cameron was glad she didn't say it out loud, because he had no idea how he would respond. Yes, he had wanted to fight bad guys when he had joined Omega Sector five years ago. And at the time, it had been the most important thing in the world to him. He and Sophia had been at the beginning of their relationship. No promises, no real commitment. They hadn't even slept together.

Casual. At least that's what Cameron had told himself. But he had known they both were taking it seriously. Every morning when he had met her at the little diner for breakfast, he had known they weren't casual.

And with five years of perspective, Cameron could see exactly what he had given up. Having Sophia standing here right in front of him, and having no way of getting her out of the danger, made him think perhaps it wasn't worth it after all.

After a moment, Sophia turned to Cameron. "So Omega Sector deems arresting Mr. Smith more important than getting us out? I mean, I can understand you wanting to get him because of your partner. But if you've decided to cut out? It sounds like you maybe just moved from one jackass-infested place to another."

Cameron gave her a half smile. "Actually, I haven't told you everything."

Sophia closed her eyes briefly and shook her head. "Of course you haven't. What's new?"

"Arresting anybody in DS-13 has become secondary in this op. Instead, it's something in his possession that Omega Sector has deemed more important than either of our individual lives. And they're probably right to feel that way."

Now Cameron had Sophia's attention. "What is it?"

Cameron explained to her the details of Ghost Shell. How, if used by terrorists, it could cripple computer and communication equipment of law enforcement and first responders, basically by using their own communication equipment against them.

"They'd be pretty paralyzed against any sort of terrorist attack or anything like that," Sophia whispered after Cameron finished explaining.

"Yes." Cameron walked over to her at the window.

"It's not an actual weapon, but in some ways this technology is more devastating than any one weapon. Law enforcement's reliance on computers and communication technology is pretty heavy."

Sophia nodded. "How did Omega Sector find out about it?"

"I'm not sure exactly. Somebody, evidently a law-abiding computer scientist person, who had been working on something similar, reported it and the report made its way to Omega Sector."

"And they found out DS-13 has it?"

"Yes. But DS-13 isn't interested in using it against law enforcement. They don't have any political or religious ambitions—they're only interested in money. They want to sell it on the black market. Absolute chaos, available to the highest bidder."

"Oh, my gosh, Cam. In the wrong hands…" Sophia shook her head.

"I know. So like I said, I can understand why Omega Sector said no to us getting out. But I don't like it."

Neither of them said anything for a few moments. Sophia turned and took a step toward him.

"Is the Ghost Shell drive here?" she whispered finally.

"If not right now, then definitely soon, when Smith arrives. Although I don't know exactly where. Omega is afraid if they come in here full force, someone from DS-13 could escape with Ghost Shell."

She looked up at him, having to crane her neck to do so. God, she was so tiny. "Then we'll find it. And we'll get out of here," she said.

Cameron framed her face with his hands. "Soph, I

can't ask you to risk your life like that. They killed my partner because they found out he was undercover. They won't hesitate to kill us, too."

"No offense, Cam, but my life is already in jeopardy. I might as well do something useful."

Cameron shook his head. He didn't like it; Sophia in the line of fire was definitely not his first choice. But it didn't look as if he had any choice at all.

Unbelievably, Sophia smiled at him. "You know, when I interviewed for my job as a graphic artist for the FBI four years ago, one of the first things I asked my boss was if I would ever be in life-threatening situations. I was assured I wouldn't be."

Cameron chuckled softly. "You mean they didn't list this situation in your job description? Hard to believe."

Sophia took a step back from Cameron. "I'll try not to get in your way, but I'm definitely not cut out for secret-agent spy stuff." She shrugged and used her hair to hide her face. "I'm hardly capable of walking inside my own closet to pick out clothes without having a panic attack, much less do anything courageous."

"Hey." Cameron tucked her brown hair back behind her ear. "Don't talk that way. You've done a damn good job so far."

Sophia just shrugged again. "I'm going to take a shower. I feel like I've got grime under my grime," she told Cameron. He didn't stop her from pulling away.

"You might want to take a soak in the tub. It's huge."

Sophia sighed. A soak in a tub sounded like the most wonderful thing she had ever heard in her entire life. "That's definitely where I'll be."

"Okay." Cameron smiled at her. "Then we'll go find something to eat. I'm starving."

"Me, too."

Cameron watched as Sophia made her way to the bathroom and closed the door behind her.

He could hear the water running from her bath, and tried to think of every possible other thing in the world except Sophia naked behind that bathroom door.

Cameron wasn't sure he'd ever found a task so difficult in his entire life.

A sharp rap on the room's other door drew Cameron's attention. He quickly pulled his shirt over his head and grabbed his SIG from the nightstand.

"Yeah?" he asked from the door without opening it.

"It's Thompson, Mr. Cameron. I've got some food for you and Ms. Reardon."

Thompson knew Sophia's name. Cameron wasn't sure if that was good or bad. He needed to be prepared for either.

Cameron opened the door and Thompson walked in with a tray of food. Thank God Sophia was in the bathroom, out of sight and earshot.

"Thanks, man." Cameron was once again struck by how much Thompson looked and acted like a butler. But he could see how lightly the man moved on his feet and how perfectly balanced he was when carrying the tray and setting it down.

Cameron had no doubt that Thompson was much more than just a butler. The suspicion was confirmed when he saw the older man glance around the room subtly, taking in all details.

This man, more than any of the goons Cameron had

hung out with in DS-13 for the past eight months, was dangerous. No doubt that was why Mr. Smith kept him around.

"Something I can help you find?" Cameron asked.

Thompson looked at Cameron and tipped his head slightly, as if respecting that he had been caught snooping, but not apologizing for it.

"Will Ms. Reardon be requiring anything?" Thompson asked as he set the tray of food on a small table by the closet.

Cameron did not want to talk about Sophia with this man. "No, she's fine."

Cameron answered a little too quickly. He cursed silently as he saw that Thompson realized it, too. The last thing he wanted to do was show DS-13, especially this man whom Cameron was beginning to suspect was much higher up in the food chain than he had thought, that he cared about Sophia. They wouldn't hesitate to use her against him.

Cameron wandered nonchalantly over to the food. He picked up an apple and took a big bite.

"I can take care of her just fine, if you know what I mean." Cameron gave the man a wink. "She's in the bathroom relaxing in that swimming pool you call a tub. Working out the kinks."

Cameron saw Thompson's eyes narrow in distaste before the man hid his response. Good. Better for Cameron to seem crude and obnoxious than as if he had some sort of attachment to Sophia.

"Mr. Smith and his other guests have arrived. Mr. Smith would like to meet with you and Ms. Reardon in one hour."

Cameron took another bite of his apple. "That's cool, man. Whatever." And because it seemed to make Thompson so uncomfortable before, Cameron winked at him again.

"Yes, well, good. Until then, please stay in your room and keep Ms. Reardon here with you."

Thompson turned and made his way out of the room quickly and efficiently.

Cameron looked over at the elaborate tray of food Thompson had brought in. Fruits, cheeses, meats and breads for sandwiches. Quite the spread. All laid out on a large silver platter with oversize handles.

Cameron began moving the food, piece by piece, off the tray. Based on what he had observed about Thompson, Cameron was willing to bet there was some sort of surveillance device somewhere on this tray. Once all the food was off the tray and he was able to turn it over, he saw a transmitter. But something about how large it was and how it sat in the handle was a little too obvious to Cameron.

Sure enough, Cameron kept searching and found it a couple minutes later: a tiny transmitter under the lip of the least descriptive part of the tray, where you would hardly think to look, especially if you found the first device.

Sneaky little bastard.

Thompson had almost caught them unawares. Cameron decided to leave the transmitting device where it was, fully functional, since it was sound-only. He and Sophia could use it to their advantage. But the larger, more obvious device, Cameron removed.

"Screw you, Thompson, and whoever else is listening. I prefer not to have an audience, you perverts," Cameron said into the piece of equipment. He then threw the transmitter on the ground and stomped on it.

So now they thought he had no idea they were listening. Good, he had no problem exploiting their overconfidence.

SOPHIA FELT LIKE a new person after her long soak in the tub. She had to put the same clothes back on, so that wasn't great, but at least her muscles were easing. Somehow being taken hostage by a crime syndicate group tended to make you tense and tight. Go figure.

Sophia came out of the door, her head wrapped in a towel, ready to boast to Cameron about the miracles of a hot tub. "Hey, seriously, it's almost like we're on a..."

She was cut off by him pushing her back against the wall and kissing her. Thoroughly.

Her arms, almost of their own accord, traveled up his arms to his shoulders. The towel around her hair came loose then slipped from her head and fell to the floor. Sophia forgot everything but the heat and strength of the kiss.

She stood up on her tiptoes to get closer and wound her fingers in his hair. She didn't care where they were anymore or the danger they were facing. She wanted Cameron now and he wanted her. That was all that mattered.

Cameron's lips moved over her jaw and up to Sophia's ear. She shivered with every light kiss he placed. His hands grasped her waist and pulled her closer to him. Sophia found herself melting into him.

"They're listening to everything we say," he murmured almost silently against her ear.

It took a moment for the words to penetrate. Sophia's arms fell to her sides. Cold washed over her where moments ago there had been such heat.

Cameron wasn't kissing her because he wanted to. He was kissing her to keep her quiet. It was just as effective as the backhand at the warehouse. And just as painful.

Sophia nodded jerkily. Cameron tried to kiss her again, but she turned her head away. There was no need to kiss her—she got the message: don't say or do anything stupid.

Or maybe do anything *more* stupid than throw herself into a kiss that meant nothing to the other person.

Sophia nodded again and reached down to get the towel that had fallen from her head. She was so cold. And she needed to be away from Cameron. Immediately.

"That's a big tub they have in there." Sophia didn't recognize her own voice as she said it, wasn't even sure how she got the words out of her mouth.

Thankfully Cameron stepped away from her.

"There's some food over on the table, if you're hungry. Thompson brought it while you were in the bathroom." Cameron pointed toward the table.

So that's how they could hear now but couldn't before—something on the tray. Sophia nodded, not quite making eye contact with Cameron—she couldn't stand to do that yet, not after the fool she'd just made of herself—and went to the table.

Although she'd totally lost her appetite, Sophia

forced herself to eat. She chewed bite after tasteless bite, forcing the needed nutrients into her system.

But damn it, she felt like an idiot. Cameron was undercover. She needed to get that through her evidently very thick skull. Arresting this Mr. Smith guy and getting back Ghost Shell were the most important things to him.

And her safety, she had to give him that, too. But he was undercover; nothing he said or did should be taken at face value.

"I'm glad you liked the tub," Cameron finally said from across the room.

"Yeah, I could definitely get used to that sort of luxury," Sophia responded. Cameron nodded encouragingly and spun his finger in a circle, gesturing for her to continue that line of conversation.

"Someday I want to own a giant tub like that one," Sophia continued as she ate another bite of a sandwich from the tray.

Cameron started talking, making up a crazy story about a hot tub he had once snuck into with his brothers while in high school and the shenanigans that ensued. At least Sophia *thought* he was making it up. She knew Cameron had two brothers and a sister, so maybe it was true.

Without ever missing a beat with his story, Cameron walked over to Sophia and led her away from the tray to over near the bed. He let out a loud guffaw as he finished the story and Sophia laughed along with him.

"Soph," he said in a low voice that wasn't quite a whisper, pulling her closer. "Smith is here. Ghost Shell is probably with him."

"Okay. That's good, right?" she whispered.

"Don't whisper," he told her in that same low tone. "Just speak very low, if you don't want them to hear. Whispers are actually easier for surveillance equipment to pick up than very low tones."

Sophia nodded.

Cameron brought his voice back up to normal range. "Mr. Smith wants to meet us in an hour. So it's probably good that you went ahead and took a bath already."

Cameron looked at Sophia, gesturing with his head that she should say something. "O-okay…" she said tentatively.

Cameron leaned closer, dropping his voice so the surveillance couldn't hear. "Remember, you want this meeting. That's how I convinced Fin to let you come here, by telling him you had information to give to Smith."

Sophia nodded. "Yeah, good." She said in a louder voice, "That's what I'm here for, to meet Smith. I just want to make this exchange and get out of here."

Cameron nodded with enthusiasm.

"I don't like the mountains," she continued. "I'm more of a beach person." That was totally not true, but seemed like a reasonable thing to say.

"Yeah, me, too," Cameron said. "Why don't we go on a little vacation after all this?"

Sophia had to remind herself that Cameron wasn't really talking to her; this was just part of his undercover story. She refused to allow herself to wish he wanted to spend time with her. When this was finished, he'd be gone again, just like five years ago.

"Yeah, sure." There was decidedly less enthusiasm in her tone.

Cameron's head cocked to the side as he studied Sophia with questioning eyes. She didn't dare explain to him what was really bothering her, even if there wasn't a bug in the room.

A knock on the door saved the moment. She saw Cameron reach for the gun he evidently had tucked in the back of his jeans. He walked silently to the door, gesturing for her to move back toward the bathroom.

"Yes?" he asked without opening the door.

Something was murmured that Sophia couldn't quite catch, but whatever it was caused Cameron to relax and put his gun away. He opened the door, and someone handed him a package.

"Here, this is for you." Cameron tossed the box onto the bed.

Sophia frowned and walked over to it. Pushing the tissue paper to the side she found clothes: a pair of stylishly cut black pants, and a soft gray sweater. Undergarments, socks and shoes completed the outfit. All of them were the perfect size for her.

Sophia looked up at Cameron. "What? Where did this come from?"

Cameron pointed over at the tray to remind her they were being listened to. "Beats me. I didn't have anything to do with it. But I guess you couldn't meet Mr. Smith in my T-shirt, now could you? So it's a good thing."

"Yeah, I guess so." Sophia turned toward the bathroom, more disturbed than she cared to admit. Did Smith just keep women's clothes sitting around? Probably not. Which meant someone with a very good eye had taken her measurements and gotten clothes up to this remote location pretty darn quickly.

Somehow the arrival of these clothes, more than any of the other things—much more dangerous things—that had happened to her over the past two days, made it hit home the power of the people Cameron was dealing with. They had resources. They had manpower. And they had a scary attention to detail.

Plus, they were murderers.

As Cameron came into the bathroom with her and started providing details about Ghost Shell in a hushed tone, Sophia clutched the box of clothes to her chest and listened as best she could. When Cameron had given her all the info he could, he left, closing the door behind him so Sophia could dress.

She did so, hoping the clothes provided by a murdering crime syndicate wouldn't be the last ones she ever put on.

Chapter Ten

There was no more Cameron could do to prepare Sophia, even though he knew it wasn't enough. Time was up. Eight months undercover had all led up to this.

And it was all out of his hands and completely in Sophia's.

Cameron knew that wasn't quite accurate, but it certainly felt like it as they followed Thompson down an extended hallway of the large house to a set of rooms in the back. By their very location, the rooms were less accessible, discouraging any wandering guests from finding them. Not hidden, exactly, just not advertised. And something about Thompson just kept nagging at Cameron.

Cameron watched Sophia from the corner of his eye as she walked beside him. She was glancing around nervously, as if looking for exits. She rubbed her fists against the legs of her black pants. Cameron wished he could catch her hand and hold it, but knew strolling in like lovers was not the way they should meet Smith.

Cameron looked over at Sophia and smiled. Sophia gnawed on her lip a moment more before taking a deep breath and straightening her shoulders.

"You okay?" Cam whispered.

"Doesn't really make a difference now, does it?" Sophia said without looking at him.

Not exactly the reassuring answer he was hoping for.

Cameron tried to go through multiple possible scenarios in his head. What he would do if Sophia freaked out. How he could help her keep it together. Their best route of escape if they had to run. Weaponless and outnumbered, none of the options were good. Cameron prayed Sophia wouldn't panic. But they were walking into a situation that would make even the most seasoned undercover agent wary. He could only imagine the terror Sophia was feeling.

Again, not reassuring.

Thompson led them to a door at the farthest end of the hallway. Cameron pretended not to watch as the older man used a card to swipe a lock on the wall. Cameron wondered who else might have a key card to this office.

Cameron looked over at Sophia again. She was no longer clenching and unclenching her small fists, so that was good. Thompson opened the door for them and Cameron gestured for Sophia to walk in ahead of him. Showtime.

They walked into the expansive office, Cameron taking in as much as he could about the room without actually looking as if he was. Sophia made no such pretense. Most of the walls were lined with deep cherry bookshelves and cabinetry. The far wall was made up of windows, showcasing the wondrous view of nature outside. A large desk took up the area near the window, with a black luxury office chair behind it. The chair was currently facing the windows, away from the desk.

Slowly the large chair swiveled around so the man in it was facing Cameron and Sophia. There was no doubt this man was related to Fin—his build, facial structure and coloring were all similar, yet he was older and flabbier than Fin. This was it; the moment Cameron had waited over a year for.

"I'm Mr. Smith," the man said in a somewhat squeaky voice that belied his overweight size. His Yankee accent was thick. His eyes small, close-set, almost beady. "Go ahead and sit down."

Cameron's lips pressed tight and his shoulders slumped as he sat. *This* man was one of the top members of DS-13 and had eluded law enforcement for years? Somehow he just wasn't what Cameron had expected. But perhaps nothing short of an absolute monster would've lived up to Cameron's expectations.

Regardless of whether the man fit the image Cameron had built in his head, Cameron was tempted to arrest him right there, everything else be damned. Omega could figure out another way to get Ghost Shell. Only the thought of Sophia trapped in the middle of all this halted him. Cameron settled back into his seat, clenching his jaw.

Thompson came around to stand next to the desk, close to Smith's side. Out of the corner of his eye Cameron noticed Smith glancing at Thompson and Thompson giving a slight nod. Immediately Cameron was on high alert. Obviously some sort of signal had passed between the two men, but what did it mean? Cameron wished to God that Thompson hadn't done a weapons check back at the room. Cameron felt naked without his SIG. Were he and Sophia about to be assassinated while Cameron was able to do nothing?

But neither Smith nor Thompson made any aggressive moves. Instead, Smith settled back in his chair and Thompson remained watchful and alert where he stood. Maybe Cameron had imagined the entire thing.

Cameron leaned forward in his chair and offered Smith his hand to shake, although he really wanted to break the offending hand. "Mr. Smith, it's a pleasure to finally meet you." Cameron managed not to choke on the words.

"Likewise, Cam," the older man answered as he shook Cameron's hand with his large sweaty paws. Cameron resisted the urge to wipe his palms on the legs of his pants.

Mr. Smith continued, "I realize you've worked with DS-13 for a long time, Cam, without meeting me. I hope you understand the necessary security precautions." Smith glanced at Thompson again.

"Oh, sure, Mr. Smith. Everybody has to be careful in this day and age." Cameron nodded enthusiastically, trying to be friendly.

"Yes, well, I have enemies on multiple sides," Smith continued in his squeaky, accented voice. "I try to always take time to thoroughly check out anyone who works for me. But I must admit you have arranged a lot of good deals for me in the past year."

Cam smiled. "Lucrative for us both."

"Glad to hear it." Another glance at Thompson.

Whatever silent communication was occurring between Smith and Thompson was causing alarms in

Cameron's head. It was as if Smith kept asking Thompson for permission to talk, or checking to make sure what he said was okay. Which made absolutely no sense whatsoever.

Unless…

All of a sudden everything clicked in place for Cameron. Before he could help himself he straightened in his chair and looked over at Thompson. Really looked. And found the man studying him in much the same way.

Mr. Smith seemed oblivious to it all and kept talking. "We really appreciate the work you've done for us. And I thought it was time to bring you up here to meet me and a few more of my associates—"

"It's okay, Jacob, you can stop. I think Mr. Cameron has figured out our little ruse."

Cameron heard a slight indrawn breath from Sophia. Evidently she had noticed something, too.

"Sorry, Mr. Smith," the other, squeaky-voiced Mr. Smith said. "I was thrown off a little bit by the woman being here."

"Don't worry about it, Jacob," Thompson told the other man, who was getting up from the desk chair and giving his seat to Thompson. "The lovely Ms. Reardon could distract any man."

Thompson sat and turned to Cameron and Sophia. "You'll have to excuse all the subterfuge. I have found over the years that when meeting someone new, sometimes a stand-in is my best option. Jacob here has been with me for a long time. The idea came to me because both of our last names happen to be Smith. So when Jacob introduces himself as 'Mr. Smith,' that is actually the truth."

Cameron had to admit, it was a pretty great plan. And using someone like Jacob—lumpy, not very personable nor clever—probably gave Smith a distinct edge when dealing with others. Most people would do as Cameron had initially done: write off Smith as not much of a threat. Because Jacob Smith wasn't much of a threat.

But Thompson Smith definitely was. *This* was the man Cameron had been waiting to meet; Cameron could feel it in his bones. Thompson Smith was the one who had killed his partner; the man Cameron had sworn he would bring to justice.

"And then, when I'm here with certain unknown guests, I like to pretend I'm some sort of butler. It allows me to better observe those around me. You'd be amazed what people will say and do when they think they're just around hired help." Thompson Smith shook his head with a tsk. Jacob—the other Mr. Smith—went to stand closer to the window, obviously no longer part of the conversation.

"I must admit, you figured it out quicker than most," Smith told Cameron.

"Uh, yeah. Well, that guy—" Cameron gestured toward Jacob "—is obviously related to Fin. But Fin never mentioned that his uncle was the head of DS-13. I've known Fin for a long time now and I don't think that's something he'd keep to himself for too long." Cameron pulled his cover identity around him like a blanket. It was time to be Cam Cameron now—kind of bright and organized, but not too much of either. The last thing Cameron wanted to do was put Smith on the defensive. This whole thing was already precariously balanced.

Smith seemed to buy it. "Yes, Fin has always loved to run his mouth." He then turned to study Sophia. "You, Ms. Reardon, have caused somewhat of a brouhaha around here."

Cameron forced himself not to tense up. It became more difficult as the seconds ticked by and Sophia didn't respond. Cameron shifted in his chair as casually as he could manage so he could glance over at Sophia. She was staring down silently at her hands folded in her lap.

Cameron didn't know how to help her. Was she overwhelmed and couldn't figure out how to respond? Afraid of messing up? Cameron was well aware that Sophia was not a trained agent. But if she was totally frozen and out of commission, things were about to spin out of control fast.

Cameron cleared his throat and gave a little laugh. "Sophia here is a little tired…."

Cameron didn't get out the rest of his sentence as Sophia looked up from her hands and at Mr. Smith. "Yeah, I tend to cause a little bit of a brouhaha no matter where I go."

Mr. Smith chuckled slightly and Cameron barely succeeded in keeping his jaw from dropping.

"I imagine you do, Ms. Reardon. We weren't expecting your presence here or in the warehouse yesterday," Smith told her.

"I gathered that from the multiple times your men threatened to kill me." Sophia looked Smith right in the eye as she said it.

Smith reached down to his desk and held up a file. "We did a little checking on you, of course. As I said, vetting everyone I come in contact with is standard procedure."

Sophia nodded. "Find anything interesting?"

Cameron had to give it to Sophia, she was handling herself like a pro. No nervous giveaways. Maybe it was possible they would make it out of this room alive.

"Nothing in particular. Except perhaps for the fact that you work for the FBI."

Damn.

Cameron flew out of his chair as if he had received an electric shock. "What? She's FBI? I swear I didn't know, Mr. Smith. She just said she knew something about this Ghost Shell thing and that you would want to hear it."

"It's all right, Cam. Ms. Reardon works for the FBI, but as a graphic artist, not an agent."

"Oh." Cameron sat back down slowly, feigning shock. "That's okay?"

"As soon as Fin reported that you had brought Sophia here back to the house in DC, I had her thoroughly checked out. Actually, having a record that so clearly linked her to the FBI helped ease my concerns a bit. Nobody trying to work undercover would be so easily linked to the FBI."

Smith turned and looked at Sophia. "And so you are still alive, my beautiful Sophia. And now there's no need to keep your FBI connection a secret."

Cameron didn't like how Smith was looking at her at all, but knew he couldn't do anything about it. Saying anything would just draw undue, and definitely unwanted, attention.

"Yeah, well, your henchmen didn't really seem like

the type to take anyone associated with the Bureau to meet you," Sophia said.

Smith nodded. "Yes, and I must admit, if Fin had been able to get in touch with me yesterday, I would've denied him permission to bring you here. And what a shame that would've been. So, although I had to have some harsh words with Fin about security, I'm glad we had a little lapse today so I could meet you."

Sophia shifted uncomfortably in her chair.

"But, on to business." Smith leaned back in his chair. "Fin and Cam tell me you have particular knowledge about the Ghost Shell technology."

Here came the real test. Cameron's breath stuck in his throat.

"That's right." Sophia nodded. "And for the right price I'm willing to give that information to you."

Smith folded his hands on his desk. "Why don't you tell me exactly what you know, so I can determine what that information is worth."

Sophia mimicked Smith's relaxed pose, but with her hands in her lap. "I don't think so. I'm sure as soon as I do that my life won't be worth much. I'm not as stupid as some of the morons you surround yourself with around here." Sophia made a vague gesture toward Cameron.

Cameron sat up straighter in his chair. There wasn't much he could do to help her, but this was one thing: insulted lover. "Hey, I'm not a moron."

Smith chuckled and gave Cameron his attention. "Well, you certainly can pick them, Cam."

Cameron decided defensiveness was his best play. "I was just looking for a good time. Then I found out she knew some stuff about that Ghost Shell thing and told Fin she should tell you about it. That's it. I'm not, like, vouching for her or anything."

"Look, Cam was just the most attractive foot in the door for me. One of your other hired thugs was my next option, but not as appealing—no offense."

Smith didn't move from his casual position. "Is that so? I understand there was quite a bit of carrying on in Cam's room at the house last night, including screaming."

Sophia shrugged delicately. "What can I say? I like it rough. Cam does, too."

"That worked out well for both of you, then." Smith laughed crassly.

Cameron chuckled, too, although he felt a little sick when he thought about the circumstances that had led to Sophia's screams back at the house. He glanced at her again. Her jaw had definitely tightened, but she gave nothing else away.

"Tell me, Sophia," Smith said after a few moments, "as delightful as you are, what is keeping me from just forcing the answer from you? I'm sure my men could find a way to be rougher than even you like."

Sophia sat up straighter in her chair, as did Cameron. The threat of torture wasn't to be taken lightly.

Out of the blue, Smith slammed his fist down on the desk, causing both Sophia and Cameron to startle. "You will tell me right now what you know." He never raised his voice, but his lower tone was all the more frightening.

Cameron prayed Sophia wouldn't panic. They were in too deep now.

"Ghost Shell has a fail-safe," Sophia said, barely

above a whisper. "A code that has to be entered to make it work outside of its design parameters."

Smith nodded, but his eyes were icy. "Go on."

"You probably know Ghost Shell was designed by a government contractor. To keep it from being used against the US government, a fail-safe code was created. If someone tries to use Ghost Shell without the code, it won't work."

Cameron was impressed. That sounded realistic even to his ears, and he knew the truth. Too bad whoever had created Ghost Shell hadn't thought of something similar.

"There's only one chance to enter the code. You have to do it at a certain time, in a certain order and even in a certain tempo. Anything is off in the pattern and you've basically got a useless piece of junk on your hands."

Cameron almost missed Smith's glance over at the wall to his left. A small tell, but definitely a tell. Ghost Shell was probably in a safe there. And Smith was believing Sophia's story.

Smith glared at Sophia. "You're playing a very dangerous game here, Ms. Reardon."

"I'm not playing any games. I just want to get paid. Two million dollars. I know how much Ghost Shell is worth, and the amount I want from you is a fraction of that."

Smith's lips flattened and his nostrils flared the slightest bit. Cameron knew they were walking an even more precarious edge than he had thought.

Sophia glanced at her watch. "It's too late to enter the code today. The deadline has passed. That much I'll tell you in good faith."

Smith nodded and Sophia continued, "Tomorrow

night I will enter the code for you. I'll get half the money before, and half afterward. Everyone can walk away happy from this, Mr. Smith."

Smith seemed to relax, and Cameron imagined it was because the amount Sophia was asking really was minute compared to Ghost Shell's black market value. But his eyes remained cold. "All right, Ms. Reardon, we have a deal. Tonight you and Cam will join me and my guests for the soiree, and tomorrow we shall deal with the business end of things."

Cameron nodded. "Sounds good."

"Just remember—" Smith leaned forward on his desk, menace clear on his face "—if you are lying to me, Sophia, about any part of this, you will beg for death before you finally die. That much I'll tell *you* in good faith."

Cameron watched as the color seeped from Sophia's face. She flinched when Smith repeated her words back at her.

Before their eyes, Smith's menace vanished and he was back to being the handsome host. He stood and Cameron and Sophia took their cue from him, and they all began walking toward the office door.

"Sophia, I assume the clothes I had brought in for you are acceptable?" Smith asked as if he hadn't threatened to torture and kill her just moments before.

Sophia nodded a little jerkily. "Yes, thank you." The words came out as a whisper.

"I hope you enjoy the gown I had picked out for you for this evening's festivities. It will suit your coloring and figure well, I believe," Smith said, reaching out to touch her on her elbow. Sophia seemed frozen.

Cameron was close enough to Sophia to see her pale and feel the fine tremor run through her body. He knew she wouldn't be able to hold it together much longer. He put himself between her and Smith.

"Yeah, thanks," Cam told Smith, struggling with all his might to grin. "She would've looked funny at the party running around in my shirt and pants." Cam ushered Sophia out the door. He turned back to Smith. "It was really great to finally meet you, Mr. Smith. And I hope you'll remember that I got Sophia here and helped save the day with Ghost Shell."

Smith nodded. "I won't forget your association with Sophia. It won't bode well for you, either, if she's lying."

"Oh, she's not, I'm sure," Cameron said, trying to put him at ease. "We'll see you tonight at the party."

Smith nodded and turned back into the office. Cameron took Sophia's arm and headed down the hall, grateful nobody was accompanying them. Sophia's breath was becoming more labored.

"Hang in there, baby," Cam whispered. "Just till we get back to the room."

They made it across the house to their room, with Cameron supporting most of Sophia's slight weight by the end. Cameron had barely closed the door before Sophia beelined to the bathroom and threw up everything she had eaten.

Chapter Eleven

Sophia felt relatively confident that she would never live through this day. Cameron kept praising her quietly, telling her what a remarkable job she had done with Smith, but Sophia just felt exhausted. They still couldn't talk freely because of the bug that Thompson—or Mr. Smith or whatever you wanted to call him—had placed in their room. That man gave her the freak-outs.

After she had completely lost the contents of her stomach, Cameron had helped Sophia from the bathroom, onto the bed. He was sitting beside her, stroking her hair back from her face, as he had been for the past twenty minutes.

"I wouldn't worry too much about what Mr. Smith said," Cameron told her in a voice loud enough for the surveillance to clearly hear him. "You'll just give him the information tomorrow, he'll pay you and it will be all over."

"Yeah…" The word came out all croaky so Sophia started again. "Yeah, I just don't like people threatening to kill me."

A knock on the door brought them both to attention. Sophia stayed where she was as Cameron went to open the door. It was Fin carrying two separate hanging bags of clothes. He was also sporting a nasty bruise on his jaw.

"These are from Mr. Smith," Fin said gruffly, thrusting the bags into Cameron's arms.

"Which one? Your uncle or the real Mr. Smith?" Cameron scoffed. "What happened to your face, Fin?"

"Your girlfriend is what happened to my face. Mr. Smith didn't like it that I allowed Sophia to arrive with us without contacting him first, even though she has something he wants," Fin spat. A vein pulsed in his neck as he turned to glare at Sophia on the bed. "You should've told me you were FBI."

Sophia recoiled from the venom in Fin's eyes. "I'm not really FBI. I just happen to work at the FBI building. Plus, I'm sure you would've just killed me if I had mentioned it."

Fin didn't respond to that, just turned and marched out the door. Cameron unzipped and held up the contents of the bags. One contained dress pants and a light gray shirt for Cameron. The other contained a black gown that looked quite lovely and demure in the front. But then Sophia turned it around on the hanger and saw that it was backless almost down to the waist.

Sophia cringed. It was beautiful, but definitely not something she would've ever picked out or worn. "Looks like we have our costumes for tonight."

Cameron nodded. "You okay?"

"I don't like having to wear what he picks out for me. But I guess it's better than a shirt and jeans." Sophia turned and went into the bathroom to build her resolve. If this dress was her only option then she'd make the best of it.

A couple hours later they were on their way to the main part of the house. Sophia was glad to be out of the room—having to monitor every word that came out of their mouths was stressful. She was constantly worried she was going to let something slip.

The dress was on, fitting her perfectly. Her hair was up in a sophisticated twist. She'd made full use of the makeup that had arrived with the dress. Sophia knew she looked good.

But she hated every bit of it.

Even seeing Cameron's expression when she had walked out of the bathroom—and Sophia had to admit that watching his jaw almost drop to the ground had been pretty thrilling—she still wished she wasn't wearing this dress.

Or that she was wearing it under very different circumstances.

She and Cameron made their way to the main section of the house, where people were already milling around and talking. The sun had set, taking with it the gorgeous views outside, but the party room itself was beautiful enough.

They joined the crowd, talking and mingling with different people. Sophia received multiple compliments on the dress, which she barely acknowledged. And she absolutely hated the way Smith had nodded with approval when he had seen her in it. She didn't think Cameron noticed. He was busy thinking like an agent.

"I wish I had facial-recognition software here, or at least a camera," Cameron grumbled as they moved through more people. "I know there are people here that Omega should be aware are associates of Smith's. But I'm pretty useless."

"I might be able to help a little bit," Sophia told him. "Obviously I can't remember everyone, but if you see a few people who you want to remember, I can study them and draw them later."

"Really?" Cameron smiled down at her. "That would be unbelievably helpful."

Finally something Sophia could do that would be helpful. Good. She was tired of feeling like an albatross.

She and Cameron wandered around chatting, watching Smith and who he interacted with. As Cameron would signal to her about a certain person to remember, Sophia would do her best to memorize features. Sophia felt so much more comfortable doing that than trying to convince Smith she knew some secret information about some computer virus or whatever. Studying people, remembering features, drawing them, even days or weeks later—*that* she could do.

But Sophia definitely didn't like the way Smith would look at her whenever he could meet her eyes. As if he owned her.

The veiled malevolence in Smith's eyes wouldn't be easy to capture in a drawing. Sophia hoped she never had to try. She didn't even want to think about tomorrow when she wasn't able to put in any sort of password.

What had Smith said? That she would beg for death before she finally died? Amazing how that would sound so melodramatic under any other circumstances, but sounded so credible coming from Smith. Glancing at him again across the room Sophia could easily imagine he knew many ways to make someone beg for death.

Sophia could feel nausea pooling again in her stomach.

"You doing okay?" Cameron whispered.

"Smith." She gestured toward the older man with a tilt of her head. "He makes me nervous."

"If he keeps looking at you like that, things might get ugly around here really quick," Cameron said.

Sophia shivered. "I know. Can we just get out of here? Do we have to stay for the entire evening?"

"No. We don't have to stay. As a matter of fact, I think I have an even better plan than staying here." Cameron smiled at her in a way that made Sophia's insides start to melt.

Sophia swallowed hard. The only options were basically staying here or going back to the bedroom. Was that what Cameron wanted?

Sophia knew that was what she wanted. If there was one thing she had learned from this whole…*adventure*, it was that you never knew how many days you had left. Especially when someone waited in the wings looking for an excuse to kill you.

She hadn't made love with Cameron five years ago because she thought she'd had all the time in the world. That ended up not being true. She wouldn't make the same mistake now, especially when tomorrow hung so very precariously in the balance.

Sophia smiled up at Cameron. "Okay, I'm ready to go whenever you are."

He reached down and squeezed her hand. "All right, we should stay here a little bit longer, then we can start to make our way out as inconspicuously as possible."

His smile took her breath away. Sophia never thought she could feel this way in a situation like this. Just for tonight she wasn't going to worry about tomorrow. Because she didn't even know if she'd have a tomorrow.

Cameron subtly started angling them toward one of the doors. They spoke briefly with a few people as they made their way out and Cameron stopped to tell Fin they were leaving. She noticed Cameron awkwardly bump into Fin when a waiter came by. Cameron apologized, but Fin stormed off to the other end of the room. Obviously Fin was still mad at them for getting him in trouble with Mr. Smith. Sophia was glad when they didn't go anywhere near Mr. Smith to say their goodbyes; he was busy talking to other people anyway.

Once they made it out of the main room, Sophia finally felt as if she could breathe without panic pushing at her chest. She just wanted to get back to the room.

Cameron wrapped an arm around her and hugged her to his side. "Thank you for doing this."

Okay, odd. "Um, you're welcome."

"We're not going to have much time, so we'll need to hurry."

Now Sophia was really confused. "Why? Are you expecting them to come barging into our bedroom?"

"No," Cameron told her as he walked quickly with her down the hallway. "I mean breaking into Smith's office while everyone's at the party to see if we can find Ghost Shell."

SOPHIA HAD SOME sort of strange look on her face and Cameron couldn't blame her. Not with the way Smith had been looking at her all evening. Cameron didn't blame Soph for wanting to get out of there.

Cameron had that itchy feeling on the back of his neck all evening—the one that told him things were not going the way he'd planned. He didn't get the feeling very often, but over the years, first as a US Army Ranger then as an undercover agent, he had learned to pay attention to it.

Things were about to take a turn for the worse.

During this party, while everybody was occupied, was the best time to try to get into Smith's office and get Ghost Shell. Once they had that, Cameron could get Sophia out, on foot if he had to.

The more time he spent with her, the more he was coming to realize how much she meant to him. He wanted to get this case finished as soon as possible. And he could admit Sophia was his primary reason for that.

He wanted to be with her outside of this lunatic situation. Cameron glanced at Sophia as they walked down the hall. The strange look was gone. Now she seemed focused and determined to get the job done. Her grit was downright sexy.

But hell, everything about her was sexy. Especially in that almost-backless dress she was wearing. Cameron hated that Smith had picked it out, but had to admit Smith's choice was flawless.

They quietly made their way back to the locked door of Smith's office. Cameron pulled out a swipe card for the lock and held it up. He had taken it from Fin a few minutes ago when he had bumped into him. "Not a good day for Fin. We're probably going to get him fired."

Sophia snickered. "My heart breaks for him."

Cameron closed the door behind them but left it cracked just a little so they could get out quickly if they needed to.

"Okay, so what exactly are we looking for?" Sophia asked him as she made her way over to the desk. Cameron was right behind her.

"Ghost Shell is an external hard drive. The encryption device contains too much data to fit on anything too small, so it's about the size of a hardback book."

Sophia pulled out the desk chair, sat down and began searching through drawers on one side of the desk. Cameron began looking around a wall of bookshelves.

"It's not going to be in a drawer just out in the open," Cameron said softly. "I saw Smith looking over at this wall earlier when we were talking about Ghost Shell. There must be a safe."

Cameron continued to look around the wall, but couldn't find anything. Every minute they were in this office put them in more danger. He quickly joined Sophia at the desk and started to feel around. He ran his hands along the sides of it then under the writing surface. Sure enough, a button lay hidden in the corner. No one would ever know it was there unless they were looking for it.

"I've got it." Cameron pressed the button and watched as one panel of books began to move.

They both saw it at the same time. A lamp that had been placed in front of the panel to make it less conspicuous.

"Cam, the lamp!"

Sophia and Cameron both dived for it, but were too late. The lamp fell to the floor with a loud crash.

Damn.

The crash seemed deafening in the otherwise silent room. All color drained from Sophia's face.

"What do we do?" She looked around frantically.

Was it possible that nobody had heard the lamp fall? In the party nobody would have heard it, but was anyone nearby? Cameron held his breath, then cursed when he heard a door open down the hall. Someone was coming, blocking their only route of escape.

It was too late to get them anywhere safe. Cameron looked at Sophia, who was watching him with a fully panicked look in her eyes.

Cameron burst into a flurry of activity. He pushed the button to close the panel in front of the safe, then quickly picked up the lamp that had fallen to the hardwood floor—thankfully, it hadn't broken—and put it back on the shelf in front of the closed panel.

He grabbed a crystal vase that rested on the desk and put it on the floor. Sophia just watched him, not understanding at all what he was trying to do.

She looked even more shocked when he began unbuttoning his dress shirt, pulling it from where it was tucked into his pants. Then he lifted her by the waist and set her on the desk. Before Sophia could ask what he was doing, Cameron climbed on top of the desk and began kissing her.

Cameron peeled her dress as far down one shoulder as it would go, baring a great deal of skin. He threaded his fingers in her hair and pushed her back fully on the desk. He pulled up one of her legs and hooked it around his waist and slid his hand over her breast, grabbing it roughly.

He heard Sophia whimper against his mouth in protest of the hard kiss and felt her pull her torso away from him. Cameron opened his eyes to find her wide green eyes staring at him.

She was frightened.

Cameron stopped immediately. He couldn't stand that look in her eyes. True, Cameron was trying to put on a show for whoever was about to come through that door, but this was Sophia. He didn't want her frightened of being close to him.

He brought his hand back up to stroke her cheek. He leaned his weight on his elbows and gazed gently down at her.

"Sorry, baby," he whispered, and stroked her cheek once more. "Let's try this again, slower. Kiss me."

This time Cameron brought his lips gently down to hers. He teased her bottom lip with his nipping little kisses, then gave the same attention to the upper one. He heard Sophia sigh and watched as her eyes closed.

Cameron deepened the kiss as Sophia responded. Her arms came up and wrapped around his neck. A knot of need twisted in him as he drew her closer.

Cameron tried to remind himself that this was all an act, that any moment now someone from DS-13 would walk through the door and have to believe that the only thing going on in here was hot sex. But as he kissed Sophia again he realized that there was no acting about it.

This time when Cameron's hand moved onto her beautiful body again it was because he couldn't stop himself, not because he wanted to put on any sort of show. Cameron shifted so he could get closer to Sophia.

She moaned and held on to him, her fingers threading through his hair.

Just a few moments later the door to the office flew open and the lights flipped on.

It was Rick. Damn it. And he had his weapon in his hand.

"What the hell are you doing in here?"

Cameron subtly shifted so he was blocking more of Sophia from Rick's view.

"What the hell does it look like we're doing, Rick? Get out."

But Rick wasn't backing down. "You're not supposed to be in here."

Cameron decided to try a different route. "Dude, we're just having a little fun in the boss's room. You know, a little danger." He gave Rick a knowing grin. *"Capiche?"*

Rick's dark eyes narrowed. Cameron didn't know what the younger man was going to do. If Rick decided to get Mr. Smith, things would become much more complicated.

"Let me off this desk." Sophia pushed out from under him. "I told you we should just go back to the room, jackass."

Sophia wiggled completely out from under him and straightened her dress over her body, but not before Rick caught a glimpse of some tantalizing flesh, Cameron was sure. She looked over at Rick without flinching. "What's the matter with you, never seen a woman before?" she snapped at him with a jutting chin. She turned to Cam. "Can we please go back to the room now? I don't like having an audience. At least, not him."

Cameron watched as Sophia began to walk toward the door. Whatever suspicions Rick had were obviously lost as he looked at Sophia with cruel lust in his eyes.

Rick grabbed her arm as she walked by. "Maybe you and I will get our turn soon." Cameron could see Sophia wince, but he didn't intervene.

Fighting a man with a gun in his hand would not work out well for any of them. Plus, it would be completely out of character for Cam Cameron. Instead, Cameron leaned down and put the vase he'd set on the floor earlier back on the desk.

"Yeah, I don't think so." Sophia all but spat the words.

Rick grabbed her other arm and pulled her up against him fully. "We'll see about that."

Cameron walked over casually. "All right, Romeo, that's enough. We'll see you in the morning."

Rick smirked, but he stepped back so they could get through the doorway.

Cameron wasn't sure what Rick's weird smile was all about, but he wasn't sticking around to find out. They had dodged a bullet, literally and figuratively. Cameron grabbed Sophia's arm and they made their escape.

Chapter Twelve

As they reached their room, Cameron signaled for Sophia to wait right inside the door. The bug was still there. It was time to get rid of that thing.

He just hoped that Rick would keep his mouth shut about seeing them. Cameron supposed it was possible. The way Sophia had shunned Rick, he probably wouldn't want to announce that to anyone very soon.

Frustration gnawed in Cameron's gut. They had been so close to finding Ghost Shell. If they had just had a few more minutes—and if that stupid lamp hadn't fallen—he could've cracked the safe. Then he could've gotten Sophia, and the device, out of here.

Which was what was best, Cameron knew. But after what happened on the desk, Cameron was torn between wanting her to go and wanting her to stay.

Basically just plain wanting her.

He wanted her still. It was physical, definitely, the desire he had for her. But after the way she'd totally kept it together over the past forty-eight hours, it was more than that. Cameron found himself realizing that Sophia had courage and backbone, things he never knew she had. He suspected she never knew she possessed those qualities, either.

And her strengths were so very attractive to him. Everything about her was becoming more and more attractive to him.

And the way she had kissed him back on the desk… There was definitely an attraction and it was definitely affecting both of them. And Cameron planned to do something about it.

But first they needed to talk. That definitely could not happen with the bug still in the room. Cameron walked over to the tray. Sophia stood just inside the door, seeming unsure as to what she should do.

Cameron took the tray and set it on the floor out in the hallway, closing the door again behind him. He signaled for Sophia to remain quiet as he got out his Omega equipment and made sure no other bugs had been placed in the room while they were gone.

None. Finally, a break.

"Now we can talk." Cameron didn't speak at full volume, but at least they didn't have to speak in low tones.

"Won't they wonder about the tray?"

"I'll tell them there was a funny smell and it was bugging me."

Sophia smiled crookedly. "Okay."

"Are you all right?" Cameron walked over to her, stopping just short of touching her.

"Do you mean in general or after what just happened?"

"Both, I guess. But specifically I was referring to what happened a few minutes ago."

Sophia shook her head. "You mean Rick? I guess

I shouldn't have egged him on. But I couldn't help it. That guy gives me the creeps."

"Yeah, no kidding. Rick definitely has a cruel side." Cameron saw Sophia shudder. "But I was actually talking about what happened between you and me. On the desk."

Sophia took a step back from Cameron, then turned and walked over to the bed, sitting down on the edge. She didn't speak for a long moment. "Don't worry about it, Cam. I understand."

"Well, explain it to me, because I don't understand." Cameron didn't like the way she was looking down, as if she was too embarrassed to make eye contact with him.

"At the desk, you were undercover. You thought fast. It was a good plan, and it worked. It seemed to fool Rick."

"Sophia—"

"I get it, Cam, I really do. It was like earlier when I came out of the bathroom and you kissed me. Again, smart, quick thinking on your part. You probably saved our lives."

She looked up at him then, and shrugged her shoulders wearily. Cameron most distinctly did not like what he saw in her eyes: wariness, embarrassment, resignation. He walked closer to her, but she held out an arm to stop him.

"There's no need to keep up the pretense now, Cam. There's no bug in the room or creep coming down the hall about to catch us where we're not supposed to be."

Sophia stood up. "I'm going to take another bath, okay?"

Cameron had heard enough. He strode purposely

over to Sophia and threaded both his hands into her hair. He tilted her head back so he could look directly into her eyes. A shocked sound came out of her throat at his sudden movement.

"Let's get something straight here, Soph. Yes, I am undercover and yes, this situation is beyond complicated."

"Listen, Cam…" Sophia tried to step back, but Cameron wouldn't let her.

"No, you listen. I have to be *on*, all the time here. My life, your life, the success of the mission, getting justice for my partner, all depend on me staying focused."

Sophia dropped her gaze. "I *know*, Cam. I understand that."

Cameron bent his knees so he could catch her eyes again. When she finally looked at him, he continued, "Well, know and understand this—you blow my focus all to hell. I want you in a way I have never wanted any other woman."

That got her attention. "Wh-what?"

"You really think I'm just acting when I kiss you, acting during what happened on the desk?"

"You're not?" Her shocked tone told him all he needed to know.

"Baby, if Rick hadn't come into that office, we'd still be on that desk. Hell, I should probably thank Rick so that I won't forever have to try to forget that our first time was on the desk of the man who killed my partner."

"It's just so hard for me to tell, Cam. To know what's real and what's not with you."

Cameron brought his lips down to hers and kissed

her gently. "Know this is real," he whispered against her lips.

He felt the moment Sophia gave in to the kiss. Her arms came up and entwined around his neck. Cameron bent his knees again so he could wrap his arms around her waist, then lifted her so she was face-to-face with him.

"You always were a tiny little thing," he told her, still kissing her.

Her arms wrapped more firmly around his neck. "I'll have you know, I'm the absolute perfect size."

"Oh, I don't doubt that at all, Ms. Reardon." Cameron began backing up until her legs rested against the side of the bed, then lowered her feet back to the ground. He trailed kisses down the side of her neck and delighted as it caused her to break out in goose bumps. He reached down and slid both sleeves of her dress off her shoulders, and because of its open back, it slid to the floor and pooled at her feet.

"Perfect size, indeed," he murmured as he removed his own shirt.

"Cameron…" He loved the sound of her voice as she said his name.

Cameron stood and picked her up again, lowering her onto the bed slowly and with a great deal more finesse than he had before. His mouth found hers again. Her hands clenched into his shoulders.

Cameron wanted to take things slow, to make sure not to frighten her as he had on the desk. Cameron moved on top of her, propping his weight up on his elbows, holding back. But evidently Sophia had other plans.

She pulled his weight down to her, making quick

work of removing his clothes and the rest of hers. Passion was building to a fevered pitch. This was definitely real; no acting involved whatsoever.

That was Cameron's last coherent thought before he lost himself in the fervor and heat that consumed both he and Sophia.

THE NEXT MORNING Sophia made good use of the giant bathroom again, this time to take a shower. Cameron had joined her in there—good thing there had been more than room enough for two—although him joining her had greatly prolonged the length of the shower.

They were both toweling off now, in the steam-filled bathroom. "I so don't want to ask this, but did Smith provide any more clothes? Anything casual?" Sophia didn't want to put on the ball gown again or yesterday's dress pants.

"I'll check." A few moments later Cameron, having gotten dressed in jeans and a soft black sweater, brought in a new package and set it on the counter. Sophia opened it, relieved to see a pair of jeans and a navy blue T-shirt. Underclothes, socks and a pair of casual shoes completed Smith's wardrobe for Sophia today.

Sophia still hated having to wear what that psycho chose for her.

Speaking of psycho… "So what's our plan when I meet with him tonight for the code? I don't think I'm going to be able to bluff my way out again." A shudder went through her as she put on the jeans.

"I'm going to contact Omega and insist on an extraction for you this evening. Your life is definitely in jeopardy, so they won't refuse again."

"Just for me? You're not coming, too?"

"We'll see. If my cover's blown, then yes, I'll be extracted, too. No point staying here just to be tortured and killed."

Sophia rolled her eyes. "Some people have no sense of adventure."

Cameron gave a soft bark of laughter and walked over to kiss her. "We have a few hours. A lot can happen in that time. But either way, I'm getting you out before this goes any further. You'll never have to see Smith again."

Sophia felt as if a huge weight was lifted. Not having to see Smith again was just fine. She tried to pull the T-shirt on over her head and winced from the pain in her arm.

Cameron helped her bring her arm back down, staring at the jagged cut on her shoulder and upper arm from the nail. "That's starting to look pretty infected. Does it hurt?"

Although she hadn't really noticed it in the midst of last night's activities or in the shower this morning, Sophia could definitely feel an ache now. She looked over at the wound. The skin around where she had scraped against the rusty nail was puffy and a fiery red.

"It's a little sore, but not unmanageable."

"When was your last tetanus shot?"

Sophia had no idea. It wasn't something she thought about regularly. "I don't know. High school, maybe?"

Cameron grimaced. "That's not great, but it's still within the ten-year mark. Let's get that bandaged." He helped her up to sit on the marble bathroom counter.

Cameron applied an antibacterial ointment and began

wrapping her arm in gauze, both items from his duffel bag.

"You're like a Boy Scout with that duffel bag of yours."

Cameron smiled and winked at her. "I try to keep as much in there as I can without carrying anything that would arouse suspicion if someone goes through it."

"Do they go through your bags a lot?"

"I don't know, but I never assume that they don't. I stay more alive that way. So yeah, I have a lot of junk in there. It helps camouflage the important stuff."

"Like that cell phone thing you used to communicate with Omega?"

"It wasn't actually a cell phone, but yes. Like that." He finished wrapping her shoulder. "Okay, you're all patched up."

He helped Sophia ease the shirt over her head. Sophia tried not to provide any indication at all that her arm was hurting her. Then she forgot all about any pain as Cameron grabbed her by the hips and scooted her to the edge of the counter and kissed her.

"Remind me again why we didn't do this five years ago?" he whispered against her lips.

Sophia smiled. "If we had known it would be this good, I don't think we'd have been able to wait."

Sophia thought about Cameron when she had known him before. She had been finishing college then, with her degree in graphic design. He had just been coming out of the US Army Rangers and had told her he wasn't sure what he was going to do with his life.

Sophia pulled back from him. "You lied to me before. You told me you didn't know what profession you'd end up in."

Cameron made a *hmm* noise in his throat. "I didn't really lie to you."

Sophia lifted a single eyebrow.

Cameron had the good grace to at least look sheepish. "Yeah, Omega approached me while I was still in the army, so I knew I was going to work for them. But I wasn't sure exactly how I would fit in with the organization and what I would be doing. So I wasn't technically lying..."

"You know, for a while after you left, since you didn't say a real goodbye or anything, I thought it was because I hadn't had sex with you," Sophia whispered.

"What?" Cameron's head jerked back.

Sophia shrugged. "Well, for the first couple months with all our breakfasts together, I knew you didn't expect anything. But when things started building between us and we started going out on dates and stuff..."

"Let me get this straight." Cameron's jaw clenched and his eyes tightened. He removed his hands from Sophia's waist and placed them on the counter on either side of her legs. "You thought I left because you didn't put out?"

Sophia tried not to let Cameron's looming chest intimidate her. She slid back on the counter a bit. "It was a possible theory, yes. After all, I had no idea why you had left, did I?" Sophia poked him in the big, looming chest.

"*That* had nothing to do with it."

"Yeah, well, I didn't know that. All I knew was everything seemed to be going fine between us and then all of a sudden you were gone. No goodbye from you, just a cryptic message on my phone when you knew I wouldn't be home."

Cameron's shoulders hunched. "Yeah, I guess you're right." There was a long pause. "I couldn't tell you about Omega Sector, Soph. And they told me I had to break ties as cleanly as possible."

"You mean no one at Omega has any outside relationships? No marriages or anything like that? It seems a bit extreme."

"No, they do. A bunch of people are married and have families in Omega. It's just…" Cameron turned from facing her to leaning against the counter next to her.

"What?" Sophia asked when Cameron didn't keep talking.

"All casual ties had to be severed."

It took a second for the pain to set in, but when it did it stole Sophia's breath. What could she say to that? She had thought he was the one. He had thought of her as a casual tie.

"Oh," she finally managed to whisper.

"Soph, I'm sorry. I never thought of you—of what we had—as casual."

"But you told Omega Sector it was." It wasn't a question.

"They asked about the nature of our relationship. How long we'd been together and stuff like that. They needed to know how often I spent the night at your house. If I was going to work for Omega, and I was in a solid, committed relationship with you, then you'd have to be closely scrutinized, also."

Sophia waited but didn't say anything.

"On paper it looked like we had breakfast together all the time and had been on a few dates," he said softly.

"Casual," Sophia whispered.

"Soph, that time we spent together. All those mornings at the diner. The dates, the kisses. They were important to me, too."

"But not important enough to make you stay. Or to tell Omega that I wasn't a casual relationship."

Cameron was standing right next to her, but the gap between them was almost insurmountable. Sophia slid a little farther away from him on the counter. She was afraid if he touched her right now she might shatter into a million pieces.

Cameron pinched the bridge of his nose, his eyes closed. "If I could go back in time to five years ago, there are so many things I would do differently."

Chapter Thirteen

Cameron would give every paycheck he'd ever get for the rest of his life if he never had to see that look on Sophia's face ever again. He had known he'd screwed up when he walked away from her five years ago. But he had never dreamed it had hurt her as much as it had hurt him.

Cameron didn't know exactly what he had thought. Maybe that she would move on quickly because they hadn't been too physical. Maybe that she was young and that a clean break would be easy to recover from.

"I had to choose. At the time I thought I was making the right choice." Cameron knew he had to make her understand, but the right words seemed to fail him.

Sophia turned her head away and it almost broke his heart. "I understand," she whispered.

He grabbed her chin firmly and forced her to look at him. "I'm pretty sure you don't understand at all. There's not a day that goes by that I don't regret that decision." He sighed, releasing her chin and turning away. "But it's complicated. I know I've done a lot of good work with Omega—maybe even saved a lot of lives. But…"

Cameron wasn't even sure what the rest of that sentence was. Silence hung between them.

"But you wonder, deep inside, if it was worth the price you paid personally," Sophia finally said.

Yes, that summed it up perfectly. Sophia had always understood him.

"Every. Damn. Day." Cameron turned around to face her again. He reached up and trailed the back of his fingers down her cheek. "And always because of..."

They both jumped a bit at the pounding on the door.

Cameron reached over and kissed her briefly and went to answer their bedroom door. It was Fin.

"Mr. Smith wants to see you in his office to talk about business stuff. She—" he gestured at Sophia "—doesn't need to go."

"Right now? It's eight o'clock in the morning."

"Yes, now. Mr. Smith is an early riser."

There was nothing particularly bad about what Fin was saying, but Cameron still felt tension pooling in his stomach. "But Smith doesn't want to see Sophia?"

"No, just you. For stuff having nothing to do with her. She can stay here and somebody will bring a breakfast tray." Fin gave nothing away, probably because he knew nothing.

Cameron wasn't sure which way to push. He didn't want to be away from Sophia and leave her here by herself, but on the other hand keeping her as far from Smith as possible was probably the best plan.

"Okay," Cameron finally said. "I'll go to Mr. Smith's office in just a few minutes." Maybe it was time to get Sophia out of here right now.

"I'm supposed to wait for you right here and take you," Fin told him.

So much for getting Sophia out right now.

Did Smith know they had been in his office last night? Had Rick told them? Surely they would've already been summoned, *both* of them, if that was the case. Maybe this really was just a routine meeting to discuss details. Cameron nodded. "Give me just a second."

Cameron closed the door and Sophia came out of the bathroom. "Everything okay?"

"Yeah, I think. Fin just came to tell me Smith wants to meet with me."

Cameron could almost see the tension that flooded Sophia's body. "Why? Is there a problem? Do you think Rick told him about us in the office?"

"No. We'd have already been dragged in there if he had."

Sophia still looked worried. "Then what?"

"Just a meeting. After all, I am his employee. Business details, Fin said." Cameron walked over to his bag and got out the SIG he had hidden there. He tucked it into the back of his jeans. He hoped he wouldn't need it, but this close to getting Sophia out, he wasn't taking any chances.

"Do I come, too?"

"No. You're supposed to stay here. They're going to bring up a tray with some breakfast. Eat as much as you can."

"Okay." Sophia looked as hesitant about this plan as Cameron felt. He walked over to her and pulled her into his arms.

"Just hang in there a few more hours," he whispered into her ear. "Let me go act normal with Smith and I'll be back in a bit. Then we'll get you out of here."

Sophia reached up her hands to frame his face. "Be careful." She stood up on her tiptoes to kiss him.

Cameron stepped back after a few moments even though he wanted nothing more than to stay there in her embrace. "I will. Stay here in the room. Get the tray when it's delivered, but otherwise keep the door locked."

Sophia nodded and Cameron turned and walked out the door.

Fin was still waiting, as promised. They silently walked together to Smith's office.

Unlike yesterday, Cameron could tell Smith's office door was already open from down the hall. As they got closer, Cam could hear Smith talking—and laughing—with another man. Cameron walked into the office, Fin following right behind, but staying by the door. He obviously was still not in Smith's good graces.

"Cam, come in," Smith said good-naturedly.

Thompson Smith, when playing the role of DS-13 leader, looked polished and friendly, not at all like the butler Cameron had mistook him for yesterday. Having seen him play both roles, Cameron could understand how he had eluded law enforcement for years. But no matter which role he played, Smith's eyes were still cold and hard.

The eyes of a killer.

"Good morning, Mr. Smith. Fin said you wanted to meet with me about some business."

"Yes, yes." Smith nodded. "A few very important details. First, this is my associate Mr. McNeil. He came up this morning to discuss some business, also. Fred, this is Cam Cameron, about whom we were talking earlier."

Talking about him could be good or bad, Cam knew. He also noticed no details were provided by either men as to what type of "associate" McNeil was. But McNeil stuck out his hand for shaking, so Cameron assumed it was good. "Nice to meet you."

Cam shook the hand and responded, "You, too, man." McNeil faded over to the side of the room and propped himself up against the wall, obviously to get out of the way of whatever business Mr. Smith had with Cameron.

"I trust you had a good time at the party last night?" Smith asked.

Cameron tensed for just a moment then forced himself to relax. Had he been wrong and Smith did know about them breaking into the office? If so, he'd have to think of a way to play this off quick. His best bet was probably to pretend to be the bad boy—wanting to have sex in the boss's office.

Disrespectful, sure. But better than announcing he was a federal agent.

"Yeah. Lots of fun. Plenty of trouble to get into," Cameron told him, providing what he hoped was a charming grin. Charming was hard to pull off when all you wanted to do was arrest the bastard sitting across from you and see that he rot in jail for the next 150 years or so.

"Yes, there's always lots of trouble with my parties." Smith chuckled. "And I trust our lovely Sophia had a good time, also? She looked beautiful last night."

Smith wasn't giving away much. Cam grinned again. "She didn't seem to have any complaints."

"Glad to hear that. Tell me a little more about Sophia. You seem quite taken with her. You met her for the first time a few days ago at the warehouse?"

These questions were not going in the direction Cameron had wanted. He couldn't quite determine their purpose. Did Smith know something? Was he setting up Cam? Or did he just like the sordid little details of other people's lives?

He wouldn't put any of it past Smith.

Cam decided to play it on the assumption that Smith didn't really know anything. It was his only real option anyway. To make up some sort of history between he and Sophia now would just be suspicious. "Yeah, at the warehouse, where Marco found her."

"And you think she was there to try to sell us the information she had about Ghost Shell."

"Yeah, that's what she told me. Honestly, really, I just thought she was hot. I wasn't thinking much past that." Better to come across as careless, rather than a traitor.

"But when Fin and Rick were about to eliminate her, you stopped them."

Cam looked at Smith then over at McNeil, who still was leaning against the wall. "Yeah, it seemed like a waste." Cam shrugged. "She knew stuff that was helpful about Ghost Shell so I thought we should bring her to you and let you decide."

"I see." Smith sat back in his chair.

"I mean, I know she wants you to pay her money, Mr. Smith. But at least Ghost Shell will still work with her help. And it sounded like you would make much more from selling it than what she was asking." Cameron injected a bit of nervousness into his tone, which wasn't difficult.

"Yes, that's true," Smith responded, leaning back in his chair. "The problem is that I have Mr. McNeil here, who tells me that the information Sophia provided was not correct."

Cameron looked over at Fred McNeil. "Oh, okay. Are you a computer specialist guy or something?" Cam added just a little bit of mockery. Perhaps he could discredit this guy. But it was a long shot.

Fred snorted. "No. I am definitely not any type of computer geek."

"Then how do you know that Sophia isn't telling the truth?"

Mr. Smith answered for Fred. "Because Mr. McNeil is on my payroll and has been for years. He works for the FBI."

This was not what Cameron wanted to hear on multiple levels. First, because a mole selling secrets to DS-13 was never good, but more important, because this meant Sophia was really in trouble. Tonight was going to be too late to get her out. She'd be dead long before then.

Cameron shot from his chair. "Whoa. FBI? I don't want to have anything to do with an FBI agent." He had to stall. Figure out what to do.

His sudden movement had put McNeil on the defensive. His hand was already at his weapon.

"Calm down, Cam," Smith told him. "Obviously, Fred is not here to arrest anyone. He wouldn't be much use to me if he was, would he?"

Cam pretended to process that. He sat back down

slowly. "No, I guess not." He glared over at Fred. "Sorry. Not a big fan of law enforcement."

Fred just rolled his eyes and Cam could tell that he'd just written Cameron off as being just another dumb thug. Good.

But Smith didn't seem quite as quick to lump Cam in that category. "Fred informs me that what Sophia said about some secret fail-safe code is not accurate."

"Maybe she knows something he doesn't."

Fred pushed himself away from the wall and came to stand closer to Smith's desk. "Look, Sophia Reardon is a *graphic artist* for the FBI. She's not an agent. She's not in the cyberterrorism division. She made up all that crap about a special code."

"How do you know?" Cameron asked.

"Because I was the person who acquired Ghost Shell for DS-13," Fred sneered. "Some goody-goody computer scientist at a technology company contacted us a few months ago in fear that something like Ghost Shell was being developed. Guess who happened to be assigned that call?"

"You?" That would explain a lot. How Ghost Shell got into DS-13's hands so quickly. And why the FBI was so clueless. The FBI may not even officially know that Ghost Shell existed. Omega Sector knew of its existence, but Omega had resources and connections the Bureau didn't have.

Agent McNeil rolled his eyes. "Yes, obviously. Me. So when I say your lady friend is lying, I know what I'm talking about. I know things that are going on in the FBI, the CIA and even some agencies you've never even heard of."

Things had just gone from bad to hell-in-a-handbasket. Obviously discrediting Agent McNeil wasn't going to work. And his bragging about unknown agencies—was McNeil referring to Omega? A mole in Omega would be ugly. Life-threatening, not only to Cameron, but also multiple other agents. Agents that included his family and friends.

Mr. Smith stood up. "Fin, get Rick and have him fetch Ms. Reardon and bring her here." Smith smiled over at Agent McNeil. "Rick has a nice cruel streak I find useful in these types of situations."

Cameron didn't turn around as he heard the door click behind him. He had to do something, fast. But pulling his SIG out now wouldn't do anything but get him killed.

"You were the one we couldn't figure out, Cam." Smith turned his attention back to Cameron. "Whether you were working with Ms. Reardon to cheat me of money."

Cam held his hands out in front of him. "Whoa. I just met this chick a couple of days ago! I thought I was helping you, Mr. Smith, honest. I had no idea she was trying to scam you."

Smith walked over to one of his large bookshelves. "I actually believe you, Cam. Not because of what you're saying right now, but because given the timeline of the development and our acquisition of Ghost Shell and Fin's ability to account for your location during that time, I believe you when you say you just met Ms. Reardon. Although I must admit, I hope you're not too fond of her, given what's about to happen."

Cameron watched as Smith reached over, pulled

down a book from the bookshelf and opened it. Inside was a cleverly hidden keypad and biometrics scanner, into which Smith punched a code and provided his thumbprint. The entire bookshelf spun and opened.

This was much more than the safe he and Sophia had found last night. And with the security measures Smith had, there was no way they would've been able to break in. Obviously he and Sophia hadn't been as close to discovering Ghost Shell as Cameron had thought.

Smith looked at Cameron and Agent McNeil, obviously happy to show off a bit. "Gentlemen, my panic room. Although, I rarely panic so I haven't had much use for it in that sense." Chuckling, Smith walked into the room. "It's fabulous, isn't it? And here is the Ghost Shell drive for which Ms. Reardon is determined to try to cheat me out of two million dollars." Smith reached over and pulled an external hard drive from one of the shelves. It was black, not too big. So benign-looking.

Cameron knew instantly what he had to do; he wouldn't get another chance like this. He could grab Ghost Shell and get Sophia out. It meant not being able to arrest Smith, but it was a trade-off Cameron was willing to make.

Cameron pulled his weapon out and pointed it at Agent McNeil. He knew that man was armed. Smith he wasn't sure about, but knew not to take him lightly.

"Sorry, Mr. Smith. But I'm going to have to take Ghost Shell off your hands." Cam decided to try to keep his undercover identity intact. Let them think he was just stealing from them out of greed. Both Smith and McNeil spun to look at Cam. McNeil made a move toward his weapon. "Nope, Agent McNeil. I need you to keep your hands right in front of you where I can see them. You, too, Mr. Smith."

Cameron kept the weapon pointed at McNeil as he walked over and took the man's gun from its holster.

Anger radiated from Smith's cold eyes. "So you did know Sophia?"

"Nope," Cameron told Smith, popping the *P* in the word as he reached over to take the hard drive from his hands. "But let's just say she convinced me of Ghost Shell's true value and that I could make a lot more money selling it on my own."

"Cam," Smith said, obviously trying to get his temper under control. "This isn't what you want to do. DS-13 is not an enemy you want to have. Even if you kill me, others will hunt you down."

Cameron knew Smith was stalling for time. Fin and Rick would be back with Sophia any minute and Cam would lose the advantage. "I think half a billion dollars will buy me pretty ample security." Cameron looked around the panic room. He had no idea what sort of communicative measures it had. He destroyed what he could see: ripping out a landline telephone and all the cords attached to a computer that sat in a corner. Cameron was sure there were other ways to communicate from inside the panic room, but hoped this would give him enough time to get Sophia out of the house.

Cameron stepped backward until he was just inside the door, weapon still pointing at the two men. "You're going to regret this," Smith spat at Cameron.

"Maybe," Cameron responded and then fired his gun at the keypad inside the door, blasting it into little pieces. Hopefully that would keep McNeil and Smith in there at least a little while.

Now the countdown had really started—somebody was bound to have heard the shot. Cameron stepped all the way out of the room and pressed the button that closed the door on the hidden book keypad. Smith's eyes were still shooting daggers at Cam as the door closed with a resounding thud. Cameron wasted no time and ran out of the office, Ghost Shell hard drive firmly in his hand.

He was carefully heading back down the hall toward the bedroom when he heard Sophia screaming his name in terror.

Chapter Fourteen

When Cameron left to go see Smith, Sophia decided to be ready. Ready for exactly what, she wasn't sure. But when he got back, she wanted to be ready.

Her shoulder was bothering her more than she had let on to Cameron, and it was becoming more stiff and difficult to move. Bending down to put on her socks and shoes caused a throbbing in her shoulder, but Sophia ignored the pain as best she could. A tap on the door startled her.

"Yes?" she asked as she walked slowly over to it. Sophia didn't want to open it, although recognized the lock on the door wouldn't keep anyone out if they were determined to get in.

"A breakfast tray for you, Ms. Reardon," a female voice said from the other side of the door. Sophia opened it hesitantly, but saw it was indeed just a woman with a tray in her hands. Moving aside, Sophia allowed the woman to bring in the tray and watched as she set it on the table and left without another word. The woman closed the door with a resounding thud as she left.

Was it just Sophia's imagination, or had the woman seemed hostile and suspicious? Did she know something Sophia didn't? Did everyone know who she and Cameron really were?

Or was it a woman just doing her job who had other tasks to get back to and didn't want to waste any time? Also a perfectly reasonable explanation.

See? This was why Sophia wasn't meant to do undercover work. Save that for the trained agents. It was too easy to reflect her own paranoia onto others' actions when there was no tangible reason to think they suspected something.

Sophia walked over to the table where the woman had set the tray. She reached down and took a spoonful of the fruit salad. Poison momentarily crossed her mind but Sophia shrugged and kept on eating. At this point either it was poisoned or it wasn't; she wasn't going to worry about it.

A knock at the door again startled Sophia. Had the woman forgotten something?

"Yes?" Sophia asked as she opened the door. But it was Rick leaning in her doorway, not the woman with the tray.

Sophia tried to shut the door again, but Rick easily blocked it. When he took a step toward her, Sophia jerked back. She realized the mistake instantly—backing up allowed Rick to enter the room and shut the door behind him.

She heard him click the lock and knew she was in trouble.

"You've got on quite a bit more clothes than when I saw you last night."

Sophia ignored that. "What are you doing here, Rick? Cam's not here."

Rick's grin was predatory. "Oh, I know. He's in a meeting with Mr. Smith." He took another step toward Sophia and she backed up again, but realized she was getting close to the bed—absolutely the last place she wanted to be near with Rick in the room—so she turned and strode over to the tray with the food.

"Yeah, that's right, he's with Mr. Smith. But he'll be back in just a minute." Sophia prayed the words sounded more confident than she felt. She picked up a grape and popped it in her mouth in what she hoped was complete nonchalance.

Rick smirked. "I don't think so. Mr. Smith had some pretty important stuff to talk to him about."

"Oh, yeah? Like what?" Another grape. Anything that kept Rick on the other side of the room talking.

The gleam that entered Rick's eyes told Sophia she had asked exactly what he wanted her to ask. "This and that. But mostly about you."

Sophia tried not to react.

"What about me?"

"Evidently you haven't been telling the truth about everything, have you?" Rick made a tsking sound. "Mr. Smith has some FBI agent guy who *really* knows about that Ghost software thing and he basically called you a liar." Rick glowed with glee.

Sophia felt paralyzed with indecision. Did Cameron know what was going on? Had Smith already done something to Cameron? Sophia thought about what had happened to Cameron's partner—Smith had had him assassinated. She couldn't bear to think of anything like that happening to Cam so she pushed the thought aside.

Should she run? Try to find Cameron? Rick was

strutting closer, that perverse smirk still blanketing his face. Sophia knew one thing: staying in this room with Rick was not a good idea.

"Whatever. This is just a misunderstanding. I'll just go set Mr. Smith straight right now." She headed toward the door, until Rick stepped right in front of her.

"Oh, don't worry, Mr. Smith sent me in here to get you. Looks like you need to be questioned with force and he knows I'm the best man for that job." Rick chuckled darkly, cracking his knuckles. Sophia felt bile pooling in her stomach. "But I thought you and I could have a few minutes in here first. So I could get a taste of what you were teasing me with last night."

Sophia darted to the side to run around Rick but he was too fast. He grabbed her by both arms and threw her toward the bed. Sophia let out a loud moan at the pain in her injured arm, and spun for the door again. But Rick was ready for her.

"Oh, no, you don't." He grabbed her from behind, wrapping both arms around her. His breath was sour at her cheek. Sophia tried to get away but couldn't and knew that Cameron was too far away in Smith's office to hear her scream. Screaming would only bring more of Smith's men in here. "C'mon," Rick said softly. "I'm not asking for anything you haven't already given Cam. What's the big deal?"

"Let. Me. Go." Sophia held herself absolutely still, since the only other option was wiggling all over Rick. "Why would I do anything with you when you basically just told me you were going to torture me for Smith a few seconds ago?"

Rick's grip loosened just a little. Maybe he never

considered the fact that him informing her of upcoming torture wouldn't make her want to jump into bed with him. Sophia shuddered. As if she would jump into bed with him for any reason.

"Maybe we can work out some sort of a trade-off," Sophia whispered, turning. "I give you what you want now and you see what you can do to take it easy on me a little later."

Rick considered that then nodded enthusiastically. "Um, yeah, that sounds good." The lie was plain to see in his eyes and Sophia barely refrained from rolling hers.

"Great. We've got a deal." Sophia forced herself to slide her hands up his arms, as if to embrace him. Rick's foul breath hitting her full in the face was almost more than she could stand. Rick slid closer to kiss her, and although she knew she should let it go further than this without running, Sophia could not force herself to kiss him. She took a slight step back and brought her knee up as hard as she could into Rick's groin.

Rick cried out and dropped to his knees, releasing Sophia. She ran toward the door, cursing as the lock slowed her down. Her fingers felt useless as she tried to get the lock to release. It finally did and Sophia frantically pulled the door open, only to have it slam back shut. She turned to find Rick's hulking form looming over her.

"You're going to regret that," he sneered.

Sophia tried to run, but couldn't get around him. His backhand came without warning and the blow threw Sophia to the ground. From the throbbing in her face,

Sophia knew she had to get help. Anybody—no matter who a scream brought in. Rick was going to kill her.

She opened her mouth to scream, but Rick moved quicker than she thought him capable. He was on her in a moment with his meaty hand covering her mouth. "Shut up," he growled.

Sophia immediately panicked. The need for air, to get the hand off her face so she could breathe, consumed her. She clawed at his hand, his face, anything she could reach. Vaguely she heard vile curses emanating from Rick, but paid no attention. Her only thought was for air.

Rick's full weight was on her body now, making everything worse. She bucked and twisted sharply, causing Rick's hand to slip off her face for a moment. Sophia screamed as loudly as she could.

"Cam!" The yell reverberated through the room, but she wasn't sure how much farther into the house the sound went.

It was only a moment before Rick hit her again. The whole world seemed to spin as Sophia fought to hold on to consciousness. Rick wrapped one hand around her throat. "You will shut up or I'll kill you right now." He squeezed to prove his point and Sophia felt everything begin to dim.

Sophia didn't know how to fight someone this much bigger and stronger than she. She clutched at his hand on her throat, but it didn't seem to affect anything. She just tried to drag air into her lungs past the hand intent on keeping that from happening. It seemed to be a losing battle.

And then out of nowhere Rick's body flew off her. Sophia sucked in gulps of precious air, scampering as far away as possible. Her vision cleared and she realized it was Cameron who had tackled Rick and gotten him off her, and was now in the midst of pummeling the other man. Rick had both height and weight on Cam, but Cam had caught him by surprise. And he obviously wasn't interested in showing Rick much mercy.

A sickening crunch brought a howl from Rick before he fell back onto the floor, completely unconscious. Cameron immediately stopped hitting him. He looked over at Sophia. "Are you okay?"

Sophia nodded, still trying to breathe as deeply as possible. Cameron rushed to her side, wincing and gently touching the bruise she was sure was forming on her cheek from where Rick had hit her. "I'm okay. Just… panicked. No permanent damage done."

Cameron reached over and kissed her on her forehead. "Good, because we have to leave. *Right now,*" he told her as he helped her up.

"Smith knows about me." She pointed at Rick's unconscious form. "Rick took great delight in letting me know Smith wanted me brought in to be tortured."

Cameron went over to a large dresser that sat against one wall. "Are you okay enough to help me move this?"

Sophia grabbed the other end of the dresser. "Sure, I think. Why?"

She understood a few moments later when they slid the chest directly in front of the door. Getting in that way would be difficult for anybody.

"I've got Ghost Shell. We've got to get the hell out of here."

"How did you get it?"

"I locked Smith and his little FBI friend in his own

panic room. But that's not going to hold him for long." Cameron rushed over and grabbed a jacket out of his bag as well as the Omega Sector gadget thing he'd used earlier. He tossed a sweatshirt to Sophia. "Here, you'll need this. Sorry I don't have anything else. I'm not sure how long we'll be outside."

"Can't you just contact Omega and have them pick us up?"

"No. We have to go on our own." He headed over to the sliding glass door that led to the small deck.

"Isn't Omega our quickest route out of here?" Sophia followed him to the door.

"Normally, yes. But Fred McNeil—the FBI agent Smith has on payroll—knew way too much. Made me think we might have a mole inside Omega, too." He turned and looked at Sophia, trailing a finger gently down her cheek. "I can't be sure either way right now. But I won't take a chance with your life."

"So how are we getting out of here?"

Cameron slid the door open and stepped out onto the deck. The brisk fall air was instantly chilling. "We're going to get as far as we can on foot. I'm going to have someone I trust meet us."

"Can't we steal a car here or something?"

Cameron shook his head. "No. I'm sure Smith would be able to track them with GPS. Almost all newer vehicles can be tracked. Plus, it would take way too long to drive out of here. Air is our best option."

Sophia grimaced. "Okay, on foot to the airfield it is, then."

Sophia followed Cameron outside. She was glad the clothes Smith had sent for her this morning had been casual: jeans, a sweater and lace-up flat boots. She imagined if Smith had known she'd be running from him he would've provided her a skirt and heels. Cameron climbed over the deck railing and jumped the few feet down to the ground, then helped as Sophia did the same. He took her hand and led her around the back of the house carefully.

Sophia could hear some sort of commotion at the front of the house. They didn't stop to see what it was. Cameron just took advantage of it and they ran deeper into the woods. Sophia knew it wouldn't be long until Smith's henchmen would be after them. She held on to Cameron's hand and ran as fast as she could.

Chapter Fifteen

Running as fast as they could while not leaving a trail any six-year-old could follow was a delicate balance. They needed to put as much distance as possible between them and the house. Cameron knew by now Smith and McNeil would've gotten out of the panic room and would have every available person looking for them.

The terrain was all downhill—it was difficult to run and hard on the body. Cameron caught Sophia as she tripped over an exposed tree root.

"Sorry," she said through breaths, gulping air.

"You okay? Let's take a rest."

Sophia shook her head. "No. I know we need to keep going. I'll be all right." But her pale features and clammy hands argued differently.

But she was right, they did need to keep going. These early hours were the most important if they were possibly going to have a chance to escape. Cameron gave Sophia a brief nod, but slowed down a bit. He kept hold of her hand as they continued to work their way downhill. It was unbelievable how tough Sophia had been the past couple of hours. Cameron knew trained agents who couldn't keep plowing on the way she had. She had every right to complain or ask for him to at least slow down, but she hadn't.

It was impressive. Hell, everything about Sophia was impressive. When this was over, when Sophia was safe, Cameron planned to rectify the mistakes he'd made five years ago. He'd walked away from her once, but he wouldn't make that error again.

But first he had to get her to safety. Her breathing became more ragged so Cameron slowed down. They'd been running for well over an hour. He glanced at the sky overhead—it was starting to look ugly. It wouldn't be long before a storm hit. That was both good and bad. Good because it would make it harder for DS-13 to find them. Bad because the temperature was already pretty brisk. Being soaking wet was definitely not going to be comfortable.

"Where are we trying to go?" Sophia asked now that they weren't running at breakneck speed.

"Back down to the runway where we landed."

"Do we have a plane? Did you change your mind about contacting Omega?"

Cameron was torn. "Honestly, I don't know what to do about Omega. There may be a mole, but if there is one, I have no idea who it is."

"So how are we going to get out of here?"

"I'm going to get a message to one of my brothers. He used to be part of Omega, but got out a couple of years ago. He has his own small airplane. Runs a charter business."

"Okay." Sophia sounded relieved. Cameron didn't blame her. Knowing there was an actual plan made the running a little easier, but not much. Cameron looked up at the sky again. Definitely looked worse than it had just a few minutes ago.

"Ready to pick up the speed a little more? We need to get as far as we can before this storm hits."

Sophia just nodded. Cameron took her hand again and began adding speed to their downhill scamper. They ran silently, talking definitely not a possibility when expending this much effort. Cameron was winded himself, so he couldn't imagine how Sophia was feeling. She never complained, but he could hear her breathing become more and more labored.

The rain came at first in a gentle sprinkle and was almost welcome for its cooling effect at the pace they were keeping. But then the skies opened and it really began pouring. They tried to continue but after falling twice, Cameron knew they had to stop. When he looked closer at Sophia he realized they should've stopped much sooner. There was absolutely no color in her face and she was swaying dizzily on her feet.

"Sophia?" Her eyes looked at him without really focusing. "Soph! Are you okay?"

She nodded but obviously wasn't really hearing anything he was saying. Cameron took a step closer to her. "Soph? Hey, can you hear me?" He said it loud enough to be heard through the pouring rain. Sophia just looked at him blankly.

Cameron put his hands on both her cheeks and was shocked at the heat radiating off her. This was definitely more than just the exertion from running. Sophia had a fever—a high one. Cameron wiped her hair from her forehead, where it was dripping water into her eyes.

"It's okay, baby, you don't have to run anymore. Let's find a place where we can have some shelter." Cameron gently led Sophia over to a nearby tree that had fallen. The huge root that had come out of the forest floor provided a slight overhang. It wasn't much, but it would keep Sophia a little bit drier as Cameron looked for something better.

He bundled her as far back into the tree root as he could and knelt down beside her. "Sophia…" Cam spoke slowly, deliberately. "I'm going to find us some better shelter. I'll be right back. I don't want you to move from here. Okay?"

Sophia seemed to understand. She nodded weakly. "Okay."

Cameron didn't waste any time. Getting Sophia somewhere warm and dry, and figuring out what the heck was wrong with her, was the most important thing. It wasn't long before he found what he needed: a small cave. It wasn't big, barely room for two people to sit up in it, but it was dry. Cameron checked it for animals and critters, delighted when he found only a couple of squirrels, which he quickly chased out.

Sophia was exactly where he had left her, propped against the large root. It didn't look as if she had moved at all from the moment he'd left. As a matter of fact, with her eyes closed, lying so still she almost looked…

Cameron rushed over and knelt beside her. "Soph? Honey, are you okay?" When her eyes didn't open immediately he felt for her pulse at her throat. It was there. Although finding her pulse flooded him with relief, its rapid fluttering concerned him. This was more than just exhaustion from running down the mountain.

Cameron pulled her arm around his shoulders and slipped his arm around her waist. He stood, bringing her weight with him. Sophia didn't wake up but a low moan escaped her lips. Cameron cursed under his breath when he realized he had grabbed her injured arm. Jostling her as little as possible, he brought her slight weight up into his arms and carried her to the cave. Feeling the heat radiating from her—she definitely had a fever if he could feel it through her layers of clothing—Cameron moved as fast as he could without putting either of them in danger of falling. The rain continued to blanket them in its cold misery.

Sophia's eyes opened just a bit as he laid her as gently as he could into the small cave opening. "I don't think I can run anymore," she said, her voice barely louder than a whisper.

Cameron brushed her hair back from her face. "You don't have to run anymore, sweetheart. You have a fever, probably from that cut on your shoulder getting infected. We're just going to rest here for a while."

Sophia struggled to sit up. "I'm sorry I'm slowing you down. I just don't feel very good."

Cameron stopped her minimal progress and helped her lay back down, even though rain was still pouring down on him. "Don't try to sit up. I'm going to crawl in behind you and scoot us both back."

Sophia didn't answer and Cameron wondered if she had passed out again. He tossed his small backpack over to the side of the cave, mindful of the Ghost Shell hard drive in the bag. Then he crawled inside, joining Sophia but careful not to jostle her in any way that might cause her pain. The cave was not very large. It was difficult for Cameron to fit himself into the dark area—he couldn't even sit up to his full height. But at least it was dry.

He eased himself behind her then pulled her backward as gently as he could so her back could rest against his chest. She didn't say anything or make any sounds, just slumped hard against him and continued shivering. Cameron caught her forehead with his hand and laid it back so it rested against his shoulder. He felt the heat radiating from where he touched her, although the rest of her body was racked with chills. He tucked his legs more securely around the outside of hers in an effort to share more of their body heat.

Cameron had some ibuprofen in his backpack. He would allow Sophia, and himself, a chance to rest for a little while, then would give her some. It wouldn't fight the infection, but it would lower her fever for a little while. But he didn't have many of the painkillers, so getting some antibiotics into her system as soon as possible was critical.

Holding Sophia snugly against his chest with one arm, Cameron reached over to his backpack with the other. The Ghost Shell hard drive was still safe inside, and he reached for the Omega communication system. Cameron still wasn't sure who he could trust inside Omega, so instead he made a call to his oldest brother, Dylan. He knew Dylan would be loath to get involved with Omega Sector—or any government undercover work whatsoever—after what had happened to him, but his brother would do it anyway if Cameron asked. And Cameron was definitely asking. The fact that Dylan had his own Cessna airplane at his disposal was a huge plus because no cars were getting up this mountain anytime soon.

Cameron's plan was to get Sophia out with Dylan and back to safety. Cameron wouldn't go with them. Instead he would meet the Omega extraction team at dark and go back to headquarters with Ghost Shell. If there was some sort of mole inside Omega, Cameron wasn't taking a chance with Sophia's life. He knew Dylan, or any of his three siblings, could be trusted. That was as far as Cameron was willing to go when it came to Sophia's safety—only the people he absolutely trusted without a doubt.

Cameron punched his security code into the communication unit. It was so much more than a phone, but in this case Cameron was using it for the simplest of calls. He pushed the digits to call his brother Dylan. He picked up after just two rings.

"Branson."

"Dylan, it's Cameron."

"Cam? Hey, little brother. Haven't heard from you in a while."

"I've been working. You know, the usual."

Dylan did know. He had enough background with Omega Sector that Cameron didn't need to explain further. "Are you done with that…project you were working on?" his brother asked.

"No, Dyl, I'm not. As a matter of fact the project became a great deal more complicated over the last few days. I need your help."

"What's going on, Cam?" Cameron could tell he now had Dylan's full attention.

"I came across some information today that suggests

that someone within my company might also be...working for a competitor. Problem is, I'm not sure who that person in my company might be or if it is anyone at all."

Dylan paused for a moment and Cameron could tell he was processing what Cam was trying to tell him. "And you're worried for your safety?"

"No," Cameron told Dylan softly, looking at the small woman lying in his arms. "I can handle myself. But someone else has gotten involved and I don't want her to have anything to do with anybody in my company if there's a problem."

"Roger that. What do you need?"

That's what Cameron loved about his family. They had each other's backs, without needing a bunch of details. That didn't mean they wouldn't needle the details out of Cameron later—him asking Dylan to fly out a lady friend was something he was going to get ragged about pretty hard—but right now all Dylan wanted to know was how he could help.

"I'm about to send you some coordinates. It's a small unlit airstrip in northern Virginia. It's smack in the middle of the mountains. You won't believe it's there until you're right on it. I need you to take my friend back to DC and stay with her. That's it."

"Where will you be going? You staying there?"

"No. I'm heading to DC also, but I'll be getting a ride with my company. It's already planned."

"All right. What time?"

"Dusk." Cameron knew Dylan landing his airplane at the unlit airstrip after dark in terrible weather was risky. They'd be cutting it close, but this would be their best chance. "I'll be looking for you around eighteen hundred. And if mountains and oncoming darkness aren't enough of a challenge for you, the weather here is absolute crap. Pouring buckets. Hopefully it will clear out."

"Sounds like a party. Can't wait."

"Dylan, I need you to get some antibiotics. She's got an infected cut and is running a fever. I don't want her to have to go straight to the hospital when a round of antibiotics will do. She's been through a lot."

Dylan didn't ask where he was supposed to get antibiotics without a prescription. But Cameron knew his brother would have them when he arrived. "Anything else?"

"No. And, Dylan, thanks."

"You owe me one for this, bro." Dylan chuckled. "But what's new?"

They disconnected and Cameron sent the coordinates to Dylan.

Sophia was still asleep lying against him, but moaned softly and was obviously uncomfortable. Cameron decided to give her the ibuprofen to help get her fever down, then maybe she could rest a little easier. He got the small tube out of his bag—it wasn't much but hopefully would help her feel more comfortable until Dylan got there with the antibiotics. He grabbed a water bottle, too.

"Here, sweetheart," Cameron whispered as he put the pills up against Sophia's lips. "Take these. They'll help make you feel better."

"Cam?" Sophia obviously was groggy. "What's going on?"

"This is aspirin, baby. It will help your fever go down and make you feel better."

"Okay." She opened her mouth for first the pills then the water. "Sleepy," she murmured, then almost immediately slumped back against him again. Cameron took a sip of the water himself then recapped the bottle and returned it to his backpack. He zipped it up so it would be ready to go if they had to leave in a hurry.

"That's fine, go back to sleep." Cameron couldn't blame Sophia for wanting sleep. God knew the past few days hadn't held much sleep for her—for both good reasons and bad. A few hours of rest would probably do him some good, too. Cameron felt his eyes grow heavy as he snuggled Sophia more firmly in his arms.

Chapter Sixteen

Cameron awoke suddenly. He held himself perfectly still. Something had definitely disturbed his subconscious. Had Smith's men found them? He reached over and grasped the SIG he had left lying on top of the backpack.

After a few moments he realized it wasn't a noise outside that had woken him, it was Sophia's labored breathing.

"Soph, are you awake?" He felt her forehead with his hand. She seemed much cooler than she had before they had fallen asleep, her fever much lower. But there was something definitely wrong.

"Yes," she said curtly. Cameron could feel tension bowing her body.

"What's wrong? Is it your arm? Are you sick?"

"I… I…" She couldn't seem to get the words out.

"Is it pain?" Cameron wished he had something stronger to give her. He tried to get her to look at him, but she seemed focused on the entrance to the cave, staring at it intently. "Did you hear something? See one of Smith's men?"

Sophia shook her head, but tension fairly radiated

from her. She was clutching at his hands and arms, which were wrapped around her, her breath sawing in and out of her chest, the sound loud in the cave, even with the rain. "What is it, Soph? Tell me, please." Cameron didn't know what to do to help her if he couldn't figure out the problem.

"I can't breathe." She finally got the sentence out.

Cameron cursed under his breath. He had completely forgotten about Sophia's claustrophobia. Evidently she had been too sick to notice the small confines of the cave when he'd pulled them in a few hours ago, but now that she was feeling better…

Cameron immediately released her, unwrapping his arms from around her body so she could move if she needed to. She slid away from him, her eyes still focused on the small entrance to the cave.

"Soph, it's okay. C'mon, let's go back outside." There was no point in making her suffer in here even if it was still raining out there.

Sophia nodded tersely and started scooting toward the entrance. Cameron went with her in case she needed any help. They were almost to the small entrance when Cameron heard it. Some of Smith's men talking. Right outside of where he and Sophia were hidden.

If she went out now, it would mean death for both of them.

Cameron knew not to grab Sophia, but he doubted she heard the men talking over her own labored breathing. He scampered around so he was in front of Sophia and they were face-to-face. She immediately began to go around him so she could get to the entrance he blocked.

"Sophia, look at me, sweetheart." She glanced at him for just a second before her eyes darted back to the entrance. Cameron reached out and as gently as he could, careful not to restrain her in any way, put his hands on both her cheeks. "Sophia, Smith's men are right outside. If you go out there now, they're going to kill both of us."

Cameron watched, heartbroken, as Sophia's eyes darted back and forth frantically between him and the cave entrance. But at least she stopped moving toward it.

"That's right, sweetie," Cameron murmured. "Just look at me. Watch me breathing. There's plenty of air in here. Plenty. Can you feel the breeze?"

Sophia nodded hesitantly. Cameron stayed right in front of her, his face only inches from hers. "Breathe with me. In through your nose, out through your mouth."

For long minutes they stayed frozen right there doing just that. Cameron could hear Smith's men still nearby, and kept his SIG ready in his hand in case he needed it. Why were the men concentrating so hard on this area? Why hadn't they moved on? If Cameron hadn't taken the time to camouflage the entrance to the cave, the men probably would've found them already.

But at least Sophia didn't seem about to rush out there and announce their presence any longer.

"I think I'm okay," she whispered.

"You're doing great. You're amazing. Courageous." Cameron trailed his finger down Sophia's cheek.

"Yeah. It's amazing that a grown woman gets freaked out in a place that obviously has plenty of oxygen and almost gets us both killed. So courageous." She turned away, disgusted with herself.

"Hey," he said, grabbing her before she could get far. "Courage isn't about not having fears. It's about how you handle the ones you do have. You were panicked, but you got yourself under control."

Sophia shook her head and refused to look at him. "No, you don't get it. It's taking everything I've got right now not to burst through that entrance. I'm still not sure I'm going to be able to keep myself from doing it."

"Soph, look at me." He didn't think she was going to, but she finally did. "Even if you handle it one second at a time, you're still handling it. That's all anybody can ask."

Cameron could tell she still wasn't convinced. He cupped her cheeks with his hands again. "I don't care if you can see it or not. You're still amazing." He brought his lips down to hers.

Cameron worried for just a moment that kissing her wasn't a good idea—what if this just compounded her claustrophobia? But the way she kissed him back eliminated those fears quickly.

When they broke apart Sophia's features were a little less pinched. She still constantly glanced over at the entrance, but didn't seem quite so much as if she was going to bolt for it at any moment.

"I wasn't always claustrophobic, you know," Sophia whispered. "Just since the car accident."

"What accident? Did someone hit you? Was it bad?"

Her eyes darted to him briefly. "Yeah, it was pretty bad." Cameron could see tension heightening in her again. He was about to change the subject when she spoke again. "But no, nobody hit me. I was driving alone—too fast—and I was upset. It was raining and I took a curve too hard and went over an embankment."

That was much worse than Cameron had thought. "That sounds pretty awful. How badly were you hurt?"

Sophia didn't say anything for a while then started wiggling around. Cameron realized she was trying to take off her sweatshirt, although he had no idea why. He helped her slip it off. "Thanks," she told him. "Being cold actually helps me to feel like there's more air. Totally a mental thing, but…" She shrugged. "As for injuries…broke my femur, a couple of ribs, pretty heavy concussion."

Cameron's breath whistled out through his teeth. He'd had no idea. They sat in silence for a few moments before she continued. "When my car went over the embankment it rolled over multiple times." Sophia swallowed hard. "It finally stopped when it hit a tree. It completely crushed in the passenger side of the front seat, and I was trapped. Fortunately, another car saw me go over and called 911, but it took them a while to get the emergency vehicles there. I was hard to get to."

Cameron could see Sophia doing a breathing exercise as she told her story—in through her nose, out through her mouth. "I was trapped there about two hours—although believe me when I say it felt much longer. The car had crushed around me, and I was pretty sure I was going to die. I kept hyperventilating and passed out a couple times, which was a blessing, until I woke back up to that enclosed space."

Cameron understood now why she had panicked waking up in the cave—too much like waking up in that car. "I'm so sorry, Soph." He'd come so close to losing her. Cameron had to touch her; he couldn't help himself. He put his arm around and scooted as close to her as possible, relieved when she didn't move away. He put his face against her neck and breathed in her scent.

He'd almost lost her, and he'd never even known.

Sophia leaned in closer to him. "Physical injuries were pretty bad—I was in the hospital for about a week. It was a long recovery, lots of PT. But I found the mental issues, this overwhelming claustrophobia, to be ongoing. I've been seeing a therapist once a week for almost five years. You'd think I'd have made more progress, right?" Sophia smiled ruefully.

Cameron felt as if he had been punched in the gut. She'd been seeing a therapist for *five years*? He thought the accident had happened recently. If she had been in therapy for five years then…

"Soph, when did the accident happen?"

Cameron could feel Sophia's attempt to huddle into herself. Silence, except for the rain and an occasional sound from one of Smith's men, surrounded them. Cameron thought maybe she wasn't going to answer—which was an answer in and of itself.

"The day after you left," she finally whispered.

Cameron struggled to keep himself under control. He wanted to punch the nearest wall or howl in some primitive rage. It wasn't hard to put two and two together. Sophia had been upset because he had left and then she had been in a life-threatening accident. Cameron moved away from Sophia, trying to process it all and his obvious blame in it. Cameron couldn't seem to figure out how to form words. What could he say anyway?

"Soph, I'm so sorry. How can you not hate me?"

Sophia reached over and grabbed his hand. "It wasn't your fault, Cam. Just a really poor set of circumstances—bad weather, bad emotional state, bad road to be driving on. Bad luck all the way around."

Cameron shook his head. Maybe Sophia had come to that point, but he couldn't—not yet anyway. He thought of after the accident; Sophia had no family, no one to help take care of her. And he hadn't been around, had actually made sure he was completely unreachable, when she needed him most. Had she tried to contact him? Even if she had wanted to, he had left her no information whatsoever.

"Soph, I'm so sorry," he repeated. Although how could words ever make up for what had happened? He couldn't believe Sophia was willing to even sit here holding his hand. Willing to be with him in any shape or fashion after what had happened.

Sophia turned more fully toward him. Cameron found he couldn't quite meet her eyes. "Cameron Branson, look at me," she told him and he did, reluctantly. There was no trace of claustrophobic panic in her features now. Just gritty determination. "What happened, happened. The accident was not your fault."

"But—" Cameron began. Sophia put her hand over his mouth.

"No 'buts,'" she said, and, miracle of all miracles, actually smiled. "I'll admit, I was mad for a while—at you, at circumstances, at life in general. But I became stronger because of it all." She gestured around the cave. "And yeah, I still struggle with claustrophobia, probably always will. But I'm learning how to work through each situation one at a time. It's like someone once told me,

'Courage isn't about not having fears. It's about how you handle the ones you do have.'"

Even with Sophia parroting his words back to him, Cameron was going to need more time to process all this. And they were definitely going to need to talk about it more. Sophia had had five years to come to peace with it, but it was a new and gut-wrenching blow to Cameron. But one thing was becoming more and more clear to him: when this op was complete, things were definitely not going to be over between he and Sophia. He wasn't sure he was ever going to have the strength to walk away from her again.

He just prayed, after everything that had happened, he could talk her into allowing him into her life permanently. Because he didn't think he could live without her.

He looked at Sophia more closely. Her face had lost the tension. Her breaths were slow and easy. "You seem to be doing okay right now."

"It's like my therapist says—sometimes it's just about refocusing. In the middle of a panic attack that can be difficult to do." She shrugged and smiled. "But I'm learning."

Cameron couldn't help it. He reached over and kissed her again. He didn't care about Smith's men outside or the rain or their dire situation. He just had to have Sophia in his arms right damn now. When they broke apart they were both breathing hard.

"Now, that's what I call refocusing." Her eyes all but sparkled. "I'll have to remember this next time I'm having issues."

Cameron pulled Sophia closer to him, loving the way

she snuggled into his side. Her breathing was calm and even now. They both watched the entrance of the cave, but not with any panic.

Every once in a while they could hear one of Smith's men talking. Cameron grimaced. They were still around here. Why? Passing through in an effort to search for them—sure. But they seemed to be spending more time here than would be expected. And yet they couldn't actually seem to find him and Sophia.

"Why are they still here?" Sophia evidently had the same thoughts as Cameron.

"I don't know. Maybe we left more of a trail than I thought." Cameron shrugged, trying to figure it out. "I covered the entrance pretty well, so unless they get right up to the overhang, they won't see it. I hope." He made sure his SIG was right beside him. It wouldn't do them a whole lot of good, especially if they weren't trying to take him and Sophia in alive, but it was better than nothing.

"Maybe they'll start looking for us somewhere else soon."

Cameron nodded. "I hope so. Getting to the landing strip in this weather will be hard enough without having Smith's men standing right on top of us."

"How long before we need to leave?"

"Pretty soon. It's going to take us at least another couple of hours to get to the landing strip. My brother Dylan is coming with his plane to get you. I talked to him while you were asleep."

"Where is he taking us?"

"He's going to take you back to DC. But I'm not

going with you. I have to get Ghost Shell to Omega Sector HQ."

"Oh." Sophia's voice was small. "I guess that will be it, then."

"You mean for us?"

Cameron could barely make out Sophia's slight nod in the dimness of the cave. But he could definitely feel her easing away from him. He reached his arm around her and snatched her back to his side.

"As soon as I get Ghost Shell settled and am debriefed you can expect me to show up at your doorstep. Don't doubt that."

There was silence for long moments. "I want that, too, Cam, so much." A huge *but* hung in the air between them. Sophia definitely had more to say and Cameron was pretty sure he didn't want to hear it. Finally it came. "But I'm not sure our worlds blend. I'm not sure that we're right for each other."

Cameron had been right. He definitely didn't want to hear this. Panic began to bubble up within him. "Soph…" He turned to her so he could look her in the eyes. "I know I hurt you before. I left and then the accident… I can never make up for not being there for you."

"But that's not really it, Cam." Sophia made eye contact, then looked away. "I don't expect you to make up for the past. The accident wasn't your fault and even leaving wasn't something you did to deliberately hurt me. The past is done, and we both have to move on. I'm talking about *now*."

"Sophia…"

"Your world is dark," she continued without letting him speak. "Your life—what you've chosen to do as an undercover agent—is so important and admirable. But it scares me, Cam." She gestured around the cave. "All of this scares the hell out of me. The girlfriend of an undercover agent needs to be braver than me, more capable than me."

There were so many things Cameron wanted to say in response to that, he hardly knew where to begin. He barely refrained from rolling his eyes. "Are you kidding me? Sophia, you have been thrown into a situation here that is impossible. And without any training you've stepped up and done as well or better than many agents I've known."

He grasped her chin to force her to look at him. "So I don't want to hear you talking any more junk like that. There is not one instance in this entire situation that I've regretted your actions. Except for maybe when you came back for me that first night. That was stupid. But so, so brave." He punctuated the sentence with light kisses on her lips. "And besides, I'm not asking you to become my undercover partner. I just want to be with you."

Sophia gave him the sweetest, softest smile. Cameron could feel his heart squeezing in his chest. *That* smile. That was the one he wanted to wake up to every day for the rest of his life.

His own thought startled him. But then he realized the thought was exactly right: he didn't want to spend another day without Sophia.

"What?" she asked. "Did you hear something? You got a panicked look for a second."

Cameron smiled and kissed Sophia again. "Nope, no panic. Just reality shifting to the way it should be."

"I don't understand." Confusion was clear in Sophia's green eyes as she gazed up at him.

"I know." He smiled. "Just don't kick me out when I show up on your doorstep in a couple of days, okay?"

"Deal." Sophia sighed and snuggled in toward him a bit. "Can we rest for a little longer? I'm still pretty tired for some reason."

"For some reason?" Cameron reached over and smoothed a lock of hair on her forehead. "Your body has been battling through life-or-death situations for the past three days. You've hardly had any rest." He grinned down at her. "Part of that is my fault, I'll admit. Plus you have some sort of infection. How are you feeling?"

"Better. Much better than when we were running."

"Yeah, you were running a fever. The ibuprofen brought it down." Cameron got the remaining pills out of the bag. "Here, take these. We're going to have to head out in just a little bit, in order to meet my brother on time."

"Okay. My arm is pretty stiff. I don't think I'm going to be able to run very fast."

Stiffness wasn't good; it meant the infection was more pronounced than Cameron had thought. "It's okay. We'll make it. Dylan is bringing a dose of antibiotics so we can get that into you as soon as you're on the plane."

"I wish you were coming with us."

"Me, too. But it's better this way."

Cameron prayed he was telling the truth.

Chapter Seventeen

Everything in Sophia's body hurt, but her heart felt light. They were about to make it out of this nightmare. She wasn't in Smith's clutches anymore. She didn't have to make up lies and pray they were the right ones and wouldn't cost her and Cameron their lives. And, come tomorrow, she wouldn't have to wear the clothes that creep picked out for her. For some reason that weirded her out most of all and she wanted out of these clothes Smith had chosen for her as soon as possible.

And speaking of being out of her clothes… Cameron. Sophia felt a little like a giggly schoolgirl. *Cameron Branson* wanted to go steady with her. He was so dreamy. A little chuckle slid out from where she was perched against Cam, trying to rest.

"What?" he asked. She heard the amusement in his voice.

"Nothing." There was no way in hell she was telling him her thoughts.

Sophia had never been able to forget Cameron. She didn't dwell on the past, but he had never been far from her thoughts. She had always imagined they would meet again, but definitely not under these conditions. This entire situation was surreal.

But Cameron wanted them to spend time together when everything wasn't crazy. Sophia thought back to all those talks they'd had together at the diner before he had joined Omega Sector. Those times together hadn't been sexual—although there had certainly been a sexual undercurrent—but they had been special. Important. She looked forward to having times like that again.

And knowing Cameron wanted them also made it all even more special.

Sophia could've gladly stayed in the cave all day under different circumstances, listening to the rain, snuggling up against Cameron. Her therapist had definitely been right about the refocusing exercises because nothing about the enclosed nature of the cave was bothering her now.

It seemed like just a moment later when Cameron nudged her. "Are you ready to go?"

Sophia nodded and began to put the sweatshirt back on. It was still wet and not very comfortable, but at least it would provide a layer of protection against the rain. "Yep. Are they still out there?"

"I haven't heard anything for a while, but that doesn't necessarily mean they're gone. We're going to have to be as quiet as possible."

They made their way to the edge of the overhang. Cameron gently moved the branches he had used to camouflage the entrance. Motioning her to stay where she was, he headed out of the cave, gun in hand.

Sophia waited, mentally preparing herself to run if needed. Cameron came back a few minutes later.

"I didn't see them. Hopefully they're gone. But try to stay right behind me and be as quiet as possible just in case."

Sophia nodded and made her way out of the cave. The rain still came down in a steady drizzle. She followed along behind Cameron as silently as she was able, but every step they made seemed terribly loud to her.

"We've got about four miles to go and just a little over an hour's time to get there," Cameron told her a few minutes later. "We'll need to pick up the pace. If those guys are anywhere around the airstrip when my brother is landing, he'll be a sitting duck."

"Is Omega Sector coming to the airstrip, also?"

"No, they'll get me out via helicopter. There's a number of places they can do that. I'll establish a place with them soon."

They began a light jog, much less quickly than their run earlier, but it didn't take long for every step to cause a jarring pain in Sophia's arm. And the rain didn't help; it just made her totally miserable. She grimaced but didn't say anything to Cameron. What could he do? She'd have to gut it out until she got on the plane. She could do that.

Thirty minutes later keeping that promise to herself was becoming more difficult, but still she tried. She was relieved when he called for them to slow back down to a walk.

"Hey, you okay?" Concern was written all over Cameron's face. He walked over to her and rubbed his hands gently up and down her arms. Sophia leaned forward until the top of her head rested against his chest. She just needed a break. Just a couple of minutes.

"I'm okay. It's just..." Sophia trailed off. She didn't have to say it.

"I know, sweetheart. You're doing great." Sophia all but snorted from against his chest. "Seriously. It's less than two miles. Let's keep going at a walk."

Walking she could do. More than that? She just didn't know.

"Okay."

Cameron slid Sophia's hand through the crook of his elbow and they began again. He kept his other hand around hers. She must really look like hell if he was keeping this close to her. It definitely wasn't the most stealthy way to travel. She knew he was afraid she would fall flat on her face again.

Sophia could admit she was afraid of the same thing.

Cameron let Sophia set the pace and she moved as quickly as she could. Every step was agony.

They both heard it at the same time. A small propeller plane. Circling not far overhead.

"That's Dylan. Damn it."

"How far are we from the landing strip?"

"Less than a mile. But if any of Smith's goons are in the area, they're going to hear him, too."

Sophia took a deep breath. "Let's move faster. I'll be okay."

Cameron reached over and kissed her hard and quickly. His hands framed her face. "You are amazing."

Sophia tried to smile, but couldn't quite succeed. "Tell me something I don't know. Now quit flirting and let's go."

Cameron took Sophia's uninjured arm and wrapped it around his shoulders. He put his other arm around her waist, anchoring her to his side. He took off at a brisk run, not nearly as fast as he could go, Sophia was sure, but fast enough to take her breath away. She focused all her energy into putting one foot in front on the other and not slowing Cameron down. She'd never forgive herself if something happened to Cameron's brother because of her.

Sophia wasn't prepared for Cameron's sudden stop a few minutes later before they even got to the landing field. She would've fallen to the ground hard if he hadn't had such a tight hold on her. He wrapped his arms around her and swung them both behind a tree and slid to the ground.

"What's happening?" Sophia asked between breaths.

"I saw one of Smith's goons." He shook his head with a grimace and Sophia knew something beyond just seeing one of the men was troubling him.

"What? Is he blocking our path?"

"No. That's just it. He's heading back toward *us*, not the airfield."

"That's bad."

"Yeah, it's bad. Plus, it doesn't make any sense. If he's that close, he should've heard Dylan's plane, too. I have no idea why he isn't trying to intercept Dylan."

"Maybe he has other orders or something."

"Maybe." But Cameron shook his head again.

"Can we go around him?"

"We'll have to. Stay close behind me. But we have to move fast. If the other men know Dylan is here, they'll be headed toward him."

They moved as fast as they could and were both careful to be silent. Sophia could tell when Cameron would spot the man, flinging them both to the ground or behind some sort of forest cover. With every bounce her arm throbbed.

Backing around one of the trees, Cameron cursed under his breath. "We can't catch a break. It's like he knows where we are."

"Could he be tracking us?" Sophia didn't know what sort of equipment DS-13 had, but the ability to track them seemed feasible.

"I thought of that, but if so, they should've found us at the cave. I don't know."

Cameron reached into his backpack and pulled out the communication unit thingy. He punched in digits while dragging himself and Sophia lower onto the ground.

"You landed?" he asked without greeting.

Sophia couldn't hear what was being said on the other end.

"Good. Anybody around?"

More talk from the other end.

"New plan. We've got a tail I can't shake. I'm going to get her to the end of the field and let her run to you. I'll lead whoever's attention I can get off in the other direction."

Sophia caught the word *stupid* from Cameron's brother.

"Yeah, I know. Just get her out. I'll take care of myself."

Cameron hit a button and threw the phone back into his bag. "Are you ready? We're going to make a run for it."

"Um, I was right here. Don't you mean *I'm* going

to make a run for it and you're going to get yourself killed?"

"Soph, I'll be fine."

Sophia shook her head. "Didn't I just hear your brother call this plan stupid?"

Cameron grinned and winked at her. "Actually, he was calling me stupid in general, not the plan. We've got to go, baby."

"There has to be another way." Sophia would not allow Cameron to sacrifice himself for her.

"Sophia, listen. I promise I will be fine. Once I get you on the plane, I will be a ninja—fast, silent, stealthy. They won't catch me."

Sophia knew she was slowing him down. If he had to fight or make a real run for it, he'd be much better off without having her to worry about. But she still didn't like it.

"Promise?" His face was right next to hers and she took the opportunity to kiss him briefly.

"Absolutely. Ninja pinkie-swear."

She would've chuckled if she wasn't so scared. "Okay, let's go."

He led her the rest of the way to the airfield as quickly as possible, continuing the darting between trees and zigzagging. Sophia only once caught a glimpse of the man who was following them, but he was very definitely only a couple hundred yards away.

Sophia saw the small airplane at the end of the runway. Cameron's brother had obviously tried to make the plane as inconspicuous as he could, but that was nearly impossible.

"Okay, you need to make your way down the tree

line to the end of the runway. Don't cut over to the plane until you have as much of a direct route as possible. Use the tree cover to your advantage. Do what we've been doing—darting back and forth between trees."

Sophia's head nodded like a bobblehead doll. "Okay. What will you be doing?"

"I'll make sure I have our tail's attention and head the other way."

"I still don't like this plan."

"You'll be fine."

"It's not me I'm worried about!" Sophia barely remembered to keep her voice to a whisper. "I'm the one about to get on a safe, dry plane."

"I'll be fine. Ninja, remember? I'll be catching a ride with Omega in just a few minutes and will see you in a couple of days." Something caught Cameron's attention in the distance. "But I need you to go *now.* And I need you to keep going no matter what you think you hear or see."

Now Sophia was really scared. But she had to trust that Cameron knew what he was doing. Her head nodded again, but she couldn't force any words through her clogged throat. Cameron took her gently by the shoulders and turned her around then gave her a gentle push toward the plane. Sophia began to run as fast as she could. She pushed past the agony in her arm and the weariness. She knew that the faster she made it to that plane, the sooner Cameron would start thinking about himself and get safely picked up by Omega Sector.

Sophia darted from tree to tree as Cameron had told her. She never saw anyone, but didn't let that change her plan. When she got to the point that the plane was directly perpendicular from her she dashed out of the trees. She wasn't out of the tree line for five seconds before the propellers on the plane started. But not before she heard the *pop* of gunfire. Sophia wanted to stop and look, but didn't. Had Cameron fired or had he been fired at? Sophia had no idea. She ran faster.

The door that became stairs to the plane was lowered and waiting for Sophia. By the time she got there—gasping for air—a man looking remarkably like Cameron, but a little older, was standing at the top. He helped her as she made her way up the stairs and onto the plane. Quickly, he secured the door and showed Sophia where to sit—right next to him in the cockpit—which was open to the rest of the small plane.

Immediately he eased the plane forward and they began to gain the speed needed for takeoff. Sophia scanned frantically through the windshield, looking for Cameron, but found nothing. She told herself not seeing him was a good sign—much better than seeing him lying wounded, or worse, on the ground—but it didn't ease her mind. As the plane pulled into the air, Sophia continued to look but never saw him. She told herself she should be thankful that at least the plane was away safely. Cameron had a much better chance on his own. But she couldn't quite make herself agree.

Cameron's brother took a pair of corded headphones and handed them to Sophia. She was so exhausted and in so much pain that she could barely understand his gesture for her to put them on.

"Hi. I'm Dylan, Cameron's older and much more handsome brother. So you're the gal who has stolen my little brother's heart..."

Chapter Eighteen

Cameron was willing to consider that perhaps this plan was pretty stupid after all. Or at least it seemed that way as a bullet flew past his head and into a tree just beyond him. He dived to the ground and crawled backward so he could return fire if needed.

At least Dylan had gotten Sophia away in the plane. No matter what happened now—honestly, even if he was captured or killed by Smith's men—Cameron wouldn't be sorry. Knowing Sophia was safe made all the difference. Of course he had no intention of getting captured or killed.

Ninja, baby.

He had made sure he was able to be seen as Sophia was making her way to the plane, pretty much making himself an open target as he saw her streak out of the tree line in a dead run. He was just glad Smith's henchmen had taken the bait and gone after him. Until he'd almost gotten shot in the head. Then he hadn't been so glad. As soon as he saw the plane beginning its trip down the runway, Cameron had dashed for the cover of the woods. For a minute Smith's men seemed undecided about what to do, go after Cameron or the plane—which told Cameron that Smith wanted them taken in alive. The men's indecision had given both Cameron and Sophia the chance to get away without injury.

Cameron peeked his head out from where he was taking cover behind a tree for a split second before pulling it back. Sure enough, a moment later the area around him was riddled with bullets. There were definitely two people trying to pin him down, possibly even three. He had a good idea where one of them was and crawled a few feet away to take cover behind a different tree. Then he came around from the opposite side and fired three shots. A howl of pain reassured him that he had hit his target.

One down. But he knew there were at least two more still out there.

It was time to set up the extraction with Omega. He had to get Ghost Shell far away from DS-13 hands. Cam got as low as he could and belly-crawled for hundreds of feet to put more distance between himself and the shooters after him. It felt like old army ranger times. He pulled out his sat-com device, but could not risk the noise of a voice call. An electronic message was less secure, but his only option in this case.

Cameron punched in his identification code and the code to send a message directly to his boss, Dennis Burgamy. The man was a jackass, and he and Cameron—hell, Burgamy and *any* of the Branson family—rarely got along, but he could get things done and that's what Cameron needed right now.

Situation changed. Imminent danger. Request immediate extraction.

Cameron didn't say it would only be him. He'd deal with that after he figured out if there was a mole or not. After a few moments Cameron received his reply.

Affirmative. ETA 17 minutes.

Burgamy provided a location based on the coordinates of Cameron's sat-com's GPS. Not far, but under fire it would take the entire seventeen minutes to get there.

Warning: hostiles present. May be coming in under fire.

Cameron put the sat-com back in his bag and began crawling forward. It was slow progress, but hopefully it meant he had lost his hunters. Cameron reached the small open area where the helicopter would land just moments before it did. As it lowered to the ground, Cameron could see the agents inside ready to lay down cover fire so he could get in. Cameron took off in a sprint to the helo. It left the ground just seconds after he was on board. No shots came from the woods behind him. Cameron was both relieved and confused.

Cameron sat back on the bench and put on the headset as the helicopter took off. One of the agents who had been standing guard in the doorway of the helicopter with his automatic weapon sat across from him.

"Thought there was going to be two of you."

"Change of plans," Cameron told the Omega agent. "Had to get her out another way."

The man just shrugged. "Thought you said you'd be

coming in hot, too." The man looked more upset about that than not having the second person on board.

Cameron didn't know why Smith's men hadn't fired at him. As a matter of fact, he wasn't sure they had even still been following him by the time he had made it to the opening. Cameron hadn't seen anyone since he'd wounded whoever he'd hit before sending the message.

But why would they have stopped following him? That didn't make sense. Had they stopped to help the wounded man? Maybe. Something about all of this was strange. But Cameron was out, had Ghost Shell in his possession, and although he wouldn't be able to use it with DS-13 again, his cover as Cam Cameron wasn't blown. They thought he was a thief and bastard, but definitely didn't think he was an agent. All in all, not a bad day.

DYLAN BRANSON WAS as charming as his brother Cameron, but in a quieter fashion. He had a silent confidence; definitely not chatty, but not unfriendly, either. They had been in the air for about twenty minutes when Dylan reached back to his bag and pulled out a syringe kit.

"Amoxicillin. A shot in the arm or leg," Dylan said. "Cameron said you needed it for an infected cut. And if you don't mind me saying, you look pretty bad."

Sophia felt pretty bad. The fever was definitely back. She took the syringe and injected it in herself without qualm. An injection was definitely the best way to get the antibiotics into her system quickly.

"There's some aspirin or something in my bag, too. For

your pain," Dylan told her. Sophia took three and swallowed them with a bottle of water he found in the bag.

She leaned over to the side of her seat. She was so exhausted. "I'm just going to rest my eyes for a few minutes," Sophia told Dylan. She knew it was rude, but couldn't seem to help herself.

"That's no problem at all," Dylan reassured her. "Rest is probably the best thing for you. It will take us a couple of hours to get there."

He might have said something else, too, but Sophia had no idea what. Her eyes had already drooped shut.

She woke with a start to Dylan's hand gently shaking her elbow. It took her a moment to remember where she was and who she was with, but all in all she felt much better. Or at least less as if she was about to keel over and die any moment.

"Sophia, it's Dylan." He was talking very slowly as if he was dealing with someone with an impairment, which probably wasn't far from the truth. "I've let you sleep as long as you could, but you've got to get up now."

"Are we there already?" It all came rushing back to her. "Did you hear anything from Cameron? Did he make it out?" It was pitch-dark out now. Surely Omega Sector would've already gotten Cameron out by now.

Dylan smiled. "Yes, I got a message from Omega. Cameron made it out, no problem."

Sophia sagged with relief. He had made it. She knew he had promised he would, but when she had heard that shot as she had run to the plane… Thank God Cameron was safe.

"Do you work for Omega, too?" she asked Dylan.

It was like watching a machine turn all the way off, the way Dylan's features completely closed down. "I used to. Not anymore." This topic was obviously not open for conversation.

Sophia was desperate to change the subject. "How long have I been asleep?"

Dylan chuckled and his features relaxed. "Well, the entire two-hour flight, plus landing, plus a couple hours while I did my postflight checklist, talked to a few buddies who work here and even supervised the refueling for my flight tomorrow."

She'd slept through all that? Holy cow. "Sorry." Sophia felt her cheeks burning.

"Think nothing of it. You needed the sleep. If I had any other business to do here, I'd do it. But this is a tiny county airport and there's not much happening around here after dark. And I didn't think you'd like to wake up and find yourself in some strange plane and hangar with nobody around for miles, or believe me, I would've let you sleep as long as you liked."

"Uh, no, I probably wouldn't. Good thinking on your part. I'd like to get back to my own bed."

"I've got my truck around the back of the main hangar. Let's get you home."

Dylan helped Sophia out of the plane and they walked toward the main hangar. As Dylan had told her, there was no one else around, just the two of them. Which, when Sophia caught the reflection of herself in a window and saw how horrible she looked—as she had run down a mountain in the rain and slept in a cave—was probably for the best. She'd hate for anyone else to see her like this.

They stopped to grab a soda and some crackers out of the vending machine in the hangar, all her traumatized stomach could handle. Dylan excused himself to go check on something about his flight tomorrow in one of the small offices and Sophia sat down at the table to consume her meal.

The door at the back of the hangar opened and closed quietly a few moments later. Sophia looked over in the direction of the door but couldn't see anything in the darkness.

"Hello?" she called out. Had Dylan gone over that way and she hadn't realized it?

Nobody responded. But Sophia sensed someone else in the hangar with her. Someone who worked there?

Sophia stood up. She'd go to the office and find Dylan. If this turned out to be nothing then they could just laugh about her traumatized nerves.

"No need for you to get up on our account, Ms. Reardon."

Oh, hell, it was Smith.

Sophia ran. Maybe they didn't know Dylan was in the office and she could lead them away. She bolted for the door, but one of Smith's men—Rick—caught her. He threw her against the door hard.

"Now, Sophia, why are you running?" Smith was grinning wickedly as he walked toward her. She could see Fin and Marco with him. Marco was wearing some sort of sling on his arm. "I thought we were friends."

"How did you find me?"

Smith's laughter was far from reassuring. "Now, that happens to be a funny story."

Smith walked all the way up to Sophia until he was

standing just inches from her. Sophia tried to back up but Rick was right behind her. Smith reached up and touched her neck. Sophia flinched and tried to move to the side, but Rick wouldn't let her. Smith's hand continued its trail to the side of her neck, then her nape, then finally reaching down inside her shirt's collar. Sophia shuddered at Smith's touch, struggling to keep down the crackers she had just eaten. Smith flipped up her collar. He brought his hand back out and held it in front of her face.

Some sort of tracking device. Damn it.

"So this—" Smith waved the tracker right in front of her "—was supposed to keep me apprised of everywhere you went. After I had a visit from a very trusted source who assured me that everything you were telling me about Ghost Shell was untrue, I decided I better keep close tabs on you. And since I was providing your clothes, this seemed like the easiest way, yes?"

Sophia tried to shy away from Smith again, but he moved closer.

"But, and here's the funny part, it seems that when it gets wet, this little tracking device doesn't work correctly. Quite the defect. So when you were running all over the mountain in the rain, this thing would provide only intermittent, imprecise signals. Not terribly useful. And very frustrating for poor Marco here, who got shot by your boyfriend in the midst of this fracas."

Better Marco than Cameron. But Sophia kept her thoughts to herself.

Smith continued with a flourish, "Once you were on the plane and your clothes eventually dried, the tracking device began working perfectly again. So here we are."

Sophia racked her brain for a way out of this. She wanted to protect Dylan, who she knew would be reappearing any moment. But she also knew what Smith wanted: Ghost Shell. And she didn't have it. And honestly couldn't even tell Smith where it was, even if she wanted to. It was at Omega headquarters and she had no idea where that was.

Sophia didn't see any way that she was getting out of this alive, but she didn't see why she would need to take the brother of the man she loved down with her.

"Well, I guess you found me. Congratulations."

Smith finally backed away from her the slightest bit. "Let's just make this easy for all of us, my dear. All I want is Ghost Shell. No need for drama."

Sophia rolled her eyes, not even trying to hide it. She had no doubt whether she gave Ghost Shell over to Smith or not, he was still going to have her killed. "Unfortunately, there's going to have to be a little drama, Smith. I don't have Ghost Shell. Cam does. And I have no idea where he is."

Sophia didn't see the blow coming, but Smith's slap nearly knocked her to the ground. She could taste blood where her teeth cut against her cheek.

"I really don't have time to play games, Sophia. I believe you when you say Cam has Ghost Shell. What I don't believe is that you don't know where he is."

"I'm sorry, but that's true. It seems that the bastard has double-crossed both of us. We split up to get away from you, but were supposed to meet here hours ago. Why else do you think I'd still be here at this tiny little airport?"

She could see that gave Smith pause. But then he

shook his head. "I think not. I saw the way Cam looked at you at the party. There is no way he abandoned you. Not even for all the money he could make doing so."

She looked over to see Fin nodding in agreement. Damn. She needed to think of a way to steer them out of the building before Dylan returned.

But she was too late. Dylan stepped out of the shadows. She could see his training—so similar to Cameron's—as he took out Fin with two short punches and an elbow to the chin. Fin dropped to the ground before Smith or his men could even figure out what was happening. Dylan had Fin's gun in his hand and was pointing it at Smith in the blink of an eye.

Marco and Rick both drew their weapons and pointed them at Dylan. But Smith only laughed. He pulled out his own gun, but instead of pointing it at Dylan, he stepped behind Sophia and pointed the gun directly at her temple.

"Oh, just look at this." Smith laughed gleefully. "You just have to be Cam's brother. You two look exactly the same. Exactly the same."

"Yeah, that's right, he's my brother. Why don't we all just put our guns down. Everyone can walk out of here without any injury." Dylan nudged Fin with his toe. "Except maybe this guy here."

"I don't think so." Smith grabbed Sophia's arm to hold her more closely in front of him. The movement jarred her shoulder and she let out a moan before she could help herself. "Oh, I'm sorry, my dear. Is that the hurt shoulder Fin told me about?" Smith turned to look at Dylan. "I'm going to need you to put your gun down." Smith grabbed Sophia's shoulder and dug into it with his fingers. Her screams echoed through the whole hangar. She struggled not to lose consciousness.

"Okay, stop," Dylan told Smith. "Here." He laid the gun on the ground and kicked it over to Smith.

"Unfortunately, your brother has something that belongs to me. I need to get that back." Smith motioned to Rick, who walked over to stand in front of Dylan. At this point Fin was dragging himself off the ground, too. "Bring him outside."

Sophia saw Rick hit Dylan in the face and then the stomach. As Dylan was doubled over, Fin brought his knee up into his face, knocking him all the way backward. Smith grabbed her arm and began marching her toward the door.

"Please, Mr. Smith." Sophia was crying now. "I swear I don't know where Cam is. I would tell you."

Smith walked Sophia all the way to his car. She watched as Fin and Rick dragged Dylan outside, taking shots at him when they could.

"Oh, I believe you," Smith told Sophia. "But if that's his brother, he knows where Cam is, or at least how to get in touch with him."

Fin and Rick dumped Dylan's nearly unconscious form at Smith's feet. Smith squatted down so he could get closer to Dylan. "Tell your brother he has until midnight tonight to bring Ghost Shell to me at the warehouse from the last weapons buy. He'll know where that is. Tell him we start cutting her into pieces at midnight."

Sophia sucked in her breath as both Rick and Smith chuckled. There was no way Cameron would be able to get Ghost Shell to that warehouse. Even if he decided her life was worth the trade—which he wouldn't—

Cameron wouldn't even have Ghost Shell anymore after giving it to Omega. Plus, it looked as if Dylan was barely breathing. How in the world was he supposed to get to Cameron? A whimper escaped Sophia.

Sophia was so worried about Dylan lying bleeding in the parking lot that she barely noticed Smith's slight nod to Rick and didn't pay much attention to Rick when he came and stood right in front of her. She finally looked up at him just as his meaty fist hit her in the jaw.

Sophia felt everything go black around her, as she sank unconscious to the ground.

Chapter Nineteen

"All I'm saying is that it would've been better if you had brought in Ms. Reardon, too, so she could be debriefed," Cameron's boss, Dennis Burgamy, argued. Again. In his whiny, nasally tone.

"She will be, in a couple of days. She has a wound that needs treating, and then I'll bring her in." Cameron wasn't about to say anything regarding the suspected mole at Omega. Not with this many people in the room.

Exhaustion and coffee flowed through Cameron's veins. Since his arrival at Omega Sector hours ago, he'd been talking, reporting, debriefing nonstop. Dennis Burgamy was thrilled to get his grubby paws on Ghost Shell. Cameron knew the man would be on conference calls either tonight or first thing in the morning, if he didn't send out a sector-wide email, somehow taking credit for the whole thing, first. What a kiss-up.

But Cameron's real problem was that he hadn't been able to get in touch with Dylan. He hadn't expected to communicate with him while he was en route, but they should've been on the ground now for a while. Cameron told himself there was no need to panic. Dylan and Sophia hadn't been out of pocket for that long, and a number of things could've caused the lack of check-in. Cameron had been without a good sleep for a long time, and under a constant level of high stress since Sophia had walked into that warehouse a few days ago, not to mention the headache he'd carried around pretty constantly since he'd had her clock him. He needed to take all these parts of the equation into consideration and not just assume the worse.

"We have medics here who can treat wounds, Branson." It was Burgamy again, but damned if Cameron could remember what they were talking about. He stared at his boss blankly. "For Ms. Reardon's wound?" Burgamy continued.

Oh. Cameron willed his exhausted brain to form a pithy response, but nothing. He just sat there staring at his boss.

"Okay, everybody out of the pool. Party's over, kiddies."

It was Sawyer. Oh, thank God. Cameron had never been so thankful to see his charismatic little brother. Sawyer patted Cameron on the shoulder and gave him a friendly wink, then proceeded to herd everyone else out of the debriefing room, including Burgamy. Cameron sat down wearily in the chair behind the table, watching his brother work his magic. Sawyer spoke to everyone jovially, slapping backs and cracking a couple of jokes. People almost always did what Sawyer asked them to do, and with a smile on their faces.

Cameron shrugged as his brother led the last person out, asking the woman about her child by name. Cameron had worked here just as long as Sawyer, but didn't even know the woman had a child, much less the kid's name. Sawyer had a way with people Cameron just didn't have. Hell, hardly anybody had it.

"You're a popular guy," Sawyer said to Cameron as he closed the door behind the woman who had just left.

"No kidding." Cameron leaned his head all the way back in his seat and closed his eyes, stretching his long legs out under the table.

"I just heard you were back or I would've been here sooner. So, mission accomplished?"

Cameron shrugged. "Not the way I had hoped it would go down. Smith and DS-13 are still fully active, which pisses me off to no end after what Smith did to Jason. But yeah, I recovered Ghost Shell, so I guess Burgamy considers that a win."

"And this girl I keep hearing about?" Sawyer came to sit down on the other side of the desk. If there was one thing Cameron could count on it was that Sawyer would definitely be interested if a woman was involved.

"Sophia Reardon." Cameron peeked out at Sawyer through one eye.

"*The* Sophia Reardon? The one you have categorically refused to talk about for the last five years?"

Cameron closed his eyes again. "Shut up, Sawyer."

Sawyer chuckled. "So where is she?"

Cameron opened his eyes and sat up straighter in the chair. "She's with Dylan. I had him come get her and fly her out separately." Now he had Sawyer's full attention. "I didn't mention this in the debriefing, but I think we have a mole in Omega." Cameron explained the meeting with Agent McNeil and what had put him on guard.

"Holy hell, Cam. If that's true, we've got a really big problem here."

Cameron nodded. A really big problem indeed. "So Dylan's going to take her home and keep an eye on her until I can get there." Cameron looked down at his phone again. Still no message from either Dylan or Sophia. "He should've touched base by now. I don't know what his malfunction is."

The door to the interview room burst open, startling both men. A young man whom Cameron recognized, but whose name he didn't know, was breathing hard, having obviously run from somewhere.

"Um, Agent Branson. You're needed downstairs in the lobby. Like right now," the man huffed out.

"Which one of us? We're both Agent Branson," Sawyer said.

The man hesitated for just a second. "I guess both of you. But he's asking for you, Cameron."

Cameron and Sawyer both stood. "Who's asking for me?"

"I've never met him, sir, but someone said it's your brother." He looked over at Sawyer. "Your other brother, who used to work here. He's down in the lobby and hurt pretty bad..."

Cameron was sprinting out the door at the first mention of his other brother. Sawyer was right behind him.

DYLAN SAT IN a chair surrounded by security personnel. Although *sat* really wasn't the right word. Cameron's heart dropped into the pit of his stomach when he saw the shape his brother was in. One eye was swollen shut, his nose was most definitely broken and Dylan perched in the chair at a peculiar angle with his arm wrapped around his middle. That pose suggested broken, or at least cracked, ribs. And security was surrounding Dylan as if he was some sort of threat.

Cameron scanned the room and noticed immediately that Sophia was nowhere to be seen.

Sawyer uttered a vile curse when he saw Dylan, and his face echoed the shock Cameron knew lay on his own. Someone had worked their oldest brother over in a way Cameron and Sawyer had never seen. And getting the drop on Dylan was damn near impossible.

Both men lowered themselves beside Dylan's chair so he wouldn't have to look up at them.

"You." Cameron turned back to the young man who had come to get them and pointed toward the main entrance. "Medic. Right damn now." He turned to the security workers. "And you two, stand down."

"He came in with no ID asking for you, Agent Branson. We didn't know who he was. He was barely conscious," one of the security guards said.

"He's our brother," Sawyer told them. "You did the right thing. We'll handle it now."

"Dyl, what the hell happened to you?" Cameron gave no more thought to the security team and gave all his attention to his brother. "Where's Sophia?"

"They got her, Cam." Every word was obvious agony for Dylan. "Smith showed up with his goons at the airport and they got her."

Cameron felt the bottom of his very existence fall out from under him. He all but fell into the chair next to his brother. "Is she dead?"

Dylan shook his head gingerly. "No. No, they plan to keep her alive to flush you out."

Cameron let out a huge breath he hadn't even known

he was holding. He was almost dizzy with relief. She was alive, at least for now. Cameron planned to do whatever he could to keep it that way. He couldn't lose her now. Not when he had just gotten her back and realized she was the missing piece in his life.

Dylan shifted in the chair and a moan of pain escaped him. "They want you to bring Ghost something." He tried to shrug but failed miserably. "They said to bring it to the warehouse from the last buy or..."

Cameron finished for him. "Or they'll kill Sophia."

Dylan winced. "The main guy said he'd start cutting her into little pieces if you weren't there by midnight."

Midnight? Cameron glanced at his watch. That was only an hour from now. There was no time to get a team together and prepped for the site. He struggled to tamp down the panic building inside him. Panic wouldn't do any good now.

"You do know what he's talking about, don't you? The Ghost thing?"

Cameron made eye contact with Sawyer. Yeah, he knew what it was, but getting it was going to be much more difficult. Especially now that his boss was probably taking selfies with it in his office at this very moment. There was no way Burgamy was going to give Ghost Shell back to Cameron. Not even for Sophia's life.

"Ghost Shell, yeah. I know what it is, bro."

"Cam, you know this is a trap. Whatever it is they want, as soon as they get it, they're going to kill you and her both. There's at least four of them." Dylan's voice was getting weaker. They needed that medic quick. A glance at Sawyer told Cameron he was worried about the same thing.

"They won't kill us if we have anything to say about it. I've got skills you've obviously lost, big brother," Sawyer chimed in.

"Please," Dylan muttered, his eyes drifting closed. "I could take you right now."

"Dylan." Cameron moved closer so his brother was sure to hear him. He had to know the answer to this, although he was afraid to ask. "Had they hurt Sophia?"

Dylan opened one eye. "The last I saw her, the beefy guy clocked her and they threw her in the trunk. But no permanent damage."

Two medics came barreling through the lobby. Cameron stepped back so they could do their job. After just a few moments they announced that Dylan needed to be taken to the emergency room immediately.

"Hell no," Dylan muttered. "If you two morons are going after DS-13, I'm coming with you."

"You're not going anywhere." The medic turned to Cameron. "We're looking at probable internal bleeding and a collapsed lung. The hospital is not optional," she told him.

"Sorry, bro, you'll have to listen to the pretty doc," Sawyer told him. "No more partying for you today. Although for the first time I wish I could trade places with you." Cameron rolled his eyes as Sawyer gave the medic his megawatt grin.

Cameron leaned in to Dylan one last time. "We'll handle this, bro. You've done enough. We'll see you soon after we get Sophia."

Dylan nodded weakly. Cameron stood up and grabbed Sawyer by the arm. "Let's go talk to Burgamy." After a few steps Cameron turned back to Dylan. "Thank you, Dylan."

But his brother was unconscious.

Sawyer and Cameron jogged to the elevator and pressed the button for the floor Burgamy's office was on.

"You know Burgamy's not going to give up Ghost Shell," Sawyer told him.

"Yeah, I know." Cameron rubbed the back of his neck.

"How well does DS-13 know Ghost Shell? Could we pull off a fake?"

"I don't think so. Maybe with enough time, but not by midnight. They're going to want to test it before making any sort of trade. At least that's what I would do. And they've got a pretty high-ranking FBI agent on the take. If he's there, we definitely can't fool him." The elevator door opened and they began walking down the hall.

"So we need the real Ghost Shell," Sawyer said.

"Yeah."

"Did I mention Burgamy's going to say no when you ask him for Ghost Shell? Not even to save someone's life."

Cameron ignored his brother. He had no intention of asking Burgamy for anything. His weapon was holstered on his belt. Cameron knew this was going to cost him his career and maybe even cause him to spend time in prison, but he didn't care. He was going to force Burgamy to give him Ghost Shell and then was going to get Sophia. And, by God, he was going to get her out alive.

He'd deal with the consequences later.

Cameron knocked briefly on Burgamy's office door then walked in without waiting for a response. Burgamy had one hip propped against his desk and was talking on his office phone.

The Ghost Shell drive was sitting on the desk right next to him. Thank God.

Burgamy shot them both an annoyed glance. "Let me get back to you tomorrow, Director. I'll be sure to give you the whole story then."

Cameron barely refrained from rolling his eyes. Although, why bother hiding his annoyance with this conceited boss when Cameron was about to have much bigger insubordination issues. He put his hand on his holster.

Burgamy hung up and stood, obviously ready to light into Cameron and Sawyer.

"Hey, Burgamy." Sawyer started walking toward the man before Cameron could do anything. "Did I ever tell you about the time I met this ridiculously hot blonde in an elevator at the San Francisco FBI field office…?"

Cameron watched as his brother got to Burgamy's desk, seemed to trip and "accidentally" coldcocked Burgamy in the jaw. Hard. Burgamy fell to the ground completely unconscious.

"What the hell?" Cameron asked.

"Hey, that was better than whatever you were about to do there, Clint Eastwood." Sawyer gestured to Cameron's hand that still rested on his weapon. "Now grab Ghost Shell and let's go."

Cameron shook his head, still a little in shock at what had just happened. "How did you know?"

"Because, sweet heaven, could you have any more

of the 'I'm going to get her out no matter what it costs me' look broadcasted all over your face? Seriously. Why don't you audition for a melodrama or something?" Sawyer rolled his eyes. "Save me from people in love."

Cameron followed Sawyer out the door, grateful for his brother's theatrics. There would still be consequences, but not nearly as bad as with Cameron's initial plan. As they jogged to the stairs it occurred to Cameron that it hadn't even bothered him that Sawyer had said Cameron was in love.

Because he was.

Chapter Twenty

Sophia awoke in a dark place. She immediately closed her eyes again but could feel her heart rate accelerate and her breathing become more shallow. Every muscle in her body tensed. She reached around with her hands, immediately recognizing where she was from the tight fit and continuous movement underneath her body.

She was in the trunk of a car.

Sophia's first response was near panic. She stretched out her legs, her arms, twisting all around, trying to see if anything would give or open. Nothing did.

Sophia fought—hard—to stay in control of her own body and mind. She didn't open her eyes. There was no point really; it was dark anyway. Instead she concentrated on breathing in through her nose and out through her mouth. She fisted and unfisted her hands, trying to give the tension coursing through her body somewhere to go.

Refocus.

Sophia thought of Cameron this afternoon in the cave and how kissing him, just being with him, had helped her get her panic under control. He wasn't here now to help her, but she knew Cameron believed in her strength to handle this.

Sophia continued her breathing exercises while she tried to take stock of the situation. She was in Smith's car. The trunk wasn't that small—Sophia felt her breathing and heart rate hitch again, better not concentrate on that—and the car was still moving.

Sophia scooted herself over so she was all the way to the back of the trunk and put her face up against the metal. It was cold, which felt good on her overheated skin, and she could feel just a hint of air flowing in from outside since the car was moving.

That little bit of air helped her to calm down even more. Remembering that it was fall and night—there was no way she was going to overheat—helped even further. Sophia turned at a diagonal so she could stretch out her legs a little more, thankful for the first time for her short stature.

Although she wasn't feeling calm, Sophia wasn't feeling panicked. As long as she was in this car and it was moving, as uncomfortable as it may be, she was at least out of Smith's clutches. Sophia thought of Dylan and shuddered. When she saw him last he had barely looked alive. Sophia thought about how much her jaw hurt after her run-ins with Rick. She couldn't imagine the shape Dylan was in. Would he even be able to get the message to Cameron?

And how would Cameron be able to get Ghost Shell to trade for her life? No law enforcement agency would be willing to risk something like Ghost Shell falling back into DS-13's hands. Omega Sector would be no exception. Not to save one single person's life. And Sophia couldn't blame them.

She had to face the fact that she might be on her own. Yeah, Cameron would try to help, if Dylan had even been able to get the message to him, but without Ghost Shell there was no way they were walking out of there. But she had to face it, even *with* Ghost Shell there was no way Smith was going to let them walk out of there.

Sophia shifted again to allow her torso to stretch out and felt something hard up against her hip. She reached back to shift it out of her way. A tire iron.

A tire iron.

She brought it in front of her and clutched it like a baby. It wasn't much, but it was something. She wasn't going down without a fight.

They drove for a long time before the road got rougher and they slowed. They must be getting near the warehouse. Sophia wondered how long it was until midnight. She had no idea how long she'd been in this trunk. Soon the car pulled to a stop. Once again Sophia had to focus on keeping calm. Without the air flowing through the crack she'd found in the trunk, it seemed so much more difficult to breathe. Sophia focused on her breathing. She had to be ready. She'd only have one chance to take them by surprise when they opened the trunk. She couldn't—she *wouldn't*—allow panic to overwhelm her.

THE CLOCK WAS ticking in more ways than one. It was getting close to midnight—Smith's deadline. But it also wouldn't be much longer before his boss figured out what was going on. All Burgamy would have to do is talk to one of the medics who treated Dylan, or the security team who escorted him in, and Burgamy would know where they were headed. Either way they had to get this done, and soon.

He and Sawyer were outmanned and outgunned. Under any other circumstances Cameron would also admit they were walking into a situation where the hostage might already be dead. But he refused to even entertain that notion right now. Sophia was not dead.

He could barely stand the thought of her being trapped in the trunk of a car. After what he saw with her today, in a cave that comparatively was much more open than a trunk, Cameron could only assume Sophia would be paralyzed by fear and panic. His white-knuckled grip on the steering wheel became even tighter.

"So what's the plan?" Sawyer asked him. They were only a few minutes from the warehouse.

"To be honest, man, I don't have a good plan."

"A good plan being where we all make it out alive and DS-13 doesn't end up with Ghost Shell?"

"Yeah. Got any ideas?"

"My good ideas started and ended with clocking Burgamy in the jaw." Sawyer chucked softly.

"I think our best bet is for me to drop you around back, then you try to get somewhere that is hidden but you can pick off one or two of them," Cameron told him.

"But Dylan said there were at least four of them. You think you're going to be able to take down two or more before they get you?"

Honestly, no. Cameron didn't think that. But what choice did he have? His primary objective was to allow Sophia to make it out alive. Making it out himself would just be a bonus. But Cameron knew they couldn't let Ghost Shell get taken by Smith. They would use it to trade for Sophia's life, but definitely not let DS-13 leave with it.

"Sawyer, no matter what, we can't allow DS-13 to leave with Ghost Shell in its fully functional form. Even though we took it from Omega, I just want you to know that I'm aware of that. It's more important than any of our lives."

Sawyer leaned over and winked at Cameron, grinning. "Don't sweat it, brother. I plan to pop a cap in some DS-13 ass if it comes down to it. That hard drive will not make it out of the warehouse in one piece if DS-13 has it."

Cameron shook his head. Sawyer was crazy, but he understood what was at stake here.

Cameron pulled the car behind the warehouse next door and dropped Sawyer off so he could make the rest of the way on foot. Then he drove slowly to the warehouse where Smith and his men waited. It was five till midnight.

Smith had pulled his vehicle all the way into the warehouse so Cameron did the same. Was Sophia still in that trunk? Had she passed out? Hyperventilated? Was she wounded? Injured as Dylan had been? Cameron pushed those thoughts aside; he couldn't let his concern about Sophia cloud his decision making. He just needed to get her out alive. Anything else she could heal from.

But Cameron did wish he knew what sort of physical condition Sophia was in. Would she be able to run? Would she need to be carried? If he had to stay behind, would she be able to get out on her own? With her having been trapped in the trunk he could only assume the worst.

The only saving grace in this entire situation was that Smith and DS-13 were desperate to get their hands on Ghost Shell in working condition. It would be of no use to them if it was damaged. Ghost Shell would be Cameron's hostage.

He prayed it would be enough.

Smith was standing beside his vehicle. Rick was sitting on the trunk, which was facing Cameron's car, a big grin on his face. Marco, arm in a sling, stood perched beside Rick, leaning against the car. Cameron couldn't see Fin anywhere around. He hoped Sawyer had eyes on him, and anyone else who might be up in the rafters.

Cameron took out his weapon and threw the holster onto the seat next to him. He picked up Ghost Shell and held the drive directly in front of his chest. As he got out of the car he wanted to make sure that everyone in DS-13 knew if they shot him, he was taking Ghost Shell down with him. It was the only protection he had.

"Cam, right on time. How professional of you," Smith announced in a pleasant voice that didn't fool Cameron for a second.

"Well, my brother said you asked so politely."

Smith gave a condescending smile. "I do find violence so distasteful, Cam. But it was so important that we give the right message and your brother was quite useful for that effect." Rick snickered from his perch on top of the trunk, but Cameron kept his attention focused on Smith.

Cameron could feel tension cording his neck and struggled to hang on to his temper. This bastard had killed his partner, had nearly killed his brother and was standing there looking positively gleeful only ten feet in front of him. Cameron was sorely tempted to put a bullet in Smith right here and now, and then let things happen as they may. Only the thought of Sophia getting hurt—or worse—kept him from doing so.

Cameron kept his SIG pointed directly at Ghost Shell. "Let's just make one thing clear from the start. If I go down, this—" Cameron rocked Ghost Shell back and forth with his hand "—gets blown to bits. Remember that. And make sure Fin and whoever else is up there knows it, too, wherever they are."

Smith looked annoyed now. "I'm sure everyone knows how important Ghost Shell is."

Damn. Cameron had hoped Smith would call out to Fin. So much for pinpointing Fin's location. Cameron just hoped Sawyer would find him. And soon.

"Where's Sophia?" Cameron asked.

Now Rick chuckled again and used his weight to make the trunk of the car bounce up and down. "She's in here, Cam. She's probably not real excited about that, do you think?" He banged on the trunk loudly with his fist, obviously enjoying the thought of Sophia's terror. When there was no response from inside, Rick continued, "Nothing. Must have gotten scared and passed out. Poor thing."

Rick didn't even know the half of it since he wasn't aware of Sophia's claustrophobia. Cameron longed to wipe that sneer off Rick's face.

"Look..." Cam took a few steps closer to them so he wouldn't have to yell. All three men drew their weapons and pointed them at him. "Whoa, everybody simmer down. I just wanted to say that I'm sorry. I obviously made the wrong choice teaming up with Sophia and I got greedy. And I don't expect you to trust me again or do any business with me anymore. All I want is for Sophia and me to get out of here alive."

"Well, you give us Ghost Shell right now and I don't see any reason why you both can't walk out of here," Smith told him. Cameron didn't believe him for a second. "Why don't you go ahead and give us Ghost Shell and then we'll let Ms. Reardon out."

"Um, I don't think so. Why don't you let Sophia out *then* I'll give you Ghost Shell." Cameron hoped Sawyer was in the ready position. Once Rick opened the trunk and Cameron was able to see what condition Sophia was in, he could figure out a plan. She hadn't made any noise from inside the trunk. If she was unconscious or nonfunctional—which was all that could be expected after being locked in a trunk for hours—Cameron wouldn't be able to assist her and keep his gun pointed at Ghost Shell.

At best Cameron was hoping to get Sophia to his car before giving Smith Ghost Shell and the shooting started. At worst… Well, there were a lot of scenarios that fit the "at worst" profile. Especially with three drawn weapons pointing directly at him.

Smith gestured to Rick and he jumped down from the trunk. He turned and unlocked it, pulling it up. Cameron could see Sophia's still form lying there unmoving. Her eyes were closed. He prayed she was just unconscious.

Rick motioned to Marco. "She's passed out. Help me

get her out of here." Marco moved in to help as best he could with one arm in a sling.

Cameron had no warning, but neither did any of the other men. With both Rick and Marco leaning over the trunk to get her out, Sophia came up swinging a tire iron. She hit Marco on the side of the head and he fell instantly to the ground. She hit Rick, too, but only his shoulder. He fell to the side of car, cursing vilely.

Cameron instantly recognized this for what it was: the only chance for success they were going to have. He turned his weapon at Rick and fired two shots into his chest just as the man was pulling his own gun up to shoot Sophia. Cameron dived for the cover of the car as bullets began flying from up in the catwalk of the warehouse. He felt a searing burn in his shoulder, but pushed away the pain. A few moments later Cameron heard a scream and the gunfire from above stopped. Wherever Fin was, Sawyer had found him. That left only Smith.

"Soph? Are you okay?" She was still in the trunk.

"Yes, I'm all right. I think." Cameron had never been so relieved to hear anyone's voice in his entire life. She sounded freaked out—who could blame her?—but she was alive.

"Can you stay in there for just a little while longer?" Cameron whispered. "Smith is still around here somewhere."

Sophia's voice was strained. "Hurry."

Cameron tried to apply pressure to the wound on his shoulder as he got up. He kicked Marco's and Rick's guns away from them as he walked by their motionless forms, just in case. Outside Cameron could see the flashing lights of law enforcement vehicles on their way. Evidently Burgamy had figured out where they were. Cameron still had Ghost Shell in his possession.

"Cops are coming, Cam," Smith called out from behind Cameron's car. "Time for both of us to go."

"I don't think so, Smith," Cameron responded. Now that he knew where Smith was, Cameron began to make his way across the warehouse, silently. No more talking from him.

"The only way we get out of this is together, Cam. If we both get caught, I've got connections, but you don't. I'll make sure all this gets pinned on you and Sophia. You don't want Sophia to go to jail, do you, Cam?"

Just keep talking, jerk. Cameron was almost to him.

"Give me Ghost Shell, we'll all get out of here and let bygones be bygones. You can see the lights, Cam. They're almost here. No need for us to get arrested."

Cameron stepped around the end of his car and brought his SIG up against Smith's head, since Smith was still looking the other way, thinking Cameron was with Sophia. Keeping his gun firmly against Smith's skull, he reached over and grabbed the man's weapon out of his hand before he could turn it on Cameron.

"Actually, you're right, Smith. There's no need for *us* to get arrested. Just you. You're under arrest, you son of a bitch, for the murder of a federal agent, kidnapping, assault and a whole slew of things too long to even mention here."

Chapter Twenty-One

"All I'm saying is that watching you come flying out of that trunk, tire iron swinging, was the sexiest thing I've ever seen." Cameron sat in a reclining hospital chair, one arm wrapped around Sophia with her snuggled up against his uninjured side. His other arm was in a sling from the bullet he'd taken at the warehouse, which fortunately hadn't done any permanent damage.

Sophia wanted to get up to make sure she wasn't hurting Cameron or making him feel uncomfortable, but every time she made any sort of movement away from him he would tuck her more thoroughly back to his side.

Not that she wanted to be anywhere else.

"True story," Sawyer called from his seat across the room.

"There's no way you could've seen it from where you were," Cameron scoffed at Sawyer.

"I don't have to have seen it." Sawyer winked at Sophia. "A woman like Sophia, jumping out swinging? Hell yes, that's sexy."

Sophia felt her cheeks burning.

"Don't let them embarrass you, Sophia." That much

softer sentence came from Dylan in his hospital bed. He seemed to be out of the woods, but still recovering from the beating he had taken at the hands of Smith's men, two of whom were now dead while two, Smith included, were in custody. Ghost Shell was safely back at Omega Sector, although Sophia understood there was some sort of *incident* where Sawyer had tripped and accidentally punched his boss.

Sophia had been told about the incident earlier today by Juliet, Cameron's sister. She also worked at Omega, although not as a field agent. At least not anymore. She had stopped by earlier to check on her brothers and promised to be back later that day after she tried to smooth things over with their boss for her brothers as best she could.

"So, are you guys going to get fired?" Sophia asked, desperate to turn the topic of the conversation to anything but her and the tire iron.

"Nah." Sawyer's confidence was reassuring. "Like I put in my initial report, I am just such a clumsy bastard. I tripped over my own size twelves and just happened to catch Burgamy in the jaw on the way down. Bad luck all around. Then everything just happened so fast. We were trying to call a medic and Dylan here came stumbling in and we just made a judgment call."

Sophia looked up at Cameron from her nook in his shoulder. "Really?"

Cameron just shrugged.

"Besides," Sawyer continued, "we had it all under control from the beginning at the warehouse. Perfect plan, perfectly executed."

Sophia saw Cameron roll his eyes. Whatever the

plan had been, it definitely hadn't been perfect. But she didn't push it any further. She just didn't want Cameron or Sawyer to get in trouble because of her.

"All right, kiddos, I'm out for a few hours if you're going to be staying here for a while, Cam." Sawyer stood up. "I better go help Juliet keep Burgamy from torching my desk. I'll be back in a bit. Try to stay out of trouble while I'm gone."

Cameron nodded. "No problem. Let me know if you need me to come help put out fires."

Sawyer walked over to the chair Cameron and Sophia were lying in. "Sophia..." He held his hand out to her. Sophia tried to get up from Cameron's side, but Cameron wouldn't let her. Sawyer saw it all and chuckled. "No, don't fight him. I'm glad to see Cameron's finally got the good enough sense not to let someone like you go. Better late than never. Welcome to the family." He winked at her then turned and headed out the door.

Sophia was mortified at what Sawyer had said. Would Cameron think Sophia meant that as a clue about where she wanted their relationship to go? "Um, I'm sorry Sawyer said that. I don't know what he meant."

"I do," Cameron told her, head laid back peacefully against the chair, eyes closed.

"You do? Oh, good." Sophia was all but stammering so she stopped talking. But then couldn't help herself. "What? What did he mean?"

Cameron turned so they could look face-to-face at each other. "He meant that I'm in love with you and I'm going to spend however long it takes to make you understand that and convince you to marry me."

"Uh…uh…" Sophia couldn't seem to remember any words in the entire English language.

"It doesn't have to be right now," Cameron continued, smiling at her and stroking her hair away from her face. "We can take as long as we need. As long as you understand that I'm not letting you out of this chair until you say yes."

There was a chuckle from the bed. Sophia had totally forgotten that Dylan was there trying to rest. But she didn't care about Dylan being there, didn't care if the entire hospital could hear them.

"Do you really mean that? You didn't suffer any sort of head injury last night, did you?"

Another chuckle from the bed.

"No." Cameron chuckled a bit, too, but then his laughter faded. "I promise I am of very sound mind. Soph, when I found out Smith had you, it had never been more clear to me that you are the most important thing in my world."

Sophia started to speak, to assure Cameron of the same thing, but he put his finger over her lips to hush her. In his eyes were all the emotions she had always wanted to see. "I've lived without you for five years, and have cursed my own stupidity each day. I don't want to live without you anymore, Sophia."

This was the man she had loved for years, whom she had given up on ever having a future with. Sophia scooted up so she could press her lips to Cameron's. "Then don't."

* * * * *

OVERWHELMING FORCE

To Allison, my editor. You gave me my first shot and I'll forever be grateful. Here we are, ten books later, and you still haven't gotten a restraining order against me yet. I'll consider that a win. Thank you for all you do.

Chapter One

She'd watched him for a year.

She'd traveled all over the country going wherever he went. Others might call it pathetic, but she didn't think so. Besides, what else did she have to do since he'd taken everything from her?

Joe Matarazzo had cost her the man she'd loved. Losing everything after that—her job, her friends, her home—had been his fault, too. Joe Matarazzo had cost her the future.

So now she journeyed around and watched him. Or when she couldn't travel she scoured the internet for information about him.

Whenever she heard his name on a police scanner she prepared to rush to the scene. She had no doubt he would save the day once again.

Why couldn't he have saved the day when it had mattered the most?

Fire had taken the man she loved. Joe Matarazzo could have stopped it, but he hadn't. Hadn't tried hard enough, not like he would today. Not like how hard she'd seen him try in all his other successful situations. He had the most important job: rescuing those who couldn't rescue themselves. Leading them to safety. Putting their lives before his own.

But he hadn't done his job a year ago. Almost exactly a year ago now. On that day he hadn't tried hard enough. Hadn't cared enough about those he tried to help.

Since that time she had observed him, followed him, studied him. She knew everything about him. Because of that, she could say with a clear conscience that he was guilty.

The time had come for Joe Matarazzo to atone for his wrongdoings. To suffer for the lives he'd lost.

He'd paid no price for what he'd done. Instead, he had women, he had money, he had everything. But soon that would change. She would see to it.

First, Joe would fall. And as he did, he would know the pain of losing what he cared about most.

Then he would burn.

Just like the fire that had taken her love.

"CASANOVA HAS STRUCK AGAIN. I know it's hard, fellas—don't be jealous just because Joe Matarazzo looks better on your girl than her outfit."

Joe rolled his eyes and tried to snatch the newspaper clipping out of Derek Waterman's—Joe's Omega Sector Critical Response Division colleague—hands. Derek shifted slightly, holding the paper just beyond Joe's reach since they were both strapped into the bench seat of the twin-engine helicopter.

Who even read a physical newspaper anymore? Joe hadn't looked at a news report that wasn't on his smartphone or computer for years. Not that his dating life was *news*, print version or otherwise.

Joe had no idea why so many people would want to read about his love life. Yeah, his family had money—a lot of it—and yeah, he'd grown up with some Hollywood A-listers and ended up photographed a lot.

And yeah—he grinned just a little, glancing out the helicopter's window as Derek continued to read and the seventy miles between Colorado Springs and Denver whirled past—Joe tended to be a bit of a bad boy. Had a reputation with the ladies.

So what? He liked women.

"The lady du jour was Natasha Suzanne Bleat, daughter of British diplomat Marcus Bleat…"

Joe tuned out as Derek read Natasha's impressive list of family credentials through the headphones that allowed all of them to communicate with each other. Jon Hatton and Lillian Muir—the first an Omega profiler and the second Omega SWAT like Derek—listened raptly from the pilot and copilot seats where Lillian controlled the aircraft.

Seriously, Joe's colleagues loved this stuff, ridiculous as it may be. They had a whole scrapbook full of Joe's clippings.

Joe had grown up with press and had learned to pretty much ignore it. The press had their own agenda and nobody's best interests in mind but theirs. He learned that lesson a little too late, but learned it.

And it wasn't like paparazzi followed him around. Yet for whatever reason, gossip sites and society pages loved to report on his dating life. A dating life he had to admit was pretty extensive. Everyone called him Casanova. The press and even his colleagues at Omega.

Joe wasn't offended. It took a hell of a lot more to offend him.

"…the redhead beauty was last seen entering the Los Angeles Four Seasons with Joe, arm in arm."

Joe raised his gaze heavenward with a long-suffering sigh and waited for the rest, but that was it.

"Last seen?" Joe finally succeeded in snatching the paper away from Derek. "They make it sound like I killed her and hid her body."

"Oh, it sounds like you did something to her body, but I don't think anyone figures you killed her. At least not literally." Lillian snickered from her pilot's seat.

"I have no idea how you get so lucky, dude." Derek closed his eyes and leaned farther back on the bench seat next to Joe. "No matter what city we're in, the women throw themselves at you."

Joe could've pointed out that speeding their way to a hostage negotiation scene was probably not the time to discuss the press version of his love life. But he knew this sort of distraction helped keep the team loose and relaxed.

There would be plenty of time for tension and focus when they landed and assessed the scene.

Joe shrugged. "What can I say? I'm #blessed, man." He made the hashtag symbol with his hands, tapping his fingers together.

Everyone groaned.

"Don't make me shoot you. I'd catch flack for shooting an unarmed man." Derek didn't open his eyes as he said it.

Joe was the only unarmed person in the helicopter. Although he was trained in the use of a number of weapons, he almost always went into situations unarmed.

He was Omega Sector's top hostage negotiator. And he was damn good at his job.

Joseph Gregory Terrance Matarazzo III didn't need a career. At least, didn't need one for a salary. He'd been born with money, had known its benefits his entire life. Had used those benefits for a carefree, fun-loving existence until about six years ago when he'd turned twenty-five and decided maybe he'd like to do something with his time besides sit around and look good.

The laid-back, playboy, slacker and media darling had decided to become a better man.

Joe had skills. Not the same skills Derek had in his ability to formulate the best tactical advantage in any given hostile situation. Or the ones Lillian had with the many ways she could kill someone not only through the use of weapons, but just her scary, tiny, bare hands. Or Hatton with whatever he did, which was pretty much overthink everything and come up with scenarios and means of handling crises.

Joe's skills rested with people. He had a charming way with others. He knew it. Everybody knew it. Joe excelled at talking to people, listening to them, making them feel comfortable. He was likable, a cool kid. The type of person people wanted to be around.

It wasn't an act. Joe honestly cared about people, even the hostage-takers he was sent to talk to. So he tried his damnedest to connect with the people in these situations, to listen to them and see what he could do so everyone could leave the situation alive. If Joe did his job right, nobody had to get hurt.

If he didn't do his job right, the Dereks and Lillians with the guns came in with a different solution.

Most of the time Joe successfully completed his mission and nobody was harmed. Sometimes there was no other way and the bad guys got wounded or worse. Joe was trained—and wasn't hesitant—to make the hard call when he knew he wasn't going to be able to neutralize the situation and SWAT needed to step in and take the tangos out. That situation wasn't Joe's preference, but he didn't lose sleep when it happened.

Every once in a while something went terribly wrong and innocent people got hurt. Joe touched a burn scar at the base of his neck, one that continued over his shoulder and partway down his back. Innocent people had been hurt that day a year ago. Innocent people had died.

Joe planned to use his skills today to make sure another situation like that didn't happen again.

Derek and Jon began arguing over the name of the woman the press had spotted Joe with a few days before Natasha during an Omega case in Austin, Texas.

"Her name was Kerri. I'm telling you." Jon's voice came crisply through the headphones. "Kerri with an *i*. I remember it clear as day."

"No," Derek said. "That was the one before. Austin was Kelli. But also with an *i*."

Joe wondered what Derek's brilliant wife, Molly, the crime lab director at Omega, and Jon's fiancée, Sherry Mitchell, a hugely talented forensic artist, would have to say about their men's topic of conversation.

No doubt they would find it as ridiculous as Joe did.

Joe remembered both Kerri and Kelli. He'd had dinner with one, a drink at a bar with the other. Nothing more. Just like the night at the hotel with Natasha when Joe had walked her, admittedly arm in arm, to her room. And left her there.

Because, hell, nobody could be as much of a Casanova as the press wanted to label him. God knew he wasn't a monk, but sometimes the women he was with were just pleasant company—clothes *on*—and nothing more.

But Joe hated to deny his colleagues their fun.

"Would you like me to settle this, boys?" he asked, sighing.

"For the love of all that is holy, please yes, Matarazzo, settle this." Lillian's higher voice cut through the baritone of the three men.

"You're both wrong. It was Kerri *and* Kelli. Both of them in Austin. *Together*." Joe smiled as he told the lie.

If they wanted Casanova he would give it to them. He knew he probably shouldn't since it reinforced what his colleagues already thought to be the truth about him: that he was less part of the Omega team and more like a novelty. But Joe was great at figuring out what people needed and becoming that, at least for a little while. A distraction en route to a troublesome situation? No problem.

Hatton and Derek both groaned, neither knowing whether to believe him.

"I'm going to check some of the gossip sites when I get back to HQ," Hatton threatened.

"You do that," Joe responded. "Because you know everything they publish can be taken as gospel."

Silence fell as they flew the last few miles and Lillian landed the helicopter on the roof helipad of a building that had been cleared two blocks from First National Bank of South Denver. Temporary home of two bad guys and a dozen or so hostages.

Lillian landed and switched off the rotors. "Time to go to work, boys."

Joe slid the door open and he and Derek both ducked their heads and briskly made their way down the stairs, out of the building and over to the bank. Jon quickly joined them as they found the officer in charge. Lillian would be there after she took care of the helicopter. Jokes and talk about Joe's exploits ceased. Omega now had a job to do.

The older man shook everyone's hand. "I'm Sheriff Richardson. We appreciate you coming out so quickly."

"We need the most up-to-date intel you have," Derek told the sheriff. Joe was glad the locals had called Omega and egos hadn't come into play. Situations like this tended to be delicate enough without law enforcement working against each other.

Richardson nodded. "We have two men in their midtwenties holding, as best as we can tell, sixteen people hostage inside the bank. Two of those hostages are children. They've been inside for two hours and we haven't been able to speak with them, despite trying multiple times."

Richardson turned from Derek to Joe. "You're the negotiator, right? The city has a good one of our own, but she had a baby a couple of days ago. She was still going to come in but I put a stop to that immediately."

Joe nodded. "That was the right decision. I won't let

you down, Sheriff. I'll do my very best to get everyone out safely."

"Do you have building plans for the bank, Sheriff?" Derek asked.

"Yes." He gestured over to a younger man who brought them over. Lillian joined them, and she, Derek and Hatton were soon poring over the plans.

Joe took a deep breath, looking out at the small bank. He couldn't see anything happening inside. The Denver County police didn't have a sizable SWAT team, but it did appear like they had a couple of marksmen. He knew Derek and Lillian were both expert sharpshooters also.

He hoped it wouldn't come to that.

Why were the hostage-takers here at this particular bank? Had they tried to rob it then got stuck so took hostages? Robbing a bank wasn't a very smart move and didn't have a high success rate, but people did desperate things sometimes.

There were kids inside. That upped the ante a lot. Joe's natural inclination was to march up to the door right now, even without backup. But he knew to set wheels in motion before Derek and the team were ready could spell disaster for everyone.

"Derek, there are kids, man," Joe said softly. He knew he didn't have to remind his friend of that—with his pregnant wife, it would be in the forefront of Derek's mind, too—but couldn't help himself. "They've already been in there a long time. Let me know which direction you'll be coming from if it goes south and I'll get started. At least get the kids out."

"There's not a lot of good options with a bank this

old that was built in the fifties," Derek muttered, studying the plans more intently. "It looks like the roof will be our best bet. Probably a ventilation shaft. We might have to send Lillian through alone if it's too small."

Lillian alone would be plenty enough to put down two tangos. Joe nodded at her; she winked at him. Despite her beauty, he had never tried to make a move on her. He knew better than to hit on a woman who made a living shooting people.

"Okay," Joe said. "What's today's go-signal?"

The team always had a phrase and action, both meant only to be used as a last resort, that Joe could use to signal SWAT that the situation inside was out of hand and they needed to use deadly force.

"Word is *sunglasses*." Derek glanced up from the plans. "Action is putting your sunglasses on your head."

Joe's shades were in the pocket of his shirt. Unlike the other Omega members, all wearing full combat gear and bulletproof vests, Joe was wearing a black T-shirt, jeans and casual brown boots. It was important that he seem as normal and nonthreatening as possible when he approached the hostage-takers.

"Be careful in there, Joe." It was Jon who looked up from the building plans this time. "We've got a lot of blinds here. I know you're good on the fly, but watch your six."

Joe nodded, already beginning to walk toward the building. "Those kids and their mother will be coming out first. Be ready for them."

He blew out a breath through gritted teeth, forcing his shoulders then jaw to relax. Coming in tense—or at least looking overly tense—never helped. There were two guys in there who needed to be heard. Joe wanted to do that. But even more he wanted to get the hostages out safely. Every one of them.

Joe walked up to the glass door of the bank and knocked, then held his hands up in a position of surrender so they could see he wasn't armed. And he waited.

He was about to become best buddies with two potentially dangerous guys.

Just another day at the office for Joe Matarazzo.

Chapter Two

Laura Birchwood should've sent her assistant to the bank to get these stupid papers signed.

But *no*, Laura had wanted to get out of the office, get some nice fresh air on this relatively warm, sunny April day in Colorado. It had been a long, cold winter and it had snowed even as late as a week and a half ago.

So when it had been in the upper 60s on a late Friday afternoon and her Colorado Springs law office—Coach, Birchwood and Winchley, LLP—had needed the signature of a bank manger here on the outskirts of Denver, Laura had offered to make the trip herself. Her assistant had Friday night plans; Laura didn't. Laura decided she would have dinner in Denver while she was here. She'd be by herself, but that wasn't anything unusual.

The two guys pacing frantically with big guns, stopping every once in a while to wave them around and scare the people sitting on the bank floor, were going to ruin her dinner plans.

As pathetic as the plans were.

Laura refused to let herself panic, even when the guys glanced over in her direction. Hysteria wasn't going to help anything in this situation; as a matter of fact, she was pretty sure the hostage-takers would just feed off it and become more aggravated.

"I have to get them out of here," Brooke, the young mother sitting next to Laura, whispered. "They're going to get hungry soon. Get upset."

She referred to the two girls the mom had with her, a baby maybe eight or nine months, not old enough yet to be crawling, thank goodness, and a five-year-old. Both had done remarkably well so far. Brooke herself had done great. She'd fed the baby a bottle and given the older girl, Samantha, a box of crayons and a coloring book she'd had in her diaper bag.

Most of all she'd stayed calm. Her daughters had picked up on their mother's cues and had also stayed calm. Laura wasn't even sure Samantha really understood what was happening.

"Police will be coming, Brooke," Laura whispered to her. "I have a packet of peanut butter crackers in my purse for Samantha. That will buy us some time."

"I need to make another bottle." Brooke gestured to the baby currently sitting in her lap, playing with some teething toys. "And I know her diaper is wet. I'm going to have to talk to them."

"No, I'll talk to them—"

Laura flinched as one of the two men, the loud one, let out a loud string of obscenities. "Shut up over there!" he yelled, pacing more wildly.

Samantha looked up from her coloring. "He said a bad word," she whispered to Laura.

He'd said a bunch of them. Laura wasn't sure which one the girl meant.

"You're not supposed to say *shut up*," Samantha stated primly, then went back to her coloring.

Laura couldn't help but smile. It was nice to meet a kid whose definition of foul language revolved around the words *shut up*.

She had to get Brooke and her two beautiful daughters out of here. She knew drawing the men's attention to her by asking them to release Brooke and the girls could be dangerous. Laura had no idea what the men wanted. To be honest she wasn't even sure these men knew exactly what they wanted.

The local police had tried calling the bank. The men had made the employees unplug all the phones and then had hit the assistant manager on the head with their gun. The man was conscious but still had blood oozing down the side of his face. They'd forced everyone to put their cell phones in a trash can and placed it in the middle of the room.

If the robbers decided to start killing hostages, Laura didn't want to put herself at the front of the line. But she sure as hell wasn't going to let Brooke do it. And now that there was no way the police could contact the men to see what they wanted, Laura didn't know how the police could help.

She reached over and squeezed Brooke's hand.

"Laura, wait, don't—"

Laura was standing up when a knock on the bank's front door suddenly drew everyone's attention. She didn't have a good angle to take in the whole scene but could see the upheld arms of a man standing there. She quickly sat back down.

The robbers went ballistic.

"Who are you? What do you want?" one screamed at the person at the door, voice shrill.

"We'll kill everyone in here. Every last one of them. Get away!"

The man outside didn't move except to gesture to them to unlock the door.

The two men began frantically talking between themselves. Laura couldn't hear all of it, but knew one of the men at least understood that the man at the door was a hostage negotiator.

Hopefully the guy was a good one.

Finally the two men broke apart from their huddle. The negotiator was still standing arms upstretched by the entrance. Laura still couldn't see his face.

"You." One of the hostage-takers pointed over to the bank manager. "Get over here and open the door."

The manager got shakily to his feet and walked to the door gathering a large ring of keys from his pocket. The robber got behind him, using the man as a human shield, and put the gun directly to the manager's temple.

The baby started fussing and Laura reached over to hold her so Brooke could get out another bottle. Plus, if bullets started flying Brooke could grab Samantha and Laura could try to protect the baby.

"You better pray that this guy doesn't try anything. Because you'll be dead before you hit the floor if he does. Open it just a crack," the man holding the manager said.

The manager nodded as he put the key in the door. Rivers of sweat rolled down his face. The room remained silent.

"P-please don't do anything," the manager said to the man outside. "He'll kill me if you do anything."

"Nah, no plans to do anything to make anybody nervous." The negotiator's voice was clear and friendly. And oddly familiar to Laura. "I swear to you all, I am unarmed and just here to talk. To see what we can work out. To find a solution where all of us get out of here without getting hurt."

"How do I know you're not armed?" the robber yelled from behind the manager, keeping his head down.

"I'm going to reach down now and lift up my shirt and turn around. You'll see. No weapon at all. No earpiece. Nothing."

She still couldn't see his face, but Laura and the rest of the bank were treated to the sight of rock-solid abs as the man lifted his shirt and turned around slowly. Under any other circumstances Laura would've just enjoyed the view.

"You could have a gun in your pants," the other man said. "An ankle holster or something. We're not stupid."

"No, you're right. You're smart to think of that. Most people wouldn't."

The negotiator was good. He'd already tuned in to what the robbers needed to hear: that they were smart, in control. The man ripped off his shirt and dropped it to the ground.

"I'm going to take off my jeans, okay? Not trying to give anyone a show, but you're smart to check and make sure I really don't have any weapons."

Strong muscular legs came into view as the man kicked off his boots and socks and then took off his jeans. Black boxer briefs were all that was left on the negotiator. Laura sort of hoped the robbers would let him in, not only so he could negotiate them out of this mess, but so she could see his face. Would it be as impressive as the rest of him?

"Miss Laura—" Samantha giggled "—that man only has his underwear on."

Laura smiled. "I know, sweetie. He's silly." She bounced the baby on her legs, thankful she wasn't crying anymore.

"So as you can see," the negotiator continued, "no weapons. Well, *one*, if you know what I mean. But I generally only bring that one out for the ladies." Laura could hear the smile in his voice. "Do you mind if I come in and talk? It's a nice day but still a little chilly out here in just my drawers."

"Fine," the guy behind the bank manager finally said. "Get in here. But if you do anything suspicious at all, I'll start killing people."

The guy grabbed his pile of clothes and quickly squeezed through the door. The manager relocked it and the bad guy got away from the danger of the door and pointed his gun at the negotiator.

Laura could feel her jaw literally drop when she got her first full look at him.

Standing there in his boxer briefs was Joe Matarazzo.

She never thought she would see him again. Had *hoped* she would never see him again. And now it looked like her life was in his hands.

Just went to prove that behind every worst-case scenario, there was a *worse* worst-case scenario.

JOE KNEW HE would never hear the end of this little striptease from his Omega colleagues. But he'd been certain he couldn't get into the bank any other way. These two guys were paranoid, frantic. Joe knew immediately he needed to put himself in a position of seeming to be the beta. Let them feel like they were alpha.

Joe's pride, his true feelings, his personality, didn't matter. All that mattered was getting everyone out of the bank safely.

If they had asked him to take off his boxers, he would've done that, too. But he was glad they hadn't.

Joe quickly assessed one half of the bank as he put his jeans back on. The bank manager seemed scared to death and had some bruising on the side of his face—probably took a punch—but otherwise appeared fine. An injured man, also a bank employee, sat propped up against the wall. Looked like he also had received a blow to the side of the face. Bloody, but not life-threatening.

All the bank employees being alive was a good sign. It meant these two guys probably didn't want to hurt anyone. Probably had planned to rob the bank and things had escalated.

No one was dead yet, so that meant there was a very good chance that Joe could get everyone out unharmed.

"I'm Joe, by the way," he told the two men as he pulled his shirt back over his head.

"You expect us to tell you our names so you can get a bunch of information on us? No way, man." Both men had their weapons aimed directly at Joe.

Joe wanted to point out the flaws in their logic: how was he supposed to get any information? He'd just gotten almost naked in front of them so they knew he didn't have any communication devices. And even if he did, what would a bunch of information do versus two very real guns?

But pointing out the logic flaws would only put them more on the defensive.

"No, nothing like that. I was just wondering what to call you."

"You can call me Ricky and him Bobby," the older of the two men said, sneering.

Joe recognized Ricky Bobby. "Yeah, I saw that movie." Joe smiled. "The kids, Walker and Texas Ranger. Hilarious. *Anchorman* was my favorite though."

The men's weapons lowered just the slightest bit. Good. Just keep them thinking about Will Ferrell and movies. Based on their coloring and size, Joe guessed Ricky and Bobby to be brothers.

He turned casually in the opposite direction so he could see the other half of the bank as he crouched down to put his shoes back on.

There were the kids. Good. A little girl alternating between coloring and watching what was going on and a baby in her mom's lap. Joe glanced at the mom's face to see how she was holding up.

And found the angry eyes of Laura Birchwood.

Joe felt the air leave his lungs.

Man, she hadn't changed at all in the six years since he'd seen her, well, except for the two kids part. She still had wavy brown hair and a face more interesting than it was traditionally pretty. But it was still the face he'd never been able to ever get out of his mind.

The pain that assaulted him at the knowledge that Laura had moved on so completely from him took him by surprise. She obviously had found herself a husband

and had a couple of kids, given the cute little baby who bounced on her knees.

After what he'd said to her when their relationship ended, Joe couldn't blame her for moving on. It still hurt like hell though.

Joe stood from putting on his boots and looked at the two men. He needed to focus.

"Ricky, Bobby, I want to help you guys. They sent me in here to figure out what we can do to work this out peaceful-like." He carefully didn't use the word *cops* in case that was some sort of trigger word for the two men "There's nothing that has been done here yet that makes the situation terrible. You guys and I can walk out of here right now and everything can be made right."

That wasn't totally accurate. Ricky and Bobby would be doing some jail time for this little stunt. But it would be much worse if they killed someone. Joe didn't really think they were just going to walk out with him, but it was worth a shot.

"No," Ricky said. "They'll shoot us as soon as we come out. Or at least arrest us."

"Nobody wants to shoot you. I promise you that," Joe quickly interjected. He needed to keep the level of paranoia as low as possible.

"Well, we're not going out there. Not until we have what we need." Bobby looked over at the bank manager.

Okay, so they did want something. Probably money. That was good, something Joe could work with, something he could talk to them about.

Something that provided him leverage.

"That sounds reasonable. Is what you need going to hurt anybody?"

If what they needed was to blow up a bank full of people while the press was watching to make some sort of political or religious statement, then it was going to be time for Joe to pull out the sunglasses to signal SWAT awfully quick. But Ricky and Bobby didn't seem to be the political statement types.

"No," Bobby said. "What we want is ours. We just want it back."

To the side, Joe heard Laura's baby start to cry. He needed to get her and the children out of here. Right now. He couldn't stand the thought of Laura being hurt again. Or especially her innocent children.

Joe had hurt her enough once. Maybe he could begin to make that right by getting her and her family out of danger.

"Alright, I can do that. That's why I was sent in here. To see what it is you need and help find a way to get it for you. That's my only job here, figuring out a way this can end okay for everyone."

Again, that wasn't actually true, but the baby's cries were getting louder. Ricky and Bobby both turned to glare at the child and Joe briefly thought of trying to take both of them down physically himself, but he decided not to risk it. Somebody might get hurt. Plus, it was too early in the negotiation process. If Joe broke their trust now, he would not get it back.

"She's got to shut that kid up," Bobby told Ricky.

"Listen, guys…" Joe took a small step closer so they would turn their attention—and weapons—back on him and away from Laura's side of the room. "I think we can solve a couple of problems here with one action."

"What are you talking about?" Bobby's eyes narrowed.

"Like you said, that baby is a huge headache. Plus the people outside—" Joe again was careful not to call them *law enforcement* or *police* "—would take it as a sign of good faith if you let the kids and their mom go. Works for everyone. You get rid of a screaming baby, and the people outside know you're reasonable. Win/win. You've still got plenty of people left in here for whatever you need to do."

Bobby looked over at his older brother and Ricky finally nodded. Joe felt like a hundred-pound weight had been lifted off his chest. Now, no matter what happened, at least Laura and her kids would be safe.

Keeping his eyes on Ricky and Bobby, Joe motioned for Laura and the kids to come over.

"Get the manager to open the door again," Ricky told him, so Joe turned to the man. The heavyset manager got to his feet and moved to the door.

Joe turned back to reassure Laura as best he could but found another woman taking the baby from her. Clutching the infant in one arm and holding the hand of the little girl in the other, she made her way to Joe.

"You're their mom?" Joe asked. "I thought the other lady was holding the baby."

"She was just helping me," the woman whispered. "Thank you for getting us out."

Joe squeezed her shoulder. "When the door opens, walk straight across the street. Don't stop for anything."

The woman nodded.

"Okay, are we ready?" he asked.

Joe turned to Ricky and Bobby and fought back a

shudder when he saw that Bobby now had Laura held right in front of him in a choke hold, gun pointed at her temple.

"If anyone does anything I don't like, I'll put a bullet in her," Bobby said.

Joe ground his teeth. It took quite a lot to get him to lose his cool, but he was finding that a gun to Laura's temple did it very quickly. He forced the anger down. He needed to stay calm.

The manager opened the door and Joe watched as the woman sprinted across the street, the little girl doing her best to keep up. They were safe. He squeezed the shoulder of the bank manager as he relocked the door.

"Thank you for not trying to run," Joe said in a low voice. The man could've taken off when the door was open. Could've saved himself at the cost of other lives. Joe had seen it happen before.

"I couldn't let them kill someone else because of me." The manager rubbed his hands down his pant legs. "But I can't give them what they want. I don't have what they need."

Joe's smile suggested a calm he didn't really feel. "We'll work it out."

Joe finally felt like he could breathe again when Bobby had released Laura and she had sat back down against the wall. She didn't seem to be hurt in any way or even too scared.

As a matter of fact her hazel eyes were all but spitting daggers at Joe. She looked like she might grab Bobby's gun and shoot Joe herself.

Joe winced. Guess she hadn't forgiven him for what he'd said to her six years ago.

He didn't blame her. And he had to admit, as much as he wanted Laura safely out of harm's way, his heart had actually leaped in his chest—seriously, he'd *felt* the adrenaline rush through him—when he realized those children belonged to another woman. Not Laura.

It was time to get this situation resolved so he could move on to more important things. Like talking Laura into dinner with him.

He had a feeling that might take more negotiation skills than even he possessed.

Chapter Three

Joe Matarazzo working in law enforcement. Who would've *ever* figured that would happen? Certainly not Laura.

But she had to admit, he had quite deftly handled the situation in the bank with Ricky and Bobby. They had come there to steal the last remaining copy of their father's will.

Evidently dear old dad had realized what jerks his sons had become and had decided to leave his "fortune" as Ricky and Bobby called it, a sum of just over twelve thousand dollars, to the local 4-H club.

Two grown men had broken into a bank, held sixteen people—including *children*—hostage, and had threatened to kill them all to get a will. A will that ultimately would only get them twelve thousand dollars if they were successful.

The perfect storm of idiocy.

The bank manger hadn't had the other key. Every safe-deposit box needed two keys and the manager only had one. That's when the problem had escalated. Ricky and Bobby thought they could just come in, show some

ID and have the box opened. But not without the second key.

Demanding the manager open it by pointing a gun at his head hadn't changed the situation. He still couldn't open it with only his one key.

Somehow Bobby and Ricky just hadn't understood that. They got loud. Someone called the cops and next thing they knew they had a hostage situation on their hands.

Laura had no idea what would've happened if Joe hadn't shown up and defused the situation.

He'd sat down with the two men and the bank manager. The manager swore he would open the safe-deposit box if he could, but that the bank had put security measures in place long ago that required two keys. It's what kept managers from being able to walk in at any time and take anything they wanted from the boxes.

Finally Joe was able to make Ricky and Bobby understand that. He'd then helped them figure out where their dead father's key might be. Explained they needed to surrender so they could come back to the bank another time.

That time was going to be after years in prison, and by then the 4-H club was going to have some pretty nice 4-Hing equipment, or whatever a 4-H club used money for, but Joe had left that part out.

Both men had exited with Joe and had been immediately taken into custody. Everyone inside could hear Ricky and Bobby screaming at Joe, claiming he'd lied about being arrested. Joe hadn't lied, he just hadn't announced all the particulars of the truth. As a lawyer, Laura could appreciate the difference.

Cops and medical workers then rushed into the bank to see who needed help. As they tended to people, Laura watched with a sort of amazed detachment as one of the large air-conditioning grates on a wall about ten feet off the ground moved and a small woman, in full combat gear and rifle, eased her way out, hung as far as her arms would allow her, then dropped to the ground.

She'd been there, probably since not long after Joe arrived, silently ready to move in if things had gotten desperate.

But they hadn't, thanks to Joe.

The woman had just made a quiet sweep of the area with her eyes then walked out the front door. Most of the people inside didn't even notice her.

A uniformed police officer entered and made an announcement. "People, I'm Sheriff Richardson. Right now we're just trying to ascertain who is injured. If you have any wounds at all, or feel like you're having any chest pains or anything like that, please let us know so we can get a medic to attend to you immediately."

Laura's chest hurt a little bit, but she was pretty sure that was indigestion caused from seeing Joe again.

"Otherwise we ask that you stay in the immediate area of the bank so we can take your statement. Certainly you are free to go outside and get some fresh air. Also to call anyone you need to let them know you're okay. This event will make the supper-time news, for sure, and you won't want any family worrying about you."

Laura doubted her parents or brother would hear about this back in Huntsville, Alabama, but she would text them anyway and let them know she was okay. She would not mention the fact that Joe Matarazzo had gotten her out of the situation safely. Her dad and brother might catch the first flight to Denver and take Joe out themselves.

They'd have to get in line behind her.

The image of Joe stripped down to his boxers and smiling charmingly at the two hostage-taking morons popped into her head unbidden.

Damn, he still looked good. Nothing about that had changed, not that she would've expected it to. His tall, lithe body was absolutely drool-worthy: broad shoulders, hard abs that all but begged you to run your fingers over them, trim hips that eased down into long, strong legs.

And that face. Crystal blue eyes and strong, sharp cheekbones and a chin that gave strength to a face that would've otherwise been too pretty. Brown hair with natural sandy highlights, straight, a little long with a half curl that always fell over his forehead.

And his smile. Joe Matarazzo had a quick, easy smile for everyone. The man loved to smile, and had gorgeous sensuous lips and perfect teeth to back up his propensity.

His cheeks were clean-shaven now, but Laura knew firsthand how quickly the stubble would grow and exactly how the roughness of his cheeks would feel as he kissed her all over her body.

She stopped the thought immediately. For six years she'd been stopping those types of thoughts immediately. Instead she fast-forwarded to the last memory she'd had of Joe. Him standing outside her apartment and telling her their relationship wasn't going to work anymore.

That he'd liked her and all, and the last couple of months had been great, but that, let's face it, she just wasn't the *caliber* of woman someone like Joe—with his money and connections and good looks and charm—would be in a long-term relationship with.

Mic drop. Matarazzo out.

Laura could make those little jokes now, almost without wincing. Six years ago she'd just wanted to crawl under a rock and die. Joe may not have used those actual words, but basically said she wasn't attractive enough for him. Silly her, she'd thought the fact that they'd always had a delightful time together, had the same quirky sense of humor and wonderful conversations had meant something. For the six months they had dated, Joe had led her to believe that he thought it was true, too. Until he just changed his mind out of the blue and ended it.

Not the caliber of woman...

So no, she was not going to let the sight of Joe Matarazzo in just his skivvies get her hot and bothered.

"Um, ma'am?"

Laura looked over at the young police officer who had evidently been trying to get her attention for a few moments.

"Yes?"

"Were you hurt in any way? Perhaps a head injury?" The young officer looked confused.

The only damage to Laura's head was in her thoughts about Joe. "No, I'm fine. Just reliving the situation. It's a little painful." She didn't state which situation.

"Do you feel up to giving me your statement? Otherwise we can have you come down to the station tomorrow."

Laura shook her head. No, she didn't want to have to come back. She gave the officer her statement, telling how Ricky and Bobby entered while she was finishing a meeting with the bank manager to get his signature on some financial paperwork for a client.

If Laura had just beelined it for the door she wouldn't have gotten caught in the hostage mess at all. But then she thought of Brooke and little Samantha and the baby. Laura had been glad she'd been able to help them.

The officer took down Laura's information and told her they'd be in touch if they needed anything else, and that she shouldn't hesitate to contact them if she thought of something more she remembered. She was free to go.

Now all she had to do was make it to her car and get away without having to talk to Joe at all. Not that he'd try to talk to her. After all, what was there left to say?

She supposed she could thank him for doing a good job today and getting them all out alive. She'd been especially impressed at how he'd immediately gotten Brooke and her girls out.

Laura was thankful, but she wasn't willing to actually talk to Joe to tell him that. Maybe she could send the sheriff's office a letter with official thanks. Better. More professional.

She stepped out into the brisk April air of Colorado, closing her eyes and breathing it deep into her lungs. She was alive. She was unhurt. She even had the signature she'd originally come to this bank for. Everything was good.

She opened her eyes and found herself staring directly into the gaze of Joe Matarazzo.

The Rockies in all their stark majesty framed the area behind him. The bright cobalt sky made the perfect matching backdrop for the overwhelming force of his gorgeous blue eyes.

It was ridiculous. Like he was something out of a John Denver song or Bob Ross painting.

"Hey, Laura."

And must the deep timbre of his voice match the sexiness of every other part of his being? Of course. Had God realized he'd given an abnormally large chunk of good genes all to one person? Height, charm, good looks and wealth all wrapped up in one sexy package. Seemed unfair.

"Joe." It was all she could manage.

"It's good to see you. I was thrown off guard for a minute when I spotted you in there."

Laura took a slight step back. He was too close. Anything under a mile was probably too close.

"Well, thanks for getting us out." She waved her arm like she held a wand. "For doing whatever magic you did and working out the situation so no one got hurt."

Joe shrugged. "Just doing my job."

"Wow, a job?" She tried for light laughter, but it came out tense and brittle. "That's new, right? I didn't think you would ever need a job."

Joe looked over to the side of the bank where the press and bystanders had been roped off. Laura hadn't even realized they were there, but saw dozens of smartphones recording them. Recording everyone coming out of the bank.

"Let's go around to the side, so everything we say doesn't end up online." Joe walked away from the crowd, around a corner, leading Laura with a gentle hand at the small of her back.

She could feel his hand through her blouse as if it seared her. That small touch stole her breath.

And pissed her off.

She didn't want to react this way, didn't want to feel anything when he touched her except maybe disgust. She stepped away from his hand, glad there was now no one else around to witness any of this.

"How have you been? It's been a long time," he said when they were out of earshot of everyone else.

She just stared at him. She wasn't sure what to say. If this was some sort of police follow-up to make sure she was okay, then that was fine. Otherwise she didn't want to make small talk with him as if they were old friends who had just lost touch.

"Seeing you here, like I said, it sort of threw me," he continued. He shifted a little nervously, but his friendly smile never wavered.

"Well, you did great. You were amazing with Ricky and Bobby."

He rolled his eyes. "Wasn't up against mastermind criminals there, that's for sure."

"They still had guns and could've hurt a lot of people. So I'm glad you were able to get them to surrender. Although they seem pretty mad at you for it."

They stared at each other for long moments. Laura felt the flare of attraction she knew was only one-sided and realized she had to get out of here. All the damage repair she'd done over the last six years was crumbling down in mere minutes in Joe's presence.

She took another step back. "I've got to go. I gave my statement to one of the policemen inside the bank, so he cleared me to leave."

His blue eyes seemed to bore into her. She looked away.

"Laura—"

"It was nice talking to you. Glad you seem to have a job you like. Take care, Joe." There. A reasonable, polite statement.

Now get out.

She took another step back and to the side. Her car was around the other corner, but she'd walk around the entire block out of her way if it meant she could make a clean getaway from Joe.

"Laura, let me take you out to dinner tonight."

"No." She knew she was too abrupt, but reasonable, polite statements seemed beyond her now.

Joe put his large hands out, palms up, in an endearing, entreating manner. "Just to catch up. It's been what, six years? It's great to see you."

She shook her head. "I can't."

"Why?" He took a step closer and she immediately took a step back. She had to keep some sort of physical distance from him. "Are you married? In a relationship?"

"No."

The attraction was still there for her. She didn't want it to be, but it was. Laura had done her best not to think about him for the last six years while also having to admit that the man had shaped her life like no one else.

Because of him the whole course of her career and even her thought patterns had changed.

One brief, cruel conversation with him six years ago had made her into the woman she was today.

"Then why?"

Was he really asking this? Couldn't figure it out on his own? "I just can't. There's too much…" She almost said *ugliness*, but that reminded her too much of what he'd said to her that night. "There's too much time and distance between us."

Faster than she would've thought possible his hands whipped out and grabbed both of her wrists. He held them gently but firmly. "There's still a spark between us."

Laura's laugh was bitter, unrecognizable to her. She wasn't a bitter person. Even though Joe's words six years ago had shredded her she'd never let herself become bitter, even toward him.

"Spark was never the problem, at least not on my end." She wrenched her arms out of his hands. "The fact that you thought I wasn't attractive enough to be in a relationship with you, *that* was the problem."

Chapter Four

Joe watched Laura hurry down the corridor between the bank and the coffee shop next door then round a corner. He wanted to run after her, to stop her, to explain.

To explain what, exactly? That he'd been a jerk six years ago?

Seemed evident she already understood that pretty clearly.

How about that he'd been a fool? That he'd realized long ago how stupid he'd been to let her go? That Laura's honesty, authenticity and love for life had been something he'd missed day in and day out for six years?

Perhaps he could tell her that he'd nearly called her dozens of times. Had stood outside her house in Colorado Springs like a stalker more times than would make anyone comfortable. That every time he got a little tipsy out with friends it was her number he wanted to drunk-text.

That he'd never stopped dreaming about her even when he'd forced his mind not to think of her while awake.

When he'd seen her holding that baby today, an icy panic had gripped his heart. Because she'd been in danger, but more because he'd thought he'd been too late to right his wrongs. She'd met someone else and fallen in love and made sweet beautiful babies.

When Brooke had stood up and taken the baby from Laura and he'd realized they weren't Laura's children, something had snapped into place for him. He hadn't realized it at that moment but he sure as hell realized it now.

He wasn't waiting any longer. He had to make things right with Laura. He didn't know why he'd waited until now to start trying.

By her own admission Laura wasn't married or seeing anyone. Joe planned to change that. If he could convince her to forgive him. That was a huge if.

But he planned to try. Fate, in the form of two moronic bank robbers, had brought them back together. It gave him the perfect opening to ease back into her life, to apologize in every way he knew how. And think of a few new creative ways if needed.

That would be his pleasure.

And if he couldn't talk her into giving their relationship a try, he could at least prove himself a friend to her. To erase from his mind forever that haunted, shattered look that had taken over her features when he'd let the press and gossip columns get the best of him and convince him he could do better than Laura Birchwood.

News flash: he couldn't.

He wouldn't blame her if she would never become romantically involved with him again, but he was going to try to convince her.

Starting tonight. He'd take a note from his get-whatever-I-want past playbook and follow her home. He'd charm her into going out with him.

He began walking back toward the bank. As soon as he cleared the building he could feel eyes on him. Press and bystanders were all taking pictures and recording the scene and him. Most weren't looking at him, just knew something exciting had happened at the bank.

But a few people in the crowd knew who he was. He could feel eyes following him in particular. It never failed to make him a little uncomfortable when people seemed to be hostage "groupies."

Derek, Lillian and Jon were talking to the sheriff when Joe walked up to them.

"We'll get the rest of the statements and proceed from there. It looks like the manager and assistant manager of the bank were the only ones injured and neither of them seriously." Jon nodded at Joe in greeting.

That was good. Hopefully the judge would take that into consideration when sentencing Ricky and Bobby, aka Mitchell and Michael Goldman.

"Lillian, Joe and I are going to head back to Omega HQ since you seem to have everything under control," Derek said, shaking the sheriff's hand.

"I'm going to stay around for the rest of the evening, if that's okay," Jon told the sheriff. "I work crisis management in a lot of cases for Omega and may be able to help you with press or any questions you have."

"We appreciate Omega sending you so quickly." Sheriff Richardson turned to Joe. "And we especially appreciate what you did in there. That you kept it from becoming bloody."

Joe shook the man's outstretched hand. "The Goldman brothers didn't really want to harm anybody in my opinion. They just made some bad decisions, which led to panicking and more bad decisions."

"Either way, me and my men are thankful for how the situation got handled today. I'm sure the hostages are, too."

Jon and Sheriff Richardson turned back toward the bank while Lillian, Derek and Joe began walking the blocks to where the helicopter had been landed.

"Alright, mission completed. Let's get home," Derek said.

Lillian nodded as they began to make their way up to the roof. Joe wanted to move quicker, to rush them, so he could get back to HQ and back to Laura. But he knew it wouldn't accomplish anything but cause them to dig into why he was in such a hurry. Joe was rarely in a hurry.

But getting to Laura, seeing her again? Touching her again in any way she would allow…

His urgency continued to grow.

He wanted to give her as little time as possible to fortify walls against him. That was why he was going to see her tonight.

Derek rode in the copilot seat next to Lillian, leaving Joe in the back by himself. That was fine. He felt some of the pressure inside him start to loosen as the overhead blades began to whirl and they became airborne.

"Hey, did anyone get video footage of Matarazzo in just his undies?" Lillian asked. "I didn't have a great view from where I was in the elevator shaft."

"Oh, you better believe it, sister." Derek's amusement was obvious. "I wouldn't want anyone at Omega to miss that."

Joe didn't even care.

LAURA WALKED INTO her small house in Fountain, Colorado, just south of Colorado Springs, an hour and a half after leaving Joe standing by the side of the bank building.

What a day. She didn't know which shook her more, two idiots running around with guns or facing Joe again.

She was a liar; she knew which shook her more. But she had kept it together, talked to him reasonably, calmly, like an adult.

And then turned and ran away like a five-year-old.

Laura sighed. She could've handled the situation with more aplomb, more pride, more professionalism—all of which seemed to have evacuated her presence when Joe entered her personal space. Thank goodness that only happened every six years so far.

She changed out of her business suit of a black pencil skirt and blazer coupled with a white blouse and slipped on brown leggings and a chunky-knit, cream-colored sweater. She looked at herself in the mirror. The person she saw looking back at her didn't cause her to cringe or turn away. Laura knew who she was. Not gorgeous by any stretch of the imagination, but she was reasonably attractive—brown hair, hazel eyes, a nose just a touch too small, lips a touch too big. Her five-foot-four-inch frame was just average. As a matter of fact everything about her looks was just sort of average.

Nobody was going to stop and follow her down the

streets whistling and catcalling because of her looks, but no one was ever going to run away screaming either.

It was only when you placed her against the backdrop of someone as gorgeous as, say, Joe Matarazzo, that anyone looked at Laura and used words like plain Jane, doleful, or *reverse beauty and the beast.*

All of those had been said about her when she'd dated Joe. Mostly by people in gossip blogs. Joe had told her to ignore all press, so she had. She thought he had, too. Until he'd proved otherwise by ending their relationship so suddenly.

That had hurt, mostly because the blow had been so unexpected.

When they'd first met she'd expected it. She'd worked nights waiting tables so she could go to law school during the day. He'd come in with a couple of buddies and flirted outrageously. She'd laughed him off, not taking him even the least bit seriously.

After all, how could someone who looked like Joe Matarazzo be interested in someone like her?

But he'd pursued her. Her twenty-three-year-old, slightly socially awkward self hadn't had a chance against Joe when he'd set his sights on her.

And she would admit, he didn't have to pursue her long. She gave in. When else would she get the opportunity to have a fling with someone like Joe? He'd been handsome and charming and popular, and the sparks had flown.

She'd been expecting the blow then, too. Once he'd gotten what he'd wanted physically, she thought he'd be gone. But he'd stayed.

Laura knew she had her perks: she was focused and

driven when it came to her career, but also cared about people. She tried to be honest and live by the golden rule. But she definitely wasn't someone who would be labeled as witty, or the life of the party, or a breathtaking beauty.

She didn't think she'd keep Joe's attention for long. But when weeks had turned into months and he was still always around, she'd started to believe their relationship was going somewhere.

She'd let her guard down. Let herself believe he was falling for her the way she was falling for him.

That had made the unexpected blow so much harder to take when it finally came. When he'd called off the relationship after they'd been together just over six months, with no warning at all.

Laura straightened as she focused on her reflection in the mirror, smoothing her sweater down. That was all in the past. No more thinking about Joe Matarazzo. Fate had dumped them together today, but that didn't mean anything.

The doorbell rang and Laura checked the clock. It must be little Brad next door. The seven-year-old sometimes came over to play video games on the weekends. His father was deployed in the military and his mom had her hands full with his three-year-old twin sisters.

Good. An hour's worth of Mario Kart would cure whatever ailed her.

She bounded down the stairs and swung by and opened the door, not stopping to look at Brad on her way to the kitchen. She needed some fortification if she was going to take on the neighbor boy. He was a fiend at the driving game.

"Brad, come on in. I'm going to throw a frozen pizza in the oven. It's all over for you tonight, kiddo. No amount of coins or stunt boosts are going to save you this time."

"I'm not sure what stunt boosts are, but I guess I better learn if they're needed to save me."

Not Brad's voice. Joe's voice. Laura dropped the pizza on the counter and walked back to her foyer.

"What are you doing here?"

"You don't sound as excited to see me as you did about seeing Brad." Joe's smile was charming, gorgeous. Laura had to force herself not to give in to the appeal, to keep her expression cool.

"That may be because the most hurtful thing Brad has ever done to me was launch a red koopa shell at my Mario Kart vehicle." She turned back toward the kitchen. "And even then he felt pretty bad about it."

"Laura..."

Turning her back to him had been a mistake. His long legs had closed the distance between them quickly and silently and now he was right behind her.

"What do you want, Joe?"

He touched her gently on the arm. It was totally unfair that she could still feel sparks of attraction where his skin touched hers. She didn't turn around.

"Seeing you today... I just wanted to say I'm sorry. I—"

"Apology accepted. You can go."

It hurt Laura to say the words. But it was better this way.

Joe was quiet for a long time before coming around to stand in front of her. "You have every right not to ever talk to me again. But let me just take you out one time. Let the person I've become in the last six years talk to the person you've become."

He reached down and grasped her hands; she could feel his thumbs stroking the back of her palms. "We're not the same people we were then, Laura. I don't expect you to get involved with me, but I would appreciate it a great deal if you would just let me take you out one time to apologize for my stupidity then."

His clear blue eyes were sincere. His face pleading, engaging. A curl of sandy brown hair fell over his forehead as he gazed down at her, and hope lit his features. Laura couldn't resist him when he was like this. Nobody could resist him when he was like this.

Like you were the center of his world.

But she'd been here before. She couldn't forget that. This time she'd take some control. She thought about just cooking the pizza she'd gotten out and feeding them both that. Letting him say what he had to say. But being trapped inside a house with him where there was a bed, or a bathtub, or the couch or the kitchen floor nearby was probably not a good idea.

"Fine," she told him, her breath escaping her body when his worried look turned into one of joy, lighting up his eyes. "I'll go out with you. But no place fancy. No romance and candles. As a matter of fact, I'll pick the place."

His suppressed half smile only added to his charm. Damn him. "Yes, ma'am."

She poked him in his chest. "And you keep your hands to yourself. You got that?"

His smile turned downright wicked.

She was in trouble.

Chapter Five

Joe seemed different. An hour later, sitting in the restaurant where they'd first met when she'd been a waitress and he'd come in with his friends after a night of partying, she had to admit he wasn't the same man she'd known six years ago.

He'd grown up.

Although he was two years older, in their previous relationship Laura had always been the more mature one. Now Joe seemed more balanced, more focused. She had no doubt of the cause for that.

"So Omega Sector, huh?" She leaned back against the booth across from him, having finished her meal, and took a sip of her wine. "I never would've pegged you for law enforcement."

"I didn't have much education, but I had a pretty developed skill set. I decided to see if I could put that to use."

Laura raised her eyebrow. She definitely remembered certain skills Joe had, but was pretty sure that wasn't what he meant. She tugged at her sweater feeling a little overheated. "Oh yeah?"

"I had a very observant, honest friend who pointed

out to me that I had more potential than to just be a trust fund baby. That I had skills in observation, listening, adaptability. That I was calm under pressure and that people genuinely seemed to like me."

Laura's eyes snapped to his face. *She* had said that to him. Had truly believed it. But she hadn't dreamed he would take her words and change his whole life.

"Wow," she whispered.

"Yeah, wow." He took a sip of his wine. "I repaid the favor by saying some of the cruelest, most ridiculous words that have ever left my mouth. Ever left *anybody's* mouth."

"Joe..."

He reached over and grasped her hand. "I want to make sure you know I'm sorry. That a day has not gone by where I haven't regretted those words. I've nearly called you or come to your house dozens of times, but—"

"Joe." She stopped him, shaking her head. "You were right. About us. About me not being the right type of woman for you. You were right."

"No." The hand not holding hers hit the table just loud enough to cause her to jump. "I was not right. Whatever the opposite of right is, that's what I was."

Laura couldn't help but smile. "Wrong?"

Joe laughed and sat back, releasing her hand, the tension easing from his face. "Yeah, wrong. Wrong to let myself be convinced of it, wrong to say it, wrong not to have apologized for it before now."

Laura was not one to hold a grudge. She'd learned long ago that bitterness against him only hurt herself and had let it go.

"Well, I accept your apology and even appreciate it. What you said, what those gossip sites said, helped me turn a corner. I realized I was never going to be beautiful, but that I could at least make more of an effort. Style my hair, wear more makeup, make more attractive clothing choices."

Joe's jaw got tight as he studied her. "You look great now, but you were fine just like you were."

"I was…comfortable just like I was. But I realized when I started my own law firm how important a professional image was. Like it or not, studies show that attractiveness affects your level of trustworthiness and credibility with people. I needed to change my image."

His expression grew pained. "Laura—"

She smiled at him. She wasn't trying to make him feel bad—the opposite in fact. She wanted him to know that what had happened between them had helped her. "I'm just trying to say that I grew from the situation, like you did."

"But—"

"No more talk about the past. Okay? Or at least that part. We were young. We were stupid. Let's just agree and move on."

He looked like he was going to say something more but stopped and nodded.

Joe told her about some of the training he'd had to do to become an Omega Sector agent and some of his exploits since joining them. Laura told him about her law firm and how it had grown over the last year.

The words flowed easily. Lightly. This was how it had always been between the two of them: comfortable, relaxed. Only when other people had entered the equation had it gotten difficult and complicated.

Laura became aware of eyes on them partway through their conversation but tried to ignore it. Someone like Joe always had eyes on him. How could women not stare, even if they didn't know who he was? But Laura didn't like it. Didn't like the thoughts that began to enter her head. Were they wondering what Joe was doing with someone like her?

Amazing how the blackness could creep in unbidden. No one had said anything; maybe no one was even thinking anything, but Laura could already feel her confidence plummet. She picked at the food she'd ordered, no longer able to enjoy the meal.

She couldn't do this again.

She wasn't mad at Joe, the opposite, in fact. Spending time with him just made her remember why she had fallen for him six years ago.

Which was also adding to her panic.

She'd been around him a little over an hour and she was already back to the person she'd been. Worried about her looks, about what people thought. How many different ways did she have to be told that she and Joe were from two different realms before she accepted it as the truth?

Somebody clicked their picture. The flash made Laura wince.

Joe turned calmly to the man. "Hi, we're having dinner if you don't mind." His voice was friendly but firm. Laura saw the manager heading toward their table to ward off any problems, but the man with the camera left.

It could've just been anyone who recognized Joe and wanted to snap his picture.

It could've been someone from a major gossip rag.

Either way Laura knew she couldn't stay. She put her napkin down beside her plate; she felt like she had a knot in her stomach that wouldn't ease. Joe studied her with concern.

"I'm sorry, but I can't do this. I can't be here with you, can't do this again. Thank you for dinner, thank you for the apology. I wish you the best, Joe."

She started to stand, but he grasped her hand before she could.

"Laura, you're panicking. Don't. Please." She felt his thumb brush over the back of her palm. "It was just a photograph and doesn't mean anything."

"No, what it was was a reminder. You are you and I am me. Our worlds aren't compatible. You would've thought I learned that lesson well six years ago."

"It doesn't have to be that way. I wasn't prepared tonight, but I can take measures to protect you from the press. From the gossip."

She tilted her head to the side. "Who's going to protect me against you, Joe?"

He gripped her hand more firmly. "I don't want you to protect yourself from me. You don't need to, because I'm not going to do anything that will cause you harm. I give you my word."

Laura shook her head. She believed that he meant it, but that didn't change anything. "I can't be the person who opened up to you so completely before. That person got crushed in the fray. I don't think she exists anymore."

"Then open up the woman who does exist." A moment of pain crossed his features. "I'm sorry. I know I hurt you badly. I wish I could take it all back."

Laura let out a sigh. "I'm not trying to make you feel bad, truly. It's just I don't know if I can open up to you. If I even want to." Didn't know if the price would be too high. "All I know right now is that it's been a long day. I need some space. Some time."

Joe stared at her for long moments. She knew he wanted to say more, wanted to plead his case. Part of her wanted him to, but she knew it could just lead to disaster.

He nodded and let go of her hand, leaning back in his seat. "Okay, you're right. I'm trying to rush this. To force it. And that's not what I meant to do at all. So we'll take it slow."

"Joe…" She wanted to tell him to just leave her alone for good, that she didn't want him around her, but couldn't do it. She couldn't force herself to say the words.

Because she knew they would be a lie.

He leaned forward pinning her with his blue eyes. "I'm not giving up, Laura. I'll let you go now, but I want you to know I'm not giving up."

LAURA THOUGHT ABOUT his words the entire way home, thankful she'd had the foresight to insist they drive separate cars to the restaurant. She thought about the intensity of his blue eyes and the way his entire body had leaned toward her as he told her he wasn't giving up.

She had no doubt he meant what he said.

But despite the attraction fairly simmering in her blood for him, Laura knew she couldn't go through it again. Joe Matarazzo might be the most handsome, charming, wealthy man she'd ever met, but he was no good for her.

She would have to make him understand. Make him see that she wasn't just playing hard-to-get. That her very survival depended on him choosing to leave her, and the life she'd built, alone.

But was that really what she wanted? Deep down did she hope for something different? For him to pursue her again as he once had?

She had pushed those types of thoughts immediately out of her head for so long that she could no longer even answer them honestly. Even to herself.

She wished the universe would send her some sort of sign.

It did, with a vengeance.

One moment she was driving down a relatively deserted patch of Highway 87, the next another car had slammed into the back driver's side of Laura's vehicle.

She screamed as her head struck the side window and struggled to hold on to consciousness, her vision immediately blurry. Her car flew out of control, spinning in a sideways direction almost off the road. She jerked the steering wheel but it didn't seem to do any good. She looked over her shoulder and found the vehicle that had hit her still pushed up against her Toyota.

Was the other car trying to ram her toward the safety rail on the side of the road?

Laura glanced in that direction for just a second. She knew this part of Highway 87 pretty well. The drop past that safety rail was steep. She would definitely flip if she went over the edge.

Looking back again at the car still locked against hers, Laura slammed on the brakes with both feet, causing her car to stop and the other one to separate from it and speed past. Once her car wasn't trapped by the other, Laura had control of the steering again and overcorrected, causing her to swing around backward and land hard up against the rail. Her head flew back the other way from the force of the hit.

Her breath sawed in and out of her chest. That driver had to be drunk. Idiot had almost killed them both.

In the rearview mirror Laura noticed the other driver tap the brakes and wondered if the close call with death had sobered the person up enough to realize what they had done. But the car sped farther away. Laura tried to get a glimpse of the license plate but her vision was too blurry.

She sat for long minutes trying to take inventory of herself. Nothing seemed to be broken. She definitely had a knot on her head where she'd cracked it against the window and her hands were shaking. But it all seemed to be pretty minor bumps and bruises, considering she'd almost been run off the road. Overall, she considered herself lucky.

An older couple pulled up behind her—well, in front of her since her car was facing backward—and immediately got out to help. They opened the passenger side door and assisted her across the front seats and out of the car. The police were called and at the scene soon enough.

Laura was tempted to call Joe. He would still be nearby and she knew he would come immediately.

She also knew there was no way he wasn't going to end up in her bed if she did that.

She would attend to her bumps and bruises herself. At least right now they were just on her body; if she called Joe she was sure he'd soothe all her physical aches. But the ones he'd leave on her heart wouldn't be so easily healed.

Chapter Six

Convincing Laura to let him back into her life wasn't going to be as easy as Joe had hoped. Not that he had really expected it was going to be easy. As a matter of fact, he would've sworn before Friday there was no way in hell she was ever going to let him back into her life. That she would punch him if he ever dared show his face around her again.

Although he had known she was a better person than that. She had even accepted his apology. But he knew when she left the restaurant she had no intention of ever seeing him again. The person who had snapped their picture had spooked her. Maybe she could agree that Joe wouldn't be cruel, wouldn't say unkind things to or about her, but the press?

Joe tended to be the press's darling, but he knew they could often be harsh and callous. They certainly had been to Laura.

What Joe said to her when they broke up had been unkind, but what the gossip sites had published about her while they had dated had been downright brutal.

Once he and Laura had been seen together multiple times over a few weeks, one blog had gone so far as to print a picture of her and point out her top ten flaws. Publicly and without mercy. He hoped she had never seen that, but wouldn't have been surprised if she had.

Joe had been stupid enough to begin to believe some of what was printed. The digs against her that pointed out her flaws. He would never be so idiotic as to pay any attention to gossip sites now—particularly since he knew how much those sites got wrong—but had let it get the better of him then. Let the sites, and some stupid friends who had his ear, convince him that Laura just wasn't the right one for him.

Because it was much easier to dwell on that than to face the real scenario: he'd been falling for Laura.

Complete and utter panic because he had been falling so hard and so quickly for her. She'd been real, so full of life, and honest and passionate about helping people. She'd had a smile that lit up an entire room.

She still did. Still was. All of those things.

Had he really ever thought Laura unattractive six years ago?

No, never. No matter what the gossip sites had said about her physical appearance, Joe had always found himself overwhelmingly attracted to her. The passion between them had sizzled. Looking at other women had been unappealing.

And honestly, another reason why he'd panicked. Because for the first time he was in a relationship where he wasn't thinking about who his next conquest would be. Wasn't feeling trapped or penned in, when he knew he should be.

He was too young for love. So when his friends and random websites who didn't give a damn about Joe or his happiness had told him Laura wasn't good enough, he'd latched onto that idea.

He shook his head now at the idiot he'd been then.

Getting back into Laura's life wasn't going to be easy, not that he blamed her one bit. But like he'd told her Friday at the restaurant: he wasn't giving up.

He'd sent flowers Saturday, stargazer lilies, her favorite. On Sunday he'd had four pints of Ben & Jerry's ice cream delivered to her house, picking out the ones he remembered she'd always loved when they'd sat on her couch watching football games together.

He didn't expect either of these gestures to make a difference; Laura would see straight through them. But they were a start.

It was Monday morning now and he was walking into the room that held his desk at Omega, an open area where most of the Critical Response Division team members' desks were arranged. The team wasn't at them a lot, but it was the home base. The floor-to-ceiling windows of the room provided a gorgeous view of the Rocky Mountains to the west.

At least they normally did. Today they were covered—completely, top to bottom—with photocopied images of Joe in his well-fitting, black boxer briefs. Hundreds of them, all different shots from the scene at the bank when he'd been proving to Ricky and Bobby he was unarmed.

And—*oh joy*—they all had comments. Most of them read something asinine like "he's unarmed but his weapon works just fine."

The audible snickers from the nearby desks surrounded Joe as he walked over to the pictures, studying all the different shots.

He knew everyone was waiting to see if he was going to get angry or embarrassed. He wasn't.

He took one down and turned to face his colleagues. "Hey, I'm going to use these to re-cover my bathroom if that's okay with everyone. Most gorgeous wallpaper I've ever seen."

The laughs burst out then.

"Yeah, you guys are a riot." But he smiled, beginning to take the sheets down. "I should leave these up here. It would serve you all right."

Lillian, along with Ashton Fitzgerald, another SWAT member, jumped up to help him. "It was just such a memorable occasion." Lillian smiled at him. "We wanted to make sure everyone at Omega had the pleasure of experiencing it."

Steve Drackett, head of the Critical Response Division, walked out of his office and looked around. He rolled his eyes. "I don't even want to know what this is all about. I need SWAT members in my office. We've got a situation."

Ashton, Lillian and a few others turned to follow Steve. "By the way, Joe, nice skivvies." Steve winked at him.

Joe watched as they left, glad, not for the first time, that he wasn't a part of the SWAT team. Let them go shoot all the bad people. Joe had to write up the report from Friday anyway.

He hadn't gotten very far in the paperwork when his phone chirped with an incoming email.

Sarah Conner, an old girlfriend.

Wow, that was a blast from the past. He and Sarah had dated briefly not quite a year ago. Nothing serious, just a few weeks of a good time. She hadn't expected anything from him nor had he expected anything from her. She'd ended it because she desired to have someone around more often and Joe couldn't be since he traveled so much for his job. Everything had been on good terms although they hadn't really spoken since.

He opened the email, not sure exactly what he was expecting. Maybe her telling him that she'd found someone and planned to get married. Instead, the email contained a brief, cryptic message.

I need to talk to you. It's important. Come to my place ASAP.

Joe wasn't sure what to do with the email. On one hand he wasn't at all interested in seeing Sarah, not romantically at least. But it sounded like maybe she needed some sort of help.

He called Sarah's number but didn't get an answer. He'd been to her place enough times to know where it was in south Colorado Springs.

Not quite as far south as Fountain, where Laura lived, but definitely in that general direction. He would go to Sarah's house, then after he took care of whatever she needed, he would stop by and say hello to Laura in person.

Maybe offer her one of his colleagues' pieces of art. She'd love that. He could use it to prove he didn't take himself so seriously anymore.

That would probably go further than flowers or ice cream.

Regardless he'd be able to see Laura. Even if it was only for a few minutes, he'd take it.

Joe let one of Steve Drackett's secretaries—all beautiful, intelligent women—know that he was going out to deal with some residual issues with Friday's case and would be back later in the afternoon. They knew how to contact him if there was a hostage situation for which he was needed. But it sounded like SWAT was going to be busy somewhere else.

Joe's Jaguar F-TYPE sports car made short work of the miles to Sarah's house. Although he was curious about what Sarah had to say, he was anxious to see Laura.

He pulled up to Sarah's house, a nice chalet-style place off on its own. It didn't look like anyone was home, which only made Joe happier. But he'd driven all the way here; he might as well at least try to see what Sarah wanted.

Joe parked and bounded up to the steps leading to Sarah's front door. He rang the doorbell and waited. Nothing. He rang it again, but received no response.

Well, he could at least tell Sarah he tried.

He knocked just in case the doorbell wasn't working and was surprised when the door pushed open under his knuckles. It hadn't been completely closed.

He knocked again, still staying outside, but stuck his head in slightly and called out.

"Sarah, you around? It's Joe."

Nothing.

Something wasn't right here. Joe took the slightest step inside.

"Hey, Sarah? You emailed me to come over. I just wanted to see what's going on."

Still no answer.

Joe went back to his car and got his Glock from the glove compartment. Although he didn't use it often, it was still his official Omega weapon. He was licensed to use it. Trained to use it.

He prayed he didn't need to use it now.

He ran back to the door. "Sarah, I'm coming inside. I'm armed. Let me know if you're in there so no one gets hurt."

Still nothing. Joe went from being afraid he might be walking in on Sarah in the shower to hoping it. Embarrassing, but at least she would be alive to be embarrassed.

He checked all the ground floor rooms first. When he found nothing in the kitchen or living room he slowly made his way upstairs.

He saw her immediately when he entered the master bedroom. Sarah laid sprawled facedown on the bed, naked, arm over her face as if she was sleeping off a hangover.

Except for the blood that had pooled all around her.

He rushed over to check for her pulse, just in case, but knew as soon as he felt the coolness of her skin that she was definitely dead, probably had been for hours.

Joe took a few deep breaths to center himself, focus on what had happened. He was an Omega agent, had seen dead bodies before, but never someone he'd known so personally.

Training took over. This was now a crime scene, and that definitely wasn't Joe's area of expertise. He needed to call in the specialists. Both local law enforcement and Omega.

He speed-dialed Steve Drackett's direct number.

"Joe, what's going on?" Steve said in way of greeting. Joe didn't call his direct line very often and only when there was a problem.

But there'd never been one like this before.

"Steve, I've got an issue. Dead woman, an ex-girlfriend of mine. I got a message from her earlier asking me to come by but when I got here she was dead. Murdered."

"You sure it was a murder?"

"Unmistakable."

He heard Steve's muttered expletive. "Okay, call the locals and get them there. I'll send Brandon and Andrea to see if they pick up on anything the locals might miss."

Brandon Han was the most brilliant profiler Omega had. Joe knew both him and Andrea Gordon, a talented behavioral analyst who was now Brandon's partner on most cases. Having them here would help, or at the very least help Joe's peace of mind.

"Thanks, Steve."

"Don't touch anything, okay? You should probably walk back out the way you came and wait for the locals outside."

Joe nodded, still looking at Sarah, then realized his boss couldn't see him. "Yeah, okay."

Steve sighed. "I'm sorry, Joe. It's always hard when it's someone you know. Even an ex."

Joe said his goodbyes and then called 911, reporting the death. Then he stood staring at Sarah for a long time.

He hadn't really felt much for the woman, besides a physical attraction. He wished he knew more about her, who he should call, family or whatever, but he didn't. The police would have to handle that.

Who would've wanted to kill Sarah? She was an accountant, or in public relations or something like that. Not a job that tended to develop enemies.

Had she known about the danger? Is that why she had emailed Joe? The cryptic message she'd sent didn't provide many clues.

Finally he did what Steve had suggested and moved outside to wait for the locals. He would need to identify himself as law enforcement and let them know why he was here. Otherwise an armed man at a murder scene tended to make cops pretty nervous.

Joe stood leaning against his car, still trying to wrap his head around this entire situation, when the locals came speeding in, sirens blaring. Four separate squad cars and an ambulance. Must be a slow day around town.

Joe had his Omega credentials out in his hand, extended so the officers could see that he clearly did not mean them any harm. The men stopped to talk to him and he explained the situation, gave them Sarah's info, then waited as three of them rushed in. The other two stayed with Joe, hands noticeably near their sidearms.

When the three men exited Sarah's house they were moving much less quickly. There was no hurry; nothing could be done to help her now. The officer in charge nodded at the two men who'd been tasked with babysitting Joe while the others were inside.

"Is the coroner on his way?"

"Yeah."

"Okay, let's rope this area off. Neighbors are going to start wondering what's going on."

The man in charge turned to Joe. "I'm Detective Jack Thompson. So you work for Omega Sector. Were you here on official business? Something to do with a case?"

"No. I used to date the victim, about a year ago. She emailed me this morning, asked me to come by."

One of Thompson's eyebrows lifted suspiciously. "Is that so? Did things end badly between you two when you broke up?"

"No, we were never very serious. Neither of us was upset when we decided it wasn't working out."

"I see." Officer Thompson jotted a couple sentences down in his notebook. "And did you and Ms. Conner talk to each other much since the breakup?"

"No, maybe once or twice, but not really that I remember."

"But she just happened to email you this morning and asked you to come by?" Disbelief clearly tinted the man's tone.

Joe didn't take offense to the question. He could admit it was a little weird that he hadn't spoken with Sarah for months then the day she contacted him, she winded up dead.

"Yes."

Thompson studied Joe's car for a moment before turning back to Joe. The nice vehicle obviously wasn't winning Joe any points with the detective. "What exactly do you do for Omega Sector, Mr. Matarazzo?"

"Joe is one of the finest hostage negotiators we have." The sentence came from behind him. Joe turned to find Brandon Han and Andrea Gordon.

Brandon showed his credentials to Officer Thompson. "We'll need to get inside, if that's possible."

Thompson's lips pursed and his eyes narrowed at Joe. "Fine. But I'm going in to supervise, make sure everything is handled correctly. Please stick around Agent Matarazzo, in case we have any more questions." He left to enter the house.

"Sorry about your friend, Joe," Andrea said, touching him on the arm.

"Thanks," he told the striking blonde. "And thanks for coming, you guys."

Brandon shook his hand. "No problem. We're going to go inside, see if we spot anything the locals might miss. Will you be okay out here?"

"Yeah, I'm fine. You guys do whatever you need to do to help with the case." He watched as Brandon led Andrea toward the front door, a protective hand on the small of her back.

Joe leaned back against his car and got comfortable. This was going to take most of the day; Officer Thompson had just started with his questions, and didn't seem interested in making this easy or comfortable for him. Joe wasn't going to be able to see Laura as he'd hoped. That was probably for the best; he didn't want to drag her into this anyway.

Chapter Seven

By Wednesday afternoon Laura was cursing Joe Matarazzo's name. Damn the man. Damn him because for just a split second she thought he had really changed. That he wasn't the selfish playboy he once had been.

After the accident on Friday, her aches had made her want to forget all about Joe. But then the flowers—or more importantly the fact that he'd remembered her favorite type of flowers were stargazer lilies—had caused her to think maybe Joe really had changed. Then Sunday the ice cream had arrived.

She had to admit the frozen stuff—again, all her favorite flavors—had melted her heart a little bit. Brought back memories of their time together.

She had fully expected him to show up or call on Monday. When he hadn't, she'd been okay with it, and even wondered if she should call him and tell him thanks, but decided not to. When she didn't hear from Joe all day Tuesday, she'd gotten a little miffed.

By Wednesday at lunch, Laura was disgusted with herself and Joe. If he didn't want to see her again, that was fine. But he shouldn't act like he wanted to then not follow through.

And her? How many times was she going to fall for his sexy-boy appeal and wit?

There was nothing more dangerous than a man with charm. And Joe Matarazzo had it in spades.

And Laura was just an idiot to keep trusting his not-really promises. *I'm not giving up.* It had at least been true for two days.

So she could admit she was a little short-tempered when her law office phone rang at 4:00 p.m. Her assistant was gone for the day so Laura answered the phone herself, unable to keep her irritation out of her voice.

"Law Offices of Coach, Birchwood and Winchley."

"Wow, do you always answer the phone like you're considering strangling the entire neighborhood?"

Joe. It figured that he would know she was about to write him off for good and call now. The man's timing was impeccable.

"No, I'm just considering strangling one person."

That quieted him.

"I'm sorry I haven't been able to get in touch before now," he finally said. "Things have been complicated."

"Things tend to always be complicated with you, Joe."

He gave a short bark of laughter, but there didn't seem to be very much humor in it. "Well, believe it or not, I'm about to make things more complicated."

Laura rolled her eyes. "Why don't I just save you the trouble and stop you right there. I've been thinking over the last couple of days and realize I need to stand firm on what I told you at the restaurant on Friday. You and I are better off away from each other."

"Laura—"

"This isn't about the not calling." Damn it, why had she said that? Now it sounded like she was pissy because he hadn't called. Which, of course, she was. "I just think you and I should leave the past where it was."

"Laura—"

She didn't want to hear what he had to say, knowing if he gave her an excuse, she'd believe him. "Joe, I just can't go through the back-and-forth and you changing your mind."

"Laura, *stop*." She'd never heard that particular air of forcefulness in his tone. Joe tended to always be so laid-back most people forgot how strong he could be when needed. It was enough to stop her midthought. "I am willing to discuss this all with you at a later time, because there's no way I'm going to let you run away from us. But I'm not calling about that."

"Then what are you calling about?"

"Have you had a chance to watch the news or get online to read the news over the last couple of days?"

No. She'd been forcing herself to stay too busy to even allow herself to do anything as stupid as Google Joe Matarazzo. "I haven't, sorry. I've been too busy at work. Why?"

"I'm calling because I need you as a lawyer. A woman I used to know was murdered on Monday."

And now didn't she feel like an ass? "Oh my gosh, Joe, that's terrible. But you shouldn't need a lawyer just because someone you knew was murdered. Unless they caught you in the act."

"It wasn't quite that bad, but it wasn't good either."

Okay, that didn't sound promising. "Still—"

"And then it happened again this morning."

"What?"

"Another one of my ex-girlfriends was killed this morning."

As far as excuses went for not calling, two dead ex-girlfriends in two and a half days was a pretty good one. Laura heard noise in the background.

"Joe, where are you right now? Were you arrested?"

"They haven't brought any formal charges against me, but they're holding me for questioning. I'm at the Colorado Springs downtown station."

Laura had already grabbed her purse and blazer. "Don't say anything to anyone. I'll be right there."

"Laura, there's more. Both women contacted me just before they died. And I found both bodies."

That really didn't look good. "I'm coming, Joe. Just don't answer any questions until I get there. Okay?"

"Don't you need to ask me if I did it?"

"No. Just don't talk to anyone." Laura hung up the phone and rushed out of her office.

She didn't need to ask if Joe was guilty; she knew he wasn't. Joe might be a lot of things Laura didn't like, but he wasn't a killer.

IF JOE HAD been the police, he would've brought himself in for questioning too.

When he'd received a message this morning from Jessica Johannsen, another one of his ex-girlfriends, asking him to come to her town house in the north part of Colorado Springs, Joe hadn't thought anything bad about it. He figured she'd just heard about Sarah's death, read a newspaper or saw a news report, and wanted to talk to him. To make this about her instead of Sarah.

Jessica had always been sort of clingy, not someone capable of handling much emotional stress. And she loved drama. Joe had never really been interested in her, although that hadn't stopped him from dating her for a few weeks about two years ago.

Jessica had had delicate features with long black hair and icy blue eyes. The press had delighted at what a lovely pair they'd made.

She'd bored him silly.

But he hadn't been surprised to receive a message from her after Sarah's death. Jessica would want to be held, patted, to be the center of attention even though Sarah's death had nothing to do with her.

She'd asked him to meet her this morning in her text message. He'd texted her back and told her he was busy.

He hadn't wanted to take the time to see Jessica. He'd wanted to see Laura. After Monday's incident with Sarah, he hadn't been able to call or go see her as he'd planned. He'd spent all day on Tuesday cleaning up from Sarah's death: he'd talked to her parents since he'd been the one who'd found her body, he'd worked with Brandon and Andrea to see if they could gather any leads in figuring out who the killer might be.

He hadn't wanted to drag Laura into this whole sordid mess, so he hadn't contacted her at all.

But by Wednesday, all he'd wanted to do was see Laura. To just breathe in her smile and banter with her. It didn't need to be sexual; he just wanted to be with her.

So Jessica's text asking him to meet had just irritated Joe. When he told her no, and Jessica had sent another message telling him how scared she was, he'd decided to go see her. She'd just keep bugging him until he did.

As soon as Jessica's door floated open like Sarah's, Joe should've known there was a problem. He should've stopped right then, backed out and called the local police.

But he hadn't. Instead, just like with Sarah, he'd rushed inside to see what was going on because he didn't want to be there in the first place. He just wanted to talk to Jessica and leave.

He'd honestly thought Jessica would step out in some sort of outrageous negligee at any moment. Or even be completely naked wanting to seduce him. To get him to hold her while she cried fake tears about something that had nothing to do with her.

Jessica had been naked. But she'd been dead. Stabbed, just like Sarah.

All the lousy things he'd thought about her had rattled in his head as guilt swamped him. No one would ever hold Jessica Johannsen again as she cried fake or real tears.

Joe had called the locals immediately. He'd thought about calling Omega, too, but had stopped. Steve had helped him once but that's when it was just a random murder that happened to be Joe's ex.

Joe had no idea what it meant now that two of his exes were dead. But it wasn't a problem he was going to drag the Omega team into. He'd have to deal with this on his own.

Detective Thompson and the other local Colorado Springs police hadn't been nearly as friendly this time, not that Thompson had liked Joe much on Monday. They hadn't hauled him off in cuffs, but Thompson had left someone with Joe at the scene to watch him every minute. And once they were done with the crime scene, they'd asked to escort him to the station.

Escort, as in have him ride in the back of their squad car.

Then he'd sat in the interrogation room for two hours. He wasn't sure if they were trying to intimidate him, didn't know what to do with him, or what.

All he knew was that this looked bad. Really, really bad.

They hadn't arrested him, which was good. They did read him his rights, which was bad. They hadn't taken his phone—although that probably only happened if he was officially arrested—so he'd used his cell to call Laura. They hadn't told him he couldn't use it, so he'd figured he would. He had no idea how long he would be sitting in this room by himself, although he was sure someone was watching him, waiting to see what he would do.

Joe could've had a team of lawyers here, and would have if Laura had refused, but he wanted *her*. Other lawyers may be more vicious, more predatory in their methods of keeping their clients out of jail, but Laura believed in him.

Had always believed in him, even if she hadn't liked him.

And with all her intensity and intelligence he had no doubt she was a damn fine lawyer.

Detective Thompson entered the room. "Sorry to have kept you waiting, Matarazzo."

Joe highly doubted it.

"I heard you made a call. Got a lawyer."

Joe sat back. "It's my understanding that I'm allowed to have a lawyer if I'm being charged with something."

Thompson mirrored Joe's gesture, head tilting away, mouth downturned. "And it's my general experience that only people who are guilty need a lawyer. Besides, we haven't charged you with anything. You're free to go at any time."

Joe just wanted this to be over with. "I didn't kill Jessica Johannsen or Sarah Conner. I haven't had any contact with either of them for months."

"Interesting isn't it, though, that both women just happened to contact you right before they died?"

What could Joe say to that?

He shrugged. "*Interesting* isn't the word I would use, but yes, it's strange."

"And you happened to find both bodies. Another interesting factor."

"I'm law enforcement, Thompson. One of the good guys."

Thompson moved in closer, leaning his elbows on the table that sat between them. "I know you're law enforcement, Joe. Is it okay if I call you Joe?" Thompson didn't wait for an answer. "You're part of Omega Sector, one of the top law enforcement agencies in the country."

"That's right."

"How does a guy like you end up working for Omega?"

"What do you mean, 'a guy like me'?"

"You don't need a job, right? You've got plenty of money. So working for Omega as a negotiator is more like a hobby for you."

Joe pursed his lips. No, it wasn't a hobby for him.

But he could admit, most of the people in the Critical Response Division probably thought of him that way.

Seeing Joe's face, Thompson continued. "I'm just saying, you're on the Omega roster, but you're not really a member of the team, are you? I don't notice any of them beating down the door to get you out of here."

Joe forced himself not to show any emotion. "I thought I wasn't under arrest, so why would there be a need for them to come get me out?"

But Thompson's remark had hit home. Joe wasn't part of the team at Omega. He got along well with everyone, joked with them, did his job. But none of them would call him a true member of the team.

The other man smirked. "Okay, I'll just take you at your word that they'll be here if you're arrested." But he obviously didn't believe that was true. "So you're a part of Omega. There's a lot of stress in law enforcement. Has been known to make strong men snap. Do something stupid. Add that stress to trying to balance two women and it could get a little crazy."

"I wasn't dating either of those women. And I definitely wasn't dating both of them." Joe shook his head.

"C'mon, Joe. I see some of the gossip sites. Dating more than one woman at a time is definitely not out of your realm of possibility."

"Barking up the wrong tree, Thompson."

"Alright, so you weren't dating them both. I can buy that. But did date them separately at one time. Maybe they got together and decided that you owed them something. A man could be forgiven for a lot of things when women decide to start blackmailing him. Especially someone who has as much as you do."

Joe had talked through enough hostage situations to recognize what was happening here. Thompson was trying to lull him into a false sense of security.

Joe hoped he wasn't this bad when he was doing his job. Because Thompson's contempt for him was just one step below obvious.

Joe gritted his teeth. "No. As far as I know, both Sarah and Jessica were wealthy in their own right, or at least they were last time I saw either of them."

"There's wealthy and then there's *Matarazzo* wealthy. I'm sure they don't have as much money as you do, and felt like maybe they deserved some of your wealth."

"If they did, they never mentioned it to me or implied it in any way."

"Women can just get it in their heads, you know, that a man owes them something, even when a guy doesn't make any promises. Them working together to try to bring you down, that would have to make you angry."

Joe was beginning to genuinely not like this guy. "Neither Jessica nor Sarah had anything against me. They weren't working together to blackmail me, or anything else as far as I know. They didn't even run in the same circles so I can't imagine they even knew each other."

"You're right. The only thing that links Sarah Conner and Jessica Johannsen to each other is their relationship with you." The detective sat back and stared.

Joe realized that had been Thompson's point the whole time. And Joe had walked him right to it. He should've listened to Laura when she said not to answer any questions.

"Why don't you give me a rundown on where you

were on both Sunday and Tuesday nights between 3:00 and 6:00 a.m.?" Thompson asked.

He'd been completely alone. No one would be able to validate his whereabouts. Now he knew he definitely should've listened to Laura.

But damn it, he didn't kill those women. He had nothing to hide.

But the police clearly thought otherwise.

The door to the room opened. "My client won't be answering that, or any other questions, Detective Thompson. Either charge him or he's leaving."

Chapter Eight

"I need to go talk to my boss at Omega Sector." Joe gave Laura the address and she entered it into the GPS system on her phone.

He looked out the window while she drove, tension evident in his jaw and posture. Laura had never seen him so shaken. He tried to play it off, make it seem like it didn't really matter, but obviously it did.

He wasn't inhuman; two women he had known—intimately, no doubt—were dead. Just because he hadn't killed them didn't mean he didn't grieve.

Knowing he was the only link between the two women just added stress.

"What would you have answered Detective Thompson about your whereabouts?" she asked Joe as she took the interstate exit toward Omega Sector's headquarters in the northern section of Colorado Springs.

He shrugged. "I was home alone. Both nights. No alibi."

"That probably would have gotten you arrested, you know. That's why I told you not to answer any questions."

Joe turned to study her. "I didn't do it. That's why I thought I was safe answering questions."

"Yeah, well, the legal system doesn't always work that way. Especially when there are two dead young women and law enforcement is probably getting pressure to make an arrest."

"Not to mention the lead detective having a personal dislike and possible vendetta for me," Joe murmured. He shrugged. "Doesn't matter. I didn't do it. And if they had arrested me there would still be a killer out on the loose."

"Let's give the cops a chance to do their job. They'll find something that clears you, I'm sure."

She hoped so.

It wasn't long before they pulled up to the large office complex that housed Omega Sector's Critical Response Division. It was a pretty unassuming set of buildings on the outside. She noticed construction was in process on another section of the complex.

"You guys expanding?"

"No, the forensic lab is being replaced after an explosion a few months ago."

"Oh my gosh. An accident?"

"No, deliberate. The people responsible for the Chicago bombing last May were trying to get rid of some evidence we had held there."

It suddenly hit home just exactly how dangerous Joe's job was. Somehow she hadn't thought of that last Friday when she saw him in action. He'd talked to Ricky and Bobby like she'd seen him talk to dozens of other people: as though they were long-lost buddies and Joe had nothing in the world better to do than chat with them.

But he'd put his life on the line. Did that all the time. And all the money in the world wouldn't save him if some crazy hostage-taker just decided to shoot him.

She pulled into the parking garage where Joe directed her.

"Do you want to come inside with me?"

"Do you want me to?"

"Sure. Nothing is going to be said you aren't already aware of anyway."

They got out of the car and he led her through the main entrance where a security team checked her in. They walked through a maze of offices, most of them empty since it was nearly seven o'clock.

Joe pushed the door open to a room with four desks. Three were empty but at the fourth sat one of the most gorgeous women Laura had ever seen. Long, auburn hair with creamy smooth skin. Her posture impeccable in the black dress that seemed to both fit her like a second skin and be perfectly professional at the same time.

"Hey, Joe." She smiled at him, lips with a red gloss that looked as if it had just been applied moments before, revealing, of course, perfectly straight teeth. She stood up and walked over—in three-inch heels—to hug him. "I heard about your friends. I'm so sorry."

Joe hugged her back. Of course he would hug her back. What man in his right mind would not hug this woman back?

Laura stood there feeling more frumpy and dumpy by the nanosecond.

...Not the caliber of woman...

"Thanks, Cynthia." The detached and perfect Cynthia moved back to her desk. "I need to talk to Steve. I know he's still here since, well, he's always here. You're working late tonight."

She shrugged one delicate shoulder. "I'll let him know you're here. And…" She gestured toward Laura.

"Laura Birchwood. Lawyer and friend," Joe said.

Cynthia turned her smile on Laura. "Nice to meet you."

Laura did her best to smile back naturally although it probably came out looking more like a wounded animal in the throes of death. "Thanks."

Cynthia spoke on the phone for just a moment before standing and opening the door to her boss's inner office, leading them inside.

"Let me know if you need anything, Joe." Perfect smile again. Laura managed not to ask how she managed to look so perfect after working so late, especially in those heels. She glanced down at her own functionally comfortable flats.

The man behind the desk stood up and came around to shake Joe's hand. "I heard about the second victim. I'm sorry. I was worried when you didn't come in today."

"I've been a guest of the Colorado Springs PD for most of the day. This is Laura Birchwood, my friend and, as of earlier today, my lawyer."

"Steve Drackett." Laura shook the man's hand. He was older than Joe by at least a decade, but the slight blend of silver around his temples did nothing to detract from his handsomeness.

Was everyone who worked here gorgeous? At least it wasn't just the women.

Steve turned to Joe. "I'm sure Ms. Birchwood is an excellent attorney, but I would've sent Brandon Han in if you'd just called."

Joe shrugged, leading her to a seat and taking the one next to her as Steve went back behind his desk. "I didn't want to take up Omega resources for something that's personal. Plus, like you said, Laura is an excellent lawyer."

Steve looked at Joe for a long moment. "Is it okay if you and I talk for a few minutes privately?"

"If it's about Sarah's and Jessica's deaths, then just go ahead and say it in front of Laura. I don't have any secrets from her."

"Colorado Springs PD of course called asking about you and your record here."

Laura nodded. She wasn't surprised.

"I want to help out with the investigation, Joe," Steve continued. "We have resources and personnel they don't have."

"Thanks, Steve."

Steve grimaced. "Don't thank me too soon. I think it's better if you take a leave of absence while the investigation takes place. That way no one can accuse anyone here of favoritism."

If Laura hadn't been looking right at Joe she would've missed it. The tiny crack under his easy smile.

Steve's request had hurt him.

But Joe certainly didn't show it to Steve. "Yeah, sure. I understand."

The older man looked like he felt bad. "I'm sorry,

Joe. And I know you just donate your salary here to charity, but I'll have to suspend that, too. Officially you can't have anything to do with Omega while you're being investigated."

Joe stood, easy smile firmly in place, even the slightest crack Laura had noticed now gone. "I totally understand. You've got to do what's right for everyone overall."

"This will blow over in a week or two. They'll catch the real killer and everything will be back to normal. You'll be back in your rightful place here."

"Sure. Absolutely."

Steve grimaced again. "But right now I'll just have to ask you for your badge and sidearm."

LAURA TOOK JOE back to her house.

She wouldn't have done it if he had asked her to. Or tried to put a move on her. Or even turned his charming smile on her.

He hadn't done any of those things. After turning his badge and gun over to Steve Drackett, he shook the man's hand and even made a joke.

Steve had looked relieved. Glad Joe had understood what needed to be done.

And Joe did understand. But he also had pushed his own feelings aside and given Steve what he needed.

That's what Joe did, Laura realized, for his job and also in his life. Read what people needed and gave them that. It was probably why he was such a good hostage negotiator.

After they'd left he'd told her the address of where his car was parked, still at Jessica Johannsen's house.

He wanted Laura to drop him off there so he could make his way back home.

Despite everything that had happened between them, all the hurt he'd caused her six years ago, despite the fact that he'd probably slept with the gorgeous, perfect Cynthia and that his exes were dropping like flies, Laura could not send him home alone.

"We're at your house," Joe said as she pulled into her driveway. "I thought you were taking me to get my car."

"Change of plans. No one should have to be alone after the day you've had."

His gorgeous blue eyes became hooded. Laura could feel heat spreading through her at his look.

"Whoa, boy. This offer extends to my couch only. You need a friend. I can be that."

He stuck his bottom lip out in the most adorable pout she'd ever seen. She groaned inwardly. Having him spend the night here was such a bad idea.

"It's couch or nothing, Matarazzo."

He held his hands up in mock surrender. "Okay, couch."

She got him in, got them both fed and listened while he'd called someone and had them pick up his car from the crime scene. Then she gave him a pillow and blanket and the unopened toothbrush she had from her last dentist visit. She showed him the couch and said goodnight.

She did it all trying her damnedest not to really look at him. Not to really notice the way his eyes followed her wherever she went. To definitely not think about how good the lovemaking had been between them six years ago.

She went into her bedroom, locking the door behind her. She knew that if Joe wanted in, that flimsy lock wouldn't keep him out.

She wondered if she even wanted it to.

Joe tossed and turned most of the night.

His foot hung over the edge of Laura's couch, which was obviously not meant for someone of his height to sleep on. He was also thinking of Jessica and Sarah and their deaths. Of why someone would kill them.

He was thinking about how much it had sucked when Steve had asked for his badge. How important working at Omega had become to him, even if—and it was clear by how easily Steve had suspended him today—Joe wasn't really part of the inner team.

But mostly he was thinking of Laura sleeping in her room right up the stairs.

There wasn't anything Joe wanted more than to go in there. To make love to Laura until he could forget about death and evil and blood.

But she deserved more than that. He had no doubt he could get past that small click of a lock he'd heard. He had no doubt he could seduce her into letting him stay in her bed tonight.

But as much as he wanted that, he didn't want that. Didn't want to use her in that way. At one time he would've thought about nothing except the pleasure both of them would gain if he ignored that tiny lock. Now he didn't want to risk what could possibly be a future between them for one night of sex. No matter how mind-blowing it might be.

Each moment seemed to drag into the next as Joe

lay on the couch. He realized he needed Laura. Not for lovemaking, just to hold.

He needed to put his arms around her and thank the heavens that Laura was safe and sound and alive.

Suddenly, having distance between them, a wall—metaphorically and literally—separating them, seemed totally unacceptable. Joe wouldn't try to talk Laura into sex, but he'd be damned if he was going to stay out here when everything inside him demanded having her in his arms right now.

He was crossing the room before he finished the complete thought. His hand reaching for the doorknob was stopped by his phone buzzing from where it sat on the end table near the couch.

Joe almost ignored it. Wanted to ignore it. But after everything that had happened in the last few days, he couldn't.

Olivia Knightley's name lit his screen when he picked it up. Another ex—a small-time actress he had dated for a few weeks about six months ago. He didn't know why she was calling in the middle of the night, but at least she was calling. That meant she was alive.

"Olivia?"

No response. Joe could tell someone else was on the line, but no one was talking.

"Olivia? It's Joe. Are you okay?"

Still silence. A few moments later the call ended.

Joe immediately redialed but it went straight to voice mail.

Damn it. Was Olivia in trouble? Should he call the police? Send them to her house just in case?

He was about to do just that when a text came through.

Sorry. I thought I could talk, but I couldn't.

Joe immediately texted back. Are you okay?

Yes, I'm fine. I have some info about the two women who died that I think you should see.

Why would Olivia have information about Jessica and Sarah?

Okay, fine. Can you send it? Or can we meet tomorrow?

It can't be sent. I have to show you in person. I'm leaving at dawn for a film shoot. It really needs to be tonight. Can you come now? I'm at my Colorado Springs house.

Joe didn't like anything about this, but was willing to do whatever it took to stop this killer.

Fine. He texted back. I'll be there in thirty minutes.

Chapter Nine

Olivia Knightley owned multiple houses. Two of them in Colorado, since she loved to ski. Her chalet in Vail was one of the loveliest Joe had ever seen. You could ski right in and out of it.

Her other house, her personal home, was in Colorado Springs, just north of Laura's. It was small, in an unassuming neighborhood, and Joe knew Olivia rarely invited people there. It was her hideout. Somewhere the press didn't know about.

Telling him to come to that house assured Joe she was still alive. Very few people knew about that house.

He and Olivia hadn't ended their relationship on very good terms. Mostly because of the woman sitting next to him in the car as he drove.

It hadn't taken long for the observant actress to realize the man in her bed had feelings for someone else. When Olivia had finally figured out it wasn't anyone current, anyone she could fight, but the memory of Laura that held Joe's heart, she'd cut him loose.

She'd been right to do that. Olivia deserved someone who could give her his full attention and heart. Joe's had already been partially taken.

Joe hadn't wanted Laura to come with him to Olivia's house for a couple of different reasons. First, it could be dangerous. Whatever information Olivia had, Joe knew the killer wouldn't be happy about it. Might go to great lengths to stop Joe from getting it. He didn't want to take the chance of putting Laura in harm's way.

Second, he didn't want to introduce her to an ex-girlfriend. That could be just as ugly.

If Laura hadn't had the keys to the car in her bedroom, Joe would've sneaked out without her being any wiser. But they had been in her room and she'd immediately awakened when he'd come in her bedroom door.

She hadn't thought he was looking for keys and would've been correct if he hadn't received Olivia's call and text. He'd quickly explained the situation.

"Are you sure we shouldn't call the cops?" she said now.

"We will if things look suspicious, I promise. Olivia values her privacy, especially at this house. She won't want anyone knowing about it."

Olivia would be happy to see Laura. To see that she'd been right all along about there being another woman in Joe's mind and heart. She'd spot Laura for what she was immediately.

Joe's.

For privacy's sake, Olivia's house was away from others in the neighborhood, surrounded by trees and at the end of a dead-end street. But beyond that it looked just like many of the other houses: upper-middle class, two stories, normal. Olivia loved to feel normal.

Joe parked on the side of the street. "I don't suppose I

can talk you into staying in the car. Let me go see what Olivia knows and I'll be right out."

Laura was already opening her door. "Nope." She popped the *p* sound.

Joe wished he had the sidearm he'd been asked to turn in to Steve, or at least had made it home to get one of his other weapons. Walking up to Olivia's door he prayed it wouldn't be cracked open like Jessica's and Sarah's doors had been.

Thankfully it was closed. On it rested a note.

Joe, I'm up in my bedroom working on a script. Headphones. Just come on in.

"That's pretty stupid," Laura said. "What if it wasn't you coming to the door?"

Joe agreed but shrugged. "It's a pretty nice neighborhood, plus nobody knows she owns this house. She's pretty fanatic about her privacy when she's here. Her place to unwind, she calls it."

And at least the note meant Olivia was still alive. That's what mattered most.

"Sounds like you know a lot about her."

"We dated six months ago."

"Of course you did." Laura cocked her head sideways and studied him. "Are you still seeing each other now?"

"No."

"Does Olivia know that?"

"C'mon, Laura. You know I'm not as bad as the gossip rags make me out to be. I liked Olivia. We went out for a few weeks. But then it ended."

"Why?"

The same reason all of Joe's relationships had ended.

Olivia hadn't been Laura.

"Irreconcilable differences, I guess. We weren't what the other one wanted."

Laura didn't respond to that.

"Is she going to mind that I'm here? She's not going to be waiting for you naked or anything, is she?"

Joe remembered having the same thoughts about Jessica and Sarah.

He opened the door. "No, she won't be." He entered the house, Laura right behind him. "But if she is, cover my eyes and fight for my honor, okay?"

"How about if I cover my eyes and hit you in the head with a baseball bat?"

"That works, too." Joe wasn't totally sure she was joking and prayed Olivia would be fully clothed.

Various lights were on throughout the house as Joe led them to the stairs. He wondered if he should yell for Olivia so they didn't startle her.

"Where's her bedroom?"

"Up the stairs on the left."

Olivia's bedroom door was closed so Joe knocked, loudly.

Nothing.

His stomach clenched before remembering the note downstairs. Olivia had on headphones. He cracked open the bedroom door. "Olivia? It's Joe. I'm here with a friend of mine, Laura."

Still no answer. Joe flung the door open expecting the worst. He let out a sigh of relief when no one was dead in the bedroom. He walked fully inside, Laura right behind him.

"You okay?" She touched him on the back.

He blew out a breath in a shudder. "Yeah. It's just..." His words ran out.

"This situation was like the other two women's."

"Yeah. With both Sarah and Jessica I walked into the room and found them dead on the bed."

But Olivia wasn't. So where was she? Joe gave up on keeping quiet and began yelling for her. Laura did the same. Joe searched in the bathroom and closet while Laura turned to look in the guest bedroom.

Laura's frightened cry had Joe running to her at the guest bedroom's door.

"What?"

She put out an arm to keep him from going any farther inside. "Joe, you've got to get out of here right now."

Joe felt sadness crash over him. "Oh no, not Olivia. She's dead?"

"Yes, definitely. I'm sorry."

Joe tried to enter the room but Laura pulled him back to her. "The best thing you can do for yourself is not get your DNA in this room."

Joe was looking at Olivia on the bed. Blood pooled around her naked form. Just like the other two women.

Laura's words barely registered, but her pull on him did. "What?"

She reached up and cupped his cheeks with both hands, bringing her face close to his. His eyes finally focused on hers. "Someone is framing you, Joe. Two dead women who both knew you could possibly be a coincidence. But you finding the body of three of your ex-lovers? The police will arrest you for sure."

"But I didn't kill her. I didn't kill anyone." Joe felt like ramming his fist through a wall.

"I know. But someone has done an excellent job making it look like it was you."

"We can't just leave her here. We have to call the police."

Laura nodded. "We will but—"

She stopped her sentence as every light in the house switched off.

They reached for each other in the darkness.

"What just happened?" they both asked at the same time.

"Fuse blew?" Laura asked.

"Very convenient timing. Especially for us to have just discovered a dead body." Joe half expected to look out the window and see squad cars pulling up. It was like someone was trying to keep them here until the cops arrived and Joe could be blamed once again.

"I'm your witness this time. You were with me when we found Olivia. That will count for something."

"Let's go try to figure out the fuse situation."

"You go check it out. I'm going to stay here. I feel like something's going on, Joe. I don't want to leave the body."

Joe knew what she meant. He used the flashlight on his phone to hurry out to the garage, finding the fuse box and ripping it open. The box had all but exploded.

Someone had definitely messed with the fuse box, and recently.

Joe ran back to the door leading to the house but found it locked. He pushed against it with his shoulder, but it didn't budge.

Damn it. It must have automatically locked when he came through. He jogged to the door leading to the outside and ran back around to the front of the house. As he stood in the driveway, a light in the upper window caught his attention. How could there be lights back on if the fuse box had been completely burned out?

It only took a slight flicker for him to realize it wasn't a light. The house was on fire.

Very close to where Laura had been standing.

Joe barreled through the front door. "Laura!" He ran toward the stairs then stopped as he saw fire swallowing the entire right side of the stairs.

Joe felt the tightness of the scar that covered part of his neck and back. He knew the agonizing sting of fire from his wounds last year.

"Laura!" He yelled again, but there was no response. The flames were becoming more intense now.

A fear like he'd never before experienced grasped Joe. Laura was somewhere in that fire.

Grabbing a blanket off the back of Olivia's couch, he doused it under water in the sink and threw it around himself running past the flames on the stairs.

The smoke was thick on the second floor. Joe dropped low and belly-crawled toward the front of the house where he'd left Laura. Breathing was difficult, seeing even more so. He was almost crawling on top of her before he saw her lying totally still in the hallway.

"Laura." He shook her shoulder, coughing. "Laura, wake up."

She didn't move.

Joe knew he had to get her out of here, and he prayed she was just unconscious. He couldn't even think about anything further. He wrapped the blanket around her and began dragging her down the hall. He realized after a few moments she was helping him.

"Laura, are you okay?"

"Somebody hit me."

"What?" Had she said someone hit her?

"I was watching Olivia's body and someone hit me on the head from behind."

Someone was in the house with them.

Joe pulled Laura closer. "The house is on fire. We have to get out."

"Okay, I can crawl."

The fire was worse at the top of the stairs. Joe could feel the painful singe on the back of his neck.

They needed to get out right now.

Laura wrapped the damp blanket around them both as they half stumbled half ran down the stairs and through the hall. Fire licked toward them on all sides, but they kept moving so neither of them suffered burns as they made it out the front door.

Once outside, they both collapsed on the front lawn.

"Are you okay?" His voice came out as more of a hiss than anything else. He rolled over and touched her on the shoulder.

"Yes." Laura began to sit up. "Joe, someone was in the house with us. I thought you were coming up the stairs, and someone clocked me from behind."

"The fuse box had been almost completely destroyed. That's why all the lights had gone out. Then the door locked behind me so I had to run outside to get back in. That's when they got to you."

She gripped his hand. "Someone's going beyond just

trying to frame you. It looks like someone wants to kill you. Maybe make it look like you killed Olivia, me and then yourself."

Terror gripped Joe at the thought that Laura could be right.

She began to stand. "We've got to get out of here. It won't take long before someone sees the fire and calls it in."

"You don't think I should stay and talk to the cops?"

"As your friend, I suggest you get as far away from this crime scene as possible. As your lawyer, honestly, I would probably suggest the same. Nothing can be done for Olivia now, Joe." Her voice softened. "I'm sorry you lost another friend."

Another woman had died, and now there was no denying it was because of her connection with him. He looked at Laura. She could've been a target also. Could've easily died along with Olivia.

It wasn't in Joe's nature to run from a fight or from solving a crime. Especially since he had taken an oath to uphold the law when he'd joined Omega. But Laura was right. Staying here now wasn't going to do anything but get him arrested.

Sometimes you had to break the rules if it was the right thing to do.

He gripped Laura's hand and helped her up and to the car. They needed to get out of here.

He couldn't stop whoever was doing this if he was behind bars.

SHE WATCHED THE house go up in flames, the beauty of the fire bewitching her. It had not taken Joe the way it was supposed to, but she could forgive it because of its loveliness.

He brought the woman from the bank. Laura Birchwood, the lawyer. She thought Laura and Joe had just met last weekend but realized now that was incorrect. Joe had obviously known this woman much longer. Trusted this woman.

She'd made a mistake in thinking Joe would be distraught at the loss of his ex-lovers. Killing them—watching Joe find them—had not brought out in him the emotional response she had hoped for.

But today, watching as he realized Laura *was trapped in the burning house? That had been the reaction she'd been hoping to see with the others.*

Laura was the key.

And to think she'd almost killed her last weekend when she ran Laura off the road. That would've been too quick, too painless.

Laura would play an important role in the revenge on Joe. Now she knew Laura's safety and well-being were the most important things to him.

Laura would die, but she would die in a way that would cause Joe the most pain. She would burn right in front of him.

But first Joe would fall.

Chapter Ten

After stopping at a twenty-four hour medical care clinic to make sure Laura's head wound and their smoke inhalation didn't require more serious attention, they'd returned to Laura's house. They'd both stripped naked in her garage, leaving their clothes—ruined by smoke—in there, and gone to separate showers. Laura didn't have anything that would fit Joe except a giant bathrobe belonging to her father. That would have to do until they could get him something else.

The pounding at her front door scared them both.

"You expecting anyone?" Joe whispered.

"Knocking on my door at seven o'clock in the morning? Um, no." She looked out her window and grimaced. "It's the police."

Joe muttered a curse.

"I knew they'd be looking for you, but had no idea it would be this soon." If they'd shown up fifteen minutes earlier, she would've had the smell of smoke still in her hair, a dead giveaway.

She turned to him. "Quick, go up in my room, stay out of sight."

"What are you going to do?"

"Talk to them. If they have a warrant to search my house, I won't be able to do anything. Otherwise, unless they see something suspicious, they can't come in. Don't come out." She pushed him toward her bedroom.

Pounding on the door resumed. Laura opened it. There stood Detective Thompson and two uniformed officers.

"Gentlemen, I have neighbors, if you don't mind. It's early."

"Ms. Birchwood, we're looking for Joe Matarazzo," Thompson said. "May we come in?"

"Do you have a warrant?"

Thompson's eyes narrowed. "No, ma'am."

Relief coursed through Laura. "Then no, gentlemen, you can't come in."

She began shutting the door, but Thompson held out a hand to stop it. Laura didn't want to add to their suspicions so she opened the door again. "Something else I can help you with?"

"Do you know where Matarazzo is?"

"Have you tried his house?" Laura sidestepped the question. "I'm his lawyer, Detective, not his girlfriend."

"Are you sure that's the case, Ms. Birchwood? We found these pictures online of the two of you together."

Thompson pulled out a half-dozen pictures he'd printed from the internet, passing them along to the other two officers to hold up as well as keeping two in his own hands.

She and Joe, six years ago, in full, unforgiving color. She found it difficult to look at the woman she'd been then. How much in love with him she'd been. The camera had captured it so perfectly.

She had to admit Joe looked pretty enthralled with her too in the photos. But she knew that had been a lie. Joe had never been captivated by her.

"Ancient history, gentlemen. Those photos were all taken half a dozen years ago."

Thompson collected the photos and got out another couple of prints. "How about these? They were taken last weekend if I'm not mistaken."

The photos someone had taken of them at dinner on Friday. The same ones that had reminded Laura why it was a bad idea to get involved again with Joe.

Glancing away from the pictures and back at Thompson, Laura realized she didn't need to lie. The truth would work best for her.

"It was dinner between two old acquaintances. I'm sure you heard about the hostage situation at the bank in Denver on Friday. Joe Matarazzo got everyone out safely and we went out to celebrate a job well done. You might want to take that into consideration during your search for him. Joe is one of the good guys."

Thompson ignored the last part. "This picture doesn't look like dinner between two acquaintances."

He was right. Damned if Laura didn't have that same look in her eyes she'd had six years ago. And Joe looked just as enthralled.

Laura crossed her arms and leaned against her door. "Detective, I'm sure if you dig just a little deeper into our past relationship you'll see why I would have to be an absolute idiot to be harboring him now or not cooperating with you if I knew anything about his whereabouts."

That was the honest truth. She *was* an idiot.

"And why is that?"

"The gossip sites hated Joe and I together. Said I wasn't attractive enough, polished enough, *sparkling* enough for someone like Joe. I'd be foolish to set myself up for that again."

Thompson shook his head. "Gossip reporters are vicious. No one takes them seriously."

"Joe Matarazzo took them seriously. Told me himself after a few months of dating that I wasn't the caliber of woman someone like him should be with. Why would I want to be around someone who doesn't think I am good enough for him?"

Thompson's eyes narrowed. Evidently Laura had just confirmed the detective's poor opinion of Joe. "I knew Matarazzo was an idiot. Has to be to say something like that. But you're still his lawyer?"

"He has no problem with my caliber as a lawyer. Plus, Joe is very wealthy. He made it worth my while to forget about past—" she shrugged "—misjudgments. On both our parts. So I helped him out yesterday. I imagine he'll get a full team of lawyers if all this continues. But there's nothing romantic between us and definitely nothing that would have him at my house at the crack of dawn."

"I see." Thompson nodded, but still didn't look completely convinced.

"Why are you looking for him so early? Something else must have happened or you would've charged him yesterday."

Laura knew it was risky bringing up the new murder, but it would be more suspicious if she didn't ask.

Thompson nodded. "There's been another murder.

Someone else Matarazzo dated. Killer tried to cover it with a fire, but we got an anonymous tip-off that someone matching Joe Matarazzo's description was seen around the victim's house."

Laura's lips pursed. Anonymous tip-off could've been a neighbor. But it also could've been the true killer trying to make sure Joe was arrested since he'd made it out of the house alive. Especially since no one mentioned her being there with him.

Thompson held up a picture of Olivia Knightley. "This was the lady who was murdered. Know her?"

Laura had to be careful here. "Not personally. She's an actress, right? Olivia something."

Thompson nodded. "Olivia Knightley. Matarazzo and Ms. Knightley dated six months ago."

"I wouldn't know anything about that. Now if you'll excuse me, I'm late for work."

"If Matarazzo does get in touch with you—since you're his lawyer and all—please call us. As his counsel I'm sure you would do the right, legal thing and tell him to turn himself in since there is a warrant out for his arrest."

"Of course."

"You should be aware that as an ex-lover of his, you are in danger, too. The only connection we've found between the three women so far is Matarazzo."

"I'll keep that in mind, Detective."

Thompson shot out his hand to keep her from shutting the door. "Matarazzo is a womanizer at best, Ms. Birchwood. I'm afraid he might also be a killer. Either way, women he's been intimate with keep winding up dead."

"Joe may be a jerk, but he isn't a killer, Detective. You need to keep searching for the real person committing these murders, not spend all your time looking for Joe."

Thompson's eyes narrowed and Laura feared she'd said too much. "Even if he isn't the killer, someone is targeting women he cares about, so that puts you in danger."

"Joe doesn't care about me. I'm just his lawyer and someone he knew a long time ago."

"I'm not so sure about that."

"Look at the women he dates and look at me, Detective. Olivia Knightley. Jessica Johannsen. They're stunningly gorgeous." Laura gestured to herself. She wasn't wearing any makeup, had her hair wrapped in a towel. "And look at me. No one could possibly think Joe and I belong in the same social realm together, much less that we could be a serious couple."

Thompson and the two other officers looked uncomfortable. She didn't blame them. They all knew what she said was the truth, even if they didn't want to admit it.

"Six years ago, I thought I had something special with Joe, then out of the blue he ended it with me because he figured out he could do better. He could find women superior in beauty, grace, wit and spark."

"Ms. Birchwood—"

"Well, three of those superior women are now dead. So I suppose I should be glad Joe found me so lacking then, or it might be me lying in the morgue right now."

Laura grabbed the door and pulled it partway shut.

"Joe and I aren't a good fit. That's what Matarazzo discovered years ago, and I agree wholeheartedly. I'm pretty sure I'm safe from whoever is killing the beautiful women Joe cares about."

Thompson nodded. "Again, I'm not so sure about that. Just be careful."

She murmured her thanks and shut the door, leaning her forehead against it.

Nothing like reliving all the painful details of your past to make a bad morning even worse.

JOE ALMOST SURRENDERED himself a half-dozen times while Laura spoke to Detective Thompson. It would've been easier than listening to all of that.

She was so wrong about how he'd felt six years ago. None of what she'd said to Thompson had been accurate. Not that Laura would know that.

Joe had been scared. He could admit that now. He'd been twenty-five and scared that he'd found the woman he wanted to spend the rest of his life with. Her looks, her *caliber*, had nothing to do with why he'd truly broken off their relationship.

Not that it made it any easier for her. To Laura he'd just been cruel.

Moving around the corner and seeing Laura leaning against the door destroyed Joe further. Before he could think better of it he walked over and wrapped his arms around her, pulling her back against his chest.

For just a moment she lay against him, her head resting back on his shoulder. A perfect fit, just like they'd always been. Then she stiffened and stepped away.

"I can't," she whispered. "Not right now. I don't want to touch you. To touch anyone. I just saw a dead woman lying five feet from me. Just washed smoke out of my hair from a fire that almost killed both of us. And my head is killing me."

"Laura—"

"Talking about the past, about what a fool I was? That was the last straw."

He had to try to make her understand. "That stuff I said six years ago, I didn't mean it."

She walked past Joe, careful not to touch him in any way. "You know what? It doesn't matter. You've got so many more important issues going on right now than our past."

She was right, but the pinched look on her face was still hard to swallow.

Laura walked into the kitchen. "You've got to get out of town. If Thompson doesn't have a warrant to search my house yet, he will soon. I'm not sure he believed me."

Laura's words about how she'd be a fool to get involved with Joe again had been pretty damn convincing, but he didn't point that out. "I don't want to run. I want to find out who's doing this and stop it."

"That's fine, but getting arrested isn't going to help with that plan." She rubbed a hand over her face. "I have a cabin in Park County about an hour west of here. It's in my mother's maiden name. No one would even tie it to me, much less you."

Joe shook his head. "No. I don't want to run."

"You're not running. You're retreating and regrouping. Let me finish up work today and tomorrow, then I'll join you. We can try to get a handle on this."

He didn't want to go. Didn't want to take himself

out of where the action was. What good could he do at her cabin?

"What good will you do sitting in a cell?" It was as if Laura could hear his inner monologue.

He gripped the kitchen counter. "I feel useless."

Her face softened. Laura couldn't stand to see other people in pain, even someone like him, who had caused her so much of it. "You're not useless. But we have to be strategic. And getting you out of Dodge is the best move right now."

She was right. But he still didn't like it.

"Okay. I'll go. But only if you promise to meet me at the cabin right after work tomorrow."

"I will. Hopefully, me going to work just like everything is normal will convince Thompson that we're not together. I'm sure he'll be watching me. They're probably watching my house, too, by the way. Just because they couldn't get inside doesn't mean they won't wait to snatch you as soon as you walk out."

"I'll use stealth—don't worry."

She smiled. "That robe is not going to get you any points in the nonconspicuous category."

"I'll handle clothes. Have something delivered." It was one of the perks of not having to worry about money.

All the money in the world couldn't bring back the women who had died. Joe planned to make sure it didn't happen to anyone else.

Chapter Eleven

Laura tried to act as normally as possible at work. That proved to be more difficult than she thought.

She shouldn't have been surprised. In the last twelve hours she'd seen a dead woman lying in a pool of her own blood, been knocked unconscious by an unknown assailant and had almost been killed in a fire. After that she'd lied, or at least intentionally misled, law enforcement officers, and harbored a fugitive.

That had all been before 8:00 a.m.

But all of that, as difficult to deal with as it might be, wasn't what had her utterly unfocused today. Joe was what had her unfocused.

More specifically Joe looking so lost this morning and yesterday at Omega. His whole world was bottoming out beneath him and he didn't know what to do.

Laura wanted to help him. Wanted to wipe that look off his face. She was sure most of the world would agree that Joe Matarazzo's face needed to be plastered with an easygoing smile, not lines of worried exhaustion. A quick and charming wit was what the world expected of Joe.

He wanted to fix this, stop this killer. She knew if

he could he would give his entire fortune to have the three women back safely. But neither his money nor his charm could mend this.

Joe had become a man of action. Wanting to do. Wanting to help. These women dying had hit him hard.

Omega Sector suspending him, despite it being the best thing for the organization overall, also had him reeling.

Laura had to face the fact that Joe was no longer the man she'd known six years ago. He'd grown, matured. Had begun to put others' needs—even those of people he didn't know—before his own. Working in law enforcement had changed him.

It both pissed her off and caused her heart to flutter.

She had no idea what the hell she felt for Joe. For a woman used to knowing her own mind, it was frustrating.

She had to help Joe clear his name. The thought of Joe sitting in a cell, even temporarily, made her feel sick to her stomach. And she knew if Thompson found Joe he would definitely be detained, probably arrested and charged.

But right now Joe was safe at her cabin. She had planned to join him tomorrow, but she would go tonight instead. They needed to figure out the pattern behind the killings so they could get a lead on who was committing them.

Laura spent the last couple of hours of her day clearing her calendar and rescheduling meetings she'd had for the next day.

Yes, going to meet Joe tonight was better. He needed a friend. Laura could be that for him.

Just a friend.

She rolled her eyes. Yeah, right. She must be a glutton for punishment or something, but she couldn't stay away from him.

It was after seven when she finally finished everything she needed in order to clear her calendar for tomorrow. Everyone else was gone from the building. Laura would go home, grab a couple changes of clothes and meet Joe at the cabin.

And her changes of clothes would involve no sexy underwear whatsoever. Definitely not the red thong and matching bra she'd purchased a few weeks ago on a whim.

Because she definitely did not remember how partial he was to that color on her.

She walked into the parking garage her office shared with other offices on the block, taking the stairs down to the bowels where she was parked because she'd been so late getting here this morning.

A woman stood over in the corner, looking out at the lot. She smiled oddly at Laura so Laura gave her a little wave. Maybe she'd forgotten where she had parked. That had happened to Laura before, after a particularly long day.

Laura turned the corner toward her car. Besides the red lingerie, she would need her laptop so they could try to figure out the pattern the killer was using.

The brutal shove into a car caught her completely off guard. Laura was usually much more diligent when walking into the garage alone, but she'd been so caught up in getting to Joe she'd let her guard down.

She turned and saw a masked man. Laura tried to dive to the side, away from him, but he grabbed her arm.

"Where are you going, bitch?"

Remembering the other woman, Laura let out a scream, hoping she would call the police. Although by the time they got here it would be too late.

"So he cares about you, huh? We'll see how much," he muttered, wrapping his hand around her upper arm with bruising strength.

Was this guy talking about Joe? Was he the one who had killed the other women?

Laura began fighting with a renewed frenzy. She would not let this man kill her and frame Joe for it.

She threw her arms and legs around wishing she had more background in self-defense. Her captor grunted as some of her frantic blows connected with sensitive places. He cursed and backhanded her. She fell against another vehicle.

"Let's go, Max. Hurry up!" Another masked man in an SUV parked toward the exit yelled.

Laura tasted blood in her mouth as she got up from the hood of the car where she'd fallen. Out of the corner of her eye she saw the woman again, just watching, too afraid to get involved.

The large man grabbed her by the hair and began dragging her toward the other van. She punched at him but it wasn't enough to stop him. She dropped all her weight to the ground crying out at the stinging pain in her scalp when he didn't let go. She couldn't let him get her in the vehicle.

"Help me with her," he called out to the other guy.

A few seconds later she felt the other guy grab her

legs. Laura screamed, trying to draw any attention to herself, until a meaty fist covered her mouth.

She bit it.

The man yelled and she saw fury burn in the eyes visible through the black ski mask. She braced herself for the fist flying toward her face.

Instead she and her two captors went flying to the ground as a huge force knocked into them.

Joe.

He kicked the guy who had been holding her legs in the jaw and sent him flying back. Laura scurried out of the way as the first man rolled with Joe on the cement, both of them giving and receiving bone-crunching blows.

Joe obviously knew what he was doing. These weren't just lucky punches he was getting in. And even with both of them rolling on the ground he effectively blocked many of the attacker's—a man much bigger and meatier—blows.

Laura scrambled to her feet and saw the second man rushing back at Joe with a knife in his hand.

"Joe, behind you. A knife!"

Her words gave him just enough time to spin around, the blade catching him in his shoulder rather than the middle of his back. Laura heard a sickening snap and a high-pitched scream from the attacker as Joe made short work of the knife in the other man's hand, breaking his wrist and recovering the weapon himself.

This was a Joe she had never seen before. Had never known existed. Would've sworn didn't exist if she couldn't see him with her own eyes.

There was no carefree in him now, no charm. Just deadly intent and overwhelming force.

Both men began backing away now that Joe had not only proved himself capable of handling them, but had a weapon. Within moments they were fleeing to their vehicle and speeding out of the parking garage.

Joe rushed to her, touching her lip gently where the guy had hit her. "Are you okay?"

Laura's short laugh had a bark of hysteria. "Me?" She looked at his arm where blood was dripping through the sleeve of his blue shirt. "You're the one bleeding. We need to get you to a hospital."

"No, I'm fine. Plus a hospital might ask too many questions. We've got to go."

She let him lead her to her car. "Why are you even here? I thought you went to the cabin."

"I couldn't do it. Couldn't run, leaving you alone. What if one of Olivia's neighbors had reported that they remembered seeing us *both* outside her house? The cops could've come back and arrested you. There was no way I would let that happen."

She nodded.

"Not to mention someone killing people linked to me." He gestured vaguely toward where the masked guys had driven off.

Joe opened the passenger door of the car for her, but she stopped, leaning against the side of the vehicle, closing her eyes, needing a minute. Trying to stop the spinning in her head, not just from the blows.

Joe's hand softly cupped her cheek. "Are you sure you're okay?"

"Those were the guys trying to frame you."

"I know."

"They were going to take me and kill me like the others. You would've found me dead at my house."

Joe didn't say anything, just pulled her closer to him. She breathed in his scent, feeling his lips at her temple.

"We need to leave," Joe finally said.

Laura nodded. The guys might come back, or the police. Either way, staying here was dangerous.

"We'll both go to the cabin."

THEY DROVE STRAIGHT out of town. Joe ripped a strip off one of the shirts he'd purchased and had delivered to Laura's house this morning. It stemmed the bleeding from the cut on his shoulder. Not getting stitches would probably leave a scar, but a hospital wasn't worth the risk.

They stopped only once on the way to the cabin, at a super center to get a first aid kit, some clothes for Laura and enough food for while they holed up and tried to figure out who was trying to frame Joe. The cashier had given the two of them quite a look, for once not because she recognized Joe, but because she was worried he was some backwoods husband beating on his wife.

Joe couldn't blame the cashier. Laura looked exhausted. Her lip was swollen from the punch she'd taken, her hair and makeup were a mess. Her eyes dull and unfocused.

So unlike Laura.

He paid in cash and put the bags in the cart, grabbing Laura's hand. It was icy. He rubbed her arms up and down, feeling her coldness even through her blouse.

He bent down so his eyes were right in front of hers. "You okay?"

She blinked and focused on him. "Yeah, I just..." She shrugged. "I'm sorry."

"Let's get you to the cabin." He wanted to take off his jacket and give it to her, but his blood-soaked sleeve would be too memorable. They had already drawn enough attention. He tucked Laura to his side and pushed the cart out with one hand.

Laura's cabin on Lake George, fifty miles west of Colorado Springs stood private and simple. She was right; no one would look for them here. Joe led her into the cabin, checking it thoroughly himself first, and sat her on the couch. When he came back in from carrying the bags she was still sitting exactly where he'd placed her.

This wasn't good.

He knew she was exhausted, in pain—she'd taken two hits to the head in the last twenty-four hours—probably hungry and definitely in shock. If it wasn't for his training with Omega, Joe would probably be all those things too.

He saw bottles of alcohol on an antique tray by the kitchen table. A good shot of quality scotch would probably do them both good. Hell, a finger of *any* scotch would do them good. He poured two glasses and sat down next to Laura.

"Here, drink this."

She did without comment, which just confirmed how far gone she was.

The strong burn pulled her back. "What *is* that?" she sputtered.

Joe grinned. "Whiskey."

"I think enough people have tried to kill me today without you joining the club, thank you very much." Coughs racked her body.

"Just call it liquid fortification. You were looking a little hollow there for a second."

She nodded. "I was feeling a little hollow."

He slipped off his jacket and grabbed the first aid kit. Laura helped him clean and wrap the cut on his shoulder that thankfully wasn't too deep and had long since stopped bleeding. It hurt now, but it wasn't going to cause him any permanent issues.

Joe put the first aid supplies on the side table then leaned all the way back against the couch next to Laura. "Hell of a day, hasn't it been?"

"Where did you learn to fight like that?"

"Not everybody liked rich kids as I was growing up. It was either have full-time security following me around middle school or learn how to protect myself."

"Did your middle school moves include learning to break someone's wrist?"

Joe was glad to see the liquor was working. Laura didn't seem nearly as brittle as she had before. He pulled her so she was resting next to him, back against the couch.

"When I started working at Omega Sector I ended up learning a lot more defensive and offensive tactics. Weapons training, close-quarter fighting. The whole works."

"Well, it showed today."

"Thank God for that."

She let out a huge yawn and he slid to the side of the

couch, pulling her with him, until they were both lying flat, her tucked against him. He felt her stiffen.

"You're okay. I'm okay. Let's just rest," he murmured. "I don't need anything you're not willing to give me. I just want to hold you and know you're alive."

Because she very easily might not have been. Listening to his instincts—staying in town rather than going to the cabin—had never served him better than it had today.

He felt her relax and drift off to sleep. Good, she needed it. He would just hold her here while she slept.

It was more than he'd ever thought he'd get again, anyway. He'd take it.

He slept also. He knew he did because when he woke Laura's soft sweet lips were on his.

"We didn't die," she murmured against his mouth. "When that guy came at you with the knife I thought he would kill you."

Joe reached down and grabbed Laura's hips, pulling her more fully on top of him. There. Touching him from head to toe. That's how he wanted her.

"When I came around the corner and saw those two guys trying to carry you off—" he broke away and whispered "—my heart stopped."

"Make love to me, Joe." Her fingers were already loosing the top button of her shirt.

"Laura." He brought his lips back to hers, rubbing his hands up and down her spine. "I want to make sure this is what you really want. This has been a crazy day. We don't have to do this."

She rolled her hips against his. "Are you suggesting you don't want to?"

He half groaned, half laughed. "That is obviously not the case."

"Then what's the problem? I've crawled on top of you. I'm unbuttoning my blouse. I'm feeling pretty confident about what I want. And I'm definitely not drunk if that's your concern."

What was his problem? Why was he not helping her with said blouse and moving things right along? He definitely wanted to.

He cupped both sides of her head and brought her face up so he could see her. Hazel eyes, clear and focused, stared back at him. Her little chin jutted out as if she was daring him.

To stop or go further, he didn't know.

He realized the problem. He didn't want this to just be let's-celebrate-we're-alive sex. He wanted it to mean something to her. An emotional connection between the two of them. Because as much as he wanted her—which was pretty much more than his next breath—he didn't want to jeopardize a possible future with her for a few hours of passion.

Oh, how the mighty Casanova had fallen.

He could feel Laura start to stiffen, true doubt entering her eyes. It gutted him, the thought that she doubted his desire for her. Laura wanted him. He would take her any way he could get her.

And pray it would be enough to tie her to him more completely.

He wrapped his arms around her, sitting up so quickly a little squeak escaped her. He swiveled and sat back against the couch so she was straddling his hips. He tilted his head and took her mouth.

He stopped thinking, and just allowed himself to feel. To sink into that soft, wet mouth. To trace it with his tongue, tease her warm lips apart and explore.

He kept the pace slow and easy, wanting to enjoy, to savor. Laura unbuttoned and peeled his shirt off him, careful of the wound on his shoulder. He made short work of her blouse before bringing her back in for a kiss.

The pace was much more frantic now. She gripped his waist, tugging him to her.

He couldn't breathe for the pleasure of it. All he could do was get closer. Her body was too far away even though they were plastered to each other.

He wrapped his arms around her hips and stood, still holding her to him.

"Where's the bedroom?" His words came out as a growl against her lips.

"Two rooms, both have the same size beds. Take your pick. But be quick about it."

He smiled, carrying her across the room to the first door he came to.

"This better not be a closet, or I'm not going to make it to a bed."

She giggled and he reached down and gently bit the juncture of where her neck met her shoulder. Her laugh turned into a sigh. She wrapped herself more tightly around him.

It was a bedroom. Within moments he had her on the bed, both of them naked. And he proceeded to lose himself in the woman he'd never been able to fully get out of his heart.

Chapter Twelve

The next morning Laura awoke to the smell of coffee and an indentation in the mattress where Joe had recently lain.

What had she done?

Besides having had the best night of lovemaking since…

Since she and Joe had broken up six years before.

She groaned into her pillow.

The physical side of their relationship had never been a problem. As a matter of fact, no side of their relationship had been a problem. Or at least Laura had thought as much.

Until the day Joe dumped her out of the blue.

"I can almost see your brain working at a million miles an hour." Joe walked into the room holding coffee.

He was so sexy, so rumpled and casual. Handing her a perfect cup of coffee.

Laura could see so easily why she had fallen in love with him before. She would be a fool to let herself make the same mistake twice. She should not forget that Joe—despite all the ways he seemed to have grown—could change his mind and decide out of the blue again that he didn't want her anymore.

She couldn't survive her heart shattering twice.

"Just trying to figure out how we're going to get out of this mess unscathed."

Joe's eyes narrowed slightly and Laura knew he wasn't sure if she was referring to the bedroom situation, the police situation or both.

Good. Let him wonder. She was wondering, too.

"We've got to figure out who's setting me up."

"Okay." Laura took a sip of her coffee then set it on the nightstand. She ran out into the living room, aware she was only wearing one of his T-shirts. It was too big on her, but she was still conscious of how much of her legs was exposed.

She grabbed her legal pad and pen from her bag and came back to the bedroom. "We need a list. 'Who would want to hurt Joe?'"

"I don't think I like this list."

"We can call it 'people who think Joe is an ass.' Is that better?" She smiled innocently.

He rolled his eyes, shaking his head. "I think the first one will suffice."

They worked on the list for the next couple of hours, and while they fixed and ate breakfast, forming two basic categories: people he'd helped put in jail and his ex-lovers. She didn't make him name all his ex-lovers—because seriously her heart couldn't take it—just people with whom he'd had relationships that ended badly. They'd both realized quickly that Laura would be at the top of that list so they'd moved on to the people he'd put in jail.

"Sometimes people feel like I fed them untruths. I try not to lie to hostage-takers, but my first priority is always getting everyone out alive. If I suggest no jail time will be involved and they believe me and surrender..." He shrugged.

"It can't be anyone from inside jail. It has to be someone who's out."

"It could be someone connected to someone I put in jail, but I can't remember all those names on my own. We're going to need my case files from Omega."

Laura put down her notepad. "Will they give them to you?"

Joe shrugged. "I don't know. I'm not going to ask. We'll need to sneak them out."

Why wouldn't he ask? Asking seemed much simpler than sneaking. "Steve Drackett seemed pretty reasonable. If you tell him we think—"

"No."

Laura waited for the rest of the explanation but none came.

Good thing she was a lawyer and talking sense into people was sometimes part of her job. "Joe, from everything I know and have seen of Omega Sector, it's a pretty tight-knit group. You are part of the team. Steve will help if you ask him."

"Things aren't always as they seem. There is a team, but I'm more of an outsider. Trust me—they don't want to be a part of this problem, especially now that a third woman connected to me is dead. I'm sure Steve would rather I just use my money to help get myself out of this mess."

She reached for his arm but he slid away.

"Joe—"

He reached forward and kissed her on the forehead before standing and walking across the room. "It's not a big deal, seriously. It's not like they dislike me or anything. I'm just not part of the inner core."

"That's not how it looked to me."

"Like I said, sometimes things aren't always the way they look."

She wanted to argue but didn't have the facts to back up her case. "Okay, so we have to sneak them out. Great, breaking more laws. How will we get in?"

"My ID probably won't work right now. Or will at least alert security if I enter the building since I'm on suspension. The files are in a relatively unsecured section in a different building, but getting in the front door is the problem."

"Do you have a plan?"

"Yeah." He grimaced. "But you're not going to like it."

JOE WAS RIGHT; she didn't like his plan.

They were back in Colorado Springs, at a bar not far from Omega Sector headquarters. It was actually called Barcade—as in, bar and arcade mixed—and it was chock full o' geeks. The group of particular interest to Joe were the geeks who worked at Omega Sector. Data-entry people, if Laura understood correctly.

They all knew Joe and had fallen over themselves when he'd shown up at "their" bar. Evidently he'd been invited a few times but this was the first time he'd shown up. They'd either not heard the news about him being suspended or totally didn't care.

Joe was talking to them like they were the bestest buddies he'd ever had. Not that he was being insincere—no, Joe genuinely liked people. Liked listening to them, liked talking to them. He liked *these* people.

But he had an agenda. He was using them to get what he wanted. The fact they would've given it to him willingly was irrelevant.

Three rounds of drinks and an untold number of jokes, laughs and stories later, Joe and Laura walked out of Barcade, two "borrowed" Omega IDs in Joe's back pocket.

The data-entry gang was going to see a movie. Joe told them he and Laura already had plans, but insisted they wanted to meet up with them afterward for a nightcap.

So he could slip their IDs back in their pockets, although Joe didn't tell them that.

Admiration and disgust warred within Laura as she and Joe walked the blocks to Omega after seeing the gang off to their movie.

"You're mad," Joe said, not slowing their brisk pace.

"*Mad* isn't the right word."

"Those guys are low clearance. No one could get into any highly secured part of Omega Sector with their IDs. So there's no real security breach here. But it will get us what we need."

"I'm not mad about security clearance."

"Your eyes tell a different story."

Laura took a deep breath. "I'm not mad. It's just… those people trusted you. Really thought you were interested in them."

Joe stopped walking and turned to face Laura, grabbing her arm. "Wait a second, I *was* interested in them. They're an interesting group. A little geeky, but not bad overall."

"You were only talking to them because you wanted to shoplift their IDs. Only laughing and pretending to like them because you needed something from them."

He looked affronted. "That's not true. I walked into that bar because of needing their IDs, but talking to them, listening, laughing—that wasn't fake. They're good people."

"Have you ever hung out with them before?"

Now he looked a little sheepish. "Not here, outside of work. But I've talked to them inside Omega."

Laura shrugged. It was a fine line. But she realized it was a line he walked all the time in his job as a hostage negotiator. He got people to trust him for a living. Got them to talk, listened to them, made them feel special.

"Laura, this was the quickest, least painful way to get us into Omega. None of them are hurt in the process and you and I are able to get the info we need to stop another woman from getting killed."

"You used them, Joe. Plain and simple."

Joe's face fell, became shuttered. Obviously he hadn't seen it that way.

She wasn't trying to hurt his feelings, but damn it, it sucked to be used. She knew.

And when had this become about her?

"You know what?" Laura started walking again. "Forget I brought it up. You're right—getting the info, saving women's lives is more important than how we get the info."

"Laura—"

"Let's go. We've got to be back at the bar by the time they're done with the movie."

Laura caught Joe's gaze out of the corner of her eye. He had more he wanted to say, but just nodded. They walked in silence the rest of the way to Omega. Joe turned toward a side entrance rather than the front door.

"Records are held in this section. It's not connected to the regular building. No security guards, but you need an active ID to enter." Joe's voice was no-nonsense.

"Okay."

"Try to look down as we enter because there are security cameras. I took IDs from one guy and one woman, the two whose features are most similar to ours, but we still don't want to be looking at the camera as we walk in."

"Do you even know the names of the people you took the IDs from?" Were they just two more people Joe used and discarded?

Joe stopped again. He held the cards out to Laura without looking at them. "Cory Gimbert and Carolyn Flannigan. She's pretty new, so I have to be honest, I don't know how long she's worked here. Cory's been here two years. We both love *Star Wars* and he emails me whenever new rumors or trailers or anything hit the web. We're buds."

His eyes were hard when he handed Laura Carolyn's card. "Ready?"

Laura nodded. She'd hurt his feelings. She hadn't even been aware of the level of buried hostility she'd felt for Joe. But evidently it was high.

Now wasn't the time to deal with it. "Yes."

Joe walked up to an unassuming back door, nothing like the front door with its guards and weapon scanners. He scanned his ID then walked through. Laura did the same.

He waited for her inside the door, body held at a slightly odd angle. She realized he was protecting them both from the eye of the camera.

“Do the cameras have sound?”

“Not that I know of. I have a buddy in security I chat with from time to time—that’s how I know about the security camera. But he didn’t mention sound.”

Another buddy. Laura was beginning to see a pattern. A lot of buddies. No real friends.

They kept walking down the hallway. “Hard copies of closed case files will be down here in written records storage.” He led them quickly to a door.

“Okay, you take the top half of the list, I’ll take the bottom. I wish we had time to scan the files and leave them, but to be honest, I’m not sure how long we have.”

“So we’ll just take the files?”

Joe shrugged. “Sometimes it’s better to ask forgiveness than permission. If we use these to stop the real killer, I don’t think anyone is going to question our methods. Besides, they’re all cases I worked. Technically I have access to them whenever I need them.”

If he wasn’t suspended.

“Okay, let’s get started.” There were nearly twenty cases on the list Joe had texted her. Joe used Cory’s ID to enter the written records room, which was exactly what it sounded like: rows of filing cabinets holding printed records of cases Omega had been involved with.

“I don’t have any friends who work here,” Joe said

almost apologetically. “I don’t know how their filing system works.”

“Let me see if I can figure it out.” Laura used Carolyn’s ID card to log in to the computer at the front of the room. It seemed to be a closed system, low-level clearance like everything else in this section of Omega, but it got them the info they needed.

“I can run a search with your name and the last three years.” She printed the paper listing where the files were held.

Joe took half. “Okay, let’s get them and get out of here.”

Finding the files wasn’t difficult once they understood the system, but it became obvious they were going to have quite a lot to go through back at the cabin. After, of course, they met Cory and Carolyn and the gang for one more drink so Joe could slip their IDs back from wherever he’d gotten them.

“Ready?”

Laura handed him the files she had collected and he slipped them all into his backpack. It was full. “We’ve got a lot to go through.”

“I just hope it will get us the answers we need. Or at least somewhere to start looking.”

Joe turned and opened the door to the hallway so they could exit.

There stood Steve Drackett, Joe’s boss, waiting for them.

Chapter Thirteen

Damn it.

Steve had a reputation for never leaving Omega, but it was ten-thirty on a Friday night. What the hell was he doing here?

"Hey, Steve." Joe had no idea how he was going to talk himself out of this one. He was about to go to jail.

"Joe." Steve nodded. "Ms. Birchwood."

"Director Drackett. Good to see you again." Laura gave Steve a professional smile as if they hadn't just been caught sneaking into a law enforcement building, while on the run from law enforcement, to steal law enforcement files.

Steve leaned against the door frame. "I'm sure you're aware that another woman—Olivia Knightley—was killed yesterday. Another ex-girlfriend of yours if I'm not mistaken."

Damn it. "Steve, I—"

"And with that third girlfriend being killed, there is officially a warrant out for your arrest."

"I didn't kill them, Steve. I swear."

Steve continued as if he hadn't heard Joe. "Of course,

as a law enforcement entity, I set our Omega computers to ping me if something with your name came up in any computer. Credit card use, someone spotting you and posting on their blog, arrest reports. So it struck me as weird when someone was searching your name here in my very own Omega Critical Response Division building."

Joe saw Laura wince from the corner of his eye. If she hadn't been so logical and efficient at getting them the files, Steve wouldn't know they were here.

Joe tried to sort the options out in his head. He could fight his boss, try to get himself and Laura out of the building. But Steve was no old man—forty or forty-one at the most—and despite not taking part in active missions anymore, still kept himself in top shape. He'd probably forgotten more fighting tricks than Joe had ever learned.

Joe would have to talk his way out of this. "Steve—"

Steve held up his hand. "I'm going to assume those are case files in your backpack."

"They are." Joe nodded.

"I will therefore assume that you are not the person killing these women and that you're looking at past cases for suspects."

Steve actually believed him? "Yes, that was our plan."

"I'd like to assume that this elaborate plan to sneak into the building and take these files was due to some misguided thinking on your part to protect me and Omega from ramifications with other law enforcement agencies."

"Well, yes, actually. I didn't want to—"

Steve didn't let him finish. "But what I really think is the issue is that you didn't think we would have your back."

Joe sighed. "I didn't want to drag you or anybody else into this mess. *My* mess."

"Looks like you were willing to drag Laura into the mess, as you call it."

That was true. But not because he'd wanted to. But because… Hell, Joe didn't know why he'd been willing to drag Laura into it.

"You trust her." Steve finished the thought for him. "And you don't trust your colleagues at Omega."

"That's not true. I put my life in their hands all the time."

"Because that's their job, and your job, and everyone is damn good at it. But you don't trust them to really see you as part of the team and to have your back when the going gets tough."

Because he *wasn't* really part of the team. Joe had always known that. Everyone was friendly; everyone joked with him, and even invited him out when they were getting together. But inside, Joe had always known that they thought of him as different. That his money, his pseudocelebrity status, made him different in their eyes.

That they thought of him as a great guy, laid-back, fun. But not as a member of the team.

"I got suspended, Steve. Remember that?"

Steve's eyes narrowed. "That is standard procedure when someone is being investigated for something as serious as murder. For your protection and Omega's."

Joe knew that. Logically, he knew that. But it had still stung.

Steve shifted. "Let me ask you something. How long do you think it took me to find that cabin of Ms. Birchwood's?"

Joe heard Laura's sharp intake of breath.

"Once there was a warrant out for your arrest, Omega was legally compelled to help find you. Detective Thompson was the first person here demanding info. It was a damn shame a virus ate all the information we had about you and Laura."

Steve was protecting him.

"How long do you think you could hide if I was using all Omega's resources to find you? Maybe if you took your money and got out of the country you'd be safe. But you didn't do that."

"Because I didn't kill those women." Joe felt Laura's hand slip into his. It meant everything to him.

"Hell, Joe, I never for a single second considered that you killed those women. It's my job to look at every possibility when it comes to a crime and I never considered you a viable option. Nobody here did."

Joe wasn't sure what to say. He'd obviously misjudged his boss. "Steve—"

"Take your files and get out of here. Find out who's doing this and let's stop him. I need my team back together."

Joe nodded and put his hand at Laura's back leading her down the hall.

"And give those kids back their IDs," Steve called out after them. "Tell them to be more careful or I'm going to fire their asses."

LAURA WAS, IN JOE'S humble opinion, having way too much fun with her legal pad and the list of "who thinks Joe is an ass." She'd brought up the ex-lovers again, although given that those were the people who were dying, that wasn't likely. Plus, Laura pointed out it made the list too long, so they were better off just dealing with something more manageable.

Joe responded to that by backing Laura up against the wall and kissing her until neither of them could breathe. At first she'd been stiff, but had turned soft and compliant after just a few moments.

She was still mad, Joe knew, about Cory's and Carolyn's IDs. Laura's practicality had won out overall—she had to admit it had worked and returning the IDs had been even easier than taking them—but she hadn't liked it.

She thought Joe was using the techs. And in that case, yes, Joe could admit he was. But it wasn't his normal practice. He normally didn't need people to get what he wanted. Hell, if he wanted something he could usually buy it.

He wanted Laura's trust, but money couldn't buy that. Tonight's stunt had just pushed him a couple steps backward from winning her trust.

First he'd take care of a maniac, then he'd concentrate on showing Laura she could trust him.

Now they were looking at the case files, studying the people Joe had a hand in putting behind bars.

There were a lot.

Joe grimaced, looking up from a case three years old. "Some of these people are still in prison. We can rule them out."

"Unless it's a member of their family trying to get revenge. We know there are two men involved, from the guys who tried to take me from the parking garage."

"Well, there's Ricky and Bobby, aka, the Goldman brothers, Mitchell and Michael. But they're definitely still in lockup. Although I suppose they could be out on bail."

"One guy in the parking garage called the other guy Max. So it can't be the Goldman brothers."

"He said Max? Are you sure?" Joe found the Ricky/Bobby file and opened it.

"Pretty positive, why?"

"Well, there are actually four Goldman brothers. Mitchell and Michael were the ones from last Friday, and were evidently pretty irritated at me that they were arrested."

"Why? They were the ones who took sixteen people hostage and assaulted the manager and assistant manager."

Joe shrugged. "Evidently they thought that having a good reason for taking people hostage gave them a free pass."

Laura shook her head. "Wow."

"So yeah, they're threatening revenge and all that stuff. I thought I would worry about that when they got out of jail in three to five years. But, interestingly, they have two other brothers."

Laura rolled her eyes. "Great. Just what the world needs."

"Brothers' names are Melvin and Max."

That got her attention. "Max?"

"Interesting, isn't it, that the murders started a couple days after the Goldman brothers were arrested and that someone named Max tried to kidnap you, presumably to kill you?"

"Do you really think it's them?"

Joe got out his phone and made a call. Sometimes having a lot of money at your disposal helped. During his past few years in law enforcement Joe had made a lot of contacts, some that worked inside the law and some who worked outside it.

Deacon Crandall did both.

"Deacon, this is Joe Matarazzo."

"Joe." He heard Deacon yawn. "It's seven o'clock on a Saturday morning. And, btw, you're wanted by law enforcement."

"Yeah, well, that's because my exes keep showing up dead."

"Lucky bastard. I wish some of my exes would do the same. What can I do for you?"

Deacon didn't ask Joe if he'd murdered the women. Joe didn't know if that was because he trusted Joe was innocent or he just didn't care.

"I need you to find a Melvin Goldman in the Colorado Springs area. Shouldn't be hard. He would be brother of Max, Michael and Mitchell Goldman."

"Okay. What do you want me to do with Mr. Goldman, whose parents didn't know the alphabet contained other letters besides *m*?"

"I need you to find out if he has a broken arm. If you happen to see Max Goldman, he probably will have a pretty bruised face."

"Okay. Do I need to pick them up?"

"Nope, just let me know if they have those wounds

and their whereabouts. If so, I'll want to talk to them myself. And Deacon, I'll pay you triple your normal rate if you can get me the info in the next hour."

"You can expect my call."

An hour later Joe and Laura had already received Deacon's call. Not just a call but photos of both Max and Melvin. Sure enough Melvin's arm rested in a sling and Max's face still held bruises from Joe's fists. Deacon sent them an address where the brothers were lying low.

"I'm going to talk to them." Joe grabbed his coat.

"I'm going with you."

Joe was torn. He didn't want to leave Laura alone, but he also didn't want to bring her into a potentially dangerous situation.

"I'm not staying here in the cabin, Joe. Not when something could happen to you while you're in town. You might need me as your lawyer."

He needed her as so much more than that.

"Fine."

"Do you want to call any of your Omega people? For backup, or whatever?"

Joe hesitated. He knew what Steve had said last night about being part of the team. But it was one thing for his boss to believe him, another thing for all his colleagues to just trust Joe was telling the truth when all the evidence said otherwise. He was better off not even asking.

"No. I'm going in alone."

"What about what Steve said?"

"Steve is one thing. My actual colleagues? I can't be sure they're not going to choose the job over me. I wouldn't blame them for choosing the job over me."

Laura shook her head. "I think you're wrong."

Joe shrugged. He couldn't chance it. He shook his head. "Alone. I took the Goldman brothers once. I can deal with them again."

Chapter Fourteen

Laura didn't like the thought of Joe going in alone to question the Goldman brothers, but he seemed adamant about not calling any of his colleagues.

She realized for all of his money, his nice cars, vacation houses and gadgets, Joe Matarazzo was essentially alone. He'd be the first one to laugh off her words with a joke about poor little rich boys. But that didn't make it any less true.

It wasn't that Joe didn't trust other people, it was that he just didn't want to put them in a position where they had to state outright that they trusted him.

His easygoing nature and charm were what made him such a critical part of the Omega team, but it was also why he thought no one took him seriously. That no one would take his side in this situation.

That no one trusted him. When they all would, Laura knew.

Of course, she felt a little hypocritical because Laura didn't trust him, at least personally. She was still afraid he would turn around at any moment and say that now that he'd thought about things again, his initial inclinations had been correct and they really weren't from the same worlds.

Truly, it was only a matter of time before he said that again. Laura knew it had to be true.

"Laura, I've been thinking." Joe's eyes were on the road. His voice somber.

She felt her heart catch. Was this it already? The last two nights had been amazing, but sex had always been amazing for them. Was Joe already coming to his senses?

This time she wasn't going to let it destroy her.

"It's okay, Joe. Just say it."

Now he glanced over at her, brows furrowed. "Just say what?"

Laura cleared her throat. "You know, whatever it is you're thinking."

She could take it. Yeah, her heart would crack, but it wouldn't shatter like last time.

"I was thinking there should probably be a third group on the 'who thinks Joe is an ass' list."

Okay, that wasn't what she had been expecting. She struggled to regroup mentally. "Okay. Who?"

"Families of people I've killed."

She could feel the shock rock through her. "*What?* You killed someone? Who did you kill?"

"There have been innocent people who have been killed because I couldn't make enough headway with the hostage-takers who had them." She could hear the pain in his voice. The guilt. The doubt.

"But that doesn't mean you killed them."

He shrugged. "It might be considered close enough by some grieving family members."

"Have many people been killed in hostage situations?"

"No. The SWAT team at Omega and I have a great record. Almost anyone I haven't been able to talk down they've been able to take out."

"But not always."

Joe shook his head. "Last year around this time was a particularly bad situation. Guy had a hand grenade. Killed four people. Almost killed me."

"Are those the burn scars on your neck and back?"

His hands tightened noticeably on the steering wheel. "Yeah. A much smaller price to pay than what the four hostages did. They all died."

"You know that wasn't your fault, right? The man with the grenade, the one who took the people in the first place. He was at fault."

"It was a guy who'd gotten fired. Came back into his office and walked into the conference room. I got him to release six people. But he wouldn't let his bosses or office mate leave. He said they were the ones directly responsible."

"Joe—"

"I should've known he wanted blood. He let the other people go too easily and I thought I could handle him. The SWAT team thought they could take him out in time if needed, but none of us saw the hand grenade."

Laura knew there were no words that could make this any better for Joe. She reached over and touched his knee.

He glanced at her briefly before looking back to the road. "Anyway, that should probably be another list of people who hate me. People who lost loved ones because of my mistakes."

"I'm sure they don't hate you."

"I think I might if I was them. I met with the families after last year's incident. Tried to give them as much closure as I could, explain what happened as best as I was able."

"None of them blamed you, Joe. I know it."

He reached down and grabbed her hand. "One of the men who died—the office mate—was about to become a father for the first time. His wife was three months pregnant when he was killed."

The anguish was clear in his voice.

"That kid—it was a little girl—is never going to know her father."

"Because a madman walked into a building with the intent to hurt people. To kill people. And he would've hurt and killed even more if it wasn't for you."

He tried to ease his hand away from hers but she wouldn't let him.

"A kid will still be growing up never knowing her own father."

"And that's a tragedy. But she won't blame you for it. She'll blame the man who walked into her father's offices with weapons of death in his hands."

It was plain to see Joe wasn't convinced. That he carried more than just physical scars from that particular attack.

Laura held on to his hand tighter. All law enforcement workers were heroes in her opinion, but for some reason she hadn't really included Joe in that group.

Why?

Because she'd convinced herself that his money, his charm and his charisma somehow kept him sheltered, separated from the most painful aspects of his job.

She realized with no small sense of shame that her line of thinking was the same reason Joe felt like he wasn't truly part of the Omega team. Because people thought his job as hostage negotiator was just a hobby for him. That he was doing it as some sort of charity work he could walk away from at any time.

That he wasn't invested.

Everything about the conversation they'd just had—from the words he'd said to the way he'd held himself as he'd said them—told her otherwise.

Joe was every bit as much of a hero as other law enforcement personnel. Just because he didn't need the money they paid him didn't make him any less of one. Although he'd never admit it, probably even to himself, it hurt Joe to think that other people assumed he didn't care as much as they did.

Joe did.

Laura was still pondering the man she realized she didn't really know, still holding his hand tightly in her lap when they pulled up to the address Joe's contact had provided.

"What do we do now?" She turned to look at the apartment complex where the Goldman brothers were staying.

"It's early on a Saturday morning. I'm going to assume neither of the Goldmans is leaving for a job anytime soon. So I'm going in there and you're staying out here."

She watched as he reached into the glove compartment of the car and pulled out two guns.

"I thought you had to turn in your gun at Omega when you gave Steve your badge."

Joe gave an innocent shrug then winked at her. "I had to turn in my official weapon, but it certainly wasn't my only weapon. These are both Glock 42s. Are you familiar with handguns?"

"I've been to the shooting range a few times, but not with this particular pistol."

Joe showed her the basics and left one of them with her.

"I don't like leaving you here alone, but I like even less the thought of taking you in there with Max and Melvin. Just stay here and keep your eyes open for any trouble."

"Like what?"

"Like the police, who will gladly arrest both me and them and sort it out later."

Laura grimaced. She couldn't pull a gun on the police and expect it to end well for anyone.

Joe took out his phone and showed her the info his guy Deacon had sent. It was surprisingly thorough given the man had only had an hour to put it together. Pictures of Max and Melvin without their masks—looking remarkably like Ricky and Bobby in the bank, a photo of their apartment, stats on their life—unemployed, unmarried, both in their 20s, neither with a college education.

"Do you think they're just going to confess?"

"No. But we're not dealing with rocket scientists here. All I need to do is get them to let it slip that they know anything about any of the women and then we can start hunting down details in earnest."

"Joe, questioning people is what I do for a living. I'm a lawyer. Let me come in with you."

Joe stared at her for a long time.

"You know I'm right. Having two of us there is much better than just one."

He grimaced, not liking it but having to accept the truth of her statement. "Fine. But I'm going in there first. Once I have them secured then I will call you and you can come up. You don't come up without a message from me, no matter what. Got it?"

Laura rolled her eyes. "Yeah, got it. Little woman will just sit in the car waiting for the big strong man to face all the danger."

Joe reached over and grabbed her chin, pulling her to him. He gave her a hard kiss, almost bruising in its intensity.

"I'm not taking any chances with your life. You're too valuable to me. Wait for my message."

He was out of the door before she'd even caught her breath.

WHAT THE HELL was he doing? Joe walked silently up the stairs to the second floor apartment the Goldman brothers lived in. Laura had been right in the cabin when she'd suggested he call in some Omega backup.

Going in here alone seemed like a fine plan when it had just been him. But now that he was bringing in Laura, having more good guys in the room seemed like a much better plan.

But his arguments still applied. He couldn't drag his

colleagues into this. Or, more honestly, couldn't trust they would choose to take his word over what seemed like pretty damning evidence.

Either way, it was too late now. Joe needed answers from the Goldman brothers and he needed them directly.

He knocked on the door, keeping his face averted in case they were smart enough to use the peephole in their door.

"Doughnut delivery. We have your order ready."

Joe didn't know of any places that delivered doughnuts, but it seemed less suspicious than pizza this early in the morning. All he needed was for them to open the door just the slightest bit.

He pulled his gun out from where he'd tucked it into the waistband of his jeans.

The door cracked open. "Look, we didn't order no—"

Joe flew into the door with his uninjured shoulder, sending it slamming open and the man—it looked like Melvin by his picture and arm in a sling—flying back to the ground. Joe immediately trained his weapon on him.

"Where's your brother?" Joe asked, looking around the small place without taking his gun off Melvin.

"You!"

"Yeah, me. You guys should've finished the job when you had the chance." He used his foot to push the door back.

"How did you find us?"

"Believe it or not, Einstein, finding out details about other people is not difficult in this day and age." Particularly when you had a Deacon Crandall on your side.

"Especially when you know what you're looking for. Where's Max?"

Melvin looked back and forth from one bedroom to the other.

He cocked his head to the side. "He's sleeping."

Joe eased his way toward the room Melvin gestured to and opened the door.

There was no one in the bed, sleeping or otherwise.

He caught Melvin's grin out of the corner of his eye and realized he'd made a mistake underestimating the man. Joe wasn't going to be able to stop whoever he could feel flying toward him.

Chapter Fifteen

Joe's gun slid out of his hand as Max tackled him. He must've come through the front door. Joe would've seen him come out either of the bedrooms.

He grunted as Max's fist found his face and realized Melvin would soon have Joe's gun. Things were getting out of hand quickly and the only saving grace was that Laura waited safely in the car.

"If you touch that weapon, I'm going to be forced to shoot you."

Maybe Laura wasn't safely in the car.

"And you." She turned her Glock toward Max and Joe. "Get off of him. Joe, are you alright?"

Joe pushed Max to the side and onto the floor by his brother. He picked up his own weapon.

"You suck at following directions, you know that? What part of 'stay in the car until you hear from me' didn't you understand?"

Laura rolled her eyes. "The part where I saw Max arrive after you and thought maybe I should come in and see if you needed help. Which it looks like you did."

She kept her gun trained at the Goldman brothers and damn if that wasn't one of the sexiest things he'd ever seen. He wrapped an arm around her waist and kissed her forehead.

"Thanks."

She smiled. "No problem."

Joe shut and locked the front door and checked the rest of the rooms to make sure there wouldn't be any more surprises. He found some plastic zip-ties and used them to restrain Max's arms behind his back. He swore Melvin would get the same treatment also, regardless of his broken wrist, if he gave them any problems.

"You going to arrest us like you did Michael and Mitchell?"

Joe shook his head. "Your brothers took sixteen people hostage in a bank. Hurt two of them. They deserved whatever they got. But I wasn't the one who arrested them."

"That's not what they said," Mitchell muttered.

"I was the one in there making sure the SWAT team didn't kill them outright. So the next time your brothers want to talk trash about me, you remind them that I am the reason they aren't sitting in the morgue right now, rather than in a cell."

Max and Melvin glanced at each other. Evidently the facts Joe provided didn't jibe with what their brothers had told them.

"But no, I don't plan to arrest you." Mostly because Joe was wanted by the law himself, although he wouldn't be telling them that. "I just need answers to some questions."

"You were trying to kidnap me in the parking garage on Thursday," Laura interjected. "Why? To kill me like the rest and frame Joe for it?"

"What?" Mitchell's eyes flew to her. "No. We weren't going to kill you. We were just going to hold you hostage until they let our brothers out."

Laura pointed at Melvin. "You had a knife."

The man shrugged. "I always have a knife. You never know when you're going to need it. But I wasn't planning to kill you with it." He turned to Joe. "I wasn't even planning to kill you with it. I just got a little carried away in the moment."

"What about Olivia? Or Jessica or Sarah? Did you kill them with your knife?"

Melvin looked over at his brother then back at Joe. His face had lost all color. "Dude. I swear I didn't kill nobody. Not with a knife, not with anything. I don't even know who you're talking about."

Joe grabbed Melvin by the shirt. "I think you do know what I'm talking about. I think you killed those three women because you were mad at me for bringing down your brothers, and you were planning to kill Laura, too."

Melvin was sweating now. "No. I swear, man. I have no idea who those other girls are. We were just taking her—" he gestured to Laura "—to get the police to let Mitchell and Michael go."

Joe resisted the urge to ram his fist into the other man's face. He wasn't a violent man by nature, but the thought of his exes' pointless deaths filled him with rage. A rage that had nothing on what he felt about Laura being their next victim.

It was Laura who brought him back, touching him on the arm. She kept her back to the Goldman brothers and leaned her face close to his. "Look at them. I think they might be telling the truth. Let me ask them some questions."

He didn't want to. He just wanted to pound on them until their blood covered his hands.

Laura reached up and touched his jaw. "Joe, you're not in this alone. Trust me to help you with this."

Joe nodded and released Melvin, who fell back, still sweating.

Laura turned to them.

"You boys been watching the news over the last week?"

"Nah. Our cable got cut off since we didn't pay the bill," Melvin said.

"You heard anything about three women in the greater Denver/Colorado Springs area being murdered over the last few days?"

Both men shook their heads. "No. We didn't know nothing about that," Max told her. "We've been busy trying to figure out how to get our brothers out of jail."

"And that's why you came after me."

The brothers looked at each other then nodded. But they were hiding something. Joe wanted to stop Laura, demand the men tell them what it was they were hiding. But Laura touched his arm so Joe kept quiet. She'd asked him to trust her.

A team meant trust on both sides.

"Tell me your plan once you had me," Laura demanded.

Melvin sat up a little straighter, obviously happy they weren't accusing him of murder anymore. "We were going to put a call in to the police telling them we had a hostage. Demand that Joe Matarazzo meet with us.

Once he saw it was you we had hostage he would do whatever it took to get our brothers out. Since they were innocent."

Joe barely restrained from rolling his eyes.

Laura continued questioning. "Did your brothers tell you how much Joe cared about me from when they saw us in the bank together?"

Max and Melvin looked at each other again. "Not exactly," Max responded.

Laura nodded. "That's what I thought. Because Joe and I didn't even talk to each other in front of your brothers. So there was no way they would've known he cared for me any more than he cared for anyone else. Who told you that, Max?" She turned and looked at the other brother. "You didn't come up with the plan to kidnap me yourself, right, Melvin? You boys didn't really want to hurt me. You're not kidnappers. You're not murderers. Who gave you the idea?"

Joe just sat back and watched Laura work. He had no doubt she was this formidable in the courtroom also. Melvin and Max had no chance against her.

"Some lady," Max blubbered. "She came up to us on Wednesday. Said she had seen the whole bank thing on Friday and had a way we could get our brothers out of jail."

"Yeah, like you said, we didn't want to hurt anybody," Melvin chimed in. "We just wanted to help them. She told us where you worked. Where you would be coming out and when. Told us that Joe would do anything for you, even get our brothers out of jail."

Joe stepped up and grabbed Max's shirt. "Who? Who told you all this?"

"We don't know her name. I swear."

Melvin nodded. "She knew everything about you, man. Loved talking about you and all the details she knew. All the women you dated and all the money you had. Talked about some burn scars."

"She was kind of scary." Max's voice lowered. "Wild look in her eyes, you know? Said you deserved to be punished." Max looked at Joe. "Said you deserved to burn."

"But she said first you would help us get our brothers out. If we took Laura and held her ransom, you would get our brothers out."

"More likely she would've killed all three of us and framed Joe for the murder." Laura dropped her gun to her side.

Both men's eyes bugged out.

"What did she look like?" Joe asked.

"Long black hair," Max said. "Really pretty."

"Yeah, sort of tall for a woman. Maybe five foot nine. Curvy. Nice rack."

Trust these two idiots to remember her breast measurements.

"How old was she?" Joe demanded, trying to think of women from his past who fit the description.

Max shrugged. "I don't know. Our age. Midtwenties."

"Had her hair pulled back in a tight bun."

"Joe." Laura pulled him closer to her so the brothers couldn't hear. "I know who they're talking about."

"Who?"

"I don't know her name, but she was at the garage the day they tried to grab me. I saw her. She was sort of staring at me. I thought she had just forgotten where her car was parked. But now I know she was definitely watching."

"Do you remember what she looks like? Do you think you could identify her again?"

"Absolutely."

It was a start. The Goldman brothers weren't the ones trying to frame Joe. But at least they now had something on the person who was.

They just had to find her.

Chapter Sixteen

They went back to Laura's house in Fountain, rather than the cabin. It was time to stop running, stop hiding. Joe would always have fond memories of the cabin, but the next time he took Laura there, it wouldn't be to escape police trying to arrest him.

Her house was a risk since the cops were still looking for him, but Joe was going to stay and fight.

And he'd called in for reinforcements. Laura was right—he'd be stupid to try to fight this battle alone. Upon leaving Max and Melvin's apartment, Joe had called Steve. He'd let Steve know what the Goldman brothers had told him: their suspect was a woman.

And she seemed to know a great deal about Joe's professional and private life.

The first thing they needed to do was search through any footage they had of crowds surrounding Joe's hostage cases. Omega routinely recorded the crowds that gathered at cases and investigations. Often the perpetrator couldn't resist coming back to inspect his or her handiwork.

Joe knew that woman was in the footage somewhere. But as evidenced by the number of case files they'd had to steal, Joe had worked on dozens of hostage cases in his career. It was going to take a long time to go through that footage.

Time they didn't have.

Steve agreed to send someone to pick up the Goldman brothers, keeping them out of the hands of the Colorado Springs PD for a little while, and to send someone with the digitized footage to Laura's house.

At least they didn't have to break into Omega to get the footage. Joe hadn't liked asking for anything, but Steve hadn't even hesitated when Joe made his request.

It was sort of a weird feeling, trusting someone to help him.

Laura was taking a shower and changing into her own clothes when the doorbell rang. Joe checked to make sure it wasn't the police and was surprised to find that instead of some low-level courier Joe had been expecting from Omega, it was Jon Hatton.

Joe opened the door. "Hey, wasn't expecting you."

"I have some footage Steve insisted I bring over. Not only am I one of Omega's top profilers and crisis management experts, I am now a pack mule."

Sherry Mitchell, Jon's fiancée and forensic artist, stepped out from behind him. "Don't listen to his lies, Joe. He volunteered. Plus I have doughnuts."

Joe let them through and introduced them both to Laura when she came down from her shower. Within just a few minutes Joe and Jon were getting the footage set up on multiple computers as Sherry worked with Laura to create a drawing of the woman she'd seen in the parking lot.

Sherry labored patiently with Laura for the next two

hours, asking her questions and helping her remember seeing details about the woman. She was truly a gifted forensic artist.

"My gal is something else, isn't she?" Jon asked.

"Unbelievably talented." Joe couldn't doubt it.

Jon smiled. "It's nice to see Sherry working with someone who isn't traumatized. Normally she works with rape or battery victims. Kidnappings. It's not easy for her." He walked over and kissed her on the head. Sherry just smiled up at him and kept working.

Finally they had a drawing. A clear image of a woman.

"That's definitely the lady I saw in the parking garage." Laura handed the picture to Joe. "Do you recognize her?"

She didn't look familiar at all. "She's definitely not someone I've ever dated." He rolled his eyes at Jon. "Despite what you and the rest of the gang think, I do actually remember the people I've gone out with. I would remember this woman's face if I knew her."

Jon took the picture. "I'm going to send this to Steve, see if the Goldman brothers recognize her." He snapped a picture with his phone.

"Alright. We've got a face. Let's start studying footage at crime scenes I've been involved with." Too bad facial recognition software wouldn't work from a drawing. Plus, if the woman wasn't in their database it wouldn't help anyway.

"It's going to be slow going with all the cases," Jon pointed out.

"Then we better get started."

They each had a computer or laptop and split the

cases. Then began the grueling process of pausing each video and comparing the drawing to the people in the crowds. Crowds that were sometimes hundreds of people thick.

"Steve just texted me back. Confirmed that is the woman who approached the Goldman brothers."

At least they knew they were looking for the right person. Even if it was going to take forever to find her.

The doorbell rang again and Laura's eyes flew to Joe's. They both worried it was the police.

But it wasn't. More of Joe's Omega colleagues had arrived. SWAT members Derek Waterman, Lillian Muir and Liam Goetz, Derek's wife Molly who worked at the Omega lab, even Brandon Han and Andrea Gordon, who had helped him at the first crime scene when Sarah had been found.

They were all here, on their day off, laptops in hand.

"Heard you needed more eyes." Derek slapped him on the back on his way in.

"Yes, Joe, we want to help." Molly waddled through. "Especially when this big buffoon won't let me do almost anything else. I'm pregnant, not terminally ill." She smacked Derek on the arm.

Never had Joe expected to see his colleagues here. Especially not en masse. Not to help him.

"You guys, I…" Joe shrugged not sure how to even finish the sentence.

Andrea, who he had gotten to know a little better last month when they'd watched over Brandon Han in the hospital smiled at him. "Joe, we want to help. All of us."

Of everyone here, Andrea probably most understood how Joe felt. Until recently she'd kept herself, and the fact that she used to be a stripper, far away from all her colleagues, afraid to ever make attachments.

Joe wasn't ashamed of his past, but he'd sort of done the same thing: kept himself apart, thinking they didn't really include him in their inner circle.

Although with Laura's house almost full to overflowing with people here to help him—here because they wanted to be, not because it was part of a case or an order from Steve—he could no longer use that reasoning.

He was part of the team.

As everyone settled in at a computer, Jon divvying up the cases, Laura made her way over to Joe. He could see the smile she tried to keep tamped down.

"You going to say I told you so?" he asked as she sat next to him, laptop in hand.

"I would never stoop so low." She grinned. "But maybe nanny-nanny-boo-boo."

Joe lowered his voice so no one else could hear. "I can't believe they're all here."

"You'd do the same for any of them, right? If they were in danger and needed your help? Even if it was off-the-record and might get you in trouble?"

"Sure."

"Same thing. You're part of the team, Matarazzo. Money, no money. Gossip sites or not. They have your back. Just like you would have theirs."

Joe didn't tend to be at a loss for words very often, but looking around the room, watching his friends stare at screens, doughnuts in most of their hands, he was.

"I don't know what to say to them."

Laura reached over and cupped his cheeks. "You

don't have to say anything. That's the great thing about family. They just do what needs to be done, no words necessary."

Joe had grown up with a lot of money, a lot of privilege, trips, gadgets…but he'd never really had family. The best boarding schools money could buy, but no one close.

"Family." The word seemed awkward on his tongue.

"Family isn't always blood, and blood isn't always family." She smiled. "Now get to work."

Joe looked back down at his screen realizing Laura was right. These people were his family. In every way that counted.

"I've got her." Liam Goetz's voice called out.

"Are you sure?" Joe asked.

Liam grinned. "One hundred percent. Check her out." The laptop got passed around. No one could doubt that was the woman Laura had described and Sherry had drawn.

"You're spooky good," Laura said to Sherry, who just shrugged.

"What about me?" Liam said. "I found her. Isn't anyone going to tell me how awesome I am?"

Somebody threw a pillow at him.

"What case is that?" Jon asked.

Liam put the pillow behind his back. "Jewelry store hostage situation in Palm Springs. Ten months ago."

Everyone looked at Joe. He shrugged. "I remember it, but there wasn't much out of the ordinary. No casualties. Hostage-takers stepped down without the use of force."

"Okay, let's branch out from that case, see if we can

find her," Jon said. "I'm going to send the picture to Omega, see if she blips on any of our facial recognition software. Maybe we'll get lucky."

Laura began looking through the case file for the jewelry store while everyone began searching footage with a renewed sense of purpose.

"You're right," Laura agreed after reading through the file. "I don't see anything in this case that would make someone angry at you."

"I've got her again," Lillian said a few minutes later. "Six months ago. She's in the crowd when that guy was threatening to blow himself up at the home improvement store. I remember that."

SWAT had to take the guy out. Joe couldn't help him. That had been clear early on.

"Yep, I've got her in Austin last month," Derek said. "Right at the very front of the crowd."

"Wow. Looks like Joe has got himself a stalker." Liam smirked. "Some guys have all the luck."

"I'm afraid Liam's right, Joe," Derek's wife, Molly, cut in before Joe could make a sarcastic comment to Liam. "I have her in the crowd at last weekend's bank heist."

Joe looked over at Laura. Her expression was as worried as he knew his had to be. This woman had been following him for months.

"Okay." Jon took charge. "Everybody get a screen shot of when you have her, as well as the date and location. We need to find out when she first started showing up."

Laura ordered pizzas for lunch as they continued to look. The woman was everywhere. She had been at every case Joe had worked on for at least the past year. Had traveled all over the country to watch him.

Downright scary.

"Okay, I don't have her," Brandon Han said. "I'm one hundred percent positive she's not in this crowd."

Nobody asked to double-check Brandon. The man was a certifiable genius. If he said the mystery woman wasn't in the crowd, then she wasn't.

"Okay," Joe said. "Let's check the case immediately before that. Maybe she was sick that day or something."

They didn't find her on the footage of the previous case either. Or the one before that.

"It looks like she first made an appearance at the Castlehill Offices case," Lillian said, voice grim. "I've got her there."

Silence fell over the room.

"Which case is that?" Laura asked, coming to stand by Joe.

He wrapped an arm around her. "The one we were talking about this morning. Where I lost four hostages to the guy with the grenade."

"Joe, none of us knew that guy had such a death wish and need for revenge," Lillian said. "Or that he had the grenade. I was watching through my rifle sights from the other building and didn't see it."

Derek stood. "Yeah, Joe. We were all there, and have all reviewed the footage. There was no way you could've known. Sometimes people are just crazy."

Joe shrugged. Regardless of whether the guy was crazy or not, four people had died.

"Joe," Andrea's soft voice cut in. She didn't say

much, didn't waste words, so when she did talk, everyone listened. "Look at these pictures of the woman."

Andrea brought her laptop over to stand with Joe and Laura. "Look at her at the Castlehill Offices. She's distraught, terrified." She flicked the screen to show other pictures from other crime scenes. "Now look at her as time progresses. She's becoming filled with rage. Resolve."

Andrea had a wonderful gift as a behavioral analyst. Her ability to read people's nonverbal communication and emotion was uncanny.

"On cases where you were successful and no one was hurt she's most angry. On cases where SWAT had to be used, she's less so," Andrea continued. "Regardless, she is connected to someone—probably one of the victims who died—at Castlehill. I can almost guarantee that."

Joe had thought he was on good terms with the victims' families—as good as someone who had caused the death of their loved ones could be. But evidently he'd been wrong. It was time to talk to the families again. See if any of them knew this woman.

She had watched them all come in this morning, and watched them all leave a few at a time.

She thought of setting a fire while they all gathered inside. Of barring the doors so no one could escape. But she didn't have what she needed in her van.

She pulled at her hair and rocked back and forth. She'd missed a perfect opportunity because she was unprepared.

But no. That plan would've killed innocent people. People who had no part in Tyler's death.

She had to stay focused. Punish only Joe and anyone he loved or who loved him. These people he worked with did not love him. He kept himself separate from them almost always.

She'd been surprised to see them here at all.

She counted them as they left to make sure they were all gone. Then watched, rage boiling through her veins as Joe left hand in hand with the lawyer woman, Laura.

Why should Joe Matarazzo find love when he'd killed her Tyler?

Tyler had loved her. Would've eventually made a life with her.

She forced herself to remain calm until Joe and the woman were far away, then made her way to the house.

Inside the house.

All she needed now was patience. That she had.

Joe Matarazzo would burn like Tyler did. And the woman would burn with him.

Chapter Seventeen

"I talked to all the families after the victims died, but have remained closest with Summer Worrall," Joe said as they drove toward the woman's house.

Laura didn't know exactly what her feelings were on the fact that Joe had remained close with the young widow of one of the men who had been killed under his watch.

She knew even less when Summer opened the door and invited them in.

The woman was beautiful. Slender, despite having just had a baby in the last few months, petite with auburn hair and big green eyes. She had a fragile, tragic air about her. It made Laura want to take the woman in her arms.

She could imagine that Joe felt the exact same way.

Summer took Joe in her arms instead.

"Joe! What are you doing here?" She hugged him hard. Joe looked over at Laura with an apologetic smile as he hugged Summer back.

As if Laura would begrudge him hugging someone who had gone through so much tragedy.

Laura just wished the woman wasn't quite so *beau-*

tifully tragic. Shouldn't someone with a newborn look frazzled and sleep-deprived?

"Please, both of you, come in." She turned to Laura. "I'm Summer Worrall."

"I'm Laura Birchwood, Joe's lawyer."

"She's my girlfriend, too, Summer."

Laura expected a laugh or raised eyebrow at that announcement, but the other woman just grinned. "Good. He needs someone to keep him in line." She opened the door wider so they could come in.

"How's Chloe?" Joe asked, walking toward the living room. He'd obviously been here before.

"She's beautiful. Sleeps like an angel, thank God. It makes a huge difference that I can stay home. Joe. Again, I wanted to say thank—"

Joe put a finger over the woman's lips. "You've already said it multiple times. No need to say it again. It's no trouble."

Laura almost felt like she was intruding on an intimate moment. Joe and Summer obviously knew each other and had a rapport that needed more than what a single "I'm sorry your husband was killed" visit would provide. There didn't seem to be anything romantic between the two of them, but definitely a closeness.

But Joe grabbed Laura's hand as he sat down on the sofa across from Summer, so Laura let it all go.

"We're here on business, Summer," Joe said.

The other woman looked a little surprised. Obviously Joe didn't usually come over to her house for business.

"Does it have to do with your ex-girlfriends who died?"

"Yes." Joe nodded. "But I didn't have anything to do with their deaths."

Summer stared at him as if he had lost his mind. "It never occurred to me that you'd had anything to do with it."

Anybody who knew Joe would never think he had anything to do with it. Laura had been trying to tell him that all week.

Joe brought out his phone and pulled up a picture of the woman from the crime scenes. He showed it to Summer.

"Do you know who this woman is?"

She startled them both by flying out of her chair and snatching the phone out of Joe's hand. Tears immediately began streaming down her face.

Laura and Joe both stood at the sudden movement. Laura was closest to the woman and put an arm around her. "Are you okay? What's wrong?"

"Where did you get that picture?"

"She's a woman who has been hanging around a lot of crime scenes. Particularly hostage situations where I've been involved."

Summer looked at Laura then at Joe. "You have to stay away from her. She's dangerous. Crazy."

"Do you know who she is?" Laura asked. Summer was visibly shaking. Laura led her to the sofa so she could sit down.

"Her name is Bailey Heath." Summer looked at the picture again. "She's emotionally unstable."

"Have you met her, Summer?" Joe asked. He was probably thinking along the same lines as Laura was:

Summer and her daughter might need protection from this woman.

"Not recently. Tyler and I had a restraining order against her before he died."

"Why?"

"Tyler and Bailey worked together at Castlehill for a few months. She became obsessed with him. He talked to their bosses and they transferred her to another building after looking into it."

Laura squeezed her hand. "But that didn't keep her away?"

Summer shook her head. "Then she just started showing up at the house. She would follow me around and tell me that Tyler loved her and would be leaving me soon."

"Do you think there was any truth at all to the statements?" Joe asked gently.

"No. None. I trusted him completely." Her eyes filled with tears again. "Tyler and I spent hours talking about what he might have done that gave her any impression he was interested at all, much less intending to break up his marriage for her. He hated that he had somehow allowed her into our lives."

Summer took a shuddery breath. "She's unbalanced. Would sit outside our house and watch it for days on end. That's when we got a restraining order."

Laura rubbed her back. "Definitely the right thing to do."

"You can tell she's sort of crazy after just talking to her for a few minutes. She fully believes whatever fantasy world she's living in is actual reality. There's no way to convince her otherwise."

"Has she contacted you at all since Tyler's death?"

"No. Thank God. Somebody told me she was at Tyler's funeral, but I didn't see her. And I had too much to worry about to deal with her then."

Laura's eyes met Joe's. At least it seemed that Summer and Samantha weren't on Bailey's hit list.

"Why are you asking about her?"

Joe's brows knitted. "We think she might be involved with killing my ex-girlfriends. It seems like she's got an axe to grind against me."

"She was so obsessed with Tyler," Summer whispered. "Maybe she blames you for his death. The one-year anniversary of his death was on Sunday you know."

Joe glanced up sharply. "That's when the first woman was killed."

"That could've been what triggered her. The fact that it had been a year." Laura frowned. Bailey Heath obviously was holding on to her delusions pretty tightly.

Joe came over to crouch by Summer. "I'm sorry that I didn't come by. I should have remembered."

Summer patted him on the cheek. "Joe, Tyler's death was not your fault. I have never for one moment of one day blamed you for him dying. You have to stop blaming yourself. His death was a tragedy, but not *your* tragedy."

Joe nodded and stood. Obviously this wasn't a new topic of conversation between he and Summer.

"Now that we know who the woman in the picture is we've got to find her. Stop her before she strikes again."

Laura nodded. Summer had never blamed Joe for Tyler's death, but there was a psycho out there who did.

"What was Summer about to thank you for at her house when you stopped her?"

They were on their way back to Laura's house. Joe had already put in a call to Omega. Steve had issued an APB to try to find Bailey Heath. Brandon Han was working up a profile on her based on what information they could find. Andrea Gordon was studying the footage to try to read any nonverbals she could.

The team was working overtime to try to clear Joe's name. Laura knew he appreciated it. If nothing good came of this entire situation, at least Joe would know his friends truly considered him part of the Omega family.

"No big deal. I found Summer a job."

"I'm sure there's more to it than that."

Joe rolled his eyes. "Fine. I created a job for her. She manages social media for some of the Matarazzo holdings."

"But it allows her to work at home. So she can be with baby Chloe."

He gave a self-deprecating laugh. "I tried to just give her money outright, but she wouldn't take it."

"She doesn't blame you. She would've taken the money if she blamed you."

He shrugged. "I still want to help out whatever way I can. I started a college fund for Chloe. She'll be able to go wherever she wants to go."

"The best thing we can do for both of them right now is get Bailey Heath behind bars."

"Absolutely."

He pulled up to a side road close to her house and parked. They weren't parking in her driveway in case the police came by still looking for Joe.

Laura opened the door to get out of the car but he stopped her, grabbing her arm.

"What's wrong?"

"That van over there. Do you know it? Does it belong to any of your neighbors?"

A white cargo van, pretty nondescript. "I don't think so. Somebody could be having some work done or something."

"It was parked there when everyone got here this morning. Still there ten hours later. A long time for a work van to be parked in a residential neighborhood, especially on a Saturday."

They got out of the car and Joe led them down the sidewalk away from both her house and the van. "We'll walk around the block and circle back to it."

Laura felt Joe's arm snake around her waist. She couldn't help but lean in to him. "What you're doing for Summer is admirable, you know."

He shrugged. "The least I could do."

He kept her tugged to his side, keeping their stride casual, until they came up on the van.

"Stand to the side while I announce myself as federal law enforcement. If anything goes bad, just get out of the way, okay?" He kissed the side of her head.

"Are you expecting anything to go wrong?"

"One thing I've learned with my years at Omega is to expect anything."

Once they were on the rear side of the van he turned to her, taking his gun from his holster. He banged on the back door. "This is federal law enforcement. If anyone is in there, I need you to open the door."

Nothing happened. Joe looked over at her, without

lowering his weapon. "If it's unlocked, you pull the door open and keep out of the way."

"Be careful."

He motioned a countdown with his finger and Laura pulled the handle. Finding it unlocked, she pulled the back door wide-open, stepping to the side as she did so.

In just a few moments, Joe replaced his weapon in the holster under his jacket. "It's clear. Really is a work van. Go figure."

She peeked around the door. Sure enough some paint cans and cloths lay on the floor of the van, some tools and other items strewn about.

Nothing suspicious.

They closed the door and Joe put his forehead against hers. "I'm paranoid. I'm sorry."

"Hey, I'm a lawyer. I'm all about the 'rather safe than sorry' theory. Especially when the person we're looking for has a history of sitting outside of someone's house and watching."

Joe pulled her close again and they crossed the street to her house. She handed him the key to her door. "You know, I think it's safer for you if I stay at your house until we find Bailey Heath."

He slid her jacket off her shoulders and Laura turned to look at him, smiling. "Oh yeah? And is some psychopath stalker the only reason you're interested in staying here?"

He hung her jacket on the back of a dining room chair and soon his followed suit. He turned his gaze on her. It could be called nothing less than predatory.

Everything inside her heated at the look in his eyes.

"Are you saying you might be interested in something other than me being your bodyguard?" He took a step closer.

"I'm pretty sure there's something I'd like you to do with my body, but guard isn't what I had in mind." She gripped the waistband of his jeans and pulled him closer. She took a step back until her spine was fully up against the door.

He was everything she should run from. He was everything she craved.

All she knew was if he was here, she wasn't going to waste a chance to enjoy him again. Enjoy *them* again.

She licked her lips.

He groaned and pushed his body flush against hers. "If you don't stop looking at me like that, we're not even going to make it up to the bedroom."

"Maybe I don't want to make it to the bedroom."

She felt his lips work their way up her throat to her lips. Not a gentle, searching kiss.

Hot. Demanding.

The way it had always been with them.

As Joe slipped off his shirt she saw the scar on the side of his neck more clearly now that she knew what it was from.

She had almost lost him that day and she'd never even known. The thought caused her to pull him closer, even more desperate not to have space between them. He obliged, cupping her face and licking deep into her mouth.

They both moaned and tore at the rest of the clothes between them.

Somewhere in the back of Laura's mind she knew she was letting herself fall too hard. Letting Joe mean too much to her again. The price she would pay when he finally walked away again would be too high.

But when his lips worked their way to her ear then lowered to her throat she pushed the voice of reason down where it couldn't be heard.

And let the flames engulf her.

Chapter Eighteen

Joe studied Laura as she slept beside him. It was late on Sunday morning. They'd spent the entire night laughing and talking and making love.

His heart broke at the pointless deaths of those women from his past, but part of him was grateful it had thrown Laura back into his life so completely.

She wouldn't be in this bed with him otherwise—he knew that for sure. Laura's wariness had flashed in her eyes last night when she thought he wouldn't see it. Not when they were making love—he knew for certain her guard remained down then—but other times.

Like when she had mentioned a colleague's white-water rafting trip and he'd stated they should go together this summer. She'd smiled, then smoothly changed the subject.

Laura wasn't making any future plans with him.

At first he thought it was because she didn't want to spend time with him in the future. But gradually he'd come to realize that she was waiting for him to change his mind again.

Bracing herself for the impact.

Joe would give every dime he had if he could go

back and change the stupid, panicked words he'd said that night six years ago.

But all he could do was keep Laura as close to him as possible. Love her every single day until it saturated every thought she had.

Love used to be a word that scared Joe. Not anymore. Not when it had to do with Laura.

"Hey," she whispered, her eyes opening a little. "What are you growling about over there?"

He hooked an arm over her hip. "No growling. Just determination."

To have her. With him. For the rest of both their lives.

"To catch Bailey Heath?"

The temptation to tell her his complete thoughts almost overwhelmed him. Only the knowledge that she couldn't accept it, wouldn't believe him if he started declaring his true feelings for her, stopped him.

"Yeah. There's been no word on her yet."

"How long does Steve think it will take to find her?"

"She's got the full weight of Omega's resources on her shoulders. That's a lot. They've fed her image into the facial recognition program. That thing is pretty damn scary. If she drives past a traffic light, uses an ATM, walks past any security camera that uplinks to a mobile server, she'll get tagged."

"Good. She needs to be caught."

He reached over and kissed her. "She will be, don't worry. Not many people can hide from Omega for long. Particularly someone with no covert training."

"Speaking of not hiding anymore, I think you ought to consider turning yourself in to the police."

"Won't they arrest me?"

"I don't think so with the new evidence that has come to light. We'll show them what we have on Bailey Heath. The Goldman brothers are in custody and can attest to her hatred for you and that she had suggested my kidnapping. Plus, we'll have Steve call and back up everything you're saying."

A couple of days ago Joe would've been loath to ask Steve to do even that, but this situation had changed everything.

"I can't be in a cell. Not right now, not with her still out there. I won't leave you unprotected." He pulled her over to lie against his chest.

"Why don't we call Brandon Han and get his opinion? He's a great lawyer and I think he'll agree with me. Plus, walking into the station of your own accord, rather than being picked up, goes a long way toward proving you have nothing to hide."

"Alright, I'll call Brandon." The other man might be on a different case—along with being licensed to practice law, he was also one of the best profilers in Omega—but he would come if he could.

"We just need everybody in law enforcement looking for her. Not wasting any time or resources looking for you."

He reached in and kissed her. "I agree. And if both you and Brandon feel confident that they're not going to throw me in jail then I'll go."

"Even if they do, we could expedite a bond hearing and get you out on bail by tomorrow."

Joe would have to think about whether he was willing to risk leaving Laura even for a night. He would have to trust his friends at Omega to keep her safe.

Could he do that?

He ran a hand down Laura's cheek. He realized that he could do it. He could trust them. Trust her. Not that he'd have a good night's sleep being apart from her, but he could trust the team to guard Laura if it became a necessity.

Because what was important to Joe was important to them.

It was nice to know someone had his back. And that it had nothing to do with his money. His team wanted nothing in return.

She cupped his hand where it rested against her cheek. "Okay, as much as I'd love to lie naked in bed with you all day, that's not going to get your name cleared with the police."

She slipped out of bed and Joe leaned back against the pillows with his arms linked behind his head enjoying the view as Laura put on yoga pants and a T-shirt. "Actually, I'm pretty sure if you showed up at the precinct naked they would give you anything you wanted."

She smiled at him and he literally felt his breath being taken away. Laura might never be a beauty in the classic sense but damn if she wasn't the most gorgeous thing he'd ever seen.

"Maybe I'll try that at my next court case."

"I'll be sure to clear my calendar." And clear the courtroom so he'd be the only one able to lay eyes on a naked Laura. "I'm going to take a shower."

"I'll get coffee and breakfast going then we can call Brandon."

She bent to tie on a pair of sneakers and he patted her bottom on his way to the bathroom. The temptation to do more, to drag her back to bed and remove the clothes she'd just put on, almost overwhelmed him. But she was right, they needed to go to the police and get his name cleared.

Joe turned the shower on and stepped in before the water could even turn warm. The cold helped get his raging body under control and Joe didn't fight it, despite preferring to handle it a much more pleasurable way.

He wanted his name cleared. Wanted the women from his past—and his much more important present—to be safe. He wanted this behind him so he could court Laura properly the way he desired. The way she deserved.

The water turned warmer and Joe quickly finished his shower. Now that he had a plan in place he didn't want to waste any time putting it into action. After toweling off and getting dressed he grabbed his phone off the bathroom counter and put in a call to Brandon.

"Hey, Joe, how are you hanging in there?" Brandon answered by way of greeting. "Any news on Bailey Heath?"

"Nothing that I've heard so far."

"It won't take long with all of Omega's resources utilized in the hunt."

"That's my hope. Laura thinks I should voluntarily submit myself to the Colorado Springs PD." Joe explained what he and Laura had discussed. "She wanted to know if you could come over to review anything she might be missing."

"Well, I'm sort of in the middle of something." Joe heard Brandon whisper something to someone at his house.

Of course. It was Sunday morning. Brandon would be with Andrea.

"Brandon, I understand. Seriously, man—"

Another conversation Joe couldn't quite hear.

"Never mind. We'll be there in thirty minutes. Andrea says we'll bring brunch."

Joe smiled. "Thanks, Brandon."

"Hey, you sat with me in a hospital after a psychopath tried to turn me into Swiss cheese. This is the least I can do."

Joe laughed, saying his goodbyes and ending the call.

"Hey, Laura," he called out to the hallway as he put on his shoes. "Brandon and Andrea are coming over and bringing food. So it's okay for you to leave your rightful place in the kitchen for a little bit."

He waited for a smart-aleck remark from her but got no response.

Joe chuckled. Obviously she hadn't heard him because there was no way Laura would let that slide.

He bounded down the stairs. "You're not waiting to clock me with a frying pan, right?"

Still nothing. He would be worried that Laura was truly irritated but knew it would take more than one silly sentence to get her mad. It was one of the things Joe liked most about her: her sense of humor.

But that didn't mean she wasn't about to jump out and pour a bucket of water over his head or something.

"Okay, I surrender." He held his arms up in front of him as he entered the kitchen. "I promise I will do all the cooking for the rest of our lives if you don't kill me now."

Actually he would do that for the rest of their lives

if Laura would agree to share hers with him. Maybe he should start trying to get her to agree to those terms.

She wasn't in the kitchen.

Now things were a little weird.

"Hey, Laura?"

He poked his head around the corner to see if the bathroom door was closed, but it wasn't.

All humor fled. *Where was she?*

"Laura? Answer me, honey."

She wouldn't hide from him in jest, not now, not in the situation they were in. Joe pulled the door open to the garage, but she wasn't there. He systematically searched each room. Laura wasn't anywhere on the ground floor.

He ran back up the stairs to make sure she wasn't in one of the rooms up there. Nothing. He entered the bedroom where they'd spent the entire night together.

His eyes flew to the nightstand.

His Glock was missing.

It had been there when he'd gone into the shower; he knew that for a fact. He'd grabbed his phone and brought it into the bathroom with him, not wanting to take a chance on missing a call from Steve if they found Bailey Heath.

Had Laura taken his gun for some reason? Why would she do that?

Joe slipped the phone from his pocket. He hit redial. Brandon answered just seconds later.

"Brandon, Laura's missing."

"What? Are you sure?"

"She's not anywhere in the house. It had to have happened in the last twenty minutes. While I was in the shower, or when I called you."

He heard Brandon murmur something.

"Joe, don't touch anything. I'll call Steve and let him know what's going on. Andrea and I will be at Laura's house in five minutes."

Joe didn't say anything, just disconnected the call. He ran back down the stairs to look at the kitchen again.

His heart plummeted when he saw the cups of coffee that had been knocked over on the table. The only signs of struggle whatsoever.

But they were definitely signs of struggle.

Laura had been taken.

A maniac who had sworn revenge on Joe now had the one person he cared about most.

Joe tried to remain calm, but rage and terror fought for dominance inside him. All he could see were visions of dead women left for him to find. Stabbed, lying in pools of their own blood.

That could not happen to Laura. Joe couldn't survive if it did.

Chapter Nineteen

After last night with Joe, Laura had decided she just wasn't going to worry so much about their relationship anymore.

She had to face the facts: she was in love with him. Had been in love with him six years ago. Was still in love with him now. Worrying about their relationship wasn't going to change that.

In the six years she and Joe were apart, Laura had dated. Had even gotten a little serious with a couple of guys. But it had never worked out.

Because they weren't Joe.

And it didn't have a single thing to do with his money. Joe could work at the local 7-Eleven and Laura would still love him. She wanted him despite his money, not because of it.

So she wasn't going to worry about it anymore. If Joe changed his mind in two months again, decided a serious relationship wasn't for him—*again*—Laura would have to deal with it.

She rubbed a hand across her chest. It would hurt—God, how it would hurt—but she would deal with it.

Right now she just wanted to concentrate on keeping

him out of jail. Joe would call Brandon when he got out of the shower and get his opinion about turning himself in to the police. Brandon was a brilliant attorney; she and Joe both would be fools not to listen to his advice.

But first coffee. After the night she and Joe had shared—she smiled just a little thinking about it: her boyfriend was so dreamy—they needed the coffee. Laura made her way down the stairs.

She got the coffeepot going and stood next to it with two mugs in hand. She heard some thumping upstairs over the sound of the water and rolled her eyes. What was Joe doing, break dancing in the shower? She wouldn't put it past him.

A minute later she could breathe in the blessed caffeinated aroma and soon poured two cups, turning to set them on the small kitchen table.

Right behind it stood Bailey Heath. A gun in her hand pointed straight at Laura.

Laura jerked and knocked one cup over, vaguely feeling the burning liquid slopping onto her hand. The rest of it spilled onto the table.

"What are you doing here?"

The woman looked dirty, unkempt. Madness danced in her eyes.

"I'm here for you. I'm here to make Joe pay. He has to burn like Tyler did. Joe took Tyler away from me."

Tyler. Summer Worrall's husband. The man who had gotten a restraining order against Bailey. Joe hadn't taken Tyler away from Bailey. He'd never been hers to begin with.

Of course pointing out any of that probably wasn't a good idea.

But Laura knew she needed to stall.

"Joe's upstairs in the shower. Why don't we wait for him to come down and we can talk about it."

Bailey shook her head. "No, the time for talking is over. It's now time to burn. You need to come with me."

"What if I don't?"

"Then I'll kill you right here. Since this is Joe's own gun, I'm sure that will be enough to put him in jail for a long time, right?" Bailey brought the gun up so it was pointed right at Laura's head. "Your choice."

Laura nodded. She couldn't see any way around it. It was better to give Joe time to find her than for him to come down now and discover her dead.

Laura knocked over the other coffee cup, trying to get any signal she could to Joe that there was a problem. Bailey's eyes narrowed as she cracked Laura in the back of the head with the gun. It wasn't hard enough to make her lose consciousness, but Laura still cried out at the throbbing in her skull.

Bailey grabbed her arm. "Let's go. And if you try anything on the way out, I will kill you. Killing you in the street then watching Joe find you will be much more satisfying than watching him find those other women. He didn't care about them at all."

Pain rocketed through Laura's arm from Bailey's punishing grip as she pulled her down the hallway and out the front door. Laura tried to figure out how the woman had even gotten into her house at all. The front door they'd just gone through had been locked. She and Joe had checked all the doors.

Bailey pulled her across the street and into the very

van Joe had found so suspicious the day before. He'd been right; it didn't belong there.

Bailey threw Laura in and stepped in behind her. Laura winced as Bailey bound her arms behind her back.

"Time to go."

Bailey was crazy. Being this close, Laura could smell the woman's body odor. She obviously hadn't showered in at least a couple of days. Laura couldn't help but make a face.

"Do I smell?" Bailey asked. "Hiding in vans and attics will do that. Showers aren't easy to come by."

"You've been in my attic?" So she hadn't gotten through locked doors.

"Ever since all Joe's little friends left yesterday. It's not comfortable, but it works."

Laura just stared at the other woman. She obviously couldn't be reasoned with.

"The Goldman brothers were supposed to snatch you and lure Joe out. I would've been able to kill you both then and blame it on them, but they couldn't even get you out of the parking garage." She rolled her eyes in disgust.

Bailey pulled a piece of cloth from a shelf and wrapped it around Laura's mouth as a gag.

"I lost you for a couple of days, but then picked you back up again when you showed up at the Goldmans' apartment. I've been watching you both ever since, waiting for a time to plant myself in your house."

Bailey shoved Laura to the side. Without her hands free to catch herself she fell hard onto the van's floor.

"It's time for Joe to pay for what he did to Tyler. I've

been waiting a very long time for this. Your death right in front of him will just be the icing on the cake."

Bailey smiled. A bright, beautiful one, like she'd received a precious gift.

If Laura had any doubts that smile erased them all: Bailey Heath was a psychopath.

"We've got one more stop to make before I call Joe and the game begins." Bailey pulled out a canvas sack and placed it over Laura's head, cutting off her vision. "Although I'm not sure it can be called a game. Not when there's no chance of anyone winning except me."

Laura struggled to breathe through the gag. Through the panic. The other women Bailey had killed had just been a warm-up. Killing Laura while Joe watched would be the grand finale.

And Laura had no idea how Joe could possibly stop her.

JOE WOULD NEVER doubt he was part of the Omega team again.

They showed up in minutes.

They *all* showed up to help figure out what had happened to Laura.

Steve had arrived not long after Brandon and Andrea. Joe knew investigating a crime scene wasn't his strength, so he just tried to stay out of the way.

Joe couldn't stop staring at the spilled cups of coffee. They were the only signs of struggle at all. If it wasn't for them, he might have thought Laura had just decided to get out. Get as far from the situation—and him—as she could.

He wished like hell that was the case as he attempted to keep his panic pushed down.

Joe had already called his non–law enforcement contact Deacon Crandall. Explained as briefly as possible what had happened. He promised Crandall a million dollars if he had any part whatsoever in finding Laura alive. Another million to the individual who gave Deacon the tip.

Joe would keep offering a million dollars until he ran out of money or they found Laura. Because every dollar he had meant nothing without her.

Steve and Brandon stepped over to Joe.

"We think Bailey Heath was hiding in the attic. We're not sure for how long." Brandon rested a hand on Joe's shoulder. "There's no sign of a forced entry at all. And Laura definitely would not have just opened the door to Bailey."

"We found some pieces of insulation from the attic on the floor, suggesting that the pull-down door had been opened recently," Steve continued. "And a hole had been drilled through the door. Probably so Bailey could see and hear at least part of what was going on in the house."

Joe thought his rage had capped out, but he'd been wrong. The thought of a sicko like Bailey Heath listening and watching him and Laura last night sickened him. His hands tightened into fists.

"As best we can tell she just waited." Brandon squeezed his shoulder. "Once you were in the shower and Laura was alone, Bailey made her way out and took her."

Joe's curse was low and pointed.

Steve nodded. "She probably had another weapon. Taking your gun was just a more convenient method of framing you."

For when Bailey decided to kill Laura. Steve didn't say it but they were all thinking it.

Joe could feel the panic working its way up his chest.

"Joe." Brandon stood in front of Joe, placing both hands on his shoulders. "I have every confidence that Laura is still alive. If Bailey Heath had just wanted to frame you, she would've shot Laura and left her here in the house. It would've fit the MO of the other crimes and would've almost certainly landed you in jail."

Joe could hear Brandon's logic, knew he was probably right, but still couldn't get the terror under control.

"Bailey has some sort of elaborate plan," Brandon continued. "It's the only logical reason for her taking Laura out of the house."

"We will figure out how to beat Bailey at her own game. I promise you that," Steve said, sincerity clear in the man's eyes.

Joe nodded, and Brandon dropped his hold. "I just want Laura back. I have money. I know you guys know that, but I'm talking about cash I can have available in minutes if that will help. I'm willing to use other channels if it means getting Laura back safely."

Criminal channels. Mercenary channels. Joe didn't care what side of the law they were on.

"Joe, don't. Don't turn to illegal pathways." Steve took something out of his pocket. Joe looked down and realized it was Joe's Omega badge and official weapon.

Steve handed him the items. "You're part of this

team. Part of this family. Give us every opportunity to get her back before making decisions you might regret."

Joe nodded. He wouldn't rein in Deacon Crandall, mostly because he trusted the man to stay on the right side of the law if he possibly could. Joe wouldn't move into dark territory.

Yet.

More of the Omega team showed up at Laura's front door. "I'm going to handle everybody here," Steve said. "Send them to HQ. A crime lab team is coming to process the house. Everyone else needs to get to work, pressing in harder to find Bailey Heath and Laura."

Steve walked over to the rest of his team.

"You going to be able to keep it together?" Brandon asked Joe.

"As long as I know she's alive, I'll keep it together. Hell, as long as I think there is any possible chance Laura is alive, I'll keep it together." He had to. For her.

Brandon nodded.

Joe looked down at the badge in his hand. "But I can't promise not to work outside the law on this, Brandon. Not if it means getting her back safely. I don't care if I lose everything—money, job, even my freedom."

Joe saw Brandon looking at Andrea across the room. "What would you do if a psycho had Andrea?"

A psycho had held Andrea in his grip just a month ago. Brandon had nearly died trying to save her.

"Absolutely anything," Brandon said softly. "Pay any price. Employ any measure. Become someone I don't even recognize."

Joe knew he would do exactly the same.

Chapter Twenty

Back at Omega Headquarters the Critical Response Division team worked like the well-oiled machine they were. Joe remembered the van, which was now gone, and Derek Waterman found it on a traffic camera in the area of Laura's house at a time fitting when Laura had been taken.

Joe computed the distance of that traffic light from Laura's house and the time the van sped through the light.

He rammed his fist down on the desk next to Derek. "Damn it."

"What?" Derek took his eyes off the screen to look over at Joe.

Joe rubbed his hand over his face. "In order for them to be at that light at that time, I must have just missed them. If I had just run outside instead of checking the rest of the house…"

Derek shrugged. "Checking the house first was the right call. I would've done the same."

But the thought that he could've stopped it burned like acid in Joe's gut.

Derek and Ashton Fitzgerald, another member of

Omega's specialized tactical team, continued the search for the van, splitting the work and using different cameras in different directions. They followed as long as they could but eventually lost it when cameras became more scarce as the van headed out of town.

Which meant Laura and Bailey could be anywhere west of Colorado Springs. Unless, of course, Bailey had thought they might catch her on camera and circled back.

A dead end.

Jon, Brandon and Andrea continued their profile of Bailey Heath, digging further into people Bailey had known. It would be helpful, but so far was just another dead end.

Others on the team watched the footage again from his crime scenes trying to pick out anything they might have missed watching it the last two days.

Joe was about to go out of his mind without something concrete to put his energy toward. When the crime lab team called into headquarters with some questions, Joe felt almost relieved to have to go back to Laura's house to clarify some things.

"Lillian is going to go with you," Steve told him. "We're not leaving you unprotected in case Bailey decides to make you a target also."

Joe nodded down at Lillian. The tiny woman could kick someone's ass more ways than most people could learn in a lifetime. She might not look like protection detail, but Joe trusted her.

"Okay. Let's go." He prayed the crime scene crew would have something that gave them a clue to where

Laura was. Every minute Bailey had her was a minute too long.

When they got to Laura's house, Joe could see the lab workers were doing a thorough job. Every inch of the attic, where Bailey had been hiding, had been searched. They ran what they could through a portable computer system at the scene. The rest would be done back at Omega headquarters.

Getting a hair sample from Joe helped them eliminate his DNA from all possible evidence sources. A pregnant Molly Humpfries-Waterman, Derek's wife, oversaw it all.

Joe answered all her questions about when Bailey could've gotten into the house and the van he'd seen outside. The crew sent someone to gather evidence in that area also.

"We're going to find something, Joe." Molly stroked his arm. "We'll get some sort of reading from all this. Some direction to send you."

But would it be in time?

Because this was also starting to look like another dead end. Like it couldn't get much worse.

Then the doorbell rang followed by a pounding on the door.

"Colorado Springs Police Department. We need you to open the door. We have a warrant for the arrest of Joe Matarazzo."

Joe let out a bitter string of obscenities and met Molly's eyes. "They still think I'm responsible for the deaths of the other women."

"And Laura being missing isn't going to help your case."

He nodded. “I can’t let them take me right now. They’ll confiscate my phone. What if Bailey calls? Or Laura? I’m going out the back.”

Lillian moved silently from the rear of the room to Joe and Molly. “No, you’re not. They’ve got uniformed cops coming up the back. No way out that way.”

“Damn it.” Joe slammed his fist against the wall.

“Steve will make some calls. He’ll have you out as soon as possible. Hopefully in just a few hours.” But Molly’s eyes were worried. So were Lillian’s.

The cops banged on the door again. All the Omega techs stared at Joe, unsure what to do.

“Bailey didn’t kill Laura here. If she wanted just to frame me she could’ve killed Laura here with my own gun and it would’ve been the perfect setup.”

Molly nodded. “I hate to admit it, but I agree.”

“Everything in my gut tells me Bailey is going to contact me. Make some trade of me for Laura.” Or something worse.

“You and I can try to strong-arm our way out,” Lillian said. “We’re outmanned and outgunned by the locals, but we might make it.”

Joe considered it for just a moment. He squeezed Lillian’s shoulder. “Thanks for the offer, killer. If I thought it would work, I might try.”

He reached in and got his phone out of his pocket and handed it to Lillian. “Keep this. Better Omega has it than the cops, for when Bailey contacts me. Because she will.”

Lillian took it. More banging on the door. A threat to enter the premises using force.

“There’s a contact in there, Deacon Crandall,” Joe

told Lillian. "He's aware of the situation and is willing to color outside the lines if and when needed. Tell him it's probably needed. Especially if Steve can't get me out fast enough."

Lillian nodded. "We're not going to let you sit in some cell while this is going down, Joe. Believe that."

He sure as hell hoped he could. He walked quickly over to answer the door before the police decided to ram it down. He opened it, immediately met by Detective Thompson, the same man who had questioned him before.

"I'm here, Detective. No need to shoot the door down or anything."

Thompson looked a little sheepish. Perhaps they'd been about to do just that.

"Why didn't you answer?" He looked around at the crime scene investigators still working. "What's going on here?"

Joe sure as hell wasn't going to mention Laura's kidnapping if he didn't have to. He was sure Thompson would immediately add that to the list of crimes to charge Joe with.

"We're looking for possible evidence to help us find the woman who is trying to frame me for the murders of my ex-girlfriends. The real villain in this situation's name is Bailey Heath, if you happen to care."

Thompson raised an eyebrow. "You'd be surprised at how many people claim they're being framed when the police come to arrest them."

Molly joined Joe at his side. "I'm Dr. Molly Humphries-Waterman. I am the head of the crime lab at Omega Sector. I assure you that what Joe says is true. He is not the one who killed those women."

"I'm sorry, but I have a warrant for his arrest. If there is proof he didn't commit the murders, I'm sure he'll be out in no time." Thompson looked around. "Where's your lawyer?"

"She's not here at the moment."

"After the way she busted my chops at the station for questioning you, I would assume she would want to read this over before I take you in."

Joe was thankful for everyone's silence. "Doubtless. But she had business that couldn't be delayed so she's not here. I'll read the warrant myself."

Joe took the paper, well aware he was stalling. Molly had turned to the side and immediately called Steve to see what could be done. He didn't see Lillian anywhere.

"I'll need your weapon, your badge and your cell phone."

Molly looked over from her phone call. "He needs a warrant in order to go through your phone."

"Phone is listed on the warrant." Thompson grinned, beady eyes narrowed. He obviously took a great deal of pleasure lording his power over Joe.

Joe handed his weapon and badge. "I don't have a cell phone with me."

"Quit screwing around, Matarazzo. I know you have a phone."

Joe shrugged. "You're welcome to search me. Search the entire place. I lost my cell phone."

Thompson shoved Joe toward the wall. "I was trying to be nice, but if that's the way you want to play it… Hands against the wall."

Thompson searched Joe, obviously not believing him about the phone. When he didn't find anything he pulled out a pair of handcuffs.

"Is that absolutely necessary?" Molly asked. "We're all on the same side here, Detective Thompson. It won't be long until Omega gets the evidence over to your precinct exonerating Joe."

"No offense, ma'am, but until that happens, this guy—" he jerked Joe forward "—and I are not on the same side. I work for a living. Very hard. I don't think a jerk like this truly understands that concept at all. He thinks he can do whatever he wants."

Concern flew across Molly's features, "Detective—"

"It's okay, Molly," Joe cut in. "You stay here and work. Get the info we need. And tell Steve to hurry up and get me the hell out of Colorado Springs' finest's custody."

Molly nodded and Thompson led Joe out to the squad car, putting him in the backseat. Joe didn't say what was on his mind because Thompson didn't know about Laura's kidnapping, but his thoughts were dark.

If Laura died because of the detective's refusal to see beyond his own prejudice when it came to Joe, Joe would spend the rest of his life making sure Thompson had good reason to feel prejudice against him. He wouldn't physically hurt the man, but he could make his life a living hell in many other ways.

Joe sat in the squad car a long time before they began the drive from Fountain north toward Colorado Springs. The farther away they drove Joe from the action, the larger the ball of acid grew in his gut.

Lillian had his phone. She would get it back to Steve,

or whoever, at Omega. If Bailey called—*when* Bailey called—someone would be able to talk to her. What exactly they would say to an obvious psychopath, Joe had no idea. He just hoped they could reason with her, explain the situation.

He hoped Bailey would believe them and not hurt Laura because of something completely out of her control.

"How's it feel sitting back there?" Thompson gave a deep, satisfied sigh. "All your money isn't going to help you now. You're going to jail, Matarazzo. And I'm going to be known as the one who put you there."

"The only thing you're going to be known as is the jerk who couldn't see reason when it sat six inches from his face."

Thompson rolled his eyes. "Be sure to tell that to your cell mate. I'm sure he'll think it's a lovely story."

Joe ignored Thompson. Fighting with him wouldn't accomplish anything. Hopefully Lillian had gotten in touch with Deacon and the man would have the best lawyer in the state—second to Laura, of course—waiting for them when Joe arrived.

Or he would have some blackmail info on someone who could get him released. Joe had learned long ago that Deacon worked on the side of justice, not necessarily the law. Deacon knew Laura's life was in danger, knew Joe wasn't guilty, knew his arrest might cause her further harm.

If Steve couldn't get Joe released through proper channels, Deacon would make sure it happened other ways.

Joe just hoped it would be in time.

The detention building was in the northeast section of town. Joe watched as they got off I-25 onto the smaller back roads. Past the airport, in a relatively deserted section of town, they came to a red light. It turned green but an armored car, stopped in front of them, didn't move.

Even this small delay increased Joe's frustration. They needed to get to the station immediately so someone could get him out. Had Bailey called? Not knowing was killing him.

Another armored truck pulled up directly beside them and stopped, effectively blocking Thompson from being able to go around the vehicle in front of them.

"What the hell?" Thompson murmured.

The detective honked but neither vehicle moved.

"They have engine problems, Thompson. Just reverse and go around for God's sake."

Joe wasn't expecting a third vehicle to come up behind them and physically hit their car. The jolt rammed him into the seat in front of him.

Thompson cursed as two masked men ran up to the car, their guns pointed clearly at him and the uniformed officer riding next to him.

"Out of the car. Now!" one masked man—the one pointing his weapon at Thompson—said. The other kept his gun silently pointed at the other cop.

Thompson looked back at him. "Do you have something to do with this, Matarazzo?"

"What the hell are you talking about? How could I have something to do with this?" Was it people working for Bailey Heath? Had she been watching Laura's house then sent someone to finish the job?

"Get out of the car. Right now." The man shot at the engine. Everybody in the car jumped.

Thompson was sweating. "Okay, fine, fine."

Thompson and the uniformed officer opened the door and before either man could get completely out and to their feet, both the masked guys reached over and injected them quickly with something in their necks. Thompson and the cop fell unconscious onto the street.

The guy who'd spoken to Thompson reached down and got the detective's keys, then unlocked the back door. He pulled Joe out roughly and put a sack over his head.

"Let's go, Mr. Matarazzo." His voice was clear and menacing. "I hope whoever is in charge of your bank account is willing to pay or you're a dead man. Of course, you're probably a dead man anyway."

Chapter Twenty-One

The man dragged Joe over to the armored car that had stopped behind them and threw him in the back. He hit hard, unable to catch himself. Damn Thompson for insisting on handcuffing Joe.

"Don't kill him for God's sake. That defeats the purpose."

A woman's voice. Bailey Heath's?

The door slammed in the back of the armored car and they began moving.

"You alright there, Joe? Your man Deacon is quite the prince." Joe was shocked to find Lillian at his side helping him sit up and taking the bag off his head.

He couldn't stop his gaping stare. "What in the world? I thought you guys were kidnapping me. Working for Bailey Heath. That was a pretty elaborate ruse." Lillian unlocked his handcuffs and Joe rubbed his wrists where they'd chafed against the metal.

"We had to make them believe it was an actual kidnapping, so you can't be charged with anything later." Deacon had removed his mask and was now driving the armored car away from the scene.

"I'm assuming Thompson and the cop will be okay?" Joe didn't think he'd lose much sleep over it either way.

"They'll be out another thirty minutes. I wasn't sure if there were any recording devices in the squad car, so I kept up the act just in case."

Lillian shook her head. "Yeah, not because you enjoy breaking the law and risking your life. That would be crazy."

Deacon looked back at them and winked. "Anything worth doing is worth overdoing."

Lillian rolled her eyes and glanced over at Joe. "That's some friend you have there. Questionable moral compass."

Joe just shrugged. He didn't care about Deacon's moral compass, at least not in this case. They'd gotten Joe out without anyone getting hurt.

"Thanks you guys. I don't know how you pulled it off this fast, but you're amazing."

"Wait until you get the bill. You might not think me so amazing then."

Joe couldn't care less about the money.

"Were there any calls on my phone while you had it?"

Lillian shook her head. "No. I'm sorry."

She removed the overalls she had on over her clothes. "We've got to ditch this truck before Colorado Springs' finest wake up. We need to get you deep inside Omega where they can't look for you."

"I've already got it set up. Car ready for you." A few minutes later Deacon pulled up to a parking garage. "This is where I leave you, kids." He tossed keys to Lillian.

"Deacon—" Joe couldn't find the words to express the size of his gratitude as he got out of the back of the armored car and walked around to the driver's side.

"Another time, boss. I've still got a lot of feelers out all over about your woman. Hopefully you'll hear from me again soon. Right now I need to finish cleaning up this mess."

He winked at Lillian, who just glared at him, and drove off.

Lillian drove the most direct route to Omega headquarters. It wouldn't be long before the police either reported Joe missing or reported him as a fugitive. He didn't care which. He was just glad to be back actively participating in finding Laura again.

In the end none of their work helped them find Bailey Heath. Bailey decided she wanted to be found. Joe and Lillian had been back an hour when he received the call on his phone. The bustle of search tactics fell silent. Joe's phone had already been connected to a recording device. He turned it on speaker so everyone could hear.

"Hello."

"It's time for us to talk face-to-face, don't you think?"

Joe had never heard Bailey Heath's voice, and found it shrill and annoying.

Or maybe that was just because he wanted to kill her so badly.

"Is Laura alive?"

Bailey laughed. "I'm glad I finally found someone you actually care about, Joe. I was afraid I'd have to kill all your ex-girlfriends before I got the reaction I wanted."

Steve nodded at Joe. They were recording this. Bailey had pretty much just admitted to the murders and cleared Joe's name. At least now he wouldn't have to worry about the Colorado Springs police coming after him again.

But he noticed Bailey hadn't answered the question. "Bailey, is Laura alive? This conversation doesn't go any further until I have that information."

"Yes, she's alive. For now."

"Let me talk to her."

There were a few moments of silence. Was Laura dead and Bailey was attempting to figure out what lie to tell?

"Now, Bailey. Let me talk to her now."

He had to know.

"Fine." Bailey's voice became shriller.

He could hear murmuring and something brushing against the phone, obviously from Bailey's movements.

"Joe?"

He almost dropped to his knees in relief from hearing Laura's voice.

"Laura, has she hurt you?"

"No, I'm fine but she has—"

Joe heard the thud of flesh against flesh before Laura cried out.

"Laura?" No one answered. "Laura!"

A few moments later Bailey came back on the phone. "No more talking to her. Laura is, um, unavailable."

Joe closed his eyes and took deep breaths to remain calm. Laura was alive. That was the most important thing.

Thinking of ways to kill Bailey Heath was secondary.

"What do you want, Bailey?"

"A simple trade. You for Laura."

"Fine. Deal." He didn't even hesitate. He would give himself to this madwoman a thousand times over if it meant Laura's safety. "But only if Laura is alive. Do you understand?"

She rattled off an address. "You have thirty minutes. And no press that you love so much, Joe. No cameras. Not like when you allowed Tyler to be killed. And none of your friends either. If I see anyone but you, Laura dies."

"Fine." Joe had no problem telling the lie.

"You remember how Tyler died, don't you, Joe?"

"Yes." He had the burn scars to remind him every day.

"It would be a shame for Laura to die the same way. To burn."

Joe grimaced. "I'll come alone, Bailey. Just don't hurt her."

"See you soon."

As soon as Joe hung up, Steve reached over and grabbed Joe by his shirt collar. "Don't you say one damn word about going in there alone, you got it?"

"You heard what Bailey said."

"That woman is planning to kill you, Joe. It is obvious to every person in here. She aims to kill you and Laura, too."

Joe looked around the room. Everyone nodded.

"Trust us to do our job," Steve continued, his hands on Joe's shoulders now rather than his shirt. "You get in there with Bailey, buy us time to get in position. If she gives you Laura, great, we'll get her out immediately and then get you out. Maybe you can even talk Bailey into surrendering and nobody has to get hurt."

Joe closed his eyes. His boss was right. Bailey wasn't planning to let anyone live, least of all Joe and Laura. She wanted to hurt him in any way she could.

"I'll buy you the time with Bailey that you need." Joe opened his eyes. "But you promise to get Laura out first."

"Absolutely."

"Then let's go. We'll need almost the entire thirty minutes to get there."

"Alright, people." Steve walked as he spoke. "We're wheels up in five. Security alert red. And somebody get a copy of that recording to whoever Jack Thompson's boss is at Colorado Springs PD. Plus, tell them that Joe fought off his 'kidnappers' and is with us."

Everybody moved at Steve's words. Activity buzzed instantly.

"We've already pulled up the building plans," Lillian said. "SWAT will study en route."

"We need the best plan we can formulate before we get there," Steve said. "Give Joe the smallest earpiece we have."

Joe shook his head. "But what if Bailey sees it?"

"She won't. But we have to be able to communicate with you. To let you know when we've got Laura out."

Joe nodded. There were so many things that could go wrong with this mission it was difficult to consider them all.

LAURA LAY ON the ground, blood pooling in her mouth. Bailey had taken off the gag and sack to let Laura talk to Joe.

They were in some sort of warehouse or old factory or something. A large, dirty building with rafters in the high ceiling and dust on the ground.

She had wanted to get Joe information—what little of it she had—but all that had gotten Laura was a bruised face and a hard fall to the ground.

She'd tried to warn Joe he was about to walk into a trap. That there was someone else involved.

Bailey had stopped somewhere and picked up another person. Laura didn't know who—the person hadn't talked at all, and Bailey had turned the radio up so loud in the van that no one could hear anything.

Laura looked around. The person wasn't here now. Was he or she waiting to ambush Joe? Was it someone who would be keeping an eye out for the rest of the Omega team and notifying Bailey if anyone else came with Joe?

Laura hoped beyond all hope that Joe would accept help from his teammates. Otherwise he had no chance to survive this.

Laura watched Bailey douse some discarded piles of wood on the ground with gasoline.

She wasn't sure Joe had a chance even with the rest of the team.

"Don't worry. Everything else is already soaked with one sort of accelerant or another. I've had a year to study fire and know exactly what works best." A blissful smile lit Bailey's face. "Once fire touches anywhere in this building, it will only take minutes for flames to engulf it entirely."

Bailey planned to die today. And she planned to take Laura and Joe with her.

Laura tried to scoot back when Bailey walked over to her with her can of gas, but with her hands still bound behind her back, there was nowhere to go.

"No, don't—"

She stopped talking so she wouldn't get gas in her mouth as Bailey poured it on her.

"Trust me. It's better this way. It will be much quicker." Laura flinched as Bailey smoothed a piece of gas-soaked hair away from Laura's face. "But now it's time to get you in place. I'm sure Joe and his friends will be here early if they can manage it."

"But you told Joe to come alone."

Bailey rolled her eyes. "I've been watching that group for a year. They're not going to let Joe go into this building alone. He'll try to stall me while they look for you. It's like SWAT 101."

Laura realized that's exactly what would happen. "So you're going to take on all of Omega Sector?"

"No, although I have to admit, I wish I could've figured out what member of the SWAT team was responsible for not taking the shot at the man who killed Tyler. They must have had a sharpshooter somewhere who didn't do what he needed to do. I would like for that person to burn also." She shrugged. "But you take what you can get."

"What's to keep them from just shooting you, storming in and rescuing me?"

Bailey smiled. "They'll consider it. But they won't

know where you are. They'll think they know where you are, but they won't."

Laura had no idea what Bailey was talking about. She was beginning to wonder if Bailey even knew what she was talking about.

"You'll be right here." Bailey walked a few steps past Laura and opened a hatch in the floor.

Laura tried to scoot away again as Bailey reached for her. She couldn't hold in the groan of pain from her sore arms and shoulders as Bailey dragged her across the floor. Bailey stopped just as they got to the hatch. She took the gag back out of her pocket and tied it back in Laura's mouth.

"You'll be right here where all the action is, but they'll never know it."

Laura screamed as Bailey pushed her into the hatch, tears coming to her eyes as she hit the ground hard even though it was only two feet down.

"See? It's not deep. Some sort of false floor." Bailey jumped in with Laura and tied her feet together. Then grabbed a strange-looking poncho. "This material blocks your heat signature. So when Joe's friends are trying to find you, you won't show up on their equipment."

Bailey tucked Laura's legs under it. "Plus, I've given them something else to chase. They'll be happy about that. I'm not a complete monster, you know."

Laura longed to ask Bailey what the hell she was talking about.

"Bad thing about this material is that it may smother you if you're left under it too long." Bailey shrugged apologetically as she tucked it around Laura like a co-

coon. "But honestly, I think the fire will get you before that."

Bailey pulled the material up and over Laura's head. "Don't worry. It will all be over soon."

Laura didn't even try to answer. She just focused on breathing in and out in the darkness. She heard the hatch door close, but that didn't change her focus.

She had to stay calm. Had to keep breathing. Had to stay alive until Joe got here.

And pray he could outsmart a maniac.

Chapter Twenty-Two

Joe drove Steve's SUV, which allowed Derek and Steve to sit low in the backseats and not be noticeable. Under any other circumstances Joe would've found it pretty funny to see his boss and friend twisted like pretzels to fit their large frames near the floor of the vehicle.

Joe couldn't find anything humorous right now.

Two other Omega vehicles approached the address Bailey gave Joe—an abandoned lumber house that had last been used over fifty years ago—from a different direction. Steve had on the speakerphone so they all could coordinate.

"The building has some pretty vast square footage," Ashton Fitzgerald, a SWAT team member, announced. "Terrible for us, tactically."

"So heat signatures are our best bet?" Steve asked.

"Definitely," Derek responded. "Joe, you've got to keep Bailey talking. Give us a chance to find Laura and get her out."

"I will."

Joe tuned out as the SWAT team spoke back and forth to each other. Who would be coming in from what direction. That wasn't Joe's job. He'd trust that the team would have his back when he needed them.

Joe's job was damn near impossible. To go in, look Bailey Heath in the eye and pretend like he gave a damn about anything she had to say.

The only thing he cared about was finding Laura.

He could still hear her cry of pain as Bailey had obviously struck her. His fists gripped the steering wheel tighter.

"You okay, Joe?" Steve asked from the back.

"What if she's dead? That would've been a smart play on Bailey's part, right? Letting me talk to Laura and then killing her?"

"Don't go down that road. It leads nowhere," Steve told him. "We go into every hostage situation as if we can get everyone out alive. This is no different."

But it was different. It was Laura.

"You have to go in there with a cool head. Keep your training in place. Talk to Bailey like you would any other hostage-taker. I know it's hard but it's what you have to do."

Joe took a deep breath. "Okay."

"I've seen you walk into situations I would've sworn no one was coming out of alive. But you've gotten everyone out. You've listened to people as if you were their psychiatrist or priest or something. You've given them a chance to be heard. Give that to Bailey Heath."

"Hell, Steve. She's hurt Laura. I don't know if I can."

Derek knew what it was to have a psychopath hurt his woman and not be able to do anything about it. "Then you listen to Bailey not because you give a damn about her, but because it will give us time to get Laura out. We'll get her out, Joe."

Joe prayed that was true. "Alright. We're almost there."

"Pull to the side," Steve said. "I'll direct from here. Derek will join the rest of the SWAT team once we've figured out where Laura is."

"It will take us a while to manually scan a building this big, Joe. Buy us as much time as you can."

Joe took his weapon and waist holster off and put it in the passenger seat beside him. "See you guys on the flip side." He opened his door.

"We'll get her, Joe."

Steve's voice was the last thing he heard before closing the door. Joe didn't care about his own safety. Only getting Laura back. He was glad Steve and the team understood that.

He found the door and allowed his eyes to adjust to the dimness of the building before walking any farther inside.

"Bailey, I'm here," he called out. "Where are you?"

The place seemed even more vast from the inside. Bailey could be lying in wait any number of places. She could step out at any minute, dump Laura's dead body at his feet and shoot him between the eyes.

The only thing stopping her was her need for the theatrical. For Joe to burn. It wasn't a comforting thought.

He could smell the accelerants all around him. He had no doubt Bailey planned for this place to go up in flames.

"C'mon, Bailey. We can't talk if I don't know where you are."

He heard a disturbing cackle from deeper inside the lumber house. Joe began walking toward it.

"I don't know that I really want to talk," Bailey said. He couldn't see her, but could tell he was heading in the right direction.

"But you wanted me here."

"But not necessarily to talk. More to watch you burn. And your girlfriend, too."

Joe sucked in a breath and forced himself to remain calm. "Is Laura alive?"

The question was more to keep Bailey talking than to gather information. He knew he couldn't trust anything she said.

"I think so."

"What does that mean?" Joe kept walking toward Bailey's high-pitched voice.

"She's alive. I want to hurt you, not her."

"Unfortunately, I don't think that's true. You killed three other women I used to care about."

Bailey's voice was much closer now. She laughed. "Okay, you got me. I don't mind hurting her if it also hurts you. And you care much more about her than you did those other three. I was able to tell that easily."

Joe advanced into a room that looked like it was once an office. Bailey stepped out from behind the broken paneling of a wall. She had a gun in her hand. Probably still Joe's Glock.

"Hi, Joe." She smiled at him, but hatred burned in her eyes.

Along with a whole hell of a lot of crazy.

"Bailey. Where's Laura?"

"She's not here with me."

"I can see that." He fought to tamp down panic.

The tiny earpiece inside his left ear clicked on. Steve. *"That's an affirmative, Joe. There's only two heat signatures in the room you're in. You and Bailey. We're systematically searching the rest of the building."*

"Is Laura alive, Bailey?"

Bailey grimaced. "Yes. She's alive. For now."

"Let her go and you can do whatever you want to me."

Joe realized he meant it. He would die whatever agonizing death Bailey planned if it meant Laura would live.

"Oh, I have plans for you, Joe." Bailey smiled again. "Don't I get a striptease like the people did last week?"

"Are you worried I have weapons?"

"Not really. If you kill me you'll never find out where Laura is. And she will die. Of course, she's probably going to die anyway."

Joe had his first glimpse of hope that Laura was still alive. Bailey wanted drama. Maybe she planned to kill Laura in front of him as some big, painful gesture.

Let her have her plans. He would give the team the time they needed to find Laura and thwart them.

"Sure, I'll take off my clothes, if that's what you really want. But I thought you loved Tyler. I wouldn't have thought you would want to see another man naked."

The earpiece switched on again. *"We've detected a faint heat signature. In the southwest corner of the building—it's the only one. It's a weird signal, but it's definitely a person. We're going to get her."*

"I don't want you to get completely naked, Joe. Just

take off your shirt," Bailey sneered. "I want to see the burn marks from when Tyler died."

Joe began pulling his T-shirt over his head as the earpiece clicked on again. *"Ashton and Derek are trying to work their way to her. Keep Bailey talking."*

"Is this what you want?" Joe asked, walking over to her and turning his back so she could clearly see the burn scars that stretched down his neck and back. He flinched as she touched him.

"Did it hurt?"

Joe didn't know if he should lie or not. Wasn't sure what he should say to keep Bailey in the moment and give the team the time they needed.

He turned back to look at her and there was such a sadness in Bailey's eyes, he almost felt pity for her.

Bailey was crazy. Had ruined lives. Had killed people.

But she loved Tyler, and had lost him.

Joe tried to think of what he would say to Bailey if she wasn't holding the woman he loved captive.

What he would say to do his job.

"Yes, the burns hurt. But I'm sure my physical pain wasn't nearly as bad as what you went through by losing Tyler."

"Now you're just trying to manipulate me." She pointed the gun at him.

"I'll admit that was my plan coming in here. But now I'm not. Now I'm just trying to talk to you."

Bailey began to cry. "Why, Joe? Why couldn't you get Tyler out that day? I've watched you for a year now. I've seen you go into one situation after another and almost always get everyone out safely. Why couldn't you do that for Tyler?"

"I've asked myself that same question every day. If I could go back and change the past I would. Bring Tyler back for you."

Of course, Tyler would be going back to the wife he loved and his baby daughter, not to Bailey. But Joe didn't mention that.

His earpiece clicked again. *"Derek and Ashton are on the other side of a door where Laura is. But they are going to have to make some noise to get through it, and it will definitely alert Bailey that the rest of us are here."*

Once Bailey heard the noise she would certainly shoot Joe or herself or light the place on fire.

Could he talk Bailey down? Was she determined to kill him no matter what? He had to try.

"Let's hold on for a second."

"Roger that," Steve whispered.

"What?" Bailey asked, eyes narrowing.

"Let's hold on to the memories," Joe covered. "And I'm saying this not just for my sake, but for yours, too. Would Tyler want you to do this? To kill people?"

Bailey began pacing back and forth.

"I don't think Tyler would want you to pay that price, Bailey. To carry that weight."

She stopped pacing and looked at Joe. For the first time there was some semblance of clarity in her eyes.

"It's too late. I've already killed."

"It's not too late if you stop now. We can't do anything about the past. It's only the future we can change."

Bailey lowered her weapon and for just a moment Joe thought she might surrender. Looking at her he realized just how young she really was. Lost. Frightened. She hunched her shoulders and put her hands in her jacket pockets.

And something changed. Joe didn't know what or why, but when Bailey looked back up at him it was with complete resolve and determination.

All the crazy was back.

"No. It's too late. I'll do whatever it takes to avenge Tyler the way he would want me to."

She was going to kill Joe and herself and take Laura with them.

"Go, Steve, go," Joe said. No longer caring if the secret was out. Three seconds later a huge noise blasted through the air as the SWAT team took out the door at the other end of the building to rescue Laura.

He looked at Bailey expecting to see surprise or fear. She just smiled. Joe realized this had been her plan all along and somehow they had all just played into it perfectly.

"Sounds like your friends found her. Good. Believe it or not, my fight was never with her. With them." Bailey took a deep breath, holding her arms out slightly as if she was breathing in a beautiful dawn.

Joe smelled it, too. The building was on fire.

Bailey looked at him, tilting her head sideways. "And now we burn."

Chapter Twenty-Three

Joe realized Bailey must have doused just about everything in accelerants. The place was going up fast.

He pressed a hand to his ear. "Steve, report. Do you have Laura?"

"Yes, Ashton has her. She's hurt, but alive. They're carrying her out. Busting the door must have triggered some sort of ignition. The whole building is burning."

Ashton tried to cut in on the frequency to tell Joe something, but there was too much noise from the fire. Joe couldn't understand him.

Laura was safe. That was all that mattered.

"Laura's out, Bailey. Your plan failed. You and I need to get out too before this whole building comes down around us."

She brought the gun back up and pointed it at him. "Actually you and I and the woman you love burning was the plan all along."

"Laura's already gone, Bailey. You'll have to try your plan another day."

After she'd spent three consecutive life sentences in prison.

"You might want to check with your boss there, Joe. Make sure everything is how you think it is."

Something about Bailey's calm expression sent a chill through him. He pressed the earpiece closer to his ear.

"Steve? I need you to confirm that you have Laura."

"Hold. Derek and Ashton are coming out of the building right now."

Joe heard lots of coughing then the distinct sound of a baby crying. He pieced it together before he heard what Ashton had to tell Steve.

"This is Summer Worrall and her baby."

"Joe, we don't have Laura. I repeat, we don't have Laura."

Joe took the earpiece out of his ear and put it in his pocket. His friends couldn't help him now.

"You took Summer and the baby."

Bailey shrugged. "I didn't hurt her. Like I said, my fight was never with her. I understood why Tyler found it difficult to leave her. They'd taken vows."

"Where's Laura?" The smoke was getting thicker even though the fire wasn't near them yet.

Bailey stomped her foot and Joe looked down realizing there was a hatch door of sorts underneath her. "She's been with us all along. Wrapped in some material that made her heat signature invisible to your friends."

Joe took a step toward Bailey. She pointed the gun at his head. "You can get her out, but slowly."

Joe nodded, praying Laura was still alive in there. He opened the hatch door and saw a form wrapped in a blanket unmoving. He jumped in and gently started unwrapping Laura.

She was covered in sweat, skin red and blotchy, her breathing shallow. The stench of gasoline permeated the air.

Bailey looked down from where she stood, gun still pointed at them. "Yeah, sorry. The price for hiding a heat signature is material that has been known to smother people."

Joe unwrapped the gag from Laura's mouth, wiping sweat from her brow. "Laura, are you okay? Sweetheart?"

Her eyes blinked open but didn't focus. "Joe."

"C'mon, let's get you out of here." He reached back and untied her arms, forcing his thumbs into the joints at the front of her shoulders to relax them enough that they could move after being held at such an awkward angle for so long. He knew it had to hurt—saw tears roll down her face—but she didn't make a sound. He untied her feet and climbed out of the hole with Laura in his arms.

Bailey had the gun pointed right at them. "See? I knew you loved her. I'm sorry I killed those other women because that was just a waste. Laura was the only one I needed to kill to make you feel my pain in losing Tyler."

Joe felt desperation swamp him. He could smell the smoke getting thicker. They didn't have much time.

He had to get Laura out of here. He turned his back to Bailey so he could talk to Laura in his arms.

"Laura." He shook her slightly, trying to get her to remain conscious. "Can you stand, baby? Walk? Open your eyes for me."

She did, her beautiful hazel eyes focused on him this

time. "I need you to be able to walk, okay?" He set her on her feet when she nodded again.

He was going to make a deal with the devil and pray it was enough. He turned back to Bailey, one arm behind him to help Laura find strength to stand. This would only work if she could get herself out of here.

"You want me to burn, Bailey. I know you do." Joe knew exactly what Bailey needed to hear and was willing to give it to her. "I deserve to burn."

Bailey's eyes lit. "Yes, you do."

"I will stay here and burn with you. But you have to let Laura go. She's innocent."

"No!" Bailey pointed her gun at Laura.

Joe pulled Laura more fully behind him. She was still wobbly but seemed to at least be able to walk.

"Then I fight you, Bailey. You may shoot me, and that's fine. But maybe I'll still be able to get the gun from you and get away. Then I won't burn. Or maybe you kill me, but I die quickly and painlessly. Either way, are you willing to take that chance?"

Bailey cursed foully, pacing back and forth. Her need for vengeance won out. "Fine, she can go."

Joe didn't hesitate. He turned to Laura and began pushing her toward the door. Her eyes, still fuzzy and hazy from something akin to heatstroke, looked at him without much comprehension.

"Run toward the door, baby. There might be some fire, but just keep moving forward, okay? Crawl if you have to." He handed her his T-shirt. "Use this if you need it, to hold over your mouth."

She nodded. "You?"

Joe framed her face with both hands. He would've

gladly spent the rest of his life with this woman. But knowing that she would live and have a life would be enough. "I'll be right behind you," he lied.

He kissed her. The sweetest, briefest of kisses. "I love you. Now run, okay?"

He turned her and pushed. She stumbled slightly then found her footing and ran wobbling toward the other side of the room.

Joe had to believe she would make it.

He picked the comm unit out of his pocket and put it back in his ear. "Steve? Anybody? If you can hear me, Laura is on her way out the front door. Send someone to help her. She's injured."

Joe looked up as Bailey turned her gun from him to where Laura was running.

"I've changed my mind. She can't live. If she lives you haven't suffered enough."

Joe ran toward Bailey but knew he would be too late to stop her from shooting Laura's retreating form in the back.

But out of the smoke stepped Steve Drackett. He shot Bailey before she could fire her gun. "I think you've caused quite enough people to suffer."

Bailey fell to the ground.

Steve walked forward and kicked the gun away from her hand.

At the sound of the gunshot Laura stopped and turned around. "Joe?"

"I'm here, sweetie." He ran over to her and put an arm around her. "Steve, let's go. This building is going to collapse any minute."

The smoke was already unbearable.

"She's still alive," Steve responded, gesturing to Bailey. "I'm going to carry her out."

Joe saw it at the same time Steve did. Bailey reached into her jacket pocket and pulled out a hand grenade.

Just like the one that had been used to kill Tyler. Bailey reached over with her other hand and pulled the pin.

"Grenade!" Steve yelled. "Get her out!"

Joe knew he wouldn't be able to get Laura to safety in the seconds they had. He saw Steve dive behind a wall in the other direction and dove with Laura back down into the false floor pulling the hatch closed over them. He wrapped the blanket around them and tucked Laura under him, shielding her as much as he could with his body.

A second later heat washed over them as well as an unbearably loud noise. Joe tightened his arms around Laura as everything went black.

LAURA TRIED TO figure out if she was dead.

It was the second time today she'd had to purposely use her brain, *force* it to work—something it usually did quite well on its own—to figure out if she was still alive or not.

She felt the same smothering heat she'd felt the first time. Unbearable heat that made breathing, moving, thinking, nearly impossible. Her breaths had come in short gasps, the effort forcing them further and further apart, until she'd been sure each breath had been her last.

Then she'd heard Joe's voice talking to Bailey. Laura hadn't been able to make out what they were saying, but she knew he was nearby.

She'd held on. Her shoulders and feet and lungs wailed in agony but she'd held on because Joe had come for her.

But at some point she'd stopped even being able to focus on his voice.

The heat, the fumes from the gas Bailey had poured on her, had pulled her completely under.

But the next thing she knew Joe was there. Carrying her out of the hot hole of death. Shirtless. That didn't help her figure out if she was alive or not. Why wouldn't Joe have a shirt on if she was still alive?

Maybe she was in heaven.

It was just that everything had seemed so far away. Even Joe. Especially Joe.

She'd screamed in torture when he'd cut the bindings off her wrists and moved her shoulders, but no sound had come out. His fingers had helped her survive it.

The pain had let her know for sure she was alive, not in heaven.

Joe and Bailey had talked but Laura couldn't understand. Couldn't process.

Joe had wanted her to stand so she'd tried her best. Then he'd asked her to run, so she'd done that too.

But first he'd kissed her. He told her he loved her.

She wanted to stay with him. Wanted to kiss him more, but he'd told her to run.

She'd known something was wrong, but still couldn't get her brain to work enough to know what it was.

But as she lay here in the dark now, her brain figured out what it was.

Joe had made a deal with Bailey: he would die with

her, if she would let Laura go. The bitch had reneged and tried to kill them both.

Joe had protected her by throwing them back in this hole and covering her with his body.

She was suffocating again, with Joe on top of her as well as the blanket. But this time her hands weren't tied; she could do something about it.

"Joe? Are you okay?"

He didn't answer. She twisted to her side, rolling him off her, and pulled the damn stifling material off them both.

Joe groaned and coughed.

It was the most beautiful sound Laura had ever heard.

Without his weight and the blanket on her, Laura could breathe more freely. There didn't even seem to be fire burning above them any longer.

"Are you okay?" she asked him again. Longer sentences still seemed beyond her.

"Yes. I think so. Are you?"

"My brain still hurts."

"You may have had a partial heatstroke from being trapped in that heat signature blocking material. It's not meant to be used indoors, or for extended periods of time."

Laura didn't like that. "Will my brain always be this slow?"

She couldn't see it, but she could hear Joe's smile. "I hope so. Then maybe I have a chance of keeping up with you."

Joe reached up with his legs and pushed against the hatch door. It didn't move. Then he touched the door with his hand. "It feels like Bailey's hand grenade actually saved us. It probably blew up so much of the roof of the building there wasn't enough to burn or suffocate us to death. It doesn't feel hot anymore, and the air seems cleaner."

"But we're trapped here."

"The team will be in here looking for us soon. We're not in any actual danger anymore. I just hope Steve made it out alive. I saw him dive the other way before the grenade went off."

Steve had been there, too. Laura's brain began to put pieces of information together. They lay there in silence while she figured it out, both of them content to just be with one another. Alive.

"You were going to let her kill you to get me out."

"Yes." Joe's voice was soft, husky.

"Why didn't you just fight her?"

"I couldn't take a chance you might get hurt in the process."

"Well, it was a terrible plan. Giving yourself over to die rather than take a chance fighting her."

Joe chuckled, wrapping an arm around her and pulling her closer. "How about next time a raging psychopath has us in her clutches I discuss the plan with you first and get approval."

"Yes. Better." She snuggled in to him. "Thank you."

"For getting you to approve the plan next time?"

"For keeping us both alive. For trusting that your team would have your back. For risking everything to find me."

"If you weren't here to share my life, it wasn't going to have much meaning anyway."

"Joe, I'm just afraid that—" She wanted to tell him

she loved him. That she'd never stopped loving him. But that she was also scared that six months from now he would decide again she wasn't enough for him.

Being trapped in an enclosed space while a building burned down around them seemed like as good a place as any for that conversation.

But damn the Omega team for being so good at their job. Moments later they heard Joe's team calling for them.

"We'll finish this conversation soon, I promise." He kissed the side of her forehead before using his legs to kick up against the door to draw the team's attention.

Moments later the hatch opened. Steve stood there looking down at them.

"Joe with no shirt on and a beautiful woman in his arms. Seems about right."

Chapter Twenty-Four

Two weeks later Joe picked Laura up to take her on what he promised would be a "special lunch date."

Considering he'd been with her almost 24/7 since the incident with Bailey Heath, and that he'd taken her on a number of luxurious dates—including a couple on a private plane carrying them to Los Angeles and New York—she couldn't imagine what "special lunch date" meant.

She got into the car as he pulled up next to her law office building. "I can't miss any more work. I have to be back in no more than an hour."

He turned, tilted his head and gave her his most charming smile. "Hello to you, too, love." He reached over and kissed her.

Between the look and the kiss, every part of her body, and certain pieces of her clothing, just about melted. She sighed leaning into him.

"Sorry," she murmured against his lips. "I just can't afford to go flying across the country today. Work has been piling up."

She'd been hospitalized for complications stemming from heatstroke and fumes inhalation, including a seizure. The doctor had released her after just two days, but strongly suggested a couple of weeks of just low stress, fun activities.

Joe had taken two weeks' vacation from Omega and proceeded to escort Laura to all the places he loved. Places he'd always wanted to show her. Some were extravagant like the Four Seasons in Manhattan. But they also went to places like Sonny's Cafe in Galveston, Texas, a tiny hole-in-the-wall restaurant that he loved.

She had to admit, it had been fun. More. It had been lovely and peaceful and healing. Just what they both needed to put the nightmare of Bailey Heath behind them.

Joe's name had been cleared, of course. Although evidently there had been some other incident with the police involving Joe—Laura still didn't have all the details. But it had all been worked out.

The gossip sites had a field day with her and Joe's relationship. But after the story with Bailey was somehow leaked, and Laura was made out to be the heroine of the story, the sites seemed to take a different slant toward their relationship.

In every picture posted of the two of them Joe looked at her with such adoration, it was nearly impossible for the sites to say anything damaging about Laura without looking like fools. Joe's looks, his gestures, his movements toward Laura spoke volumes about his feelings.

But how long would they last? She forced herself not to think about tomorrows. Joe hadn't brought it up, so she didn't either.

"I promise to have you back in under an hour." He put the car in Drive and pulled away from her building.

"Okay, so where are we going for this 'special lunch date'?"

She'd barely gotten the question out before he pulled the car around the corner and parked it in a lot, then strode around to open her door for her.

They were at the county courthouse. Laura and her law partners had specifically chosen their office building because of its proximity to City Hall and the local courtrooms.

"What's going on? Oh my gosh, Joe, are you in trouble with the police again? You should've told me so I could be more prepared. What are the charges?"

She racked her brain trying to think of what charges could've been brought against Joe that would have him at the county courthouse rather than the criminal court downtown. This court was primarily used for real estate and marital purposes.

He gripped her elbow gently and led her up the stairs. "The general charge is being an idiot for too many years."

She couldn't help but laugh. "Well, in that case you really should've given me more time to prepare." He opened the door for her. "Seriously, what's going on?"

They went through security, Joe presenting his weapon to be held in a security box since he wasn't here on official business. "You'll figure it out in a minute. I enjoy being ahead of you for once."

They walked down the hall. "Figure what out? Joe, just tell me what's going on."

He stopped them in front of a courtroom door. "Get there faster, Laura. I know you can."

He twirled something around on the end of his pinkie as he said it.

A ring.

They were here to get married.

"Oh my God, Joe, we can't. It's too soon."

"Too soon? Hell, it's six years *too late*."

"But what about..." She trailed off unable to find the words she wanted.

"What about what?" He put his forehead against hers. "You need this so I can prove I'm not going to wake up one morning and change my mind again. I need this so I can have you legally bound to me while you're still slightly addled and will say yes."

"But—"

"I want you, Laura. I want you so badly I can't think straight for it. I love you so much that the thought of life without you causes me to break out in a panic."

"Are you sure?"

He cupped her face with both hands. "I have never been more sure of anything in my entire life." He kissed her. "We'll have a big wedding soon and invite everyone we know. We'll do this here today because I want you bound to me right now. Just you and me."

She nodded. He kissed her again and opened the door to the courtroom, his hand still gripping hers.

But when they walked in they realized they were not alone. Every member of the Critical Response team was already in the courtroom. She felt Joe's hand tighten around hers.

"You guys. How?" Joe basically sputtered.

Steve stepped forward. "You work for one of the most elite crime fighting agencies on the planet. Did you think we wouldn't discover the wedding of one of our own and be here to celebrate it?"

Joe wrapped his arm around Laura. "I guess not."

"Welcome to the family, Laura," Steve said.

Laura couldn't think of anywhere else in the world she'd rather be.

* * * * *

A secret Santa is sending Chloe Clementine increasingly threatening gifts. Can cowboy Justin Calhoun save the girl he has always loved?

Read on for a sneak preview of
Rugged Defender
by New York Times *and* USA TODAY
bestselling author B.J. Daniels.

It all began with a kiss. At least that was the way Chloe Clementine remembered it. A winter kiss, which is nothing like a summer one. The cold, icy air around you. Puffs of white breaths intermingling. Warm lips touching, tingling as they meet for the very first time.

Chloe thought that kiss would be the last thing she remembered before she died of old age. It was the kiss—and the cowboy who'd kissed her—that she'd been dreaming about when her phone rang. Being in Whitehorse had brought it all back after all these years.

She groaned, wanting to keep sleeping so she could stay in that cherished memory longer. Her phone rang again. She swore that if it was one of her sisters calling this early…

"What?" she demanded into the phone without bothering to see who was calling. She was so sure that it would be her youngest sister, Annabelle, the morning person.

"Hello?" The voice was male and familiar. For just a moment she thought she'd conjured up the cowboy from the kiss. "It's Justin."

Justin? She sat straight up in bed. Thoughts zipped past at a hundred miles an hour. How had he gotten her cell phone number? Why was he calling? Was he in Whitehorse?

"Justin," she said, her voice sounding croaky from sleep. She cleared her throat. "I thought it was Annabelle calling. What's up?" She glanced at the clock. *What's up at seven forty-five in the morning?*

"I know it's early but I got your message."

Now she really was confused. "My message?" She had danced with his best friend at the Christmas dance recently, but she hadn't sent Justin a message.

"That you needed to see me? That it was urgent?"

She had no idea what he was talking about. Had her sister Annabelle done this? She couldn't imagine her sister Tessa Jane doing such a thing. But since her sisters had fallen in love they hadn't been themselves.

"I'm sorry, but I didn't send you a message. You're sure it was from me?"

"The person calling just told me that you were in trouble and needed my help. There was loud music in the background as if whoever it was might have called me from a bar."

He didn't think she'd drunk-dialed him, did he? "Sorry, but it wasn't me." She was more sorry than he knew. "And I can't imagine who would have called you on my behalf." Like the devil, she couldn't. It had to be her sister Annabelle.

"Well, I'm glad to hear that you aren't in trouble and urgently need my help," he said, not sounding like that at all.

She closed her eyes, now wishing she'd made something up. What was she thinking? She didn't need to improvise. She was in trouble, though nothing urgent exactly. At least for the moment.